Born in London in 1874, **Maurice**  a scion of a family long prom the British Empire. The son director of the Bank of Englar Bros.), he was educated at Eto the diplomatic service in 1898. ....c a journalist and reported the Russo–Japanese war in Manchuria; later he was a correspondent in Russia and Constantinople. He is credited with having discovered Chekhov's work in Moscow and helping to introduce it to the West. Baring is remembered as a versatile, prolific and highly successful writer, who produced articles, plays, biographies, criticism, poetry, translations, stories and novels. He is regarded as a representative of the social culture that flourished in England before World War I, his work highly regarded to this day for the acute intimate portraits of the time.

BY THE SAME AUTHOR
ALL PUBLISHED BY HOUSE OF STRATUS

C
CAT'S CRADLE
THE COAT WITHOUT SEAM
DAPHNE ADEANE
THE PUPPET SHOW OF MEMORY
TINKER'S LEAVE

In My End Is
My Beginning

MAURICE BARING

HOUSE OF
STRATUS

This edition published in 2001 by House of Stratus, an imprint of
Stratus Holdings plc, 24c Old Burlington Street, London, W1X 1RL, UK.

www.houseofstratus.com

Typeset, printed and bound by House of Stratus.

A catalogue record for this book is available from the British Library.

ISBN 0-7551-0099-9

PREFACE

The title of this book needs some explanation. The inscription:

"In My End Is My Beginning"

was the motto embroidered upon the Chair of State of the Queen of Scots. This inscription perplexed Mr Nicholas White, a friend of Cecil's, who, on his road to Ireland in the spring of the year 1569, paid a visit of curiosity to the Queen of Scots during her captivity at Tutbury, the house of the Earl of Shrewsbury.

He wrote as follows: "In looking upon her cloth of estate, I noticed this sentence embroidered: *'En ma fin est mon commencement'*, which is a riddle I understand not." In the same letter he wrote: "The Queen of Scots should be seen as little as possible; besides, that she is goodly personage, though not comparable to our sovereign; she hath withal an alluring grace, a pretty Scotch speech, and a searching wit, clouded with mildness. Fame might move some to relieve her, and glory joined to gain might stir others to adventure much for her sake; then joy is a lively impetuous passion, and carrieth many persuasions to the heart, which moveth all the rest."

Mr White's words were prophetic; for many, not only during her lifetime, but after she died, even until the present day, have been moved to relieve her, and to adventure much for her sake, either by the desire of fame, gain or glory, or by impetuous joy.

For, as Sir Francis Knollys wrote about her to Queen Elizabeth, when the Queen of Scots first came to England: "Surely she is a rare woman".

At the present day it is indeed to "adventure much" to write about the Queen of Scots, after so many books have been written about her and so well, by so many; both glorious and obscure. Indeed, the procession of her chroniclers, both in history and in fiction, is

Bright with names that men remember, loud with names that men forget.

Her motto was symbolic in more ways than one. Putting aside the question of whether the death of the Queen of Scots was, as some think, the triumph of a martyred saint awaiting canonization in the future, or a consummate piece of play-acting, there is no doubt that practically and politically the end of the Queen of Scots was her beginning; for at her death her son, James Stuart, became the heir to the crowns of England and Scotland, and he lived to wear both crowns.

This book is an attempt to retell, once more after many thousand times, the story of that Queen from her childhood until the beginning of her end.

It has no claim to be a history, nor is it based upon any special knowledge. I know no more about the Queen of Scots than the many writers of fiction who have grappled with this rich and perplexing theme during the last two centuries. At the same time, I, like no doubt those before me, have tried to keep as closely as possible to recorded fact, gleaned from the works of scholars, who have devoted so many years to the subject, and when possible, from contemporary record.

I have tried (and the attempt is by no means original) to retell the story, not as it appears to us now, but as it might have appeared to four friendly but not necessarily uncritical eye-witnesses. I have chosen this vehicle because, since the accounts of the Queen's story differ sometimes in essentials and often in detail, by giving the reader four narratives I have not committed myself to one particular version of the events.

The setting is fictitious; I have allowed the narrators of each story, although they and all that is said about them is as far as possible historical, to indulge in thought and comment of my own invention. But there is no direct speech in the book attributed to the Queen of Scots herself which has not some foundation in contemporary record.

After reading all that I could lay hands upon of contemporary documents, of history, and of fiction in prose and in verse, I have been left with one overwhelming impression; that the story is still, in spite of all that has been written about it, a mystery – one of those everlasting riddles that have the power to arouse and to kindle the passions of many generations of mankind; and to trouble the judgement even of the wisest and the most sober, the most tolerant, the most discriminating, the most staid and impartial, of historians.

The novice who for the first time dips into the literature which has grown up about Mary Queen of Scots will find, perhaps to his amazement, that instead of looking down upon a remote and minute puppet-show from the serene plane of an Olympian summit, he is in the lists among bitter and battling antagonists, who are at war, and ready to defend their cause to the death. He will find that the warring parties call each other "Anti-Marians" and "Mariolaters" respectively, and show no quarter.

The evidence used by the two schools is necessarily the same, because it is limited. Each school uses the same documents and, as a rule, impartially; that is to say, each quotes those which will support and those which will damage his cause; but in the appreciation of the value of the documents which they quote they are far from impartial.

The letters of Ambassadors to their Sovereigns form a large part of the documentary evidence; but the letters of Ambassadors, as we know from experience, contain gossip as well as the record of first-hand experience. Yet, in the case of Mary Queen of Scots, if this gossip casts a slur upon the Queen, her historical defenders protest that it is baseless. If, on the other hand, it is to the advantage of the Queen, and to the detriment of her enemies, her historical enemies will sometimes protest that it is a lie.

The reason of this violent clash of opinion, which subsists until the present day, is probably to be found in what Walsingham said of the Queen of Scots, namely, that "the love and hatred that was borne her" was "either in the extremest degree". The novice, when he has made himself tolerably familiar with the literature and the quarrel about Mary Queen of Scots, will, I think, come to the conclusion that her chroniclers and commentators may be roughly divided into four schools.

There are those who believe that the Queen of Scots was a martyr and a saint, who was as greatly calumnied after her death as during her lifetime; and who is now a possible candidate for canonization.

Of such was Miss Strickland.

There are those who think she was altogether evil; a murderess, a wanton and a dissembler; who agree with John Knox when he said: "If there be not in her a proud mind, a crafty wit, and ane indurate heart, against God and His Truth, my judgement fails me"; and again: "In communication with her I espied such craft as I have not found in such age."

Of such was Froude.

Then there are those who stand betwixt and between; who think that the Queen was neither a saint nor a great sinner, but a woman of fine sincerity and directness, lacking in coolness, self-control and patience; courageous, but liable to panic and folly, and at times physically exhausted.

Of such was Sir John Skelton.

Then there are the sceptics, who are frankly puzzled; and who, while they discount the pleadings of the Queen's defenders, are still more critical in their disbelief, or rather in their analysis, of the accusations of her enemies; and who find it as hard to extract and puzzle out a coherent and convincing story from the findings of the one as from the findings of the other.

Of such was Andrew Lang.

I must add a fifth school: those whose opinion has been most eloquently voiced by the poet Swinburne; they take their cue from his verse:

> *Strange love they have given you, love disloyal,*
> *Who mock with praise your name,*
> *To leave a head so rare and royal*
> *Too low for praise or blame.*

> *You could not love nor hate, they tell us,*
> *You had nor sense nor sting:*
> *In God's name, then, what plague befell us*
> *To fight for such a thing?*

> *"Some faults the gods will give", to fetter*
> *Man's highest intent:*
> *But surely you were something better*
> *Than innocent!*

They argue that Mary Queen of Scots was bad, but greatly bad, like Clytaemnestra, or Cleopatra; and that she belonged to the category of those high unfortunates and those rash importunates who, like Phaedra, Guenevere or Iseult, were the overmastered victims of the god of Love.

Those, they say, who try to excuse the conduct of such, can but diminish and belittle them. And in writing of the Queen of Scots, they cannot believe that the Queen who showed herself so great and so fearless amidst so much hardship and peril should, on another occasion, betray weakness and folly, unless an overmastering passion were the cause and the explanation.

But is there not a simple answer to this objection? Namely, that the human heart is complex, and that the elements in it not only are mixed, but inconstant; and that they respond in a different manner and in a different degree to varying circumstance. It is surely not impossible that the Queen of Scots might have been gay as a lark, as fierce as a tigress, as cold as an icicle, on certain occasions, and yet panic-stricken on others.

We know that this was true after the battle of Langside.

There is no doubt that her character, as it is interpreted by the poet Swinburne and those who agree with him, is by far the most romantic and dramatic; but it does not follow on that account that it is the more true. Supposing Shakespeare had told in his play the true story of Macbeth, who the historians tell us was a good king, a model husband, and whose family life was a pattern of domestic felicity, his play would no doubt have been interesting, but perhaps a little less arresting than it is as he wrote it.

And, as Anatole France pointed out, the historians might now bring up enough proofs of Macbeth's innocence to satisfy Rhadamanthus; it is Shakespeare's version of the story which will still be accepted by mankind.

It is possible to maintain the theories of each of the five schools I have mentioned; and it has been done over and over again, with eloquence, with brilliance, and sometimes with genius, but the result, when either of these theories is held fast exclusively, is never quite satisfactory. The case (except in that of the sceptics and agnostics) is never quite complete; there are always a few obstinate facts cropping up of a sudden which, far from fitting in with the main theory, contradict it; and the Mary of Swinburne, in spite of the brilliant rhetoric he puts into her mouth, and the gorgeous poetry with which he invests her, does not quite tally with the Mary who is revealed in her own letters.

There is another point. The Queen of Scots was slandered during and after her lifetime by George Buchanan and other writers. We know that the aspersions made in some cases are slanders, because we have the record of the movements of the Queen of Scots from day to day, and her itinerary from August 1561 until May 1568, recorded in the registers of the Scottish Privy Council and in other contemporary records. These records all historians are agreed disprove certain of these slanders; therefore if some of the slanders are known to be false, there is no reason that the others should be true.

My own impression, after reading what I have been able to read of Mary Stuart literature, is that the outlines of the story are often obscured by the fumes and dust of controversy and comment; and the voices of the eye-witnesses are drowned by the loud-speakers of the commentators, who are explaining to us what the actors in the story really did and really meant to say.

I confess, therefore, that I come armed with no theory; nor have I attempted to solve the problem, nor to pluck out the heart of that mysterious and shining opal. I have aimed only to try and dig up once more the bones of the story from underneath the mounds of controversy, and to expose them in a light which is intended to resemble that of contemporary opinion, leaving the reader to build what theory he chooses, and to find his own key to the problem.

My excuse is that the bare story is of such undying interest that it cannot be told too often.

My thanks are due to Lord Salisbury, who permitted me to consult, and to Mr Lovell, the Librarian at Hatfield, who found for me, some documents relating to the story which are among the Cecil papers, and to Mr Edward Marsh for correcting the proofs.

CONTENTS

MARY FLEMING'S NARRATIVE   1

MARY BETON'S NARRATIVE   71

MARY LIVINGSTONE'S NARRATIVE   143

MARY SETON'S NARRATIVE   213

REPORT SENT BY JANE KENNEDY
TO MARY SETON   289

BIBLIOGRAPHY   304

MARY FLEMING'S NARRATIVE

(Translated from the French)

CHAPTER I

The Queen was born in the Palace of Linlithgow. She was
crowned Queen at Stirling when she was but one year old, and
when she was yet a baby she was like a sweet apple thrown by
the Goddess of Discord into a savage world, about whom
warring factions and rival princes in several countries debated
and fought. The King of England, King Henry VIII, sought her
hand for his son, and the King of France, Francis I., wished for
the marriage of the Queen's Grace to the Dauphin's son. When
she was but five years old she was sent to the Island of
Inchmahome in the Lake of Menteith, where there was a Priory,
and she was sent thither because the times were troubled and
there was strife between England and Scotland, and battles;
and it was thought that in this time of peril she would be more
secure than in a fortress on land. For a year she was Queen of
a little garden with boxwood and plants of box, and fruit trees,
and Spanish filberts; and this was the only place where
throughout her life she reigned in peace, and the only garden in
which she took pleasure where there was no hidden threat, or
where she was not a captive. After a year she sailed for France,
for the lords determined to offer her in marriage to the
Dauphin, and to let her be educated at the Court of King Henry.

A French squadron sailed to fetch her from Dumbarton in
the month of July, passing round the North of Scotland and the

west coast, so as to escape the English fleet which would have caught her. She landed in Brittany in the month of August, and with her were the Lords Erskine and Livingstone, and Lady Fleming, her father's sister, other noblemen and gentlemen with sons and daughters of her own age, and with these last four in especial, of whom every one bore the name of Mary, being of four honourable houses: Fleming, Livingstone, Seton and Beton. She went to join the Dauphin at St Germain-en-Laye, where royal honours awaited her, and the power to grant pardons and to release prisoners had been conferred upon her. And she received the education of a Queen. For a few months she remained in a convent; but she was not suffered to remain there long. She spoke French with sweetness and elegance, and she learned Spanish and Italian. She understood the Latin tongue, but spoke it less easily. She delighted in the works of the poets, and could turn verse herself gracefully, but she was more eloquent in prose. Her singing was most excellent, aided by the sweetness of her voice; and she played well on the cittern and the harpsichord, and later on the virginals; but Sir James Melville said later that it was not flattery alone which made him tell the Queen of England that she excelled the Queen of Scotland in the playing of the virginals; and this, he said, was the only point in which the English Queen was more excellent. The young Queen danced gracefully and becomingly, for her body was exceedingly agile. She learned to ride as far as it was necessary for travelling and hunting, in which she delighted, and she managed the needle as well as the reins of a bridle, for she had royal fingers. She grew apace, and tall early, taking after her mother, who was of the largest stature of woman, and, although now and throughout all her life she could endure roughness and fatigue easily, she was frail of body and easily sick, and in France she was sick of the smallpox and cured by Fernel, first physician to the King, who punctured her face all over with a lancet and put water upon it, and saved the beauty of it from being diminished by any of its perfections. And as she was later, so was she now, ready to speak her mind even when it was imprudent, ready to lean upon others but obdurate when she had once made up her mind; wise and yet rash, thoughtful yet imprudent, bold yet easily persuaded; gentle, considerate, pitiful, yet hard as steel when offended, and cold as ice in danger. Born to rule and yet to be ruled; and whether in triumph or misfortune, in power or in captivity, queened or un-queened, yet always one who could command service and inspire worship even unto death.

She was but fifteen years of age when she was married to the Dauphin, who was sickly and feeble; and the Queen liked him well, but she thought not of inclination in this matter. She was Queen of Scotland by birth, she had been trained and educated to be Queen of France; and she regarded this destiny as being inevitable, like the march of the Seasons.

Her wedding was exceedingly magnificent. The night before it was solemnized the Queen-Dauphiness and the family of France slept in the Palace of the Archbishop of Paris, and the Queen slept well and peacefully, although from without there came all night long a noise of hammering and knocking, for the workmen were making ready a scaffold which had been built twelve foot high between the hall of the Bishop's Palace and the Church of Notre Dame. And at six of the clock on the Sunday of the 24th April, the Eve of St Mark, and the Saint for the day being the Penitent Thief, the Queen was wakened by trumpets and drums, and at eight of the clock she told her ladies that in two hours' time she would be wedded, and begged them dress her for the solemnity.

On her head she had a veil of lace and the Crown Royal; an *Agnus Dei* about her neck, and a jewel, a fair diamond called the Great Harry making a cross, with a chain of rubies and diamonds. Her gown was of white satin, whiter than the lily, and glorious in fashion and ornament, pointed, with long sleeves to the ground set with acorn buttons of gold and trimmed with pearl.

5

Her royal mantle and train were of blue-grey velvet embroidered with silk and pearls. It was six *toises* in length, and covered with precious stones.

And at ten of the clock there came a knocking at the door, and one of the Chamberlains came to tell her all was ready; and, being told that Her Majesty was at prayer, he went back and came again in a little while. And the Queen, taking from her oratory a Crucifix and a pair of beads, walked down the staircase, her ladies bearing up the train.

The common people crowded the streets and the bridges and swarmed at the windows and upon the stairs. Between the Church and the Palace, a great scaffold had been made ready, on which was a gallery built in the semblance of a cloister, with carved work representing leaves and branches, and at the end of it was a pavilion, in which there was a *ciel-royal* of blue Cyprus silk adorned with golden lilies; and a blue carpet covered the floor, stamped likewise with golden lilies.

As the clock struck ten her eldest uncle, the Duc de Guise, entered the pavilion, where the rite was to be solemnized by the Queen's uncle, the Cardinal de Lorraine, and saluted the Archbishop of Paris, and when this salutation was ended he went to the Palace to head the procession. First of all came the Queen's musicians and minstrels, in red and yellow, playing upon a variety of instruments; then followed the gentlemen of the King of France's household; next the Royal Princes; then the Bishops and the Abbots, bearing crosses before the Archbishops and the Cardinals of Bourbon and Guise, and the Cardinal Legate. Next came the Dauphin, with his two smaller brothers, the Dukes of Orleans and Angoulême, and the King of Navarre; and after them the Queen, she being led between the King of France and the Cardinal of Lorraine.

After the Queen came the Queen of France, the Queen of Navarre, only sister to the King, and other Princesses, with their Ladies.

The Queen was met at the portals of the Cathedral by the Archbishop of Paris; and the marriage rite was solemnized in the pavilion under the *ciel-royal*. And after the benediction had been given, largess was thrown to the people.

Then the processions entered the Church in the same order and walked up the nave to the sanctuary, where, under another *ciel-royal*, with a carpet of cloth of gold at their feet, they heard Mass. After Mass the processions went to the Archbishop's Palace, where there was a banquet in the hall. And at five o'clock in the afternoon the King and the rest of the Princes upon steeds, the Queen and the Princesses in open litters, went to the Palace by the Rue St Christophe, and there they partook of supper at a marble table, while the musicians played on hautboys and other instruments, and every dish was brought up by the Duc de Guise, the Grand Master for that day, in a robe of cloth of gold, with a clamour of trumpets, clarions and drums. At the end of the banquet the tables were lifted, and the Queen of Scotland, the bride of the Dauphin, took for her partner the daughter of the King, and opened the ball, dancing a pavan which ladies alone might dance. When this dance was finished, the Queens and the Kings went to the Golden Chamber, where there was pageant and triumphs, one figuring the seven planets, wherein were Mercury, the Messenger of the Gods, dressed in white satin with a golden girdle, Mars, in golden armour, and Venus. And there were horses upon which Princes were mounted, made of wicker, and covered with gold and silver trapping; and unicorns, and ships with silver masts and sails of gauze, which sailed in mimic voyage round the hall. On the morrow there were more pastimes at the Louvre, with balls and masques; and joustings were held in honour of the bridal at the Court of the Tournelle for three days.

Henceforth, after the marriage, the Dauphin was no longer styled "the Dauphin", but the "King-Dauphin", and the Queen was called the "Queen-Dauphiness", for the two Crowns of France and of Scotland were united in their Arms, and for a

while the Queen-Dauphiness enjoyed felicity unmarred by
machinations and unthreatened by coming events. She had her
own Court, which was haunted by the noblest and the gentlest
of the land, whereat were not only the gallant and the brave,
but those most versed in science and art, most famous in
poetry, and most skilful in music and the dance. There was
Monsieur d'Anville, among the gallant the most excellent, who
was enamoured of the Queen, but who soon after, and perhaps
on that account, was constrained to marry Mademoiselle de la
Marck; and his servant, Châtelart, a Huguenot of good stock, a
man pre-eminent in bodily exercises and in all elegant
accomplishments, for he made verses and sang, and in the
duelling field he was above others for prowess. Monsieur
d'Anville made him the confidant of his love for the Queen, and
this was a grievous error, for from the very first Châtelart
became enamoured of the Queen himself, although he
concealed it. And at the Court of the Queen-Dauphiness all,
whether prince or poet, or sage, or men of war, were loud in the
praises of the Queen-Dauphiness; and never has a Princess
received louder or more unanimous or more tuneful praise, so
that Monsieur de Ronsard would say that in after years men
would discredit all this acclamation and say it was but the
flattery and the ready money of Court poets; but, he said, they
will not understand because they will not have seen her. And
although many painters made her portrait, not one of them, try
as he would, could put on canvas even the shadow of her
beauty. They gave but the geography of her face as though they
were making a map, but they left out the colours of the sky and
the light of the sun. These painters were for the most part
heavy by nature, Germans or Flemish, and their fingers were
not delicate enough, nor their brush sufficiently supple to catch
that grace and that gleam. When she was quiet her eyes were
grave, and when she smiled they bewitched you, for they had a
strange twinkle, and one had a slight cast; and when she was
lively they were full of a blinding fire which dazzled you so that

you could not tell their colour, for in the morning they would appear blue or grey, and in the evening time brown or even black, like a fabulous gem. The poets and the men at the Court spoke or sang of her beauty in terms of rapture, and maybe so demented were they that their words have not the value of careful testimony. But there were none, not even her enemies, who did not think that she was very lovesome. And her lady governess, Madame de Briante, who was slow to praise and swift to mark imperfections, especially those of other women, said that the Queen extinguished all other beauties and had eyes wherewith to draw down an angel from Heaven. The Queen's happy reign as Queen-Dauphiness was first over-shadowed by the death of the Queen of England, Queen Mary Tudor; for, although Queen Elizabeth succeeded to the throne of England, the Queen of Scotland became next in succession, and from that moment in her heart was lit the desire to be Queen of England herself. This was the strongest desire in her life; and she often said, both in France and in Scotland, in after times, that either she or a child whom she would bear should wear the Crown of England. That was her prayer, and maybe it has been heard; and if it shall be granted it will have been at the price of her own doom.

The Queen, although she was gay of spirit, was serious in her soul. She gave every day some hours to study, and she was ever thoughtful; and the pleasures of life never darkened her serious intent, which was to be a Queen, and to rule, and if it might be, Queen of England. She was ready to be Queen of France, but when her husband, the King, died, and she became second person, the Crown of Scotland did not satisfy her, and she aspired to greater things.

While she was Queen-Dauphiness, Monsieur d'Anville, who excelled among the noblemen of the Court, for he was far the most comely and the most gallant, worshipped the Queen to frenzy, and she was enamoured of him. But when he was married and the Queen-Dauphiness, even after the death of her husband, although free, perceived that he was for ever removed from her reach by circumstances, she put away all thought of him, although he followed her to Scotland. For at this time at least her affections were ruled by her reason.

Her felicity lasted but a brief time. Her husband, the young King of France, was too frail to live, and maybe it was good for him that he lived no longer; for, although not without spirit, he had not the strength to be King of France at such a time, in the thick of so many warring factions and such fierce religious quarrel. And the Queen, knowing that the Queen-Mother, who now guided all, hated her, and that she could only be second person in France, and yet would never be suffered by her ambitious uncles to retire into complete seclusion, but would ever be made a pawn of, determined to go to Scotland and to assume her crown there, although that crown tempted her but little. But there was another thought which allured her; for she regarded the throne of Scotland as a stepping-stone to the throne of England, and she was encouraged by all to bear this in mind and to unite the two kingdoms; and this was the wish of the more thoughtful and subtle of the Scottish nobles.

While she was still in her dule-chamber at Orleans, the Countess of Lennox sent her son, Lord Darnley, to see her in secret, and he was a Prince of the blood royal of Scotland, of the Stewarts, and a Prince of the blood royal of England and next in succession to the throne of England after herself. In that period of dule the Queen, who was dressed all in white, and was more beautiful than she has been ever before or since, for her whiteness, which was extreme, became her, wavered for a time between two desires: the desire to pass from the life of Courts and from the world, and the desire to rule. And it was the latter which prevailed. For her spirit, which was fiery, was easily stirred, and the Queen of England refused her passport into her realm; and from that moment the Queen determined to go to Scotland, whether the Queen of England would or no. So it was that the Queen, after bidding farewell to Fontainebleau, the Palace which she loved, for, with its waters, its alleys and fountains, and its grey walls, it pleased her grave mood even more than the other and more gorgeous palaces pleased her merriment, she took her leave of the King and Queen and the nobility and set out with her uncles and many ladies and gentlewomen to Calais. And in her train went Monsieur d'Anville and Châtelart. In August, the fourteenth day, she left Calais with eight galleys and sixteen ships: the larger galley, her own, was all white; another red with two flags – another blue with the Arms of France and another white in her stern, and glistening like silver; and as her galley left the port a ship which was coming in foundered, and sank, and the greater part of the mariners were drowned; and the Queen exclaimed: *"Ha! Mon Dieu! Quel augure de voyage est cecy!"* And when the galleys left the port, a little wind arose, and sail was set, and the Queen leant with both her arms on the stern of the galley next to the steersman and shed salt tears, looking towards the port, and saying again and again: *"Adieu, France! Adieu, France!"* She remained, sighing these words, until nearly five of the clock, when it grew dark And when they came to her and begged her to partake of supper, she cried the more bitterly, and she said: "It is at this hour, my beloved France, that I shall lose sight of you altogether, since the dark night, jealous of the sight I have delighted in as long as I was able, lets down a veil before my eyes to deprive me of such felicity. Farewell, then, beloved France! which I am now losing sight of. I shall never see you any more." Then she retired, saying that she was the contrary of Dido, who had done nothing but look at the sea when Aeneas had parted from her, whereas she had looked always on the land. The Queen desired to go to rest without having eaten, and would not go down into her cabin; but she had commanded her bed to be made across the beam in the stern, and, resting a little, she told the steersman that as soon as it should be dawn, if he should see the land of France, he should not be afraid to waken her; and fortune favoured her in this; for, the wind having dropped and the men taken to the oars, they made little progress this night, so that when day dawned the land of France was still in sight, and the steersman obeyed her command; and she rose from her bed and looked once more upon the land of France as long as she was able; but as the galley passed on she said good-bye to her felicity, and she could no more see the land which she had loved. And she repeated over and over again these words: "Good-bye, France. This is ended. Good-bye, France! I think never to behold you again."

As they neared the coast of Scotland the English squadron, which had been sent by the Queen of England to intercept them, caught them up; but they were saved from being overtaken by the ardour of the men who rowed and by a fog which protected them from pursuit. For, on the morning of the day before they landed, the fog which had been between them and the Queen's ships thickened, so that they knew not where they were; and they were compelled to anchor in mid-sea and take soundings. This fog lasted all one day and all one night, and early on Sunday morning, when it lifted, they found themselves surrounded by rocks and wellnigh had perished; and the Queen said that as for herself she did not care greatly, as she desired nothing so much as death, and that she desired to live not for her sake but only for the weal of her realm, of Scotland. And when the mist lifted and all beheld the land of Scotland, there were some who augured that this mist signified that she was about to land in a realm of confusion, darkness and misfortune. And there were those who blamed the Queen for the darkness of the very face of Heaven at the time of her arrival, and Mr Knox, the preacher, feared not to say that the Queen had brought with her sorrow, dolour, darkness and all impiety. The fog continued for two days, and the mist was so thick and dark that a man could not see two yards in front of him. Nor did the sun shine for two days after her arrival.

The Queen would have proceeded to Holyrood House, but nothing was yet ready, for she had arrived sooner than was expected; so she tarried in the house of one of her subjects at Leith until the afternoon, and when everything had been prepared her brother natural, Lord James Stewart, and her brother-in-law, the Earl of Argyll, and other nobles, came to greet her and to conduct her to Edinburgh. But the Queen's horses had been intercepted on the way, for one of her galleys had been overtaken by the squadron of the English Queen, and Lord James had brought her for steeds some of the ponies of the country, which were so ill-appointed with shabby saddles and worn-out bridles that the Queen said, "These are not like the appointments to which I have been accustomed, but it behoves me to arm myself with patience".

The Queen was received by her subjects with Hosanna; and on the way to Holyrood Palace she was met by the rebels of the crafts of Edinburgh, who asked her pardon for a misdemeanour which they had committed, they having resisted the Bailies of Edinburgh, who had forbidden them to enact the play of *Robin Hood* upon a Sunday; and he who had played Robin Hood had been made prisoner by the Provost and the Bailies, and condemned to be hanged: but, when the time of his hanging came, the craftsmen and prentices flew to arms, seized the Provost and the Bailies, dragged down the gibbet, and set Robin Hood free; whereupon there was conflict, and the craftsmen were promised pardon if they released the Bailies; which they did. Nevertheless, in spite of this promise of pardon, the craftsmen feared retribution, and to prevent it asked pardon of the Queen, who accorded them her grace; and this angered Mr Knox, who declared that she pardoned these craftsmen easily for what they had done in despite of the Religion.

As the Queen entered into Holyrood Palace there were bonfires in her honour, and all night long the ragamuffins of the town sang psalms outside her window to the screech of fiddles and rebecks. The Queen said she liked this well, and willed the same to be continued; and they sang again on the second night, and again on the third. And one of the Queen's ladies said to her, that the Bishop of Valance had been wont to say in his sermons: "Is any one merry: let him sing psalms." And the Queen replied: "Alas! This is no place for mirth." And after the third day she changed her chamber from the ground floor to one higher and more remote.

CHAPTER II

On Sunday morning, after her arrival, the Queen ordered Mass to be said in the Chapel Royal; for before starting from France she had been promised freedom of worship for herself and her household; and, as the Queen's Almoner was on his way to the Chapel, Lord Lindsay put on his armour and attacked him at the head of a party, shouting: "The idolater priest! He must die the death." They would have slain him if he had not fled into the presence of the Queen, and the Queen, greatly saddened, said: "This is a fair beginning to the obedience and the welcome of my subjects; what will be the end thereof I know not, for I foresee it will be very bad."

The nobles of Scotland at first received her suspiciously, but she took their hearts with her witchery, and especially those of the young by her beauty and her winning ways.

She rode into the town upon a Tuesday, and, after dining in the Castle at mid-day, she rode down the hill and was received by fifty young men of the city, whose bodies were covered with yellow taffety, their arms and legs bare, covered like blackamoors with black hats upon their heads and black visors on their faces, and about their necks, leg and arms chains of gold. And twelve of the most honest citizens in the town, dressed in black velvet gowns with crimson satin doublets and black velvet bonnets, received the Queen under a canopy of

15

purple velvet lined with red taffety and fringed with gold, which they carried above her head while she rode upon her palfrey. And the Queen smiled upon all as she passed. And after them came a cart with bairns carrying a coffer in which was a gilded cupboard, which was to be presented to the Queen.

When they came to the butter throne, where there was a gate made of timber, coloured and hung with Arms, there were children upon the gate who sang music and played upon instruments. And from the top of the gate as the Queen approached there was the semblance of a cloud, from which a child – a boy of six years of age – came down and delivered to the Queen the keys of the town, with a Bible translated in the Scots language and the Book of Psalms turned into Scots verse, together with the keys of the gates. And the boy who delivered the Book of Psalms said by a speech that these emblems signified that she should defend the Reformed religion; and he presented her with some verses as well.

At the Tolbooth there was a double pageant, one above the other, and a virgin called Fortune, and two others, called Justice and Policy, made compliments to her there. And when the Queen came to the Cross, wine ran out at the spouts in abundance, and the people drank of the wine and threw the glasses on the ground when they had drunk of them. At the salt throne there was a pageant showing the vengeance of God upon idolaters, and Korah, Dathan and Abiram being burnt at the time of their sacrifice. They had minded to show a priest burn at the altar, at the Elevation, but this was forbidden by the Earl of Huntly; and this pageant to the French seemed contemptible. At Netherbow there was a pageant showing the burning of a dragon, where speeches were made; and after the dragon was burnt a Psalm was sung. And from Netherbow the Queen passed to Holyrood House with her convoy of blackamoors, and there the bairns who were in the cart with their present of plate made a speech concerning the putting away of the Mass; and they sang a Psalm. The cart went back to Edinburgh and the citizens who had first received the Queen presented her with the gilt cupboard, and she thanked them. And the citizens and the convoy went back to the town.

Soon after her entry into the city the Queen made a royal progress and visited the towns of Linlithgow, Stirling and other cities; and while she was at Stirling, having a candle burning by her when she was lying in bed, the curtains took fire, and she was in danger of being smothered; and people said that the old prophecy had now been fulfilled, that a Queen should be burnt at Stirling. At Perth she was well received, and was presented with a heart full of gold. There were pageants in that city which offended her by their blasphemy, and, beholding one of these as she rode in the street, she fell sick from displeasure, and was borne from her horse into her lodging. And when she returned to Edinburgh, those of the French nobles who had not already gone took leave of her.

In the month of October there was a masque at Holyrood Palace which the Queen gave to bid farewell to her uncle. Among the performers at the masque were Châtelart and his master, Monsieur d'Anville, who entreated the Queen to wed him, saying he would put away his wife. But the Queen told him this could not be, saying, "If he had been single, I might have been free to listen, but he is already married and I have a soul, and I would not endanger it for the sake of all the grandeur in the world". The masque was devised by Mr Buchanan, the learned scholar, who wrote elegant verses in compliment to the Queen. And now all the French people departed, save one of the Queen's uncles, Monsieur d'Elbœuf.

The Queen had given the guidance of the realm into the hands of her brother, Lord James Stewart; but she desired to have another there as crafty as he, and she appointed William Maitland of Lethington to be her Ambassador to the Queen of England. The suspicion with which the nobles regarded the Queen when she first came to Scotland from the French Court, a stranger and of an alien religion, was soon blown away by her

17

bewitchment, and the nobles, who at first kept at a distance, soon came to Court; but it was not long before the Queen learnt how perilous it was to put her trust in any of those about her. They soon taught her to distrust them, until she learnt, after bitter experience, that there was no one whom she could trust; whereupon they accused her of being suspicious – and this in time became true, but there is little cause to marvel. The Queen was not slow to please her new Counsellors and her new subjects, not only by her seductive ways but also by the wisdom and moderation of her policy and her love of study; for daily after dinner she read a little out of Livy instructed by Mr George Buchanan. But, do what she would, she could not disarm her enemy, Mr John Knox, who said that many were deceived in her, and prayed God daily to turn her heart, obstinate against God and His truth; or, if the Holy Will were otherwise, to strengthen the hearts of His chosen and elect to withstand the rage of all tyrants. The religious freedom she gave to others was not accorded to herself; for when she had a Mass sung upon All-Hallows Eve, one of the priests was beaten for his reward.

In the spring of the year after that when the Queen arrived in Scotland, the Earl of Bothwell, who had come with her from France, first began to trouble the waters.

During the reign of the late Regent Mother the Earl of Bothwell had fought upon her side against the Protestant Lords of the Congregation, and had taken part in many feuds and in much Border warfare. In Denmark, where he had tarried on his way to France, he had been betrothed to a Norwegian lady, whom he had carried from her home and deserted; and he had been betrothed to the niece of Cardinal Beton; and, later, he had sought the French Court and served the Queen when she was Dowager of France.

When the Queen came back into Scotland, an old feud broke out between him and the Duke of Châtelherault, Chief of the Hamiltons, and he sought to ruin the Hamiltons. He attempted to win the Lord James, the Queen's brother, who had been made Earl of Mar, to his side, but the Lord James would not trust him. So Bothwell changed sides, and he tried to persuade the Duke of Châtelherault that Lord James Stewart alone stood between him and greatness, and that if he were removed they might seize the person of the Queen, and rule the realm together in absolute power.

And the Duke's son, the Earl of Arran, who was privy to this plot and mad with love for the Queen, revealed it to Lord James; and the Earl of Arran, whether from love or from infirmity, lost his reason, and he and the Earl of Bothwell were sent prisoners to Edinburgh Castle, whence the Earl of Bothwell escaped and went to France.

During the summer there was much talk of a meeting between the two Queens of France and of England, and there were many embassies sent between the two countries about this interview. At one time it was agreed they should meet at York, but before the appointed day the meeting was prevented by cunningly fomented jealousies.

In the month of August the Queen went in progress to the North. In the North her subjects were Catholics, and the chief of them was the Earl of Huntly, who was greatly displeased because the title of Mar had been conferred upon Lord James. And the Earl of Huntly would have restored the Catholic religion, and corresponded with the Queen's uncles; but the Queen knew that in all his projects his chief aim was his own greatness, and she put no trust in him. Lord James, who had the favour of the people, had more power than the Queen herself, and she would have gladly been rid both of him and of the Earl of Huntly, but who was there to guide her who did not seek his own greatness rather than her own?

The Queen had now made her natural brother, Lord James Stewart, Earl of Moray; but the demesnes of that Earldom still belonged to the Earl of Huntly. Now, the Earl of Huntly's third son had lately broken prison from Stirling Castle, and at

Aberdeen the Earl and the Countess of Huntley, who was a witty woman, entreated grace for him; and the Queen declared that no favour could be granted him unless he would appear for his summons in the Justice Court of Aberdeen, and surrender himself into ward at Stirling Castle; and Sir John Gordon appeared in answer to the summons, and agreed to enter himself a prisoner at Stirling Castle. But the Earl of Huntly and his Lady feared to let him hazard himself in a place over which the Earl of Moray had so great power; for the Earl of Moray was their chief enemy.

In the meantime the Queen on her progress designed to visit the Earl of Huntly at his house at Strathbogie, and on her way there, during a long and painful journey in foul and cold weather, the Earl of Huntly pressed the Queen for his son's pardon. But the Queen would not yield unless Sir John Gordon should show obedience, and in the debate some words escaped the Earl of Huntly which incensed the Queen so far and caused her to be so suspicious that, although only three miles from Strathbogie, she turned another way, in spite of great preparations which had been made for her; and she went to the Castle of Balquhain.

During all this time of broil and danger the Queen was never less dismayed or more gay in spirit, and although the roads and the journey were painful and long, and, owing to the season, the weather extremely foul, so that the corn was unlikely to come to ripeness, the Queen outrode all her followers, and repented nothing but that she was not a man.

Now, the Earl of Huntly and his Lady had resolved that their son should marry the Queen, and when the Queen left them they consulted to use force, for they thought that once they had the Queen in their power, which it seemed easy to do in that country, they could carry out their designs as they pleased, and force the Queen to marry their son, who was enamoured of her and conceived foolish hopes of a marriage, although he was a married man. And they plotted that when the Queen should come to Inverness, the Captain of the Castle, who was in Huntly's service, should refuse her entry, and she, being compelled to lodge in the open town, might easily be surprised.

The Queen was refused entry by the Deputy of the Castle, he saying that he had no authority but that of his Chief, Lord Gordon, the heir of the Earl of Huntly, who was Sheriff of Inverness, and who was away. And the Queen was obliged to lodge in the town. But the Queen grew suspicious, and all that night kept a strong guard in the town, and in the case of need she had ships ready to take her away; and before the next night it was known that the Earl of Huntly and his son had taken the field with a number men. But when the Highlanders understood what was on foot they refused to march with the Earl, and the next day they came and submitted to the Queen. After this, her forces increased, and those of the Earl left him. Then the Queen besieged the Castle, and forced it to surrender. The Captain was hanged, the rest were pardoned, and the Queen returned to Aberdeen.

But the Earl of Huntly did not give up his enterprise, and he resolved to fall upon the town of Aberdeen, which was open, and take the Queen's person. In the meantime, letters from him were intercepted which discovered the whole plot. The Earl of Moray thought it time to take action himself, for he knew that the plot had been made against him; so he marched out against the Earl of Huntly, who had but five hundred men; and with the Earl of Moray were the Earl of Morton and Lord Lindsay, with nine hundred men. He marched upon Huntly and surprised him; and the fight was engaged by the stream of Corrichie, where the Earl of Huntly was defeated; and one hundred and twenty men were killed and two hundred were taken prisoner, among them the Earl of Huntly's sons: Sir John Gordon and Adam Gordon. The Earl of Huntly was taken prisoner himself, and fell dead from his horse in the press.

Sir John Gordon was taken bound as a felon through the streets of Aberdeen, and the Earl of Moray led the Queen to the window to see him pass, and the Queen wept. Sir John Gordon was found guilty of treason and sentenced to be beheaded. The execution followed swiftly, at Aberdeen, and the Queen was constrained by the Earl of Moray to witness it, in order, he said, that treason might not be countenanced. Sir John Gordon died proudly, after suffering more than one blow, and he was pitied on account of his youth, his comeliness and his carriage.

Adam Gordon, the younger brother, was likewise sentenced to death, but reprieved because of his youth. The eldest brother fled, and the rest of Huntly's friends were punished, either by banishment or fine. The Earl of Morton was made Chancellor, and the Earl of Bothwell, who had escaped from the Castle of Edinburgh, was summoned to appear and declared rebel for contumacy.

Soon after, at Montrose, Châtelart came to the Queen, sent by Monsieur d'Anville, who was pressing his suit once more. He brought from Monsieur d'Anville one letter only, but very long; and he rode on horseback with the Queen, and presented her with a book of his own making, written in verse. The Queen was pleased with his commerce, which brought back to her the happiness she had dreamt of in France. But Châtelart, under pretence of pleading his master's suit, pleaded his own, and, his love for the Queen increasing to frenzy, he entered the royal bedchamber and hid himself there, in the Palace of Holyrood House, armed with a sword and a dagger. The Queen, being informed of this, commanded him to leave the Palace and the Court, nor ever to come into her presence again.

But Châtelart was now beyond prudence and reason, and four nights later at Burntisland he hid once more in the Queen's bedchamber, and came forth, as he said, to clear himself of his ill-conduct. The Queen was in the act of stepping into her bed, and was attended by her ladies; and she called for help, and the cries of the ladies wakened the house. And the Earl of Moray came to her, and she commanded that her brother should kill the miscreant with his dagger. But the Earl of Moray said he must be dealt with according to law. And Châtelart was examined and condemned to death; and after his examination, during which he had been put to the torture, the Secretary Lethington told the Queen that he had been suborned by the wife of the Admiral Coligny and other enemies of the House of Guise to cast such a stain on the Queen's honour as should hinder her marriage with the King of Sweden, the Archduke Charles, or any other princely suitor. And whether she credited this or not, it is certain that the Queen, when many sued for his pardon, would not listen, although someone wrote upon the panel of her chamber:

> *Sur front de Roi*
> *Que pardon soit;*

And the Council hastened the execution, and he was executed at St Andrews. This was the second time that a man perished on the scaffold for the Queen.

Châtelart died as proudly as Sir John Gordon, and would listen to no consolation from the ministers of his religion, although he was a Huguenot. He walked to the scaffold reading instead from the poems of Monsieur de Ronsard – reading out for his eternal consolation that poet's *Hymn to Death*, from the beginning to the end, and dispensing with all other spiritual work or spiritual aid. When he had finished reading the poem, he turned his head towards the window where he thought the Queen might be watching, and he said out loud: "Farewell, most beautiful and most cruel Princess in all the world."

And after this day the Queen appointed Mary Fleming to be her bedfellow and to sleep in her chamber.

In the spring of this year, the Queen was at St Andrews, healthy and merry, and riding in the fields when the weather was fine. One morning, when she was about to go to the garden, news was brought her that her Secretary Roullet had

23

returned from France, and he entered, in mourning, bearing with him news of the death of her uncle, the Duc de Guise, who had been murdered. And the Queen was full of grief.

Soon after followed the news of the death of her uncle the Grand Prior, and this caused her to lament the death of her husband, the security she had enjoyed in France, and to call to her mind her great present dangers and the want of trusty friends.

Upon the 26th of May (1563) the Queen met her Parliament in person in the Tolbooth. The Queen came to it in state, the Duke of Châtelherault carrying the crown, the Earl of Argyll the sceptre, and the Earl of Moray the sword. The Queen made an oration in the Scots tongue, and there were some among the crowd who said: "*Vox Dianae*, the voice of a Goddess and not of a woman – God save that sweet face; was there ever orator spoke so properly and sweetly?"

In the hall of the Parliament the ladies sat in the galleries in full dress, and all was gay and glorious. This was the first time that the Queen had sat in her Parliament since she had been crowned as a child, and she put aside her dule-robes and wore robes of State and her royal crown, so that men said: "The fairest rose in Scotland grows on the highest bough." But Mr John Knox was angered at the state that was displayed, and the favour showed to the Queen by the people, and he said that such stinking pride of women as was seen at that Parliament was never seen before in Scotland. A few days later there was another ceremony, and an indictment of high treason was exhibited against the Earl of Huntly after he was dead, his body having been kept unburied ever since the battle of Corrichie. The body was brought into the Parliament Hall in a coffin covered with his escutcheons, and it was set upright, as if the Earl stood upon his feet; then, the treason being declared proven and the forfeiture of his lands, heritages and goods passed, the escutcheons were torn from the bier and riven and cancelled; and his dignity, name and memory were deleted forth of memory and his posterity declared incapable of office, honour or dignity within the realm.

And the Queen beheld this ceremony beneath her Canopy of State.

At this time there were rumours of the Queen's marriage, and with a foreign Prince. It was thought that the Secretary Lethington was arranging a marriage either with Don Carlos, the Prince of Spain, or with the Archduke of Austria, and Mr John Knox, hearing of this business, became alarmed for the security of the Kirk, and preached with violence about the Queen's marriage. He prophesied the vengeance of God, saying that "whensoever the nobility of Scotland, professing the Lord Jesus, consents that ane infidel – and all Papists are infidels – shall be head to your Sovereign, ye do so far as in you lieth to banish Christ Jesus from this realm".

His sermon, and his manner of speaking, offended both those of the old and of the Reformed religion; and the Queen, when she had heard reports of the sermon, summoned Mr Knox to her presence.

This was the fourth time the Queen had summoned Mr John Knox to her presence, and this interview bore as little fruit, or maybe as evil fruit, as those which had been heretofore. There were two men whom the Queen met during her life whom she was powerless to dominate; one was Bothwell and the other was Mr John Knox. When the Queen saw Mr Knox the first time, hardly a fortnight after her arrival into Scotland, she tried to win him by reason; but the wit and ripeness of her words merely sowed in him distrust and aroused his sharpness, and he suspected her of craft.

She saw him a second time after he had preached in protest to the dancing at Court, in which the Protestant nobles had taken part, saying these festivities were held to celebrate the sufferings of the Huguenots in France. And the Queen asked him to come to her if she offended him, but not to rail at her in the pulpit; but Mr Knox said he was willing to explain her the form and substance of doctrine when she willed, but his conscience would not suffer him to wait at her chamber and have no liberty but to whisper in Her Grace's ear.

The following year there was a dearth in Scotland; the harvest failed, and there was extreme famine, and many died; and Mr Knox in his sermons said this was caused by the Queen's idolatry, who had defiled the land with the abomination of the Mass. At Eastertide of the year 1563, several priests had celebrated the Mass, which was against the law, and since the Queen made no move, the Reformers had seized several Priests and threatened to punish them for idolatry. The Queen sent for Mr Knox to Lochleven Castle in April to plead with him, and he replied, as always before, that the sword of justice was God's, that the Papists were idolaters, and it was right they should be punished for idolatry, just as Elijah had slain the Priests of Baal. And the Queen gained nothing from him, either by anger or graciousness, although she used both, and although by the latter and by flattering him for the first time she won his ear.

And this time, when he had spoken against her marriage, she gave vent to her rage, and she said to him: "I have borne with you in all your rigorous manner of speaking both against myself and my uncles; yea, I have sought your favours by all possible means. I offered unto you presence and audience whensoever it pleased you to admonish me; and yet I cannot be quit of you. I vow to God I shall be avenged."

And the Queen wept, and she wept still more when Mr Knox warned her once more of the curses that should fall upon her should she marry an idolater.

In the summer, while the Queen was in the West Country, Mass was said in Holyrood Chapel for some of her servants; and there was broil and brawl, and some of the Reformers broke into her chapel. Two of the ringleaders in this turmoil were commanded by the Queen to await trial for having invaded the Palace, and Mr Knox summoned the faithful to meet in Edinburgh on the day of the trial; whereupon, his letter being intercepted and shown to the Queen, she laid it before the Council, who agreed that it was treasonable for Mr Knox to have summoned her lieges without her licence. He was summoned before the Council, and the Queen laughed, saying: "Yon man makes me weep and wept never tear himself. I will see if I can make him weep." But although Mr Knox was the persecutor and not the persecuted, he declared that he had never accused the Queen of cruelty (which was not the truth) but only the obstinate Papists who were the deadly enemies to all such as professed the religion of Jesus Christ. And he spoke of the vices of the Papists until Secretary Lethington interrupted him and told him he was not in the pulpit. But Mr Knox replied that he was in a place where he was demanded of conscience to speak the truth, and speak it he would, impugn it who list. The Queen was greatly angered; and the Lords, although Mr Knox was guilty by his own confession of what the Council held to be treasonable, were all of one accord and acquitted him.

And this proved that the Queen was no match for Mr Knox; and what chiefly angered her was the injustice of the business, and her powerlessness to resist it; for she had persecuted none of the Reformers, whereas the Reformers persecuted those of her religion, even when they practised it in the confines of the royal palace, which exemption from the law had been promised her. And from henceforth the Queen, finding that neither the Earl of Moray nor Secretary Lethington could protect and defend her and her religion from insult, turned from those of the Reform and sought aid elsewhere; but she found it nowhere.

CHAPTER III

The Queen's hand was now sought after by princes throughout Europe. She herself was desirous of finding a husband, for although there were about her men of power and craft, both captains and statesmen, she knew there was none in whom she could put her full trust; each sought his own ends, and the people in Scotland feared a foreign marriage for her, for they were afraid for their religion. And the Queen of England feared any husband for her that should be powerful; and most of all a foreign man, the Prince of Spain or the Archduke of Austria. And the Queen, perceiving the great displeasure that was caused by talk of a foreign match, Mr Knox preaching against it and the Queen of England an enemy to it, put away her foreign suitors; yet she had determined to marry.

Now each of her four Maries had made a vow not to wed before the Queen; and at Holyrood Palace, on Twelfth Night a year after Châtelart had been executed, the Queen released them from their vow. For that night there was a great ball given to the Court for the feast of the Bean, and the Bean was hidden in the Twelfth Cake; and whoever found it was to be sovereign for that night; the Bean falling to the lot of Mary Fleming, the Queen said she should be Queen indeed, and lent her her Robes of State and the Royal Crown. She was apparelled in a gown of cloth of silver, her head, her neck, her shoulders all beset with stones. And yet, in spite of her finery, it may be that Mary Beton was the fairer, clothed as in the silver of the dusk; and Mary Seton in jacket of green velvet and kirtle of green satin was the tallest; and Mary Livingstone the slenderest, in a gown of white and silver. But the Queen herself was apparelled in colours white and black, with no other jewel or gold about her, but a ring which had been sent her from the Queen of England, which hung at her breast, and a lace kerchief of white and black about her neck. And she, although unadorned, was the more splendid and the more queenly. It was at this feast that the Queen told her ladies they would not have to tarry long to be released from their vow.

The same year, at Shrove-tide, there was the grandest feast which had ever been seen in Scotland. The Queen dined with the chief of the lords and ladies, with the English Ambassador near to her; and the Queen was attended by her four Maries. The Queen wore still her dule-robes of black and white, and she was attended by her gentlewomen and her maidens, apparelled, as were the four Maries, in black and white. Three courses were brought in. With the first came a boy with bandaged eyes, acting the part of Cupid, the servants singing an Italian song which was written by Signor David Riccio, who had been brought to Scotland by the Ambassador from Savoy, and left by him in compliment to the Queen, for, he having a sweet bass voice and being useful to sing in the choir, the Queen had made him a gentleman of the chamber. The second course was brought in by a fair young maid, representing Chastity, who sang verses in the Latin tongue made by Mr Buchanan. And the third course was ushered by a child who pictured Time, and again the servants sang verses by Mr Buchanan foretelling the lasting friendship that was to be between the Queen of Scotland and the Queen of England. The Queen pledged the Queen of England, and the cup passed between her and the English Ambassador, and the toast was acclaimed by three hundred persons. After this feast and in the months that followed, the marriage of the Queen was much talked of and debated; and the Queen of England's Ambassador pressed the Queen to give her hand to her favourite, Lord Robert Dudley; others came from France to press her to wed the Duke of Anjou. The Queen declined to marry the Lord Robert Dudley; but the Queen of England pressed the suit, for she was loth that the Queen should marry a foreign Prince. In the autumn the Queen sent Sir James Melville to the Queen of England to debate upon the question of her marriage and, if he were able, to discover the Queen of England's real meaning and intention. Sir James Melville went to London in September, and when he came back again to Scotland he reported all that the Queen of England had said to him.

The Queen of England gave him audience in her garden at Westminster. She told him she was determined to end her life in virginity, and she wished that the Queen, her sister, might marry Lord Robert Dudley, as being meetest of all. For, being matched with him, it would remove out of her mind all fears of any usurpation before her death. Sir James Melville was required to stay until he should see Lord Robert Dudley made Earl of Leicester. He assisted at this solemnity at Westminster, and at this ceremony the Queen, pointing to Lord Darnley, who was bearing the sword of honour, said to Sir James Melville: "You like better of yonder long lad." And Sir James Melville answered that no woman of spirit would make choice of such a man, who more resembled a woman than a man for he was handsome, beardless and lady-faced.

The Queen of England being determined to treat with the Queen concerning her marriage with the Earl of Leicester, she promised to send commissioners to the Borders for that purpose. Sir James Melville stayed nine days in London and conferred with the Queen of England every day, sometimes more than once. She gave him a fair diamond to take back to the Queen, and she asked Sir James Melville many questions concerning her: what colour of hair was reputed best, the queen of Scotland's hair or her own, and which of them two was fairest? To which Sir James Melville said she was the fairest Queen in England, and his Queen the fairest in Scotland. And the Queen, pressing again for an answer, he said they were both the fairest ladies in their countries, that Her Majesty was whiter, but his Queen was very lovely. She enquired which of them was of highest stature, and he said, his Queen. And this pleased the Queen of England, for she said: "Then faith, she is too high." And she asked if his Queen played well upon the lute and the virginals, and Sir James having said: "Reasonably, for a Queen," the Queen of England contrived that he should hear her play upon the virginals as if by accident; and when she enquired whether his Queen or she played best, he found himself obliged to give the Queen of England the praise.

The Queen of England was curious to see the Queen of Scotland, and Sir James offered to convey her secretly to Scotland by post clothed like a Page, that in this disguise she might see the Queen, as James V had gone to France in disguise with his own Ambassador to see his would-be bride. Sir James said that none need be privy thereto except one of her ladies and one of her grooms. The project pleased her, and she said with a sigh: "Alas! If I might do it thus." When Sir James Melville came back to the Queen she enquired whether he thought that the Queen of England's fair words and messages reflected what was in her heart. Sir James Melville said that in his judgement there was neither plain dealing nor upright meaning in the Queen of England, but dissimulation, emulation and fear; that she was afraid of the Queen of Scotland, afraid that she might chase her from the kingdom. She had already hindered her marriage with the Archduke Charles of Austria, and he was confident that the earnestness of the Queen of England in offering her the Earl of Leicester, which she knew at that time she could not want, was but strategy. Nor was the Earl of Leicester deceived; he wrote wisely to Lord Moray; and his letters pleased the Queen. The Queen of England now began to suspect that the offer she had made in pretence might take effect in earnest; so she gave Lord Darnley licence to come to Scotland; and the Queen of England's counsellors approved of this licence, thinking to delay the Queen of Scotland's marriage. Thus it was that Lord Darnley was allowed to come to Scotland and licence was given to his father, Lord Lennox, who had been outlawed for many years, to come to Scotland as well.

Now there was at the Court one David Riccio, who had come with the Ambassador of Savoy. He was a Piedmontese, a man of great experience, who understood the affairs of the State, and who pleased the Queen by his wit. He was mis-shapen and ill-made, and dark, but richly dowered with many virtues of heart and of spirit, fidelity, wisdom, prudence, as well as qualities of the mind. At first the Queen had made him her Groom of the Chamber, and, later, when her French Secretary retired to France, Signor Riccio obtained his office. The favour which the Queen showed to him, for she disguised not how useful he was to her, nor how greatly his wit and his accomplishments pleased her, for he was a cunning musician and sang with a ravishing voice, soon caused him to be envied and hated of the nobility, and Signor Riccio was warned of this by Sir James Melville, and was told that the nobility were angry because he presented signatures to be subscribed by Her Majesty, and because when they entered the Queen's chamber they found him always speaking with her. Signor Riccio said he would heed Sir James Melville's advice, but afterwards the Queen would not suffer him to do it, when the envy against him increased. Sir James Melville warned the Queen, telling her that the demonstrations she gave to Riccio, a stranger and one who was suspected to be a pensioner of the Pope, would have evil consequences for her. But the Queen said she might dispense her favours to whom she pleased, and paid no further heed.

Lord Darnley came to Scotland, and met the Queen at Wemyss Castle; and she was pleased with him, saying he was the best-proportioned long man she had ever seen, for he was of a high stature and accomplished. After he had been at Court for some time he proposed marriage to the Queen, and offered her a ring. But this offended her, for she thought it over-bold, and that he should have waited for her to speak to him. The Queen was advised by Sir James Melville to marry Lord Darnley, for he thought that no marriage was more to her interest than this; and Riccio, who had fallen into acquaintance with Lord Darnley and become his great friend, encouraged the match. Rumours of the match reached the Queen of England, who declared her displeasure. And the Queen, seeing the Queen of England opposed all marriages that were offered to her, determined to delay no longer.

The Queen, against the advice of her French uncle, but pressed thereunto by Signor Riccio, married Lord Darnley in secret, in Signor Riccio's chamber at Stirling Castle, and the favour she showed Lord Darnley provoked discontent among the nobility. But the Queen obtained agreement to her marriage from the Peers of Scotland, and created Lord Darnley Duke of Albany and Knight of the Thistle. The Queen held a chapter of the Order, wore the golden spurs and the green and the purple collar, for the whole fraternity had become almost extinct during her minority; and she chose her man, and bade him to carry out the duties of the office; and she chose as her man Henry Stewart Lord Darnley, who knelt at the footstool of her throne and pronounced the Oath in which were, among others, these promises:

I shall be leel and true to my Princess, my sovereign lady, Queen of Scotland, and her successors.

I shall never fly from my Princess, Master or Fellow, with dishonour, in time of need.

The nobles, headed by the Earl of Moray and the Duke of Châtelherault, determined to withstand the marriage, and tried to take the Queen and Lord Darnley prisoner when she was on her way from Perth to Callander; but the Queen took her horse at five of the clock in the morning, and with only three women in her train, and reached Lord Livingstone's house at Callander before her enemies were abroad.

The Queen came to Holyrood Abbey, and she recalled the Earl of Bothwell from outlawry; and upon a Saturday at nine o'clock, Lord Darnley was proclaimed King by three heralds at the sound of the trumpet, and the next day, at twelve o'clock in the morning. And upon Sunday, between five and six of the morning, the Queen was conveyed by her nobles to the Chapel, and she wore her mourning gown of black and her mourning hood; and she waited in the Chapel until her husband came, who was conveyed by the same lords who had brought her. The banns were asked for the third time, and an instrument taken that no man had spoken against them. The words of benediction were spoken, and three rings put upon the King's finger; and after prayers had been said over them the Queen went to her chamber and threw aside her dule-robes, after some pretty refusals, as every man that could approach her took out a pin, and then she went with her ladies to change into her bridal robe. And after the marriage there was a banquet, to which all the nobles were convened. Trumpets were sounded, a largesse cried and given; and after the banquet there was dancing.

On the first day of August after the marriage, George Lord Gordon, who had hitherto been an outlaw, gave presence to the King and Queen in the Palace of Holyrood House, and two days later by proclamation at the Market Cross of Edinburgh he was released by the Sovereign's herald from the process of the horn, and received to peace, with licence to resort and pass wheresoever he might please in any part of the realm. Soon after he was restored to his dignity and to the Lordship of

Gordon, and in the October following to the Earldom of Huntly, and all his late father's estates and honours.

But the Earl of Moray and the Earl of Argyll and others of the Lords were in their turn declared rebels and put to the horn.

These rebels took to the field, but the Queen pursued them before they had time to assemble, and they fled to England. The Queen of England, who had supported them and sent them money, when she perceived their cause had failed, abandoned them and upbraided them for their treason in the presence of foreign Ambassadors.

From this time forward Lord Darnley became ever more arrogant, and pressed for the Crown Matrimonial, which the Queen was reluctant to grant him. And there was discord and jars between the Queen and her husband. After Christmas the King withdrew himself from the Queen and retired into Peeblesshire; but later on there were festivities at Holyrood for the French Ambassador, who came to invest the King with the Order of St Michael; and on Candlemas Day the King and his father followed with three hundred men in a procession carrying tapers. The King swore that he would have a Mass again in St Giles' Church ere long, which greatly angered the nobles; and the Earl of Morton, who was a man of two faces and the Queen's Lord Chancellor, warned the Queen that the King was unfit to be entrusted with any more power than he had, and warned her against letting him have the Crown Matrimonial, and at the same time in the King's ears he sowed suspicion. Upon the day the King was invested with the Order of St Michael there was a banquet at Holyrood House, which was reapparelled with fine tapestry, closing with a masque. And the next day there was more banquet and maskery, and the Queen and her ladies, clad quaintly, presented to the Ambassador and to each gentleman of his train, a dagger cunningly made and embroidered with gold. And at this masque, in which Signor Riccio and several others took part, the King was already plotting his death.

Already, some months before, George Douglas, called the Postulate, who was a natural son of the Earl of Angus, was continually about the King, sowing suspicions against Riccio, and urging him to give his consent to his slaughter. And while the Court was at Dumfries the King and Signor Riccio visited George the Postulate at his Castle in Lanarkshire, and all three went out in a boat to fish in the waters of the loch, which was remote and large in circumference. And while they were fishing in the midst of this loch, and Signor Riccio's back being turned to the other two, George the Postulate signed to the King that he should throw Signor David into the water; but the King was not yet ready for such a deed.

The King now became accustomed to drinking *aqua composita*, and at a merchant's house in Edinburgh, being far gone in drink, and the Queen dissuading him, he used words to her which caused her to leave the house with tears. In the month of February a wedding was solemnized between the Earl of Bothwell and Lady Jane Gordon, sister of the Earl of Huntly; and there was a banquet, and feasting, which continued for five days.

But a plot to deprive the Queen of her authority was already on foot, and Signor Riccio was moved by the King to become a party to it. But Signor Riccio would not subscribe to the conspiracy. And he warned the Queen that the nobles were plotting against her.

Now the conspiracy was in this wise. The Lords pressed the King to assume the authority of the whole Government and to have the Queen shut up in the Castle. At first the Queen would not credit Signor Riccio's warning; and later she found the conspirators together with Signor Riccio in a little cabinet, and with them was Lord Ruthven; and the King was offended with the Queen for breaking upon their council. But although Signor Riccio told the Queen what they had been there debating, which was conspiracy and treason, even then she would not heed it, but treated the matter with disdain.

The Earl of Morton grew ever more busy sowing in the mind of the King all manner of suspicions; that Signor Riccio was more familiar with the Queen than her honour would suffer, and, what hit him more sorely, that it was Signor David who had persuaded the Queen not to give him the Crown Matrimonial, which belonged to him by right, both human and divine; which if she refused to do, he promised him the assistance of the Queen of England and of the Earl of Moray, as well as his own, and of all the rest of their faction who were now waiting ready in England to come to his aid if he would pardon their former trespass and restore them to their estates. This he could do without asking the advice of the Queen, whose will should be that of her husband, for she should depend upon him and not he upon her.

CHAPTER IV

The Queen knew nothing of this conspiracy, nor of the covenants and bonds which had been signed and ratified between the Lords and the King; and she assembled the Three Estates in the beginning of March to meet their Sovereign Lord and Lady in Parliament. The Queen had given the King authority to ride in state with her to the opening of the Parliament, where she would introduce him to the Estates and obtain recognition from them. But the King would not suffer her to introduce him, saying that unless he were to open the Parliament himself he would not give his presence to the ceremonial. Thus the Queen rode alone from the Palace of Holyrood House to the Tolbooth, in wondrous gorgeous apparel, and took her seat upon the throne without her husband.

Signor Riccio, being warned that the Lords were seeking his life, spoke of it to the Queen, and the Queen told him they said this but to frighten him, but he must remain by her side for his safety's sake. The rebels first determined to kill him at Seton, where the Queen had taken her leisure, and again they debated whether to kill him while he was playing at tennis with the King, which he was wont to do frequently. And one of the conspirators said it would not be well to do it in such a place while the Queen was absent, out of regard for what the people would think; but if they killed him in her presence and in her room the people would believe that the King would have found him in such circumstances and at such a time so that the King could not do otherwise but kill him.

Upon the 9th day of March, in the afternoon, the King played at tennis with Signor Riccio. And that evening, about seven of the clock in the evening, the Queen took her supper in her cabinet, with the Countess of Carlisle, Lord Robert Stewart, Commendator of Holyrood House, the Laird of Creich, Robert Bethune, the master of the Queen's Household, Arthur Erskine, the Captain of the Queen's Guard, and certain other domestic servitors, among whom was Signor David. The Queen was taking supper quietly because it was the season of Lent, but she had been counselled by her physician to eat flesh, in despite of the season, for she had then almost passed to the end of seven months towards her day of reckoning.

Before supper they made music, and sang in parts, Signor Riccio singing the bass, and a page held the torch in front of the music; and they sang songs of France. And the Queen sat her down to supper, leaving a chair vacant for the King. And while they were having supper, Signor Riccio standing with the other servants by the buffet board, the King came up by the private stair from his lobby into the Queen's cabinet, with Anthony Standen, his page, and sat down in the empty chair. And while the Earl of Morton and Lord Lindsay and five hundred armed men occupied the entry of the Palace, Lord Ruthven came into the Queen's cabinet in a nightgown of damask lined with fur, over which he wore armour and a casque of steel. And when the Queen asked him who had given him licence to come thither at such an hour, he said he had to speak with David Riccio. And the Queen asked the King whether he knew anything of this enterprise and the King denied it. Then the Queen commanded Lord Ruthven under pain of treason to leave her presence, declaring she would bring David Riccio before the Lords of Parliament to be punished if he had

offended. Whereupon in the outer chamber there was a noise
of voices, and the Earl of Morton, George Douglas and others,
came into the cabinet. And the Queen said to Lord Ruthven, the
leader: "What strange sight is this, my Lord, I see in you? Are
you mad?" And Lord Ruthven said: "We have been too long
mad." And so saying, they pulled Signor David out of reach of
the Queen, and hurried him out of the cabinet. The Queen was
forced with the press into her bedchamber , and she thought by
her princely presence to appease the tumult. But it availed
nothing, for the Earl of Morton in her presence struck David in
the temple with his dagger, and the wound seemed to be
mortal, for he fell without speech, and there in the ante-
chamber after he was dead they gave him fifty-one more
wounds. The Queen in the meantime stood in the middle of her
chamber, environed with these savage rebels, and one of them,
Andrew Ker of Faudonside, leant a pistol against the Queen,
and said he would kill her if she spoke one word more. The
powder took fire, but not the cannon. At the same time behind
her a servant of Lord Ruthven, called Bellenden, drew his
dagger and made to strike at her left side; but Anthony Standen
turned the blow aside by laying hand upon Bellenden's wrist.
They struggled together, and fell, and the Earl of Morton came
between them and thrust Bellenden out of the chamber. The
King was looking on all this while, and laid hand to his sword
and drew it. When the tumult was somewhat assuaged, the
King and the Queen both found themselves prisoners under a
guard of two hundred soldiers.

Presently an equerry came to the Queen, and she asked him
whether they had taken David to prison, and where. And the
equerry answered: "Madam, there is no more need to speak of
David, for he is dead." And the Queen, turning to the King, said
to him: "Traitor, and son of a traitor, this is my recompense for
the honour to which I have exalted you." And, so saying, she
swooned.

Presently Lord Ruthven came again into the Queen's presence and asked for wine, for he was sick; and he declared how he and his complices were offended with her proceedings and her tyranny; how she had been abused by David Riccio, whom they had put to death because he had taken counsel for the maintenance of the ancient religion, and entertained amity with foreign Princes and with the Lords Bothwell and Huntly, who were traitors. And in the Palace the Earls of Huntly, Atholl, the Lords Fleming, Livingstone and Sir James Balfour tried to come to the rescue of the Queen and, after they had parleyed with the Rebel Lords, they escaped from their chambers at a back window by cords.

The Provost and town of Edinburgh having got wind of the tumult in the Palace, rang the common bell and came in great numbers and desired to see the Queen and speak with her, and to be assured of her welfare. But the Queen was not allowed to answer them, being threatened by the Lords, who declared to her face that if she spoke to them they would cut her in collops and cast her over the wall. The King appeared in her stead, and assured the Provost and his men that the Queen and he were in safety, and commanded them to disperse, which they did.

All that night the Queen was detained in captivity in her chamber, and the morning after proclamation was made in the King's name commanding the prelates and the other Lords to retire from Edinburgh. The Queen was kept captive all day, nor was she allowed to see her servants or her guard. And she was guarded by the rebels and eighty men-at-arms. On the evening of that day the Earl of Moray and others of the banished Lords came from England; and the Queen sent for her brother and cried out to him: "If my brother had been here, he would not have suffered me to be thus cruelly handled." And her brother wept. But the Queen did not know that her brother had signed the bond with the others for the murder of Signor David. The Earl of Morton asked audience of the Queen, not, he said, to ask pardon for the murder of David Riccio, of which he was altogether innocent, but because, knowing that the Three Estates had been convened, he did not know why she should refuse to grant the King the Crown Matrimonial. To which the Queen answered: "My cousin, I have never refused to honour my husband in any wise; on the contrary, ever since I have wedded him I have exalted him to every greatness and honour. But those in whom the King puts his trust today are the same who have ever dissuaded me from his advantage."

When the Earl of Morton said to her that the time was favourable for her to show her goodwill to the Three Estates since they were convened, the Queen answered that being a prisoner nothing that she could do would be valid. The Earl of Morton took counsel with the King and the Earl of Lennox, and they determined that the King should seek the Queen, and by pretending repentance of the murder of David Riccio he should appease her, and that they should remove the armed guards from her Palace and allow her servitors access to her. This was done, and the Queen's guard commanded to serve her in the accustomed manner. The Queen spoke to the King with soft reproach about the murder of David and of the great harm and scandal this murder would cause her, especially among foreign Kings, and in particular in France, where her reputation had been high and unspotted during the long time she had lived there. The Queen told him how miserably he himself would be handled if he permitted the Lords to bring about the Queen's ruin; and the King, perceiving the wisdom of the Queen's words, asked her what outgate there was from their sad case. The Queen then said to him that she would find an outgate if he would follow her counsel, and put his trust in her, and swear not to discover her plan to others, which he promised to her. He revealed to her at the same time all that the Lords had plotted, not only against Signor David, but against her own life, whereupon the Queen told him of her plan to escape.

The first to be trusted with the Queen's design was the Captain of the Guard, the Laird of Traquair, Lord John Stewart.

And the King having dealt with him and found him faithful, he sent Standen to the Queen, for the King might not have access to her then, to arrange the matter, which she did willingly, and added much of her own judgement. The escape was planned for midnight the next night. There was a third person acquainted with the business, and this was the Queen's esquire, Sir Arthur Erskine. These three assembled together in the Queen's chamber about eight o'clock in the evening, Erskine, Traquair and Standen, and the Queen spoke to them of the confidence she reposed in them and warned them to be secret and faithful. And after wise directions and with sweet manner she dismissed the three until midnight, so as to put all things in order for herself.

The place of tryst with the horses was near the broken tombs of the ancient kings of Scotland in the ruined abbey of Holyrood House, through which the King and the Queen came by way of the office of her butlers and cupbearers. They crept through the charnels and vaults, and at the postern gate they were met by the horses, where the Queen was mounted in croup behind Sir Arthur Erskine upon a beautiful English double gelding, and the King upon a courser of Naples. There were in all six: Their Majesties, Erskine, Traquair, Standen and a *femme de chambre* for the Queen; and being favoured by moonlight they arrived all safe at Dunbar, twenty miles from Edinburgh, in two hours, where Their Majesties entered into the Castle and rested. When the Queen had partaken of some food, she wrote to her uncle, the Cardinal of France, and subscribed the letter, "Your niece, Marie, a Queen without a kingdom".

But as soon as she came to Dunbar many of the nobility who wished her well assembled to her, by whose advice proclamations were made convening her lieges to assemble. And after remaining at Dunbar for five days, she returned to Edinburgh well companied. The conspirators fled, the Earl of Morton, the Lords Ruthven and Lindsay, into England, and others within the realm. Others fled into Argyll with the Earl of Moray, and presently the Queen, knowing herself to be surrounded by traitors, and not knowing whom to trust, pardoned Moray, and restored to him all his honours, and once more he had the guidance of the realm. This greatly angered the King, who knew that Moray had been ready to betray the Queen. But Moray and Morton and the rest of those who had taken part in the murder of David Riccio, harboured a mortal resentment against the King for having betrayed to the Queen their part in the conspiracy. The King tried to persuade the Queen to hear his suspicions of her brother, for he distrusted his very shadow, and he threatened to kill him, assuring the Queen that his death would be for the welfare of the State and the comfort of the people.

But the Queen would not do without her brother's guidance, nor without his power over the Reformers, and she determined to pardon the Rebel Lords one by one, thinking that in time she would make peace between the warring factions and between the nobles who were at enmity one with another. She did not perceive that as long as the King lived there could be no peace; for it was sure that once the Rebel Lords were pardoned they would combine to ruin the King, and his ruin must bring about her own.

Moreover, the elements she strove to reconcile were all of them fiery and at war one with another. She would not forgo support of her brother, and she could not forgo the Earls of Bothwell and Huntly, on account of the services they had lately rendered her; for they had saved her life; and the Earl of Bothwell was now once more Hereditary Lord High Admiral as well as Captain of Dunbar; and the Queen had conferred on him the Abbey of Haddington, which she had taken from Secretary Lethington. Here already was seed of quarrel enough; but there was more; for Moray hated both the Earls of Bothwell and Huntly. And not only the Earl of Moray and his faction hated the King, but it was certain that if the Earl of Morton, who was now outlawed, should be pardoned, he would never forgive the King for his betrayal. So it was that although the Queen had seemed to triumph over her enemies, and to be thought well of by her subjects, and to be at peace with all, she was walking along the edge of an abysm, which was concealed at least from those around her. It may be that she herself knew more than those around her guessed; it is certain that never was her infelicity more great; and when one day the British Ambassador spoke to her of the Queen of England's wisdom, she said: "Speak not to me of the wisdom of women; I know my own sex well, the wisest among us all is only a little less foolish than the rest," and sometimes she would say she wished she were dead.

The King was misliked by all, and by the Queen; for she, like the rest, could not forgive him his treachery.

The time of her reckoning was now at hand, and the Queen passed to the Castle of Stirling and took to her chamber; and about this time the Queen of England fell ill. And all parties in England expected her death, and determined to proclaim the Queen of Scots as the Sovereign of England. But the Queen of England's illness proved to be the smallpox, and the danger passed as soon as the rash came out. The Queen of England wrote to the Queen, asking her for the receipt which had enabled her when in France to recover from the same malady without diminishing her beauty. But the Queen could not send her the receipt, for Fernel, who had prescribed it for her, was dead, and he had been unwilling to disclose the secret. The Queen of England wrote to the Queen wishing her short pain and a happy hour; and the Queen gave birth to a son upon the 19th of June; and her travail was long and sore. At the birth of her son the Queen made a vow to send his weight in solid wax to the Church of Notre Dame of Cléry, and to have a *Novena* made there, and a Mass sung every day for a year, with a daily donation of *Treize-Treizains* to thirteen poor persons. And her son was given a nursery establishment all Scottish, and a band of four violars. The third day after the deliverance the King ordained a running at the ring, and the Queen sent a jewel to be the reward of the best runner, which fell to the lot of Anthony Standen. When the King returned to the Castle, the Queen sent for Standen and spoke to him thus: "You see here lying by me him that some day must be King of England and so yours. You have been an eye-witness of his danger and most miraculous escapes, which was a clear argument of God's providence in his preservation. Wherefore, since you yourself have been an instrument to save him from danger, and since you have loyally accompanied him from Holyrood House to Dunbar and from Dunbar to this Castle, I make you his servant."

And the Queen commanded Standen to hold up his right hand, and she ministered to him the oath of fidelity, adding further that if ever Almighty God did favour her in that which was her due, she would acknowledge in England Standen's losses at home, and his services to herself and her son abroad; and she desired the King to knight Standen, which he did.

The Queen sent Sir Anthony Standen into France to fetch horses and other furnitures which were not to be had in Scotland, and at the same time to announce the birth of the Prince to King Charles IX, who was then King there. Sir James Melville was sent likewise to the Queen of England to announce the news, as soon as he was advertised of it by Lady Boyne, who was Mary Beton. She had wedded Alexander Ogilvy of Boyne the same year, in the month of May.

Sir James Melville found the Queen at Greenwich, dancing in great mirth after supper; but as soon as the Secretary Cecil had whispered the news into her ear the Queen sat down and put her hand under her cheek, and cried out to some of her ladies that the Queen of Scots was the mother of a fair son, while she was but a barren stock.

In the month of July the Queen went by water to Alloa, the Castle of the Earl of Mar; for having no carriage on wheels, she was too sick to ride on horseback. With her went the Earl of

Moray, and while she was there the French Ambassador came to felicitate her on the birth of her son, and the Earl of Moray and the Earl of Atholl solicited the pardon of Lethington, which greatly angered the King, who told the Queen that Lethington was the vilest of traitors, and had been guilty of the murder of Signor Riccio. But Moray said that Lethington had always been very much her friend, and had been innocent of the murder; and it was true that he was the wisest and the most subtle of the Queen's counsellors. So the Queen gave him full and free remission for all his offences, and admitted him into her presence; and this greatly angered the King.

At the end of the month of August the King and the Queen, accompanied by the Earls of Moray, Bothwell and others, went into Meggatland to take the recreation of hunting. After they had returned to Edinburgh they went both together to Stirling. The Queen passed to Edinburgh, but the King abode at Stirling in a sort of desperation, saying that he was minded to go to France, and it was thought that he was unwilling to be present at the ceremony of the Prince's christening, for he feared that the French Ambassador would not treat him as King. The King was vacillating and in two minds, saying that he would leave Scotland and go to France, and yet not going.

In the month of October the Queen held an assize at Jedburgh, and while she was there she visited with the Earl of Moray the Earl of Bothwell, who had been wounded in an affray on the Border and was very sick at the Hermitage Castle. And when the Queen rode home from the Hermitage to Jedburgh, her horse sank up to the saddle girths in a morass, and the Queen lost one of her spurs, which greatly saddened her, for she said it was an ill omen. On the next day she fell grievously sick herself, and lay for many days between life and death, and her physician and the ladies around her who attended her thought she had been poisoned; for she had fits of swooning and vomiting, and her body turned cold and stiff; and her eyes closed. Nevertheless, her French physician, Monsieur

Arnault, restored her to life by rubbing her, on the ninth day of her illness. And speaking very softly she desired the Lords to pray for her to God, and entreated the Earl of Moray, if she should chance to depart, he would not be over-extreme to such as were of her religion, saying to him: "I pray you, brother, that ye trouble none." And then she began to mend.

All this while the King remained in Glasgow, hawking and hunting, and came not to visit the Queen, until the crisis was passed and she had begun to mend. He remained there but one night, during which time he spoke with the French Ambassador, who thought no better of him, and, speaking of the King's tardy visit to the Queen, he said: "This is such a fault as I know not how to apologize for it."

CHAPTER V

As soon as the Queen was in tolerable condition for travel, she set out towards Edinburgh, and on her way she viewed the town of Berwick from a distance, whence, staying first at one castle and then another, she came to Craigmillar Castle; and it was here that the Queen reconciled the Earl of Bothwell and Lethington, and made Lethington Secretary of State once more. And it was here, too, that the Earl of Moray, the Earls of Argyll and Huntly and the Earl of Bothwell, went to the Queen, and that the Secretary proposed to Her Majesty that if she would be pleased to pardon the Earl of Morton and the other Rebel Lords, they would find the means to bring about a divorce between her and the King without her having a hand in it. But the Queen declared she would not agree to the divorce except under these two conditions: one, that the same should be made lawfully, the other, that it should not prejudge her son, otherwise she would rather endure all torments and abide the perils that might chance her in her lifetime. The Earl of Bothwell said the divorce might be made without prejudice to the Prince. And the Secretary said the Nobility and Council would easily find means, and that she should be quit of the King without prejudice to her son, which the Queen took amiss, not understanding the wisdom and the goodwill of the Secretary Lethington.

The Queen was in great dejection, for from this time onwards she feared that the Lords had determined to rid them of the King, and maybe of herself as well; but whether they plotted this or no, she knew the King must ride to ruin which was like to bring about her own. The King, persuaded by the Queen not to go to France, yet left her of a sudden, and went to Stirling, not to the Castle, but into a lodging; and the Queen went to Holyrood House to make ready for the baptism of the Prince. On the 15th of December, a Sunday, at five o'clock in the evening, the Prince was carried by the French Ambassador from his chamber into the Chapel between two rows of barons and gentlemen, each holding a pricket of wax in his hand. The Earl of Atholl bore the great *surge* of wax, the Earl of Eglinton carried the *salt*, the Lord Sackville the *cude*, Lord Ross the *bason and ewer*; these noblemen were all of the Roman profession. In the entry of the Chapel the Prince was received by the Archbishop of St Andrews, and he was held up at the font by the Countess of Argyll in the name of the Queen of England; and the Archbishop of St Andrews administered the Sacrament of Baptism according to the Roman rite. The Earl of Bedford and the Nobility of the new form did not enter into the Chapel, but remained outside the door. When the rites were performed, the child's names and titles were thrice proclaimed by the heralds under sound of trumpet; CHARLES JAMES, JAMES CHARLES, *Prince and Steward of Scotland, Duke of Rothesay, Earl of Carrick, Lord of the Isles, and Baron of Renfrew.* Then there was music, and the Prince was taken to his apartment. There was feasting and triumph and mirth, which continued so long as the Ambassadors from France and England were there. At the principal banquet Bastian devised a pageant, in which a number of men dressed as satyrs, with long tails and whips in their hands, ran before the meat, which was brought through the hall upon a machine, with musicians singing and playing upon instruments. The satyrs wagged their tails, which the Englishmen, being called "lang-tailed" by the

Scots, thought was done in derision of them; and one of them said, if it were not in the Queen's presence he would put a dagger in the heart of Bastian, who, he alleged, had done this to spite the English. The Englishmen sat down upon the floor behind the back of the table, where the Queen and the Earl of Bedford, the English Ambassador, were sitting; and they made a great noise, and the Queen and the Earl of Bedford had enough to do to get them appeased.

But the King was not present at the office of baptism, nor at the public amusements, and he went to his father at Glasgow.

Upon the Feast of Kings the marriage of Secretary Lethington and Mary Fleming was solemnized, the Queen giving the banquet and the bridal gown, but not being present, for she was sick. She had sent her physician to the King, for the King, when he reached Glasgow, had been taken sick of the smallpox, which prevailed there, and which had seized him as soon as he arrived.

The Queen continued in Stirling until the middle of January, when she returned to Edinburgh, where, after she had stayed for the space of a week, she visited the King at Glasgow, tending him, so that people spoke of a reconciliation between the two; and as soon as the King was in condition to travel, the Queen conveyed him in a litter to Edinburgh. As the air of Holyrood House was thought to be damp, he was lodged in a house that belonged to the Provost, and called the Kirk of the Field. And the Queen continued to tend the King here. But in the meantime a dark plotting had been on foot.

After the baptism of the Prince the Queen, pressed by the English Ambassador and by the Lords of the Council, had given an amnesty to Lord Morton, Lord Lindsay and the rest of the banished Lords, all but two. The Earls of Moray and Morton were determined to rid them of the King, and they designed to use the Earl of Bothwell as an instrument. They courted him, flattered him and incited his ambition, for ambition and pleasure were his ruling passions. They said that it would be

51

good for the realm if the King were away and if the Queen were married again to a man of spirit. They told him that if he would remove the obstacle, they would engage themselves to make the Queen marry him, and obtain the consent of the greater part of the nobility. To this end he could procure a divorce.

Bothwell was inflamed with passion, and he coveted both the throne and the Queen, and the nobles drew up a paper promising him the fulfilment of his desire and determining the conditions, which was signed by them all. When the Queen brought the King back from Glasgow all was ready, and it was designed that the business should be carried out upon the 10th day of February, a Sunday. The Earl of Moray that morning on his way to church received a letter which he said was from his wife at St Andrews, who was dangerously sick in childbirth, and he took his leave of the Queen. The Queen begged him to put off his journey, for, she said: "Your lady will either be well before you can come there, or at least your journey will not haste the birth."

The King knew there was treachery on foot and warned the Queen of it on Saturday, for rumours of the plot had reached him, but not the whole truth. Some confederate of the Lords had told him of a plot to rid the realm of the Queen, and to give him the Crown Matrimonial, and he, unable as ever to keep a secret, blabbed it to the Queen, who, aware now that there was treachery, knew not whom to trust; for least of all could she trust the King.

When the Earl of Moray took leave of her she was yet more greatly concerned than before. On Sunday morning the Queen attended the marriage of Bastian, her servant, and later a banquet; and after the banquet, at eight of the clock, she went with the nobles to Kirk of the Field, and talked with the King in his closet, while the Earl of Bothwell shook dice with the Earl of Huntly in the larger room. About eleven o'clock the Queen said she must take leave of the King, for she had promised to be present at the masque for Bastian and his bride, and to put the bride to bed. As she took leave of the King she took from her finger a ring and put it on his finger, in token of forgiveness.

When she reached Holyrood House, after staying a little while in the chamber where the bridal was held, she went to her chamber, where she spoke with the Earl of Bothwell and the Captain of the Guard. The Earl of Bothwell left the Queen, and shifted his clothes and put on a cloak, and passed through the guard, and went to Kirk of the Field. It was said that he and a servant, one John Hamilton, who had stolen the keys, entered the King's chamber softly and found him asleep, and strangled both him and his servant, William Taylor, who lay behind him on a pallet bed. After they had strangled the King and his servant, they carried them out into the garden, and they fired some barrels of powder which had been put in the cellar of the house, and the Earl of Bothwell went back to the Palace. About two hours after midnight there was a great blast, and the magistrates rose from their beds to search for guilty persons; but only one was found, who had been drinking wine in a house hard by, and who at the noise of the blast ran out, leaving his wine untasted. And the Queen, amazed at the noise, sent for Bothwell and commanded him to go to the town and see what the business was; and he returned and told her that the King had been found lying dead. The shirts of the dead men were not singed, nor were their skins touched with fire. The Queen lay quiet in her room. The King's body was brought back by four men upon a board to the Churchyard of Holyrood House, and was buried five days later in the Chapel. But first of all there was fear and then later rumours, widespread abroad; and libels, pamphlets and satires were published accusing Bothwell of the murder. And the Queen, thinking that neither she nor her son was in safety, went to live in Edinburgh Castle, and went to her dule-chamber, and gave over her son to custody of the Earl of Mar, who should keep him in the Castle of Stirling; and after some days she passed to Seton.

Now that the Earl of Bothwell had played his part, he expected the Lords to fulfil their share of the bargain and to procure him the hand of the Queen. And this was to their advantage, for it would remove the blame from themselves, it would defame the Queen in the eyes of the world, and it would ruin Bothwell, who was the possessor of all their guilty secrets.

But before the marriage could be brought about it was necessary to clear Bothwell of the murder, and the King's father, the Earl of Lennox, continued to cry for justice against the Earl of Bothwell for the murder of his son. So Bothwell was summoned to appear and be tried by his peers. The Court sat, and most of the peers were Bothwell's friends. The sentence of the Assize was pronounced by the Chancellor, and the Earl of Bothwell was absolved by law from all damage. He immediately set up a challenge upon the Cross that if any man (his equal) would say that he was guilty of the King's murder, he was ready to clear himself by the sword. And as soon as he was acquitted and Parliament had met and risen, he invited the Earl of Morton and others of that faction to a supper in the house of Ainslie, a taverner, where they subscribed a bond in which they bore testimony of his acquittal of the King's murder, recommended him as a proper person to wed the Queen and obliged themselves to procure the Queen's consent. As soon as this bond was signed, the Earl of Bothwell determined to make himself master of the Queen, and at first he began to discover his intention to her afar off, so she said, and to essay if he might by humble suit obtain her goodwill; but his words were in vain.

But there were some who warned the Queen that she was in peril from Bothwell; but the Queen, who had never feared a man, heeded them not; and Madame de Briante said to the other ladies that in Bothwell the Queen had met her match, for he regarded neither God nor man, and least of all woman.

The Queen had gone to Stirling to visit her son, and Bothwell convened his friends and with six hundred horse went out to meet her as she was coming back. Upon the Eve of St Mark, the 24th of April, he met the Queen at Almond Bridge, took Her Majesty's horse by the bridle and conveyed her by force to the Castle of Dunbar; and she was accompanied by the Earl of Huntly and Secretary Lethington and Sir James Melville. These three only were taken captive to Dunbar, and the rest of the Queen's servants were allowed to go free. The next day Sir James Melville was allowed to go home, and he said that the Earl of Bothwell boasted he would marry the Queen, whether she herself would or no. And while the Queen was prisoner at Dunbar Castle, Secretary Lethington angered the Earl of Bothwell by defending the Queen, and the Earl of Bothwell thought to have slain him in the Queen's presence, but Her Majesty came between them and saved him.

The Earl of Bothwell kept the Queen at Dunbar Castle for nine days, until she allowed him both to accomplish the marriage and gave him remission of it, and of all other treasonable acts done by him in times past. The Earl of Bothwell at once prosecuted the business of the divorce from his wife, to whom he had only been married six months. The business was carried out after the ancient and the new established form in the Archbishop's Court, the Earl suing for a divorce upon the score of consanguinity, and in the new Court the plea was founded on the head of adultery, which charge implicated the Queen by the Earl of Bothwell having carried her off. The divorce was finished in the space of a few days. The Queen was but nine days in the Castle of Dunbar when on the 6th day of May the Earl of Bothwell carried Her Majesty back to Edinburgh, and he ordered the men there to lay by their spears lest it should seem that this was done by force of arms. But at the entry of the tower that leads to the Castle he made semblance to lead her bridle; and the people said that Her Majesty was being led into captivity. And the people thought that all had been done at the Queen's consent. The Queen wrote to the Bishop of Dunblane that he should declare on her behalf to her brother, the King of France, the Queen and her uncle, the Cardinal of Lorraine, telling how this marriage had come about, which she said was in this wise.

How the Earl of Bothwell after the Queen's return to Scotland had employed his person in furthering her own authority and in suppressing the insolence of her rebellious subjects on the Border. How his conduct had excited the envy and jealousy of others, and, causing broil, had compelled the Queen to put him in ward whence he had escaped, and passed to France, remaining there two years. How the same persons who were the instruments of his disgrace had turned rebels themselves, whereupon the Queen had called Bothwell home and restored him to his former charge as Lieutenant-General. How Her Majesty's authority had so well prospered in his hands that the rebels had been constrained to fly to England; and with what dexterity he had rid himself of those who had held the Queen captive after the murder of David Riccio. How after the death of her husband his proceedings had become strange, and how she had been deceived in him, thinking that his readiness to fulfil her commandment had proceeded from duty, whereas he, while entertaining the Queen's favour by his good outward behaviour, was at the same time in secret conspiring with the noblemen to obtain consent to the furtherance of his designs, and had obtained a written bond, subscribed by all, in which the nobles not only consented to the Queen's marriage with him, but promised to be enemies to all who would impede the marriage. How as soon as he had obtained this bond he began to discover his intention to the Queen, but afar off, and to try if he might by his suit obtain her goodwill but, finding that her answer corresponded not to his desire, he resolved to seek his good fortune and put away all scruple. How without delay, and only four days later, when the Queen was passing secretly to Stirling to visit the Prince, her son, he awaited her on her return and, accompanied with a great force, took her prisoner to Dunbar. How, there, the Queen

reproached him for his ingratitude and made all other
remonstrance which might serve to procure her deliverance.
How his gentle words had belied his rude acts, he saying that
he would honour and serve the Queen and in no wise offend
her, and asking pardon for having taken her to Dunbar by force,
saying he had been constrained by love, the vehemence
whereof had conquered the reverence which he as a subject
bore to the Queen. How thereupon he had related the story of
his life; how he had made men his enemies whom he had never
offended; how their malice had pursued him ever unjustly; how
they had pursued him with calumny in respect to the murder of
the late King; how he was unable to save himself from the
secret conspiracies of his enemies, and how he could not find
himself in safety unless he be assured of the lasting favour of
the Queen: and how the surest assurance thereof would be that
the Queen should take him for husband, he protesting always
that he would seek no other sovereignty but hers, and serve her
as before all the days of her life. How, when he saw the Queen
was minded to reject his suit and his offer, he showed the
Queen what the nobles had signed. How the Queen, finding
herself in his power, sequestrate from the company of all her
servants, and seeing that those upon whose counsel she had
hitherto depended and without whom she was nothing (for,
quoth she, "What is a Prince without a people?"), had already
yielded to his desire, was left alone, and as it were a prey to
him. How she had revolved many things in her mind, but never
could find an outgate. How he left her little space to mediate
with herself, but continued to press her with importune suit.
How in the end, seeing that she had no hope of being rid of him,
and that never a man in Scotland had raised a hand to procure
her deliverance; and seeing that it appeared, both by the bonds
they had signed and their silence, that Bothwell had won all the
nobility, she was compelled to heed his offer. How he had dwelt
on the service he had done in times past, and had promised to
continue it. How he had said the people would not suffer the

Queen to remain unmarried; that the realm, being divided into factions, could not be kept in order without authority, and that force would compel the Queen in the end for the preservation of her realm to marry; and that the people would not suffer her to marry a foreign husband, whereas of her own subjects there was none who either for lineage or worth or valour could be preferred to him. How after he had used all reasons and all manner of persuasion he partly extorted and partly obtained the Queen's promise to take him for husband; and how, not content therewith, but fearful lest she should change her mind, he would not suffer the consummation of the marriage to be delayed, nor give the Queen time to consult the King of France, her uncle and other friends; but as by bravado in the beginning he had won the first point, he never ceased until, by persuasion and importunity, not unaccompanied with force, he drove the Queen to end the work which was begun, using her otherwise than she had wished or deserved; and how, seeing that what had been done could not be undone, she must needs make the best of it.

The Queen declared herself publicly in the Parliament House a free woman. The Earl of Bothwell was created Duke of Orkney; and on the 15th day of May the marriage was made between him and the Queen at the Palace in Holyrood House, after a sermon by Adam Bothwell, Bishop of Orkney, in the great hall, according to the order of the Reformed religion, and not in the Chapel, nor was there Mass. As soon as the marriage was made the people began to cry out on all sides, and those lords who were the first to consent to the marriage and to help to contrive it were those who exclaimed the loudest. They blamed her themselves and incited the people to blame the Queen and Bothwell, and then they took horse, and retired from the Court.

The Queen knew now that she had walked to her doom; but she had seen no outgate, nor was there any; for, being constrained to marry the Earl of Bothwell after what had passed at Dunbar Castle, she must needs, as she had said, make the best of it, in truth a sorry best.

The Duke of Orkney wrote to the Archbishop of Glasgow announcing his marriage, and said that Her Majesty might well have married with a man of grater birth, but never with one more inclined to do her honour and service. Thus they wrote abroad, the Queen and the Duke of Orkney; but there was much which they left unsaid. They said nothing of the marriage, nor how it was solemnized, without wine or music, pleasures or pastimes; nor how in her dule-robes, which she still wore for her first husband, the Queen was so changed a woman in face that there were some who hardly recognized her. The day after her marriage the French Ambassador came to her, and he noted the strangeness between her and her husband; and she, to excuse herself for this, said that if he saw her sad, it was because she could not rejoice, nor could she rejoice again; for she desired but death. And the day after, while she was in the small closet with the Duke of Orkney, her ladies who were in the chamber heard her crying aloud that they should bring her a knife wherewith to stab herself; and they thought that unless God helped her she would fall into desperation. The French Ambassador counselled her and comforted her as best he could; but he knew that her joint reign with the Duke of Orkney would not continue long; for the people were determined to bring the murderer of the late King to justice; and besides the Duke of Orkney there were no nobles at the Court.

The Queen was but a month the wife of the Duke of Orkney; and during all that time she was kept a prisoner and subjected to tyranny and thraldom, and never allowed to go abroad save surrounded by the company of harquebussiers. The Duke of Orkney was both jealous and unfaithful, for during this time he went back to his wife, who remained in his castle at Crichton.

The Queen had craved all her life to find a master, but hitherto she had ruled those whom she thought she had found.

She had craved for a King, and she had found King Francis, a sickly lad, and Lord Darnley, an overgrown child, weak and petulant. But in Bothwell she had found one in whom she thought she could put her trust, who had saved her life, and who had never betrayed her, nor sold her for foreign gold; and she thought his boldness and his daring would ever be enlisted in her service; but he aimed at a higher mark, to be King; and he used her but as an instrument of his own ambition and his pleasure, and as soon as she had served his purpose and satisfied his pleasure he discarded her like a broken toy. His love had been but pretence, for he loved his wife better; and this the Queen knew.

Hitherto, she had ruled all men, and as soon as she found the one man who could rule her, he treated her like a drab.

CHAPTER VI

The Queen had sent the Prince, her son, to Stirling Castle to the care of the Earl of Mar, and she greatly desired to go to Stirling to see him; but the Earl of Mar would not permit her to do so if accompanied by more than a dozen persons. And he acted wisely, for the Duke of Orkney desired nothing so much as to draw the young Prince into his possession, aiming at the authority he would secure under the title of Regent. Stirling Castle was in the hands of the Confederate Lords, and the Earl of Morton and his friends easily seized the excuse of protecting the young Prince to revolt and to revenge his father's death; and they said more; they declared they would redeem the Queen from thraldom and cruel tyranny, saying she had been taken to Dunbar against her will, and had wedded the murderer of her late husband by compulsion.

Thus the Queen, or rather the Duke of Orkney, designed to make themselves strong at home, and to prepare against the troubles which were already plain. The Duke of Orkney thought himself secure of those who had taken part in the murder of the King, and many of them subscribed to a bond that they would defend and assist the Queen and her husband; all but the Earl of Moray, who promised to assist the Queen, but signed no bond, and he pretended business in France and left the realm, leaving the Earl of Morton to head his faction. The

Earl of Morton and other of the Lords signed the bond against the Queen and the Earl of Bothwell, which was betrayed by one of the Earls; and the Queen and Bothwell sent to the North and called their friends there to come to their aid. The Queen went with Bothwell to Borthwick Castle, Bothwell thinking to quell those who were rebellious on the Border. The Confederate Lords, being advised that forces were coming to the Queen's assistance from the North, invested the Castle with two thousand men, and Bothwell disguised in a woman's habit, and the Queen disguised in a man's, escaped in the night and went to Dunbar Castle, where they were joined by their friends, who came to them in troops. The noblemen and gentlemen resolved to march to Leith. Two days later they moved to Haddington, whence they passed to Seton. This was on Saturday, and on Sunday the Confederate Lords, thinking that the Queen and Bothwell would attack the Castle of Edinburgh, marched to Seton, and the Queen and Bothwell set out to meet them. The Confederate Lords drew out of Musselborough and lay with their army in two battles, while the Queen's army advanced to Carberry Hill and stood in order. There was about half a league between them. The Lords were halted near a little stream. Monsieur du Croc, the French Ambassador, rode from Edinburgh with only ten horse and met the Confederate Lords by the stream, and told them that he had come to see if the quarrel could be settled without bloodshed, for he said that they were acting against their Sovereign, and that if by the favour of heaven they should win the battle, they would be in as bad a case as they were now; for whoever should get the better of the quarrel, the country would be the loser.

The Earl of Morton answered that he and his followers would go the Queen and serve her on bended knees if she would deliver up the murderer of the King to justice, or abandon him; and that if the Earl of Bothwell was willing to appear single between the two armies, he would find one, or, if he wished, a dozen, from their side who would come forth and declare that he was the murderer of the King, and fight him in this quarrel; so Monsieur du Croc procured leave from the Confederate Lords to treat with the Queen. The Queen answered that the behaviour of the Confederate Lords was ill, since they were going against what they had signed, and they themselves had married her to the man whom they now accused; yet, if they were willing to ask pardon, she was ready to give it; whereupon the Duke of Orkney came up and asked out loud, so that the army could hear, whether it was he against whom the Lords had taken arms. And Monsieur du Croc told him that the Lords professed to be the humble servants of the Queen, but he whispered to the Duke that the Lords were his mortal enemies.

After a long parley the Duke of Orkney bade Du Croc tell the Lords that if there were any of them who would be willing to appear single between the two camps, he would offer combat to any of his quality. But Monsieur du Croc refusing to deliver this commission, and the Queen saying she would not suffer such a combat, the Duke said there was no use in more parley; for he saw his enemies approaching. So Monsieur du Croc took leave of the Queen, who wept; and he went to Edinburgh.

The two armies remained standing in order one before the other from eleven o'clock in the morning until five o'clock in the evening. And on the Queen's standard there was a lion, and that of the Lords was a white ensign on which was pictured a dead man near a tree, who was the late King; and a child, representing the Prince, holding a small scroll on which was written: *Judge and Revenge My Cause, O Lord.* At last there was talk in both the armies that some expedient should be found; and that the Duke of Orkney should appear single between the two armies, and offer combat. The Duke of Orkney consented, and Sir James Murray and his brother, Sir William Murray of Tullibardine, accepted the challenge; and after that Lord Lindsay; but the first two he refused as not being equal in quality, and the last was discharged by the Queen.

During this long parley the Queen's troops began to disperse in search of food and drink, for the day was hot and they were ill supplied with water. In the meantime, a new treaty was proposed, and the Laird of Grange was sent from the Confederates to treat with the Queen, with an offer that, if she would put away her husband and come to them, all would be ready to obey her.

But in secret he brought a commission from the Earl of Morton who advised the Duke to retire to some far-off spot for the time, until better fortune; and he gave assurance that if he retired, none would be allowed to follow him. The Duke of Orkney took heed of these conditions, and said farewell to the Queen, and left the field without trouble or danger. Then the Queen, upon the conditions offered, went over to the Confederate Army, her horse being led by the Laird of Grange; and the Earl of Morton received her with great respect, and she desired to send for Secretary Lethington, but this they would not suffer her to do; and she perceived that she was a prisoner.

The commanded her to go to Edinburgh, and as she passed through the army the men in buckram spoke of her with great disrespect; and the ensign bearing the picture of the King's murder was shown to her as she passed; and the soldiers cried out: "Burn the whore!" The Queen was greatly angered, and could not contain herself for tears and rage. And she was carried a prisoner to Edinburgh. It was eight o'clock of the evening when they started, and the sun was setting; and she came to Edinburgh at ten o'clock, and she was taken to the Provost's house, a tall, high building, called by the people "The Black Turnpike". The Lords would not allow her to change her apparel, so that she entered the town in a coat little longer than the knee, which was made for the fields, all bedabbled with clay and dirt; and guards were set at the door of the house, and of her room, and soldiers in the room itself, who treated her disrespectfully; and when she looked out at the window of her room, which was on the top floor, into the street, the people flocked to gape at her; some pitied her misfortune, and others reviled and mocked her, and the white ensign was brought out and stood up before her eyes.

The next day she saw Secretary Lethington passing in the streets, and she begged him for the love of God to come and speak with her; which he did, and he caused the people in the street to retire. Secretary Lethington told her the truth: that to confer with her now at this time would do her more harm than good, for she was in peril of her life, the Lords having spoken more than once of killing her.

The French Ambassador demanded to see her, and the Lords consented, and said they would send for him and have him conducted to the Queen; but in the meantime there was an alarm in the town, which lasted nearly all day, and at nine o'clock of the evening the Queen was taken on foot to the Palace of Holyrood House, and two foot soldiers carried the white and bloody ensign before her. When she reached Holyrood House she was allowed to see her ladies, who welcomed her with tears; and they sat down at supper; but before supper was ended, at ten o'clock of the night, the Earl of Morton ordered the dishes to be removed from the table, and told the Queen to prepare to mount on horseback. The Earl of Morton hinted to her that she was to visit her son; but she was taken to the Castle of Lochleven, the house of the Earl of Moray's natural brother; and she was not permitted to take other clothes than the coarse brown cassock she was wearing, nor any linen.

She was put in the charge of Lord Lindsay and Lord Ruthven, and there were others who pursued her to rescue her, but the Queen was brought to the edge of the lake before her rescuers had time to overtake her.

The Queen was kept a prisoner at Lochleven for nearly a year. None was allowed access to her. But she won the hearts of some of her gaolers, and through them it became possible for her to receive news from the outside, and to send letters to her friends and to France; and she obtained, by the aid of Sir Robert Melville and with the advice of Mary Fleming, two ells of Holland linen to make trousers; six coverchiefs worked with silk and gold thread; a dozen of handkerchiefs worked with gold and silk in different patterns; a dozen knitted collars; four thousand pins; an étui furnished with comb; a ball of soap in the shape of an apple to wash her hands; and a small square of blue taffety, corded with silver, filled with perfumed powder; and, what she needed most of all, packets of silk and hanks of gold and silver thread, together with needles and moulds for raising, so that she might embroider a screen; which she did during her captivity.

The Confederate Lords ordered the Lords Lindsay and Ruthven, who were the Queen's guards within Lochleven, to bid her renounce her crown in favour of her son, threatening her with death if she refused; and, finding her obdurate, they used her roughly, so that, overcome with fear, they extorted from her a renunciation of the crown in her son's name. She put her hand to the renunciation without either reading it or hearing it read, protesting that she would observe the articles she had signed no longer than during her imprisonment, and calling upon those who were present to be witnesses thereof.

As soon as they had obtained this renunciation, the Confederate Lords acquainted the Earl of Moray, and desired him to come back to Scotland and to assume the Government; and on the 21st day of July they crowned the young Prince King by the name of James VI, and Mr John Knox made the sermon, the King being but one year and one month old. The Earl of Moray came back to Scotland and was received with honour by the Confederate Lords; and in August he was invested with the government of the realm under the title of the Lord Regent, in the Parliament Hall, but without the presence of Parliament.

The Queen set about to be the instrument of her own release from Lochleven Castle, as she had been before when she was imprisoned by the Rebel Lords in Holyrood House after the murder of David Riccio. She persuaded George Douglas, the Regent's youngest brother, to help her to escape; and George Douglas, who was called Pretty Geordie, undertook the business; but none knew of his design except Lord Seton.

And while the Queen was at Lochleven Castle it was said that she had been sick from the result of a miscarriage of twins, her issue by Bothwell; but there were others who said later, and in secret, that the Queen in the month of February, in the year 1567–8, nine months from the time when she was taken by force to the Castle of Dunbar, had been brought to bed of a daughter, who was privately transported to France, and became a nun in the Covent of Soissons. But the Queen never spoke thereof, and Secretary Lethington, when asked whether it were true, said that it was a matter whereof he knew nothing, but, had he known anything thereof, he would hold his peace, for such knowledge was like gunpowder.

In the month of May, when the Regent was in Glasgow, the business of the escape was carried out by George Douglas, who was enamoured of the Queen. And while the Laird and the Lady of Lochleven were both at dinner, one William Douglas, who was a page in the Castle, and said by some to be the natural son of George Douglas' eldest brother, stole the keys of the Castle gates and the Queen's chamber, and brought them to the Queen, locked the gates on the outside, and brought the Queen to a boat which George Douglas had ready, the Queen being dressed in the gown of one of her gentlewomen, Mary Seton, whom she left behind, and taking with her Jane Kennedy, her *femme de chambre*. As they went from the Castle Willie Douglas threw the keys into a cannon which was planted near at hand, and when they were midmost in the lake, the Queen stood up and signalled to those on shore, who were there ready with their horses. Lord Seton, with a great concourse of gentlemen, led her to Hamilton Castle, whither all her friends flocked, and many others who abandoned the Regent, among whom was Lord Boyd, who was said ever to turn to that party which he thought was the strongest.

In a few days the Queen's forces amounted to over six thousand men, horse and foot, and they determined to take her to the Castle of Dumbarton, where they said she would be in security. In the meantime, the Regent at Glasgow assembled an army of some four thousand men, and resolved to fight before the Queen should get supplies from the North, which had been promised by the Earl of Huntly. Having been advised by the aforesaid Lord Boyd, who, having gone from the Regent to the Queen and learned her plans, went back to the Regent and revealed them to him, that the Queen must march through the little town of Langside, the Regent occupied the bridge and the town and manned the houses and the ditches with musketeers. And when the Queen's forces advanced, they found the Regent in possession of the advantage, although weaker in numbers; and the Queen's army was beaten from the field. Only some three hundred were killed, but many were made prisoners. The Queen, who had been watching the battle from an eminence near the castle, called Castlemilk, when she saw that the day was lost, lost all courage, which she had never done before, and took a great fear, and rode from the field with the Lords Herries, Fleming and Livingstone, George Douglas and Willie Douglas, the Foundling. She rode all night, and did not halt till she came to Sanquhar. From thence she went to the House of Lord Herries at Terregles, where she rested, and thence, against the advice of her friends, she determined to go to England and to seek the protection of her sister, the Queen of England. So she embarked at a creek near Dundrennan, in Galloway, and with Lord Herries and other gentlemen and gentlewomen she crossed the Solway Firth and landed at Cockermouth, in Cumberland. The Queen sent Lord Herries to London, in hopes that she would be received with honour, and she gave him the diamond ring which the Queen of England had given her in token of a sure friendship. For the Queen of England had promised that whenever and as often as the Queen of Scotland had need of her sister's help, if she would send this ring back as a token, then she, the Queen of England, at the sight of this ring, would either come in person and help her sister, or else send her assistance, with all her power.

But before Lord Herries returned, Lord Scroop, who was Warden and lived at Carlisle Castle, was commanded to carry the Queen to the Castle of Carlisle, where, with a shadow of honour, she was kept under strict guard. And God and the world know how this promise was kept and how the Queen was used.

And the Queen did not know that on the very day she escaped from Lochleven and met her lieges at Hamilton, the Queen of England was purchasing the Queen's necklace of pearls, six cordons strung as paternosters, with five and twenty separate from the rest, finer and larger, and like black muscades, from the Regent at her own price, although the lapidaries of the City of London estimated them at three thousand pounds sterling, certain Italian merchants at twelve thousand *écus*, and one Genevese at sixteen thousand *écus*.

MARY BETON'S NARRATIVE

CHAPTER I

It was upon Candlemas Day (in the year 1558) the Court attended High Mass at the Church of Notre Dame de Liesse, and the Queen of Scotland, who was that year sixteen years of age, walked in the procession, bearing a taper in company with the other princesses.

Her gown was of white damask, pointed, with mantle and train, with a small partlet ruff of point lace; and on her head she had a white veil, and round her neck and her waist a collar and a girdle of sapphires and rubies: the sleeves parted and trimmed with pearl, and finished with ruffles. She was the highest of the princesses, and bended as she walked like a lily in the wind, her small head nodding the while, and so dazzling was that highness and that whiteness, that a woman of the crowd knelt down and cried: "Are you not an angel?"

Among the courtiers who watched the procession was Monsieur d'Anville, the son of the Connétable de Montmorency. He was twenty-four years of age, well-favoured and shapely; and among the courtiers he excelled all the others.

As she passed to the Church, the Queen of Scotland looked neither to her right nor to her left, as one rapt in musing; and as she passed from the Church, she looked towards Monsieur d'Anville as if drawn by his amazement, and she smiled upon him: and never was there and never will there be aught so celestial as the smile of Mary Stuart.

And therein lay haply the seed of much misfortune; for but for Monsieur d'Anville the Queen had not deserted the pleasant land of France for shores and folk across the sea. In the same year, in the month of April, the Queen of Scotland married with the Dauphin, he being but fifteen years old; and she was thereafter called the Queen-Dauphiness.

Monsieur d'Anville soon haunted the Court of the Queen-Dauphiness. He was gallant and merry, and as some said, fair as a god. He was able of body, and excelled in all games and martial exercises, and smiling he would confess to ignorance of letters, saying he could not write his name; the truth being that he disrelished pedants, yet had an understanding of wit as well as of music; and since among the learned men at the Court there were those who flaunted a false learning, Monsieur d'Anville took pains to seem to know less: and he was the braggart of a false ignorance, whereunto the letters he wrote to the Queen thereafter testified, as well as Monsieur d'Aubigné, who in later years saw Monsieur d'Anville tear a piece of bark from a tree and write upon it six verses in the Latin tongue.

At first he was awed by the majesty of the Queen-Dauphiness, looking up towards her as to a star; and the Queen-Dauphiness gave him no more than that meed of graciousness which she bestowed upon all alike; but later he became less fearful, and the Queen-Dauphiness on her part showed that she took this not ill, and that his worship, which was patent to all, in no wise displeased her. For the truth was this: ever since that Feast of Candlemas in the Queen's heart as well as in his own a flame had been lit: for the Blind God had wounded each of them.

And for a time Monsieur d'Anville was restrained by awe, and the Queen-Dauphiness was loth to heed worship from one so young, and from one who, it was well known, was easily moved to profession of love, she moreover being used to homage; and she masked her inclination until there came a day when with no word spoken by Monsieur d'Anville or by the Queen a barrier was removed, and they entered each of them into a realm of dream and dalliance which was the more entrancing because each knew that it could not be but fleeting and insubstantial.

And this interlude, albeit it lasted nearly two years, passed swiftly as a noon.

Never was there a court more glittering and more delectable, more richly adorned with fair women and gallant soldiers, famous wits and poets, than that of the Queen-Dauphiness. There were pastimes and pleasures daily, and dance and music and song. Monsieur de Ronsard and Monsieur du Bellay, and Monsieur de Maison-Fleur, made rhymes: and lutists married the verse of the poets with music for the ladies to sing to the accompaniment of the virginals: but the sweetest voice at the Court was that of the Queen-Dauphiness; and it was a marvel to watch her as she sang to the cittern and the harp or conversed as she sewed; so deft and so delicate were her hands, so magical her speech and her song.

And when she rode at the chase through the woods she seemed to be the goddess of the hunt: the heavenly Dian come to life once more. Such were her swiftness, her radiance, and her ardour, and so easy her horsemanship. And when she walked in the alleys of Fontainebleau, she seemed to be the very goddess of the spring leading on the golden hours: and wheresoever she smiled there was sunshine, and wheresoever she gazed there was worship, and whensoever she spoke there was wit and fancy, and wheresoever she walked there was beauty and grace, and wonder akin to amazement.

And at the Court, albeit well accustomed to beauty, and satisfied with splendour, men went about saying of her that never had such a princess been seen, nor one who while she outshone the sun at his brightest, so beautiful was her body, was at the same time so wise, so well-spoken, so accomplished and so learned.

But of all the hearts which sighed in love or were mute with worship for the Queen-Dauphiness, none was so sorely stricken as that of Monsieur d'Anville; and there was none upon whom the Queen looked with such favour. They were indeed twin beings, and when Monsieur d'Anville looked up at the Queen-Dauphiness there passed from his eyes through the air a message like a shaft of sunshine.

This interval was over-fair to last. Among the ladies of the Queen-Dauphiness there was a Mademoiselle de la Marck, the granddaughter of the Duchesse de Valentinois. This lady was at enmity with the uncles of the Queen-Dauphiness, and the house of Guise, and she was desirous to strengthen their rivals, whose chief was the Connétable de Montmorency. Whereupon Madame de Valentinois pressed the Connétable to marry his son with Mademoiselle de la Marck, and the Connétable determined to bring the match to pass. But Monsieur d'Anville knowing that his passion for the Queen-Dauphiness, howsoever high in her favour he might be, was hopeless, did what he could at first to escape, and thereafter to delay the match. And for a while he was able to stay the accomplishment of his father's will, alleging the youth of Mademoiselle de la Marck; and he was aided therein by the Queen of France, who, albeit she had small love for the Queen-Dauphiness, misliked the Connétable, and feared to see him grow more powerful. Whereupon Mademoiselle de la Marck became enamoured of Monsieur d'Anville, and albeit he had paid her but such compliments as he was wont to offer to all the fair, the Connétable declared that it was due to Monsieur d'Anville's honour to marry with Mademoiselle de la Marck incontinent; his will prevailed, and the marriage was solemnized. And the news reached the Queen-Dauphiness in the month of June, when her Court was at Fontainebleau. She was with her ladies in the garden, and busy, as was her wont, at her needlework, when a messenger brought dispatches from Paris. A letter was brought from the Queen, and it was read aloud by one of the ladies. And in this letter the Queen wrote that Monsieur d'Anville was married with Mademoiselle de la Marck.

The Queen-Dauphiness sewed no more for a while, and listened to the reading of the dispatch to the end, attentively, as if it had been some other thing, and presently she said that the heat irked her, and she passed to her chamber. That night when she was holding a Court, she was exceeding pale, and fell swooning in the presence of all and she was forced to retire and to be revived with *aqua composita*, and to one of her ladies who attended her that night she said she was the unhappiest woman alive.

The Connétable rejoiced exceedingly at the marriage of his son, thinking himself to be well seated in power; but his joy was short-lived, for at the joustings given in honour of the marriage of the King's daughter and the betrothal of the King's sister the King was wounded by a shiver of a spear in the eye, and he died of the wound seven days later.

The young King was now wholly guided by the House of Guise and the Queen-Mother, and the Connétable was deprived of his high offices.

The Queen-Dauphiness was now Queen-Consort of France. She retired at first to St Germain-en-Laye, but her sickness, far from mending, increased, and fear was felt for her life, but she mended in time to go with the King to Rheims for his coronation. On the way the Court tarried for a night at Lafert, the house of the Connétable, and there were Monsieur d'Anville and his youthful bride. And the Queen when she greeted them betrayed no private feeling; but it was patent that the presence of Monsieur d'Anville had restored her to health more swiftly than all ministering.

The King was now overgrown and sickly, and distracted by the furious factions which were warring and plotting around him. The Queen's mother had died but lately in Scotland, and the Queen, who could count on the friendship of none and on the certain hatred of the Queen-Mother, knew that Monsieur d'Anville alone of all those about her was prepared to live and to die for her; but he seldom haunted the Court, for the Queen-Mother was ever on the watch. Yet those about the Queen knew that neither she nor Monsieur d'Anville had suffered a change of heart; change of fortune had rather inflamed his passion, and the Queen's sorrow; and one day one of her ladies who spoke of what was to be, said that whatsoever might befall her, the Queen would nevermore be a happy or an unhappy woman.

Thereupon followed the King's sickness, and his death at Chenonceaux, from an imposthume in the ear, he being about to reach his seventeenth year; and for forty days the Queen kept, according to the rule, to her *chambre de deuil*, at Orleans. And during her first forty days of mourning the Queen was clothed in white from head to foot, and never was she more fair: a heavenly ghost rather than a mortal; and they called her *La Reine Blanche*.

The Queen was now Queen-Regnant of Scotland, and the lodestar of hopes and schemes throughout all Europe.

The Prince of Spain and the Earl of Arran sued her in marriage: the Spanish Prince being championed by the Catholics and the Earl of Arran by the Huguenots, who were led by the King of Navarre; but this King was but feigning, for he was enamoured of the Queen himself, and he would have put aside his wife to marry with her. But while the pretenders and their factions hatched schemes, the Countess of Lennox sent her son in secret to offer condolence to the Queen while she was yet keeping to her dule-chamber. This was my Lord Darnley, who was now fifteen years of age, and the first Prince of the blood royal of England: since his mother was the daughter of Margaret Tudor, the oldest sister of King Henry VIII, by her second marriage with the Earl of Angus; and he was a cousin to the Queen. (This visit was kept secret from the

Queen-Mother.) My Lord Darnley was presented to the Queen by my Lord d'Aubigny, who had been a servitor to the Queen's mother. My Lord Darnley was a handsome youth, of a high stature, even and straight, and well instructed in all honest exercises; and the Queen received him graciously; and she wrote a letter in her own hand to his father and to his mother; and after he had taken his leave one of her Ladies said to the Queen that if Her Grace would marry with that child she should one day be Queen of England.

And when her Ladies spoke one to the other of my Lord Darnley's graces, Madame le Briante declared he could never be the Queen's master: and if she must reign as Queen of Scotland, let alone England, she must needs marry a man who could be her master.

As time went by the great love of Monsieur d'Anville for the Queen in no wise diminished. Rather it was inflamed now that the King was dead, the Queen free and her hand sought after by the Princes of Europe. But the Queen-Mother kept them apart and made use of Monsieur d'Anville's young wife to aid her in her design. Presently the Queen perceived that so long as she should live in France there would ever be a gulf between her and Monsieur d'Anville, or barriers sightless and yet so formidable that she would not be able to remove them; and so great was her love for Monsieur d'Anville and so bitter her misery at being debarred from the fulfilment thereof, and from his presence, that from this time onwards she had no more desire to remain in France.

The Queen was pressed from every side to go to Scotland, and encouraged with the hope of succeeding to the Crown of England, both the Catholics and those of the Reformed religion in her Kingdom sending her delegates entreating her to return. Her uncles, the Cardinal de Lorraine and the Duc de Guise, desired her to reign in Scotland; and the Queen-Mother wished her away from France. Albeit she was loth to stay, for each day she perceived more clearly that the Queen-Mother would not abate the enmity which she had for her and would for ever be between her and Monsieur d'Anville; she was at the same time loth to go; for she had no desire to leave France, which was her adopted country as well as the country of her heart; and it may be she would never have gone but for the Queen-Mother and the Queen of England.

While the Queen was making a sojourn at Nancy, soon after the coronation of the young King, which she was too sick to attend, she retired to Rheims, to the convent of St Peter, with her aunt, the Abbess of Lorraine. She was loth to leave this retreat, but her uncles persuaded her to follow them to Paris in the month of June; after a fair welcome she was lodged at the Louvre, and she waited upon the Queen-Mother at the Tournelle; and the Queen-Mother in her turn visited the Queen; and this visit was not without consequence.

The Queen-Mother welcomed the Queen with honeyed words, but the Queen was not deceived, for she knew the Queen-Mother was never more to be feared than when she was prodigal of fair profession. And the Queen-Mother spoke of Monsieur d'Anville, who had suffered from a fever, and she said to the Queen: "I rejoice exceedingly that Monsieur d'Anville has recovered his health. If he should fall sick again I will send to him my own physician. In the meantime you should advise him to keep away from the Court, for the late hours weary him."

The Queen had now determined to return to Scotland, and she advertised Monsieur d'Anville to be circumspect through Châtelart, his servitor. The Queen solicited a safe conduct of the Queen of England, for a free passage by sea into her own realm, to be accompanied with such favours, as upon events, she might have need of upon the coast of Scotland. About a month later the answer was delivered by her by the English Ambassador, saying that the Queen of England could not satisfy her desire for a passage home, nor for such other favours as she required.

A threat would ever steel the Queen's courage and strengthen her resolution; and she told the English Ambassador that she could pass well home into her own realm without the passport or licence of the Queen of England. Thereupon the Queen determined in her mind to depart. And she tarried two days at the Palace of Fontainebleau, in the month of July, wishing to see those alleys, those trees and those fair springs and pleasant waters for the last time.

The Queen had put off her white mourning and put on black crape; and while she was at Fontainebleau she bewitched Monsieur de Ronsard; for he met her one day in the alleys of the park thus arrayed, and her veils were lightly stirred by the summer breeze, and under the black web Monsieur de Ronsard caught sight on a sudden of her long, her frail, and her delicate hand; and he commemorated the sight in pensive rhymes. Monsieur d'Anville, through the good offices of Châtelart, was the first to learn of the Queen's determination to leave France, and he said he would accompany the Queen to Scotland.

As soon as the Queen's pleasure became known the nobility of France made ready to follow her to the coast, and some of them to cross the seas; and of the Scottish noblemen there were with her the Earls of Eglinton and Bothwell, who had been in her service during the last months.

The Queen having put forward her voyage from the spring until the end of August, it was noted by those at Court that that year the spring wherein she was first minded to leave France arrived so tardily, so sadly and so coldly, that in the month of April there was not yet a leaf nor any fair flower. So that the courtiers, making augury therefrom, declared that this spring had exchanged her sweet and pleasant season for a rough and wild winter, and had been loth to put on fair apparel of greenness, and wished to wear mourning for the departure of this Queen who was the only sunlight, and Monsieur de Maison-Fleur made upon this subject an elegy.

When autumn came, the Queen went by stages to Calais, accompanied by her uncles and many gentlemen of the Court and many ladies; and of her uncles three embarked with her; also Monsieur de Castelnau and Monsieur d'Anville, and with him Châtelart, a youth from the Dauphiné whom Monsieur d'Anville had protected and made the confidant of his passion for the Queen. And with the Queen were her four gentle-women, each named Mary; and two doctors, one of theology and one of medicine.

The voyage lasted five days and was heralded by an evil omen: for, as the Queen's galleys were putting out to sea, a vessel in the sight of all foundered on the bar, and the greater part of the mariners were drowned.

And the Queen's galleys were threatened by ships which the Queen of England had sent to prevent them; but they escaped by the swiftness of the rowers; and they were concealed by a thick mist from pursuit, and thus anchored safely in the Port of Leith.

CHAPTER II

The Queen came to Scotland sadly, even as she had passed from France; she landed sooner than she was awaited, and nothing had been prepared. The galley wherein her horses had been shipped and her palfrey whereon she was wont to ride in procession had been overtaken and captured by the Queen of England's ships; and a few sorry hackneys with mean saddles and shabby bridles were sent to meet her; and the land was covered with a mist which chilled the French company.

The Queen wept for shame that she who had ridden splendid along the streets of Paris should offer so sorry a display unto her French kin. There were bonfires to greet her entry into Holyrood upon the night of the Queen's advent; and the men of the congregation sang psalms outside her window, while they played upon discordant rebecks and fiddles: a vile screeching, which the Queen endured with patience, and she bade the singers with fair words to continue; and for three nights she could not sleep for the noise, and she was weary unto sickness.

Yet in spite of the dark weather and the rude pleasures, the Frenchmen were pleased with their welcome, and yet more glad with the greeting the Queen had received from her subjects. For it was manifest that the people were proud to have so rare a lady for their Sovereign; but the Queen perceived that her path was like to be beset with thorns.

Before she left from France the Queen had claimed for herself and for her household the liberty of conscience which she had freely given to her subjects, and yet upon the first Sunday, when she went to hear Mass in her private Chapel at Holyrood House, there was tumult and broil, and her almoner was all but slain. And Mr Knox, the Calvinist preacher, was from the first her enemy, for to him her charms were as the wiles of Satan. She summoned him unto her, and he browbeat her with hard words, so that when he took leave of her she wept; and she knew that nothing would abate his hostility.

There was banquet at Blackfriars Wynd for the French noblemen; and two days later the Queen entered her city and made progress through the streets with pageant to the Castle; but the pageant, albeit rich in devices and loud with acclamation, was marred by exhibitions of blasphemy, whereat the Frenchmen marvelled and the Queen almost wept.

The night following the Queen held a feast at Holyrood House, which had been made new by furniture and ornament brought from France: there was cloth from Arras, chiming clocks from Blois, crystal from Venice, carpets from Turkey, lamps from Italy and cabinets adorned with the needlework of the Queen and her gentlewomen; tables with cunningly wrought chessmen, and everywhere devices; the device embroidered upon the Queen's Canopy of State being:

"In my End is my Beginning."

And amidst that pride and glitter, surrounded by so many gallant courtiers and fair women, the Queen in her robe of dule was the highest and the fairest.

That night the Queen trod a measure with Monsieur d'Anville. The Queen's uncle, the Grand Prior, was to sail to France in October, and Monsieur d'Anville was to sail with him; but the nearer the time approached the more loth was Monsieur d'Anville to leave; and he declared to the Queen, that being unable to live without her, he would put away his wife and obtain a divorcement if the Queen would be willing to marry with him.

The Queen said to him that, were she a free woman, she would choose him rather than any Prince in Europe; but since Providence had determined she should be Queen of Scotland and so near in succession to the throne of England, a Queen she would be; and she must mind her duty before her own inclination: nor could she marry with a man who was already wedded, and so there must be an end to dreams; whereat Monsieur d'Anville grieved. There was maskery at Holyrood House in honour of the departing French noblemen, when at that masque the Queen bade Monsieur d'Anville a lasting farewell; yet, quoth she, should he be freed by the death of his wife, or any other fresh design of Providence, she would marry with him and with no other.

Upon the morrow the French noblemen sailed for France, leaving behind them the Queen's younger uncle, the Marquis d'Elbœuf. The Queen was distressed at this parting; she rose upon that morning to bid them farewell, and then she took to her bed again in sorrow; for she knew she had cut the chain that bound her to the land of her adoption, and that the man who loved her above all had left her, and for ever. But albeit Monsieur d'Anville had gone from Scotland, his part in the fortunes of the Queen was not yet ended: for the seeds that we sow stop not from growing because we neglect them.

Not many months later the Marquis de Moretta, the Ambassador from Savoy, came to Holyrood House. On the day of the death of her husband the King of France, the fifth of the month of December, the Queen ordered dirge to be sung in the Chapel, and she entreated her nobles to put on black that day; but not one of them carried out her wish; and the Earl of Bothwell, famous for the gaudiness of his apparel, which became him ill, was gaily clad in gold. Of such a nature were the slights that often caused the Queen to weep in secret.

The Queen had three valets of her chamber who sang three parts in her Chapel, and she wanted a bass. The Marquis had with him a secretary from the Piedmont in Italy, named Signor David Riccio di Pancalieri; a dark man, small and crooked in body; he was a rare musician, and his voice was ear-ravishing, and that day, at Mass, he sang the fourth part; and as the *Dies Irae* was chanted his voice filled the building, and pierced the senses of all present with so rich a sorrow that the Queen wept.

When Mass was ended, the Queen summoned to her Signor Riccio and complimented him, and she was pleased by his carriage and his turn of speech; and when the Marquis de Moretta went from Scotland he left Signor Riccio behind him in compliment to the Queen, knowing it to be her pleasure; and the Queen made him a Groom of the Chamber, in which office he entered with credit.

It was about this time that Monsieur d'Elbœuf and the Earl of Bothwell put the town in disorder by roaming the streets of Edinburgh in masks, which led to strife between the Earl of Bothwell and the Earl of Arran; and the Earl of Bothwell, being reproved by the Queen, met the reproof with contumacy; further broil and riot ensued, and the Earl of Bothwell was banished from the city for a month.

And in February, after the marriage of the Lord James Stewart, the Queen's brother natural (who was now her Prime Minister), the Earl of Bothwell came back and brewed fresh mischief. The Earl of Arran was demented with love of the Queen, and the Earl of Bothwell made his peace with him through the good offices of Mr John Knox, and made him privy to a design that they should both carry out together: to seize the person of the Queen, and to let her remain in the keeping of the Earl of Arran at Dumbarton Castle, while they then should rule all. But the Earl of Arran wrote to the Queen and revealed the plot, accusing his father of complicity in it.

The Earls of Arran and Bothwell were confined to Edinburgh Castle, whence after three months the Earl of

Bothwell fled to England, and thence to France. This was in the month of August, and about the same time that the Queen set out to visit her people in the North of Scotland.

At the beginning of the year the Queen had in secret given Lord James Stewart, whom she had already exalted to be Earl of Mar, the Earldom of Moray; but the demesnes of this Earldom had been granted to the Earl of Huntly, who had taken possession on the death of the last Earl. The Earl of Huntly was the chief of the Catholics in the Kingdom, and the Queen's Lord Chancellor; but the Queen regarded him with coolness, fearing his zeal; for he had complained to her uncles that she was but a lukewarm Catholic, whereat she was wrathful. Lord James Stewart was avid of money and greedy for land; having been raised from the Church and being the Commendator of two Priories in Scotland, he joined those of the Reform, but retained the Church properties and collected great possessions of land. But this did not satisfy his greed, nor did the Earldom of Mar. He coveted the demesnes of the Earl of Huntly, but these he could not possess so long as the Earl of Huntly lived; and prudent in all matters he awaited his opportunity, and it came. The Earl of Huntly's third son, Sir John Gordon, was the most comely man in the land, and, it was said, enamoured of the Queen, and plotting to carry her away to one of his castles; but the Queen had never regarded him save with coolness.

A feud between Sir John and another led to a brawl in the streets of Edinburgh, and the Queen's brother committed Sir John Gordon to the Tolbooth, in a dungeon among felons, whence he escaped and fled to Aberdeenshire.

The Queen set out on a progress through her northern Kingdom, and she was to hold a Justice Court at Aberdeen. Her brother went with her. The Queen was met at Aberdeen by the Earl and Countess of Huntly, who entreated the Queen to pardon their son, whereunto she consented, so long as he should appear at the Justice Court. But the Queen would not go to Huntly Castle, although it was within three miles of her way, and although the Earl had made wondrous preparations, both there and at the Castle of Strathbogie, to welcome her.

The Queen's household and the English Ambassador suffered from the extreme weather and the painful ways; but not the Queen; she outrode her followers, and was only sad, she said, at not being a man, to know what life it was to lie all night in the fields, or to walk upon the causeway with a jack and a knapsack, a Glasgow buckler and a broadsword.

In September they reached the chief demesne of the Earls of Moray; and here for the first time the Lord James called himself Earl of Moray; and the next day he led the Queen to Inverness, where the Lord Gordon was the keeper of the Castle. The Lord Gordon was absent, and his deputy, albeit the Castle was a royal fortress, would not surrender it without orders from the keeper; wherefore, when the Castle was taken the next day, he forfeited his life.

The Queen was undismayed by this affray; for, as ever, danger sharpened her spirit. And those around her bade her believe that the Earl of Huntly was plotting against her and designed that his son, Sir John Gordon, albeit married, should carry her off and become King Matrimonial.

At first the Queen lent credence to the whisperings of Lord James, albeit the Countess of Huntly swore by the Rood on the Altar that her husband would live and die a faithful subject of the Queen. "Had he forsaken his religion," said she, "as those about the Queen's Grace, he had never been put upon as he is now."

But these words, albeit repeated to the Queen, availed not; soldiers were sent to take Findlater Castle, and Sir John Gordon slew some and captured others. The Earl of Huntly was summoned to appear with his son at Aberdeen, and not appearing was put to the horn. Then the Earl of Huntly in his folly took to the field against his Queen with five hundred men, and he was surrounded by the two thousand men of the Earl of Moray at Corrichie, and died as soon as he was taken.

And now that the Earl of Huntly was dead and his cause ruined, the Queen's mind began to misgive her; and she wondered whether maybe he, and not her brother, were not her more faithful servant. Three days after Sir John Gordon was taken to Aberdeen and sentenced to be beheaded. He was executed at Aberdeen, and six gentlemen of the same name were hanged that day The scaffold was built opposite to the house where the Queen was lodged. The Earl of Moray, her brother, said the Queen must witness the execution: this she was loth to do, and there were high words between them. But her brother said that, since it had been bruited abroad that Sir John Gordon meditated violence on the Queen's person, and that many of her enemies believed that this was not against her own will, she must countenance the punishment in public. And her brother had the Chair of State set in the Queen's open window, and he stood beside her.

Sir John Gordon mounted the scaffold with a proud step; he was pitied and lamented, for he was a noble youth, very beautiful, and entering upon the prime of his age. And he marked the Queen, and, turning towards her, confessed that her presence was a solace at his death, for he was about to suffer for his love of her. The Queen was near enough to hear his words, and Sir John Gordon straitway kneeling down, looked long at her and with worship; and the Queen wept exceedingly. Then he laid his head upon the block, and the executioner, stricken maybe by the Queen's sorrow, or else unskilled, struck awry and inflicted a grisly wound, so that his body was drenched with blood, and he remained alive and endured several blows. And the Queen cried aloud and swooned, and she was borne from the window and laid upon her bed.

Soon after, the Queen passed to Montrose, where one evening after supper a messenger came from M. d'Anville.

The first war of religion had lately broken out in France, and Châtelart, who was of the Reformed religion, was of two minds and greatly perplexed: whether to go to Orleans and to fight with the others of his faith, or whether to stay with M. d'Anville and to fight against the Huguenots; he was loth to fight against his faith and his conscience; and he loved his master, M. d'Anville, too greatly to fight against him. Thus, he resolved to do neither, but to leave France for a while, and to let time fly until the quarrel should be ended. He told M. d'Anville of his resolution, and begged him to give him letters for the Queen of Scotland, whereat M. d'Anville rejoiced greatly and charged him with an embassy. Thus Châtelart came to Montrose with a letter from his master for the Queen. The Queen was heartened once more at receiving news from M. d'Anville and from France, and at being able to converse once more in the French tongue with one whom she had known while she was yet Queen-Dauphiness.

There was music and dance and song, and Châtelart made rhymes for the Queen, and the Queen answered in rhyme. And this was the purpose of Châtelart's embassy: M. d'Anville had written to the Queen imploring her once more to be his wife. But to this she answered in the same words as she had answered before when M. d'Anville was in Scotland. But she was loth to let Châtelart go, as his presence brought to her the gleam of the sunshine of France, and he followed the Court to Perth and Edinburgh, where for a time the Queen fell sick of the *New Acquaintance*, a disease that struck the whole Court and spared none, and was accompanied by pains in the head and a soreness in the stomach, remaining with some but three days and with others longer.

The Queen held a feast upon her birthday, and there was dancing, in which the Queen danced the Purpose, or Talking Dance, with Châtelart: they made a peerless pair; for at this Court there was not one of the Nobles who could dance in a manner fitting to match the steps of the Queen, who trod the floor as if an angel were directing her; and so sure and so swift were her movements that they seemed easy to counterfeit, and yet each was accomplished before an onlooker could say how or when it had been made.

And so fair to witness was this dance that the Court beheld it in silence; and when it was ended the Queen curtsied to her partner, bending to the ground and springing to her full tallness again in a magical trice. And Châtelard as he watched the Queen a-curtsying, seemed as one consumed by a great longing, and yet as one without hope.

Madame de Briante warned the Queen that Châtelart seemed to have forgot his mission, and was in peril of soaring too near the sun, and that he would do well to go back to France; but the Queen laughed, and said that with Châtelart, like all Frenchmen, it was a point of honour to pay homage to all women.

So Châtelart stayed on, nor did the Queen cease to converse with him, nor did she treat him more coolly; and he wrote rhymes and sonnets to the Queen, and the Queen made answer to him in verse, for she rhymed well for a Queen.

Mr Knox was greatly angered by the dancing at the Palace, and he preached a sermon inveighing sorely against it; and the Noblemen in their reports to the Queen aggravated the tenour of his discourse. The Queen summoned Mr Knox to her bedchamber, where she received him among her Lords and Ladies, and Mr Knox rehearsed his sermon; and when the Queen bade him to come to her in private if he heard anything of herself that he misliked, he replied that he was called to a public function within the Kirk of God, to rebuke the sins of all, but not appointed to come to every man in particular. And, in speaking, he addressed the Lords and the Ladies, neglecting the Queen as if she were a child, and he said that he was even now waiting at the Court when he should be at his book.

When he had departed, with a proud smile, and the Lords left the Queen alone with her Ladies, Madame de Briante said to the Queen that she was wasting words in reasoning with Mr Knox, for the better she reasoned, the more greatly he would suspect her; but that she could win him, if at all, by flattery, for he was puffed up with pride and a vain man.

And the Queen took this advice to heart.

Early in the New Year, the Queen fell sick again, and the Earl of Moray caused George, Lord Gordon, the Earl of Huntly's heir, to be arraigned for High Treason; and, albeit he had taken no part in the revolt of his father, and had been living in peace, with for his only crime the name of Gordon, he was condemned to be hanged. But the Queen would not sign this death warrant, and ordered Lord Gordon to be removed from Edinburgh to Dunbar and kept in the free ward under the charge of the Captain.

And in despite of all my Lord Moray's persuasion, she would not sign this death warrant; so my Lord Moray resorted to wile. And the Queen being sick, he brought her a number of papers dealing with the business of the day which she was wont to sign without reading, after he had told her of their purport; and among them he slipped a mandate to the Captain of Dunbar bidding him, when he should receive it, to cause Lord Gordon (now the Earl of Huntly) to be beheaded incontinent.

The Queen signed the mandate unwittingly, and the Earl of Moray sent it by a messenger to Dunbar.

Late at night, when the Queen was lying in her bed and still awake, for Madame de Cric was reading to her from the Romance of Gyron the Courteous, the Captain of Dunbar rode to Holyrood and won admittance into the Palace, but was stopped at the door of the Queen's chamber. Madame de Cric went out to him, and he told her that he came on an errand that brooked no delay. The Queen bade him brought to her bedside and, kneeling down, he said that he had obeyed her order for striking off Lord Gordon's head, whereat the Queen broke into lamentation, and the Captain showed her the mandate signed by her hand; and the Queen said: "This is my brother's subtlety, who without my knowledge or consent hath abused me in this and many other things."

The Captain then confessed that he had stayed his hand till he should hear her Grace's will from her own lips. And the Queen, greatly rejoicing, tore up the mandate and bade the Captain to credit no order save what he should receive from herself in her presence.

As time went on, it became patent to all at Court that Châtelart had quite forgot his mission, and his master, and was aware only of the Queen's presence; and when the Queen was absent he was like to a dead man, for he was enamoured of the Queen even unto ecstasy. Madame de Briante and others spoke to the Queen about it, and the Queen no longer denied it to Madame de Briante; albeit she laughed away her brother's words when he spoke of it; and she said it were better for Châtelart to go back to France, and that she would write dispatches for him to take, and this she did.

Madame de Briante warned Châtelart that he must make ready to depart, for the Queen had written dispatches for him to bear to France incontinent, and orders were given for Châtelart's voyage and all was made ready; but Châtelart said he had no longer any desire to return to France, and Madame de Briante warned him to be prudent, or he would bring misfortune upon himself and upon the Queen. And all at once he became meek, and said that he would obey the Queen in all things.

That night, whether this sharp turn of affairs had roused his passion to a frenzy, or whether he had long brooded upon his mad purpose, Châtelart was found in the Queen's chamber under the bed, with a sword and a dagger beside him, just before the Queen entered her chamber; but no word of this was said until the next day.

The next day, when the Queen was told of this, she was exceedingly wrathful, and amazed that a man so chivalrous could dare such a thing, for he knew, said she, how easy it was to besmirch a Queen's honour in a country where she had many enemies. But the matter, albeit at Court it was known, was not noised abroad, and the Queen went from Edinburgh the next day. Before leaving, she sent a message to Châtelart bidding him leave the Court and the country incontinent.

She was on her way to St Andrews, and she stayed the night at Burntisland.

Châtelart made as if he were leaving the country, but he followed the Queen in secret; and as the Queen went to her chamber that night, Châtelart, who had hidden himself in her chamber, came forth and knelt before her. The Queen's Ladies called for help and the Earl of Moray was summoned; the Queen cried in her rage: "Stab the traitor", and the Earl of Moray led him away.

Châtelart was examined, roughly some said, and tried at St Andrews and condemned to be beheaded.

And it was said by some that Châtelart, when he was examined, confessed that he had been suborned by the enemies of the House of Guise to cast a slur upon the Queen's honour, so as to prevent her marriage with the King of Sweden, or any other Prince; but the Captain of the Guard told Erskine, who was his cousin, that Châtelart had confessed nothing save his love for the Queen, and for her sake he was glad to die; for death to him was preferable to life bereft of her countenance.

Suit was made for his pardon; but the Council would have none of it; saying that if the Queen pardoned him the whole world would believe in her guilt. So the Queen consented to his execution, but she designed, nevertheless, to save his life; and she bade one of her equerries, who was a cousin of the Captain of the Guard , to contrive his escape; and this was done. Horses were got ready, and it was planned that he should fly in secret to France; but that night the gaoler, who was of the Reformed religion, was stricken with doubt, and neither persuasion nor bribes would move him. It was in vain that Erskine told him that Châtelart was a Huguenot. The gaoler said he was a Frenchman, and an idolater, and deserved to die.

And so the plan miscarried, and Châtelart was led to the scaffold. He walked as easily to death as he had walked to the dance; and, refusing the offices of the Ministers of his religion, he rehearsed Ronsard's *Hymn to Death* on the way to the scaffold, and, as he reached it, he spoke loudly the line:

Je te salue, heureuse et profitable Mort.

And before the blow of the axe fell he said:

"Farewell, most lovely and most cruel of Princesses."

The day of his execution the Queen wept sorely: tears of sorrow for Châtelart, and, in greater number, tears of rage against the Council and against her brother, who would not rest, said she, until they had been undoing.

Thus ended Châtelart's mission, and with it the Queen's commerce with M. d'Anville; and this mad adventure, with its woeful consequence, did the Queen grievous harm: for men remembered it later and blamed the Queen as having been guilty. Thus it was that M. d'Anville, the man who loved the Queen better than life, was instrumental in bringing about her bane: so true is it that the deepest wounds we receive are inflicted by those whom we love and by whom we are beloved.

CHAPTER III

The Queen's four Marys, Mary Beton, Mary Seton, Mary Livingstone and Mary Fleming, had taken a vow never to marry unless the Queen were the first to take a husband.

On the Twelfth Night the year after the death of Châtelart, the Day of the Kings was celebrated after the French fashion at Holyrood House. A bean was hid in the *galette*, which was cut and a piece chosen by all, and the piece with the bean fell to the lot of Mary Fleming. The Queen willed that Mary Fleming should be Queen indeed for the day of the festival, and she lent Mary Fleming her royal robes and her captain jewels, even the great Harry, and Mary Fleming was Queen of the feast, and whenever she raised her glass the whole company rose and cried: *La Reine boit.* That night there was a glittering ball, and it was marked that while Master Randolph, the English Ambassador, courted Mary Beton, to the disgust of Alexander Ogilvy, who loved her, and while Secretary Lethington courted Mary Fleming, Mary Livingstone was the more ardently courted of all by Lord Sempill. This was maybe the fairest of all the feasts ever held at Holyrood, and the most joyous.

Mary Fleming was arrayed in a gown of cloth of silver, and she was beset with precious stones, so that she was like an image in a shrine, enriched by unvalued treasure, and her laughing eyes and her silken skin were undimmed by the gems.

Mary Beton was dressed in *Colombe* satin; and Mary Livingstone, slender as a reed, nimble in every limb: and Mary Seton, fresh as a cherry, in her jacket of green velvet, were at the feast; and yet, as ever, the first was she, who kept apart, dressed in black and white, nor wearing a single jewel, save a ring she had received from the Queen of England, on her breast: the Queen, higher and whiter than the rest, and albeit that night discrowned, yet not unqueened.

And David Riccio said to Madame de Briante that the Queen, by putting herself at this disadvantage, knew she had nothing to lose, for without a gem she would still outshine all the treasures of Solomon.

That same night the Queen said to Mary Livingstone she need no longer mind her vow, for she was minded to release her from it soon by taking a husband herself. And Mary Livingstone took the saying to heart.

The Queen, albeit she no longer thought of love, and had put that thought away with the departure of M. d'Anville, for she knew well that nothing could reunite them, not even were she to abdicate the throne, had turned her thoughts to marriage.

Soon after Shrovetide M. de Castelnau came from France and entreated her to return to France and to marry the Duke of Anjou, the brother of the King. But the Queen answered that she would not risk her Kingdom in Scotland in order to be the second person in France, where she once been the first.

Suit had been made to her by many princes: the Kings of Denmark and of Sweden, the Archduke of Austria, the Duke of Ferrara, the Prince of Condé and the son of the King of Spain, but she would have none of them. In truth she cared no longer for her Kingdom in Scotland; it was of the Kingdom of England that she dreamed, and she had resolved to wed no foreign Prince.

But the Queen of England feared a foreign match for the Queen, and she sent her Ambassador to the Queen to urge her to marry Lord Robert Dudley, her own favourite.

The Queen answered that it was beneath her dignity to marry a subject, but, nevertheless, the Ambassador never tired of urging her to this suit. Soon after, the Countess of Lennox sent to the Queen in secret to solicit the hand of the Queen for her son, Lord Darnley, whom the Queen had seen when she was still in her *robe de deuil* at Orleans, in the first days of her widowhood.

While on his mother's side Lord Darnley was Prince of the blood royal, on his father's side he was the next lawful Prince of Scotland, of the Stewarts, and brought up as a Catholic. This match was smiled upon by the Queen, for if she married with Darnley she would be doubly the cousin of the Queen of England, and closer than before to the throne of England.

The Queen was harassed by the Queen of England's insistence that she should wed Lord Robert Dudley, angered at Mr Knox's denunciations of her in the pulpit when there was talk of a foreign marriage, weary of being thwarted by her brother, hectored by the Queen of England and encompassed by Secretary Lethington's cunning. The Queen was alone and defenceless among a host of enemies. She had none to whom she could turn, and no one whom she could converse with fearlessly, save David Riccio, and by so doing she led to his undoing. She determined therefore to marry. Thereupon she recalled the Earl of Lennox, who had been put to the horn twenty years since, to Scotland, and the Queen of England, although she commanded her Ambassador to tell the Queen she could never consent to the Queen's marriage with Lord Darnley, gave the Earl licence to go to Scotland.

The Queen's Secretary, M. Raulet, departed for France in the month of December of the same year (1566), and the Queen made David Riccio, who was a skilful scribe and could write elegantly in many tongues, Secretary in his stead. Riccio from that moment began to carry himself without prudence, and made himself many enemies.

David Riccio was a secretary without peer, untiring in his business and as swift as he was industrious. But Providence, who had made him misshapen and ungainly, with a shoulder that was awry, small of stature and with a limp, and a face that was sallow, and as if fashioned of putty, in which his black eyes gleamed maliciously, had compensated these disgraces by bestowing on him many accomplishments.

He could play upon all musical instruments, not only as well as the trained musicians, but he excelled them; he sang in all tongues, and whether he chanted Latin, as at Mass, or whether he sang a French roundelay or an Italian descant, or even some wild ballad from the Highlands or the Border – and these he sang as one who had been born and bred on the hill and in the heather – he pierced the hearts of all listeners, and bound them with a spell like to that of the sweet siren against which Ulysses was compelled to seal his sailors' ears and let himself be bound to the mast of his ship.

Moreover, he was merry, prompt and fertile in wit, invention and fancy, mischievous withal. He would have drawn laughter from the most solemn, and tears, when he wished, by his song, from the most hardened.

Thus, as time went on, the Queen found him more useful at business, and more diverting at play, and she came to rely upon him alone, and ever to take greater delight in his commerce; and this caused him to overstep the bounds of prudence. He would speak to the Queen in publick in the presence of the nobility, and he presented all signatures to be subscribed by the Queen, so that he became hated and envied.

Madame de Briante spoke to the Queen of the matter, and the Queen said to her that Seigneur David was the most observant of all her servants. Sir James Melville made representation likewise, pointing to the danger of the public demonstration of favour she gave to Riccio, who was a stranger and suspected of being a pensioner of the Pope; and the Queen answered that he meddled no further than in her French writings and affairs, as her other secretary had done, and she promised to take such order as the case required. But in spite of this the Queen continued to ask Riccio's advice on all subjects, and she not seldom followed it; nor did Riccio restrain the freedom of his carriage, and when blamed for this he said that it was Her Grace's will that he should carry himself as formerly.

His advice was often wise, for he had a great knowledge of the hearts of men, and a fine sense, like that of a physician. So it was that in spite of earnest warnings from those who were wisest and oldest at the Court, Riccio continued to behave with imprudence, and the Queen continued to countenance his familiarity. And this was fated to have sad consequences, as in the matter of Châtelart: and Sir James Melville, when speaking to the Queen, had not failed to remind her of that sorry story; but in vain.

My Lord Darnley came to Scotland from England and met the Queen at Castle Wemyss upon the day of St Valentine, and thence she returned to Holyrood House. In the month of March there were pleasures at Holyrood, for Mary Livingstone was wedded to my Lord Sempill of Beltreis at the Shrovetide Feast in the presence of the Queen and the Court, and Lord Darnley was present at the wedding. And, being by now deeply enamoured of the Queen and impatient of delay, instead of waiting for her word, he proposed marriage to her himself. This the Queen took in evil part, and refused the ring which he offered to her, and although she had come back from Castle Wemyss so well pleased with Lord Darnley that all at Court expected a royal marriage, she now told Madame de Briante and Sir James Melville that she would not wed him; he was over-headstrong, said she, lacking in discretion and apt to overstep the limits of seemliness.

Lord Darnley was now nineteen years of age. He was of high stature, too high maybe for the spirit that was in him; long and straight, fair and comely, prompt and ready in all exercises of the body, a pretty horseman and a skilful lute-player, but facile in mind, intemperate and unable to keep a secret. His person and his carriage pleased the Queen, likewise his speech and his accomplishments; but from the day he asked for her hand, instead of waiting for Her Grace to be the first to speak, as was seemly, she knew he had in him a fevered rashness that was to be feared.

The Queen's uncle, the Cardinal de Guise, wrote to her entreating her not to wed her cousin, if she valued her future happiness, for he was, he said, but a vain and puffed-up pretender, unmeet in every way to be her consort.

The Earl of Moray for a while supported the match, until Lord Darnley angered him by questioning his right to great possessions; after which he favoured the suit of Lord Robert Dudley; the Secretary Lethington was not averse to it, for he desired above all things to see the Kingdoms of Scotland and England united under one Crown.

But to all these counsellors the Queen paid little heed, for she mistrusted them one and all. It so happened that the nobles grew ever more envious of Seigneur David, and would frown upon him and shoulder him, and Lord Darnley followed their example, calling him a foreign upstart and other unfriendly names, and this the Queen was not slow to mark. One night, after she had supped and sat with her Ladies in her small chamber at Holyrood, she summoned Lord Darnley, and Riccio was present. She begged Riccio to play music on the lute and sing a ditty, whereat Lord Darnley frowned. And Riccio, smiling, and nothing loth, took his lute and sang an Italian song:

> *Ben venga Maggio,*
> *E'l gonfalon gentile.*

And Lord Darnley, who was a lover of all kinds of music, in spite of his ill-will, could not but smile, so taking was the lilt of that music, so seductive was the spell of that voice. After which he sang a ballad from the Border: a lament which ran:

> *This night is my departing night,*
> *For her nae longer must I stay;*
> *There's neither friend nor foe o'mine,*
> *But wishes me away.*

And into the rough words, and into the sad melody that accompanied them, he put such a world of grief that there were tears in the eyes of all, and Lord Darnley wept and entreated Seigneur Riccio for another song, whereat Seigneur David, in his cunning, sang a song that M. de Ronsard had made in praise of the Queen, and Lord Darnley's grief was turned to fervour, and Riccio, after that, sang many diverse songs, and with each fresh song he entranced Lord Darnley yet more.

After that Lord Darnley and Seigneur David became fast friends, and Lord Darnley made Riccio the confidant of his love for the Queen, and Riccio heartened him to pursue his suit, and he counselled the Queen to take Lord Darnley for a husband. Rumours of this match were abroad both in Scotland and in foreign lands; and there were many who made a last bid for the Queen's hand; and among them once again the Prince de Condé. And while the Queen protested she had no passion so strong as her desire of the good of her country, she was determined not to marry a foreign Prince, and, of Princes that were not foreign, my Lord Darnley was alone of those not beneath her dignity who yet pleased her.

From France she had news that M. d'Anville was busy fighting in the civil war, and had been made Governor of the Languedoc; and so it was that the Queen bade Lethington tell the Queen of England of her determination, and say she was obeying her directions in not wedding a foreign Prince. In the meantime Lord Darnley fell sick of the measles; Seigneur David, since he had cemented a friendship with Lord Darnley, had become the Queen's chief adviser, and he favoured the match, and in the month of April the Queen married Lord Darnley in private at Stirling Castle, in the room of Seigneur David, according to the Roman rite.

After this secret wedding a great change came about in the Queen's affairs. Lord Darnley, scarcely well from the measles, fell sick of an ague, and the Queen nursed him, and her liking for him grew swiftly into love, and for a time she doted on him: nor would she allow aught that he said or did to be questioned; and the Queen's love was fatal to Lord Darnley, for it stiffened his pride and loosened his arrogance, to which henceforth there were no bounds, and for which he grew to be hated of all.

Two months later the Queen met her nobles at Stirling and declared to them that she had determined to wed Lord Darnley, her father's sister's son by the Earl of Lennox, to which the nobles consented, there not being one dissentient, but the Queen of England sent the Queen her Ambassador to declare her dislike of the Queen's hasty proceeding with Lord Darnley, who had failed in his duty by acting without her consent. The Queen held a Chapter of the Order of the Thistle, and dubbed Lord Darnley a Knight, and created him Earl of Ross; and with these honours the pride of Lord Darnley increased, and he could not brook opposition, howsoever slight, and he was prone to forget himself in outbursts of anger and petulance; nor did these honours satisfy him, and he demanded the highest honour: to be made Duke of Albany, but the Queen bade him tarry a little so as not to provoke the Queen of England beyond endurance.

Lord Darnley would hear no reason, and insisted the more; but the Queen determined not to confer upon him this Dukedom until she should hear from the Queen of England. And so greatly angered was Lord Darnley, and in so high a fever of impatience, that the Queen durst not acquaint him of her determination herself, and she sent the Justice Clerk, a man high in office, and of great repute among all, to tell him, and

Lord Darnley was so angered that he drew his dagger upon the Justice.

The Queen sent her Ambassador to the Queen of England to make remonstrance, saying she had refrained from marrying into the houses of Spain and France so as not to anger her cousin, and had taken their common kinsman because she thought none could be more agreeable to her royal sister. And the Queen of England for an answer first bade the Countess of Lennox be guarded in her house and then committed her to the Tower, and summoned Lord Darnley and his father to England, wherein if they failed, they would be guilty of High Treason.

The Queen, having chosen Lord Darnley as her spouse and her sole mainstay, had now no counsellor to advise her but Seigneur David Riccio, for the Nobles held aloof, and both the Earl of Moray and the Lord of Lethington were plotting how they could rid themselves of Lord Darnley.

Madame de Briante warned the Queen that the Nobles, with the Earl of Moray at their head, were plotting Lord Darnley's ruin, and that they would not rest until they had brought it about; and she repeated to the Queen what she had heard from M. de Castlenau: the counsellors of the Queen of England had sent Lord Darnley to Scotland to bring about Lord Darnley's ruin, and with it that of the Queen, and that the Queen of England's wrath at the match was but a pretence. To this the Queen would pay no heed, for, in spite of all that was said to her, she believed that her cousin, the Queen of England, wished her well, whatever her counsellors might contrive, nor would the Queen of England, she thought, countenance the designs of those about her, should they be directed against herself. The truth being that at this time the Queen was infatuate with Lord Darnley, and was as one who is haunting a fool's paradise. And Seigneur David was of one mind with her, and said that the Scots were braggarts in words, and would talk much and do little; and in this he erred grievously, as time was to show. In the meantime, the plotting of the Earl of Moray and his followers went on apace. Lord Moray first spread abroad a bruit that Lord Darnley was plotting his murder, but when faced with this charge and challenged by the Queen to let the truth of it be determined by trial according to law, he kept aloof. After this a plot was hatched secretly by the Earl of Moray to kill Lord Darnley and his father and all others in his company, and to imprison the Queen in the Castle of Lochleven.

It was in the month of June, and the Queen was at Perth with Lord Darnley and her Court, and David Riccio was with them. The night was warm and the daylight lingered, so that they sat in the garden after supper. And that night they made merry, and the Queen and Lord Darnley played chess, the Queen winning, which Lord Darnley took ill, and he asked Seigneur Riccio to sing a ditty. Seigneur David began to sing a song that the Queen had made herself in France, but the Queen would not suffer him to finish the song, saying it was over-sad, and he sang a more lively air in the Italian tongue, which pleased the company; and with much song and laughter and talk they dallied in the garden until it was time to go to bed, and even then it was not dark. The next morning, at ten of the clock, the Queen was to ride to Callander House to be gossip at the christening of the infant heir of Lord Livingstone.

No sooner had the Queen retired to her chamber than a gentleman named Lindsay arrived in haste from Parenwell and demanded to see the Queen upon a matter of life and death, and the Queen bade him be brought to her. Lindsay revealed to the Queen that the Earl of Moray had hatched a plot against Her Grace, and that a triple ambush would lie in wait for her on the morrow to slay Lord Darnley and his father, and to kill all others that should resist, and carry the Queen away to the Castle of Lochleven. And the plotters knew at what hour she was to start.

The Queen summoned such of her counsellors who were with her, the Earl of Atholl and Lord Ruthven, and they were all of one mind, that the Queen should not hazard the ride, and yet that Perth was no longer a place of safety for her, and Lord Darnley was without purpose or plan. Then the Queen said, come what might, she would not break her word to Lady Livingstone. She would start at five of the clock and be at Callander before the rebels were in the saddle.

And so it came about, for at five of the clock the next morning the Queen was in the saddle, with her skirts kirtled, and a plume in her green velvet cap, and she rode towards the North Ferry with three of her Ladies and three hundred horsemen raised from the countryside, and she passed through Kinross and by Lochleven, and crossed the Ferry, and was at Callander House at ten of the clock.

Later, hearing while she was at Callander House that the rebels were busy at Edinburgh, she rode at the head of her men to the city, and many of the Nobles and the gentry followed her thither, and the rebels fled in dismay.

In the month of July Lord Darnley was made Duke of Albany by the Queen, and the banns of marriage were published in the Church of St Giles, Edinburgh: but Lord Darnley was still unsatisfied and demanded the title of King: and he was proclaimed King of Scotland by the King of Arms and the Heralds at the Abbey Gates, and at the Market Cross, the day before the marriage. This was solemnized according to the Roman rite in the Chapel Royal of Holyrood House. But, after the benediction had been given, Lord Darnley did not stay to hear Mass, but left with the Lords of the Reformed religion. The Queen was wedded in her gown of dule, but when Mass was ended she changed her garments and put on bridal robes.

And the Queen, being well aware that the Earl of Moray and his followers were still malcontent, pardoned the Earl of Bothwell and recalled him from outlawry; whereat the malcontents took the field, and the Queen declared the Earl of Moray and his accomplices to be rebels and called her subjects to her banners, and she took to the field herself with her Lords of Council, with pistols at her saddle bow, and under her scarlet jacket a shirt of mail, and under her hood a casque of steel. And she pursued the rebels here and there until they were compelled to flee into England for refuge.

And the Earl of Bothwell was made High Admiral of Scotland and Warden of the Southern Marches.

The rebels were aided and abetted by the Queen of England; but when they fled across the Border the Queen of England compelled them to confess upon their knees before the foreign Ambassadors, who had alleged in their masters' names that she had been the cause of the rebellion, that she had never stirred them up against their Queen; and she upbraided them for their abominable treason.

Sir James Melville petitioned the Queen to pardon the rebels, representing that, as so many Nobles were banished and were so near to the Border, and had other noblemen, kinsmen and friends at home who were malcontent, he feared they might hazard a desperate enterprise towards an alteration; and the Queen – fearless as ever – was ready to defy them; and Seigneur David, who ever disdained all danger, despised this counsel.

The Earl of Moray sued the Seigneur to obtain his pardon, and sent him a diamond ring, and Sir Nicholas Throckmorton urged the Queen to pardon the rebels and to attach those who were not of her religion to her throne: but the King of France and her uncle, the Cardinal of Guise, dissuaded her from showing any favour to the banished Lords, and the Seigneur did not think fit to offend so many Catholic Princes; thus the Queen was persuaded to act against her first intention, and she resolved at the next holding of Parliament to confirm the acts of forfeiture against the banished Lords, and to summon them to appear before Parliament for their acts of treason.

In the month of February the Earl of Bothwell was married to Lady Jane Gordon, sister of the Earl of Huntly, whom the Queen had released from the process of the horn, and there was feasting that continued five days, with joustings and pastimes.

CHAPTER IV

The feasts held at Holyrood House for the marriage of the Earl of Bothwell were the last that the Queen was fated to grace, for, from that time onward, the troubles and perils that beset her grew thicker and more pressing. Her enemies had in no way abandoned their plotting to rid the country of the King, and, indeed, they were plotting for the ruin of the Queen as well. They were minded to wrest the Queen's power from her by means of the King, and thereafter to rid them of the King, which they knew would be the easier task. At first, they tried to entice Riccio into their confederacy, offering him rewards, but Seigneur David was faithful to the Queen, and he warned her that some scheming was on foot, but the Confederates had not revealed their plot to him, to which the banished Lords and the King himself were parties.

And one night the Queen, going into his chamber, found the King busily engaged in talk with those whom Riccio suspected, and the King spoke urgently to her and accused her of spying, whereat she left his chamber.

The Earl of Morton and his defenders feared that at the next Parliament the Queen would deprive them of benefices that they had taken from the Church lands, and they plotted that this Parliament should be stayed, and the power taken from the Queen; and the cousin of the Earl of Morton, called

George Douglas, the Postulate, son natural to the Earl of Angus, who was also father to the Countess of Lennox, the King's mother, was continually about the King and put into his head suspicion against Seigneur David. But this suspicion was not needed to woo the King into the confederacy; it spurred his envy, but in no wise created it, for the King was resentful at not having the Crown Matrimonial, and although he was now King Consort of Scotland, this did not satisfy him, and he desired to go before the Queen and to lead her into Parliament. He had by now become ungentle towards the Queen and unfaithful to her, running after base amours; and Seigneur David had already incurred his enmity by not taking part in his debauches; and as his temper soured he solaced himself with deep draughts of *aqua composita*, and this made him the more pliable in the hands of the Confederates, and the more ill-humoured against the Queen.

The Confederates drew up a bond which the King and his father signed, for no man durst trust the King's word without his signet, and the Earl of Lennox proceeded to Newcastle, where a bond was signed by the Earl of Moray and the six banished Lords for the slaughter of David Riccio and others.

The Queen was warned that a plot was on foot, and Damiot, the French astrologer, bade Riccio beware of the bastard; but the Queen paid no heed to his words, scenting a threat to persuade her to stay measures against the banished Lords.

Nor would Seigneur David pay heed to the warning, thinking that Damiot spoke of the Earl of Moray, who was in England, and saying, as was ever his wont, that it was "Parole, parole, nothing but words. The Scots will boast but will rarely perform their brags."

The Estates of Scotland had been summoned to appear for the Parliament, in the Tolbooth, on the seventh of March, and the King and the Queen and their Court were at Holyrood House. The Queen was to introduce the King as her Consort and ask his recognition from the Estates as King and Joint

109

Sovereign with herself. Such was the lawful proceeding, but the King's pride and vanity could not stomach it, and sooner than be introduced to the Estates by the Queen he rode away to Leith, and the Queen opened Parliament without him, arrayed in cloth of silver, the Earl of Huntly bearing the Crown before her.

And the King, in greater choler than ever, was ready to take part in the plot, which had for purpose not only the slaughter of Riccio, but of all who had refused to grant the King the Crown Matrimonial: the Protestant Lords, the Earls of Huntly, Bothwell and Atholl and Lord Livingstone, while Sir James Balfour was to be hanged at the Queen's chamber door, and the Queen was to be slain, or imprisoned in Stirling Castle.

The King was ready for these murderous acts, but he dissembled his purpose with the smoothness of a skilled dissembler. The day after the meeting of Parliament the King invited the Seigneur David to play a game of tennis with him and asked the Queen to watch them at play, but the Queen had been enjoined by her physicians to remain quiet, for she was far gone with child, having almost passed to the end of seven months. She retired early to her small cabinet with her Ladies and the Countess of Argyll and Seigneur David, and they made music and there was singing in parts, and Seigneur David sang a soft ditty.

At seven of the clock the Queen sat down to supper, and there was flesh, in spite of the Fast, the Queen having been counselled by her physicians to sustain herself. There were with her besides the Countess of Argyll, Lord Robert Stewart, Lord Keith, Arthur Erskine, the Abbot of Holyrood House, Arnault, her physician, and Seigneur David, with the other servitors. The Queen sat at her table and the chair next to her was empty, being kept for the King; but he was supping that night with Lord Lindsay and Lord Ruthven, who was sick. The Countess of Argyll was at the Queen's table: the gentlemen of the household and Seigneur David were standing at the buffet-board. The Queen spoke of Lord Ruthven, who was mortally sick, and she said she was minded to go and visit him in his apartment, and she asked her physician after his health, and the physician shook his head. The Queen sent Seigneur David some paste from her table, when the King entered the cabinet by the limanga which led from his chamber to the Queen's bedroom. He sat down in his chair next to the Queen and embraced her, and cast his arms about her with many gentle and endearing words.

"My Lord, have you supped?" the Queen asked of him, and the King nodded and said he had no mind to disturb the Queen's meal. And, as he spoke these words, the Lord Ruthven came from behind the arras which concealed the secret passage into the Queen's bedchamber, leading to the King's lobby. He was pale from his sickness and more like a ghost than a live man, and under his nightgown he wore mail and in his hand he held a sword. The Queen started at this apparition, which was awesome in itself, and the more forbidding because it was common talk that Lord Ruthven was a sorcerer and had traffic with the Evil One. But the Queen, recollecting herself, said to him: "My Lord, I was coming to visit you in your chamber, having been told you were very ill; and now you enter our presence in armour – what does this mean?" Ruthven sat down upon a chair, and he spoke painfully, and he said: "I have indeed been ill, but I find myself well enough to come here for your good."

The Queen asked him what good he could do her, for he came not in the fashion of one that meaneth well; and Ruthven said he intended no harm to Her Grace, nor to anyone, but only to David, with whom he had to speak.

And the Queen said: "What hath he done?"

And Ruthven bade her ask the King, her husband.

The Queen turned to the King, who was leaning upon the back of her chair, and asked him the meaning of these words;

but the King said he knew nothing of the matter, and he looked away as he spoke.

And the Queen ordered Lord Ruthven to leave her chamber under the pain of Treason, and he said nothing, but stood glowering. And Arthur Erskine and Arnault laid hands upon him to thrust him out, but he shook them off and threatened them with his sword; and immediately another of the Confederates entered with a horse pistol, followed by others, and the Queen said: "Do you seek my life?"

"No, Madam," said Lord Ruthven, "but we will have out yonder villain, Davie."

And, as he spoke, he thrust at Seigneur David with his sword; but the Queen held Ruthven's wrist, and stood between Lord Ruthven and Seigneur David, who was in the bay of the window with his dagger drawn.

And one of the men who had entered had with him a rope, and said: "Here is the means of justice." And Seigneur David said to the Queen: "Madam, I am a dead man."

But the Queen comforted him and, looking at the King, said: "The King will not suffer you to be killed in my presence." And Lord Ruthven said to the King: "Sir, take your wife and sovereign to you." But the King stood amazed and wist not what to do.

There was a noise and a cry of "A Douglas", and Lord Morton and many of his followers were on the great staircase and forced the doors of the presence chamber, and the Queen's servants fled; and armed men entered the Queen's bedroom carrying torches. But the Queen would not go to the King, but stood in front of Seigneur David, and Ruthven and the men-at-arms, trying to seize Seigneur David, overthrew the buffet-board and all the candles, meat and dishes that were on it, and the lighted candles fell to the floor, and Lady Argyll caught one of them in her hand. And the Queen called out to the assailants that they were traitors and villains, and bade them begone, and Lord Ruthven cried out: "We will have out that gallant," and the

King bade the Queen let him go. But Seigneur David, with shrieks of *"Justitia"*, clung to the Queen's gown, crying out: "Save my life, Madam, for God's dear sake," and the Queen wept and entreated them all to proceed according to the forms of justice.

And George the Postulate struck at Seigneur David over the Queen's shoulder, so that the Queen's robe was dabbled with blood, and the dagger was left in him; and thus the words of Damiot, the astrologer, came true, for, as ever, the augury had a double meaning. The King forced the Seigneur's fingers from the Queen's gown and dragged him from her feet, and the Queen would have defended him yet, but the King forced her to a chair and held her there.

One of the assailants, Andrew Ker of Faudonside, threatened the Queen with a pistol, and she afterwards told her Ladies that she felt the coldness of the iron through her dress; and another, Patrick Bellenden, thrusting at the Seigneur, made as if he would wound the Queen; but one of the pages, Anthony Standen, parried the blow with the torch that he had been holding to light the music while the Queen had been singing in parts earlier in the evening, and the Seigneur was dragged from the closet into the bedchamber, where near the doorway they gave him fifty-six strokes with daggers and swords; and they dragged his body down the stairway, and the Queen was left alone with the King.

And Lady Sempill, hearing the tumult, came to the Queen's chamber, and on the way, at the porter's lodge, she saw the murderers stripping the corpse of Seigneur David, which was covered with wounds, and one of them with a laugh took the fair diamond he wore that night round his neck, which the Earl of Moray had given him.

And Lady Sempill entered the Queen's cabinet and said what she had seen, and what she had heard, and that Seigneur David was dead, and how all had been done by the King's order, and the Queen looked at the King and cried out: "Traitor, and son of a Traitor."

And the Queen swooned, and her Ladies came to her in her bedchamber; but presently she was roused by Lord Ruthven, who returned with his men and asked for and took from a page a cup of wine, saying that he was sore felled by sickness. And the Queen left the cabinet with the King and went into her bedchamber, and soon there was a clamour below and Lord Gray knocked at the door, and said that the Earls of Huntly and Bothwell were fighting against the Earl of Morton and his party. And the King said he would go down, but Lord Ruthven bade him remain where he was, and he went down himself, walking unsteadily; and Lord Ruthven invited the invaders to a parley in the Earl of Bothwell's chamber, and tried with fair words to lure him into the conspiracy; but the Earl of Bothwell and the rest would not listen, and they escaped from a back window by a rope-ladder into the garden, where the lions were kept. And Lord Ruthven, having drunk more wine, came back to the Queen's bedroom and taunted her with the miscarriage of her servants' attempt, and called them traitors, and he accused her of tyranny; and all at once the tocsin rang in the town and a great crowd of burgesses came with the Provost to the Palace and demanded to see their Queen; but Lord Ruthven would not suffer the Queen to go to the window, saying that if she attempted to speak to that muster they would cut her into collops and throw her over the walls. And the King went to the window and bade the Provost pass home with his company, for nothing, said he, was amiss, and the Queen and he were merry.

But the Provost and his men called out: "Let us see our Queen and hear her speak for herself." But the King commanded them to pass home to their houses.

And after they had dispersed, the Queen and Lord Ruthven talked for a while in the cabinet; the Queen, so faint and weary was she, could talk no more, and went to her bedchamber and asked for her Ladies; but Lord Ruthven dismissed the Ladies that were there, nor would he let any of the others nor any of her servitors come to her, and he set guards at the door, and the Queen was allowed to see her maid only and scarcely her, and all night long the Queen saw no one else.

And the next morning was Sunday, and the King made a proclamation in his own name at the Market Cross ordering that all the Lords who had a vote in Parliament should leave Edinburgh; and when he sent his Esquire, Anthony Standen, to ask after the Queen he was not allowed to enter, nor were any of his servants allowed to pass the guards that were posted at the door of the Queen's chamber, without an order from the Lords; and in great wrath the King visited the Queen himself and found her in sore distress without her Ladies. And the King ordered them to come, but this they were not able to do without leave from Lord Ruthven, who feigned to consent to the demand but failed to carry it out. And after the King had dined, at two of the clock, and returned to the Queen, he found her still desolate and unattended, and the King sent word to Lord Ruthven that it was the King's pleasure that the Queen's Ladies should allowed to come to her. And thus Lady Sempill (Mary Livingstone) and Mary Beton were permitted to go to the Queen; and Lady Sempill was able, by means of her husband, Lord John of Sempill, to bring her from the Seigneur's chamber the box in which were the Queen's letters and ciphers, and she was able to write letters to the Earls of Atholl, Argyll and Bothwell, and others.

And Lady Huntly had permission to see the Queen, and brought her a message from the Earl of Huntly, her son, that he had raised troops, and could the Queen descend from the window by a rope-ladder they would be waiting to receive her, and Lady Huntly would bring the Queen the ladder between two dishes. But the Queen said that the window proposed was watched by the guard from the other side, and she wrote a letter asking the Earl of Huntly to wait for her in a village near Seton, where she would keep tryst with him and his party the following night; and the Queen gave Lady Huntly this letter, which she hid between her body and her chemise. As they were talking Lord Lindsay, being suspicious, entered the room, and ordered Lady Huntly to leave it; and he bade the guard search her clothing as she left the room; and the guard, searching but the outside of her dress, found nothing.

The Queen saw Lord Morton and the Earl of Moray, who had returned to Edinburgh that day with the rest of the banished Lords. The Earl of Moray, close and cunning as ever, spoke fair words to her, and entreated her to receive the Lords into her presence, but, petition as he might, the Queen refused; and that evening the Lords met in Lord Morton's house, where the rebels debated on the fate of the Queen, and the Earl of Moray spoke in favour of her death, saying they had gone too far to recede with safety, and could expect no grace from the Queen, and it behoved them to take such measures as their safety prescribed. And the King came from this meeting to visit the Queen, and she met him with tears and sweet reproach, and a sad smile, so that he grew remorseful and wept bitterly, and entreated her to forgive him; and he showed her the articles drawn up between himself and the conspirators, wishing to rid his conscience of the burden, and revealed to her the full plot of the banished Lords, telling her that her life was in danger, as well as the lives of the Earls of Bothwell and Huntly and others, unless she could devise a means of escape. And the Queen told him what she had planned with the Earl of Huntly, and said she would find a means of escape, but that he must first rid her of the four and twenty men-at-arms who kept guard at her chamber door.

But this the King could not compass, for he was a prisoner no less than the Queen, and the Queen bade him come back to her that night; but the Lords plied his wine with a drug, fearing what might be the outcome of his intercourse with the Queen, and he slept, and none could rouse him until six of the clock of the morning, when he at once visited the Queen and remained with her a while; and at nine of the clock, having dressed himself in his state clothes, he visited the Queen again, and remained with her until two of the clock in the afternoon, when he went down to dine, telling the Lords that he had prevailed upon the Queen to grant them presence and remission of their offences. After he had dined he was about to pass to the Queen's chamber when the midwife came with the tidings that the Queen made as though to part with her child, and that she must be removed to some place where she should have free air, and the Ladies said the same, and Arnault; and the Lords feared this was but craft and policy, wherein they were not altogether deceived, although this was true that the Queen was faint and ill and in pain; and this rumour was part of her plan, which the Queen had devised the day before, for she had sent for the Laird of Traquair and spoken with him through the door of the King's lobby. Her purpose was to go down to the King's chamber this night, and thence to the office of the Cupbearers, from which there was a door which opened into the burial-ground. Arthur Erskine, an Esquire of the Queen's stables, was warned to wait near this door after midnight and to bring with him a gelding on which the Queen was to be mounted on a pillion, and horses for the King and his attendants. Towards four of the afternoon the King brought the Earls of Moray and Morton to the outer chamber, where they knelt, and the Queen spoke with them and told them she would accord them her Grace, and bade them to prepare their own securities which she would subscribe. And when they left her she told the King that he must obtain the dismissal of the guards, or else they could not escape.

At six of the clock, while the King supped with the Lords, the Queen spoke with Anthony Standen, the elder brother of the page (they were both named Anthony), about the hour and manner of her escape; and the King after supper proposed to the Lords that they should dismiss the guards, when they brought their securities for her subscription; but although they

117

told him he could do as he pleased, the guards were bidden to remain, and the Queen sent for Secretary Lethington, and she entreated him to obtain from the Lords the dismissal of the guards, and he promised his aid, and counselled her to summon all the banished Lords in the presence of the King and to promise them remission for all crimes bygone. And the Queen did it. She received all the banished Lords, save only Lord Ruthven, whom she would not allow to come into her presence, because he was the principal man who had come into her cabinet to commit slaughter; and she promised the remission, for which she said she would make an act by consent of Parliament when no longer a captive, and she drank to every one in special, and bade them deliver the keys of her Palace to her servants and leave her chamber to the care of her own servitors, because for the last two nights she had taken no rest; and the King promised to be her keeper for the night. And the Queen, saying she could hardly stand for weakness, retired to her chamber. And the Lords passed from the Palace of Holyrood to the Earl of Morton's house, where they supped, not putting any faith in the Queen's promises, but deeming her to be too much enfeebled to hazard an escape.

The King and the Queen went to bed, but rose after midnight, and, accompanied by the Laird of Traquair and Arthur Erskine, they went down by the secret stair, through the offices, where the butlers were French, into the cemetery, where they passed the grave of David Riccio, and at the gate of the cemetery Anthony Standen was waiting with the King's horse.

The Queen mounted on a pillion behind Arthur Erskine, and Margaret Cawood behind the Laird of Traquair, and Bastian, the Queen's servant, on another horse.

They rode towards Seton, and as soon as they left the town the King began to gallop until they reached the outskirts of Seton, where some soldiers had been posted by the nobles of the Queen's party, and the King, deeming them to belong to the enemy, spurred his horse, and flogged that of the Queen, crying out: "Come on, come on, or by God's blood they will murder us." And the Queen, being in great suffering, entreated him to have regard for her condition, and the King in a fury cried: "Come on, if this baby dies we can have more." But the Queen could bear the galloping of the horse no more, and bade the King push on and take care of himself, which he did, abandoning her in the open country, where she was presently overtaken by the Earls of Huntly and Bothwell and others, and they arrived at Seton House, whence they continued with a large escort to Dunbar, where they arrived safely, and the Queen ordered a fire to be made to warm her, and asked for some new laid eggs.

CHAPTER V

Early the next morning the news spread through the Palace that the Queen and the King had escaped, and the Ladies of the Queen told the news to Secretary Lethington and asked him also of the truth of the report that had got abroad that the Palace would be sacked, and the Secretary bid the Ladies have no fear. The news spread through the city, and the people rejoiced, and the Lords who had been in the plot took flight. A proclamation was made in several parts of the Kingdom that all persons capable of bearing arms were to proceed to Dunbar: and the Queen five days later reached Haddington well attended: and there, in the Abbey, she held a Council, before which the King declared that he was innocent of the death of Riccio, and whereat the Queen made many changes, and subscribed the remissions for the Earl of Moray and all the Lords who had returned with him from England. The next day the Queen entered Edinburgh with the noblemen of her faction, and a great muster of men, horse and foot. And the Queen lodged at the house of Lord Home in the High Street.

Lord Ruthven and the Earl of Morton were summoned to appear to answer for their offences, and not appearing they were put to the horn; and the Earl of Bothwell was made once more Lord Admiral and Captain of Dunbar, and all seemed to be quiet in the realm, and might haply have remained quiet, but for the intempestive behaviour of the King.

The King was in disfavour with all: the Lords of the Queen's faction complained of his unstable purpose; some would no longer speak to him, and others blamed him openly. The King, angry and afeared at such insult, entreated the Queen to bring about a reconciliation between him and her Lords, but these declared when she spoke for the King that for the future neither his promises nor his orders would move them.

The other faction, that of the banished Lords and the Earl of Moray, harboured hatred for him and revenge for his having betrayed their secrets.

As for the Queen, she was willing to persuade her subjects, and at first even herself, that the King had been a tool in the hands of men more crafty than himself, but there were many who took care that the Queen should see all the covenants and bonds that had passed between the King and the Lords, so that the Queen knew that his declarations before the Council that he had been innocent of the death of Seigneur David were false; nor could she forget that he had come to betray her with a Judas kiss.

And the King went about with a great dread, for he feared that if aught should befall the Queen in childbed which was drawing near, or otherwise, all factions would be avenged upon him, and he urged the Queen to grant him a pardon against all manner of treason, that if in the case of her death proceedings were instituted against him, he might produce these as a proof of her forgiveness.

The Queen granted him his wish; but she warned him that her written word would avail him little were she not there to confirm it; and she told her Ladies that she had as much to fear as the King and more, for the Lords who had assailed her once would surely assail her again, and it was her throne that they coveted, and not the King's life, for they had little esteem for him.

Great was the infelicity of the Queen at this time; and she spoke of retiring to France and leaving her realm in the hands of a Regent; but the Lords were all at variance, and there was her unborn child to be thought of, and the Queen retired to Edinburgh Castle for her lying-in.

The Queen took to her chamber the first Monday in June with the proper ceremonies; she was sorrowful in the extreme: it was not the childbed, nor the pangs of travail she feared so much as the plots of her enemies: the Earl of Morton and the rest, who would return one day, she said, to accomplish what they had begun with the murder of Seigneur David.

She feared they would slay both herself and her child; and she dreaded the King's assistance more than his hindrance. He was no more of any account to her, although she pitied him, for she said he was walking to his doom and dragging her down with him: and he, walking about as one haunted by a great fear, tried to drown his apprehension in disorder.

The Queen made her will and dispatched a copy of it to France. Joseph Riccio, the brother of David, had come to Scotland with M. de Castelnau, who had been sent by the King and Queen-Mother from France to felicitate the Queen for her escape from murderous hands, and the Queen prevailed upon him to remain as her secretary; and she confided to him a jewel which, in the case of her death, he was to take and give to one whose name he alone was privy to; and after she had made her will and received the Sacraments she gave this jewel to Mary Beton to give to Joseph Riccio, and Mary Beton knew it as being a jewel the Queen had worn on Candlemas Day a long time since in France, the day upon which she first set eyes on M. d'Anville.

And upon Tuesday night, the eighteenth of June, the pains of travail began, and the Queen was in great suffering for many hours, so that Arnault and Margaret Houseton, the midwife, despaired of her life; and in the moment of peril the Queen prayed that the child might be saved without regard to herself.

The Queen was reconciled with the King and said farewell to him; but she trusted him so little that he knew nothing of her testament, nor whom she had appointed Regent in the event of her death; and this she revealed to none.

And between nine and ten of the clock of the morning of the nineteenth the Queen gave birth to a boy; and the artillery of the castle was discharged, and the Lords and the nobles gathered in the Church of St Giles to give thanks.

At two of the clock of the same day the Queen summoned the King and Sir Anthony Standen to her chamber, and before them all, and her Ladies, taking her child in her arms, she presented him to the King, protesting to God that he was the King's son, so much his son that she feared it might be the worse for him hereafter; and at these words the King turned red. And the Queen, who had already made Anthony Standen a Knight before her lying-in, commanded Sir Anthony to lay his hand upon the cross of diamonds which the sleeping Prince wore, giving him the oath of fidelity, and ordaining him the Prince's first servant, and saying he had given the Prince his first faith and homage of the Crown of England, for she said: "This is the Prince who I hope shall first unite the two Kingdoms of England and Scotland." And Sir Anthony asked whether he should succeed before Her Grace and his father, and the Queen said: "Alas, his father has broken to me."

And the King said: "Madam, is this your promise that you made to forgive all?"

"I have forgiven," the Queen made answer, "but I can never forget."

The Queen dispatched Sir Anthony Standen to France to the King, and to the Duke and Princes of the family of Lorraine, her cousins, to declare unto them the happy coming into the world of her son, and she sent other gentlemen to the Queen of England and to the Duke of Savoy, asking them to be Godmother and Godfather to the Prince. But the King, albeit elated at the birth of his son, was ill at ease, and lived the life of a vagabond, and sometimes he went to bathe in the sea, and sometimes wandered in remote places; and the Queen was fearful of the perils that might await him, for she knew how greatly he was hated of the Lords; and he caused the gates of the castle to be open at every hour of the night, so that there was no safety for the Queen and her son, and the Queen entreated him to have care, but he paid little heed to her remonstrance; and he threatened that he would kill the Earl of Moray, whom he hated above all others; for he knew that the Earl of Moray was guiding the realm.

The King was much angered against the Queen because she had asked the Queen of England to be her gossip at the christening of the Prince; for the Queen of England did not recognize my Lord Darnley as King of Scotland. And he was yet more angered that she pardoned and gave presence to Secretary Lethington and brought about a reconciliation between him and the Earl of Bothwell, and called to her board of Council the rival Lords: the Earls of Moray, Huntly, Bothwell and Argyll.

After spending some days at Alloa with the Earl of Mar in August, and hunting the stag, with the King, the Earl of Moray and others in Meggatland, where the Queen visited the Laird of Traquair, she passed to Stirling, whither she moved the Prince and gave him to the care of the Earl of Mar, and thence the Queen passed to Edinburgh.

Preparations were now made for the Prince's Baptism, and the Queen sorted her jewels for the ceremony, and she chose the colours that were to be worn by the assistants.

In the month of October news came of trouble and disorder on the Borders; and the Queen sent the Earl of Bothwell to proceed against the offenders, and to take them in custody, until they should appear before her in the Justice Court, which she proclaimed she would hold in the second week of October at Jedburgh, on the Border. The Earl of Bothwell fought with John Elliott, of the Park, from whom he received three wounds, after the Earl had fought with him and admitted him to quarter; and the Earl, after receiving these wounds in the head, in the body and the hand, nevertheless wounded Elliott mortally with his whingar. After which affray the Earl of Bothwell was taken to Hermitage Castle.

The Assize was opened at Jedburgh the ninth of the month, and lasted six days, and thereafter Privy Councils were held, and the sixteenth of the month the Queen visited the Earl of Bothwell at Hermitage Castle and held conference with him, and that day the Queen lost her gold signet ring, whereat she grieved sorely; and riding back from Hermitage to Jedburgh her horse sank in a morass, and the Queen lost a silver spur.

The Queen misliked these omens; and it is true they were quickly followed by misfortune, for on the day after her return to Jedburgh she fell sick. She was seized with a pain in the side, which was followed by fits of swooning and fits of vomiting. On the morrow she was a little better, but very soon again the sickness seemed as if it would prove mortal. Arnault said she might well have been given poison, as a lump of green substance very thick and hard was thrown from her stomach; and on the same day news came that the Prince was sick, and that his life was despaired of, but, after being made to vomit, he mended.

The Queen made ready to die, and she asked the Kirks in the neighbourhood for their prayers. She desired to be buried with the Kings and Queens, her forefathers, and she asked pardon of God, and she forgave all who had offended her, especially her husband, King Henry, and the banished noblemen who had so highly aggrieved her; and she entreated that if they were brought back into the realm they should not have access to the Prince, her son, of whom she spake long.

And she sent for M. du Croc, the French Ambassador, and bade him commend her to the King of France and to the Queen-Mother. And she called together the Lords of the Court and exhorted them to unity and agreement, and recommended her son to their care, and bade them defend him against the King, his father, should the King wrong him as to the succession for the Crown. And she repeated the Creed in Latin.

Towards the evening of the ninth day of the sickness the Queen lost the power of speech, and her sight failed, and at eleven of the clock at night her body became cold, and her servants thought she was dead, and the windows were opened, and the Earl of Moray laid hands upon her rings; and mourning dresses were ordered. But Arnault, the doctor, detected tokens of life in one of her arms, and he bandaged her legs from the ankles upward very tightly, and poured wine into her mouth, forcing it open; and, after vehement torments which lasted three hours, the Queen recovered her sight and speech, and got a great sweating, and the fever and the sickness abated; and the Queen spoke softly, and asked the Lords for their prayers. From that time onward she mended, until the day when she returned to Edinburgh, where once more she was rid of corrupt blood and restored to health.

And all this time the King remained at Glasgow, hunting with his hawks and his hounds, and he came to Jedburgh on the day after the Queen's health had begun to mend, and he abode there one night.

And a Council was holden at Jedburgh, and four days later the Queen passed to Kelso. And later, after a progress through different towns, she came to Craigmillar Castle, which is situate two miles from Edinburgh, where she held a Court for the French Ambassador, the Count de Brienne, whom the King of France had sent to represent him at the Prince's Baptism. And after the King and Queen had tarried for a week at Craigmillar, the King, of whose behaviour the French Ambassador, M. du Croc, complained, left the Queen and went to Stirling. And at Craigmillar the Earls of Huntly, Argyll and Moray and Secretary Lethington proposed to the Queen that since the King continued every day from evil to worse, if Her Grace would pardon the Earls of Morton and Lindsay, and their company, they would find a means to make a divorcement betwixt Her Highness and the King, her husband; to which the Queen made answer that under two conditions she might be willing: that the divorce be made lawfully, and that it were not to prejudice her son; otherwise she would rather endure all torments. And when the Lords proposed that the King should leave the realm, the Queen said it were better that she herself should pass into France; and the Secretary said that the nobility would find the means that the Queen would be quit of the King without prejudice of her son, and that my Lord Moray would look through his fingers and behold their doing, and say nothing to the same.

But the Queen told them she would do nothing whereto any spot could be laid to her honour or to her conscience, and she prayed them to let the matter be abiding till God put a remedy thereto, whereat Secretary Lethington asked that the business should be guided by them and approved by Parliament; but the Queen said nay to this, and negatived the conspiracy of the nobles, whether their design were to be divorcement, or banishment, or impeachment. The Queen was sufficiently mended in health to go to Holyrood for the birthday of the King, his twenty-first, the seventh of December, and for her own birthday the next day.

The Earl of Bedford was about this time upon his journey to Scotland, also the Ambassadors of France, for the Baptism of the Prince; and the Queen passed to Stirling with the Prince for the solemnizing thereof.

And never was the Queen more pensive or more sad than during this season; and there was none to comfort her, and Sir James Melville, who was at Stirling at this time, tried to assuage her grief and pressed her to recall the banished Lords, and to pardon them; they not having, he said, a hole to hide their head in, nor a penny wherewith to buy their dinner. And the Queen listened to his words and thought fit to be reconciled to them by time according to their future deportments.

And she purposed to proceed with such a gracious government as should win the victory over all her enemies and competitors.

But the Earl of Bothwell, as soon as he heard of her merciful inclination, took occasion to make friends of the Earl of Morton and his associates, for he had already then in his head the resolution of performing the murder of the King, which he afterwards put into execution, that he might marry the Queen.

The Earl of Bedford was honourably received and lodged in the Duke of Châtelherault's house, in the Kirk of Field. The Queen held a Court for the reception of the Ambassadors from England, and there was daily banqueting, dancing and triumph. And the Earl of Bedford, on behalf of the Queen of England, presented to the Queen a silver font, gilt and enamelled, and a ring worth a hundred marks, and the Countess of Argyll acted as the Queen of England's proxy as gossip at the Baptism of the Prince.

The Baptism was solemnized at four of the clock, in the Chapel Royal, and the Prince was borne by Brienne, who represented the Most Christian King of France, as one Godfather; M. du Croc was the proxy of the Duke of Savoy, the other Godfather.

There was a double line of nobles, each bearing a lighted pricket of wax, from the Prince's room to the door of the Chapel, where he was received by the Archbishop of St Andrews in cope and mitre, and other prelates at this ceremony, which was solemnized according to the rite of the Church of Rome.

After the Baptism there was a supper in the Hall of Parliament.

The Queen rewarded the Earl of Bedford with a rich chain of diamonds, and the other gentlemen of the Embassy with fair gifts; and two days after the Baptism there was another banquet, with masking and playing and fireworks, and at the end of the evening music and dancing.

But the King was not present at the Baptism, for he would not associate with the English nobles unless they would acknowledge him as King of Scotland, and this they had been forbidden to do by the Queen of England, their mistress.

The Earl of Bedford entreated the Queen to pardon the banished Lords, as she had already pardoned Secretary Lethington; and the Earls of Moray and of Bothwell pressed her thereunto; and the Queen gave full redress to those who had murdered the Seigneur David, always excepting George Douglas, who had stabbed the Seigneur over her shoulder, and Andrew Ker, who had presented a pistol to her body, and Patrick Bellenden, who had aimed a rapier at her. This pardon so greatly angered the King that he left Stirling without taking leave of the Queen, on the eve of Christmas, and passing to Glasgow he fell sick of the smallpox; and the Queen sent to him her physician, M. Lusgerie, who had been with her in France when she had been sick of the same malady, and had aided the physician of the Court.

And on the Day of Kings the Secretary Lethington was married at Stirling Castle with Mary Fleming, one of the Queen's Ladies, being the third of the Queen's Ladies to marry; but there was no feasting nor cheer at the marriage, for the King was sick, and the Queen was herself ailing in body and sore tormented in spirit. And rumours of plots were abroad: the Queen was told by the Earl of Moray that the King and his father were assembling troops to dethrone her and to take away the Prince; and the King was told that the Queen harboured a like intention towards himself. The Queen passed incontinent with the Prince to Holyrood, and she sifted the rumours for herself, and found them to be baseless. And at this very same time the Earl of Morton came from England to Whittinghame Castle, and there he met Secretary Lethington, the Earl of Bothwell and Mr Archibald Douglas, and it was there that the Earl of Bothwell proposed to him the purpose of the King's murder. And the plotters said that it was the Queen's mind; but Mr Archibald Douglas was sent by my Lord Morton to Edinburgh with the Earl of Bothwell and the Secretary to obtain the Queen's warrant for the deed.

The Earl of Bothwell and the Secretary bade Mr Archibald Douglas tell the Earl of Morton that the Queen would hear no speech of the matter, whereupon the Ministers drew up a warrant for the arrest of the King and his imprisonment, and they presented it to the Queen; but the Queen would not sign it, saying that God would in his own good way put remedy and amend what was amiss in him.

The King sent several times for the Queen, who was herself sickly, having been injured by a fall from her horse. But, a month after the King fell sick, the Queen, after holding a Court to welcome the Ambassador from Savoy, passed to Glasgow, and she had provided that all should be ready at Craigmillar Castle, and took with her her litter, to carry the King back thither, in order that he might travel softly.

The Queen was lodged in the Palace of the Archbishop, and she told the King that preparations had been made for a cleansing course for him of medicine and bathing at Craigmillar. And at first the King said he would go with her wheresoever she pleased, but later he said he liked not the Queen's purpose of taking him to Craigmillar, and as he had no will thereunto the purpose was altered, and another conclusion was taken.

The King's health now began to mend, and two days after she had come, the Queen left Glasgow with the King, and four days later there were in Edinburgh, where it was concluded that the King should lodge in the Provost's house near St Mary's Kirk of the Field, until the cleansing time should be accomplished. And during this journey a raven followed the King and the Queen from Glasgow to Edinburgh, where it perched sometimes on the King's lodging and sometimes on the castle, and the day before the King's death it croaked for a while upon his house.

And the Ministers chose this dwelling for the King; the Earl of Moray recommending it to the Queen, saying that it was a place high situate, in good air, environed with pleasant gardens, and removed from the noise of the people.

The Queen's brother natural, the Lord Robert, Commendator of Orkney, spoke to the King in secret of a plot against his life and that of the Queen. And the King rehearsed all to the Queen, and the Queen sent for Lord Robert and bade him repeat his words. But my Lord Robert denied that he ever spoke thus, and there was choler and dispute, and the Queen called upon the Earl of Moray, who was present, to appease them.

This advertisement moved the Earl of Bothwell to haste forward his enterprise, and a train of powder had already been laid under the house where the King lodged.

On Sunday morning the King heard Mass, and at Holyrood House the marriage was celebrated between Bastian Pagez, one of the Queen's servants, and Christily Hogg; and the Queen provided the wedding dinner, whereat she was present, and promised to be at the mask the same evening. At four of the clock she and the noblemen supped at the banquet which was held by the Bishop of Argyll, whereat was the Ambassador of Savoy. When the supper was ended, the Nobles led her to the King's house at Kirk of the Field, where she brought them into the King's chamber.

At about the eleventh hour the Queen said it was later than she had thought, and rose to go. The King besought her to stay a little, and she drew a ring from her finger and placed it upon his. And as the Queen was about to leave the King's house she met Paris, a servant of the Earl of Bothwell, and his face was blackened with gunpowder, and she said to him in the hearing of all: "Jesu, Paris, how begrimed you are!"

At this he turned red, and the Queen mounted her horse and passed to Holyrood with her gentlemen and her Ladies and with a company of men bearing torches. And as soon as the

Queen arrived at the Abbey she ascended to the room where the bridal was held.

As soon after midnight the Queen retired.

The Earl of Bothwell was at the bridal, dressed in a velvet hose, passemented and trussed with silver; and when the Queen retired the Earl of Bothwell went to his chamber, and he was seen to leave the Palace in a riding cloak by the postern gate.

About three or four of the clock in the morning a match was put to the train of gunpowder under the King's house, and there was a great noise equal to a volley of twenty-five or thirty cannon, and the Earl and Countess of Bothwell were roused by Mr George Hacket, who said that the King's house had been blown up, and he trow'd the King be slain. And the Earl of Bothwell cried: "Fie, treason!" And he rose and put on his clothes, and with the Earl of Huntly and others, and their Ladies, he went to Holyrood House into the Queen's presence, and told the Queen the tidings. The Queen commanded the Earl of Bothwell to hasten to the King's house with the guards, but it was not until five of the clock that the body of the King was found, in a little orchard near the ruins.

And it was thought at first that the King's body had been blown into the garden by the force of the explosion, but there was neither bruise nor mark upon his body, nor on that of William Taylor, his servant, whose dead body lay near to his; nor was there a smell of fire on the garment; nor a hair of their heads singed.

At daybreak the Earl of Bothwell came back to the Palace and told the Queen that the body of the King had been found in the garden; and the Queen withdrew to her own chamber; and about ten of the clock in the morning the Earl of Bothwell came to her once more and spoke to the Queen by her bedside; and Madame de Briante was present with other attendants, and gave Her Majesty breakfast while she gave audience to the Earl of Bothwell.

CHAPTER VI

When the Earl of Bothwell had left the Queen's presence the Queen said to Madame de Briante and to the other Ladies that the murder of the King was the consequence of the murder of Seigneur David, and that it would be her turn next. The day after the murder the Queen received a letter from Archbishop Beaton warning her that some formidable enterprise was in preparation against her, and upon the same day, Shrove Tuesday, Margaret Cawood, the Queen's servant, was married with John Stewart, the Queen giving the bridal feast; but the Queen remained throughout that day in her darkened chamber, stretched upon her bed, and silent.

The King's body was brought to the Chapel Royal, where dirge was sung day and night until the night of the burial.

And the Queen passed from Holyrood House to her dule-chamber in Edinburgh Castle, where she tarried a week, until the burial of the King, which was at nightfall in the Chapel of Holyrood.

The following day the Queen passed from Edinburgh to Seton, and thence later she returned to Edinburgh. The Earl of Moray, who had taken leave of the Queen and passed into Fifeshire the day before the murder of the King to visit his wife, returned not now, despite of the Queen's entreaties, and the realm was wholly guided by the Earls of Bothwell, Huntly and Argyll, and Secretary Lethington.

All suspected the Earl of Bothwell to be guilty of the murder, and evil reports of him were spread abroad, to which he answered with defiance and challenge; but his enemies, having used him for ridding themselves of the King, designed to use him for ridding themselves of the Queen, whose ruin they knew must bring with it his own downfall.

They designed the Queen should marry with the Earl of Bothwell, so that they might charge the Queen of having plotted against the late King, and of having been privy to his murder. Tickets were affixed on the Tolbooth door of Edinburgh accusing the Earl of Bothwell of being guilty of the murder of the King; whose father, the Earl of Lennox, petitioned the Queen to take order in the matter. Two Privy Councils were held in Edinburgh, and the Earl of Bothwell said that he was ready to answer the charges and to justify himself. An Assize was appointed to be held in the Tolbooth, whereupon the Earl of Moray went from the realm three days before it was held, despite of the Queen's entreaties, and he passed to England and later to France; and in both countries he sowed seeds of mischief against the Queen. The Earl of Bothwell was cleared and acquitted in full Parliament, whereupon he set up a cartel declaring his innocence, and offering to maintain the same against any challenger.

The Queen, after the business of Parliament was completed, passed to Seton, and the Earl of Bothwell bade to a banquet all the noblemen who had attended the Parliament. The banquet was held in a tavern of a certain Ainslie, whereat the nobles signed a bond pledging themselves to defend and maintain the quarrel of the Earl of Bothwell against all privy or publick calumniators bypast or to come, and likewise to further advance and set forward a marriage betwixt the Queen and the Earl of Bothwell: the bond was signed by eight Earls, among whom were the Earl of Morton and the Earls of Huntly and Argyll.

After the signing of this bond the Earl of Bothwell began afar off to discover his intention to the Queen, but her answer disappointed him.

And the Queen passed to Stirling to see the Prince, and intrusted the Prince and the Castle to the care of the Earl of Mar.

The Queen passed from Stirling to Linlithgow, being delayed by illness, and on the morrow, when she was on her way from Linlithgow to Edinburgh, with a train of twelve persons, the Earl of Bothwell, with a thousand of his followers, rode out from Edinburgh and encountered the Queen at a village called Foulbriggs, within three-quarters of a mile of Edinburgh Castle, and, seizing her bridle, carried her away with him to Dunbar Castle as a prisoner, a distance of twenty miles, the Queen having already ridden that day from Linlithgow almost to the gates of Edinburgh.

The Earl of Bothwell boasted that he would marry the Queen, whether she were willing or no, and, together with the Queen, he carried away the Earl of Huntly, the Secretary Lethington and Sir James Melville, but none of the Queen's Ladies; and the Earl of Bothwell's sister was the only lady at Dunbar Castle to attend upon the Queen.

Sir James Melville was released from captivity the day after the Earl of Bothwell came to Dunbar Castle; and the Secretary Lethington was high wrought in rage against the Earl of Bothwell, and the Earl of Bothwell would have slain him in the Queen's chamber had not the Queen come betwixt them and saved him.

And never a man in Scotland moved to procure the Queen's deliverance; and when the Queen threatened the Earl of Bothwell, he showed her the handwrites of the nobles, and what they had writ in the Bond, and he gave the Queen little space to meditate with herself; but pressed her ever with continual and importune suit; and as by bravado, so the Queen said later, in the beginning he had won the first point, so ceased he never till by persuasions, accompanied not less by force, he finally drove her to end the work which he had begun.

After the Queen had been kept a prisoner for seven days, the Court came to Edinburgh, and a number of noblemen assembled in the Palace, where they subscribed a paper declaring that they judged it was much to the Queen's interest to marry the Earl of Bothwell; and now the Queen could not but marry him, seeing he had had his way with her against her will. The Earl of Bothwell caused his own marriage to be nullified by the Consistorial Court, and sent a requisition for purpose of matrimony to be proclaimed between himself and the Queen in St Giles's Church, and for a while the proclamation of the banns could not be made, for the reader, John Cairns, who spoke against the marriage, had not the Queen's warrant; but at the end her handwrite was obtained, and the Queen was taken to the Court of Session in the Tolbooth, where she declared that she had pardoned the Earl of Bothwell for his proceedings, and that she was acting of her free will. The proclamation of the banns was made twice in St Giles's Church, and the Earl of Bothwell led the Queen to Holyrood House, and he visited the French Ambassador, M. du Croc, and entreated him to be present at the wedding, but M. du Croc kept aloof.

Upon that same day the Earl of Bothwell was made Duke of Orkney in Holyrood House. And when the Queen was seated upon her throne, the heralds went out with the Earl and led him back in procession bearing a blue banner worked with his arms, and the Earl of Bothwell followed himself, in a crimson robe furred, between two Earls, and was made Duke of Orkney. Five days later the marriage was made at the Palace in Holyrood House, after a sermon by Adam Bothwell, Bishop of Orkney, in the Great Hall, according to the order of the Reformed religion, nor was there rite nor Mass in the chapel.

And the Queen was married in her robe of dule, neither were there pleasures nor pastimes, and the Queen was more changed in face without sickness than ever as yet.

And the Duke of Orkney was desirous to get the Prince into his hands; but my Lord of Mar would not deliver him out of his custody. And in the presence of the Duke of Orkney the Queen said to M. du Croc that he must not be surprised if he saw her sorrowful, for she could not rejoice, nor ever should again, for all she desired was to die; for the Duke of Orkney handled her with disdain, and with reproachful language, so that the Queen, in the presence of her Ladies, asked for a knife to stab herself, or else she would drown herself.

And her Ladies were of mind that unless God aided her she would become desperate; for the Duke of Orkney continued to visit the Countess of Bothwell, his lawful wife, who was at Crichton Castle, and at the same time he was suspicious of the Queen, and put such indignities upon her that he suffered her not to pass a day in patience without making her shed tears.

And now the same Lords who had signed the Bond setting forward the marriage betwixt the Queen and the Duke of Orkney were the foremost to cry out upon the marriage, and the Court was empty, and the Queen fell a swooning so often it was thought by some she had been stricken by the falling sickness

And all began to cry out against the foul murder of the King, and the Lords concluded at a secret meeting to take up arms to avenge that murder and the author of it, the Duke of Orkney; and the Queen, having summoned the men of the shires to convene at Melrose to proceed against the insurgents on the Border, the Lords came to Edinburgh, thinking to surprise and to capture the Queen and the Duke of Orkney. But the Duke of Orkney, having been made privy to their design, retreated to Borthwick Castle and took the Queen with him.

The Lords convened to the number of three thousand men, and set out in Council, at the Market Cross at Edinburgh, a proclamation of their quarrel, and declared they would deliver the Queen's person forth of captivity and prison, and punish Bothwell for the cruel murder of the late King, the ravishing design and detention of the Queen, and the wicked design he meditated against the Prince.

And the proclamation met with response, and the Lords, joined by Lord Hume and his men, made an assault upon Borthwick Castle that night, and they discharged volleys of musketry, and railed at the Duke of Orkney and at the Queen, using injurious reproaches, to provoke him to issue from the Castle, which he would have done had he not been held back by the Castellan and his own people.

At the end, provoked beyond endurance, and followed by forty men-at-arms, the Duke of Orkney sallied from the Castle and gained the open country, where he began to collect his forces.

The Queen was left alone with about seven or eight persons, and at midnight, dressed as a man and booted, she let herself fall from the window of the banqueting hall to the ground, and passed by the postern in the wall, where she mounted a pony that had been brought her by a cousin of one of the men-at-arms. And albeit she rode all night, she rode astray, and was met at dawn scarce two miles from Borthwick Castle by the Duke of Orkney and his men-at-arms, whence they proceeded to Dunbar.

The Duke of Orkney marched forward out of Dunbar towards Edinburgh, taking the Queen with him. The Lords, with their company, went out of Edinburgh, with desire to fight. Both armies lay not far from Carberry, and the Queen's men were posted on Carberry Hill, where the Queen dismounted; and in the afternoon M. du Croc, the French Ambassador, who was with the rebels, came to parley with the

Queen, and passed several times from one camp to the other protracting the business.

And as it grew late, deputies came to the Queen for the fourth time from the rebels, and a meeting was held between the two camps.

The insurgents protested that they had come as faithful subjects and required nothing but justice for the murder of the late King, and that the Queen should be restored to liberty. In order that this might be done, they petitioned that the Queen should deliver up the Duke of Orkney, the murderer of the King, and that she should accompany the Lords there assembled, who should reinstate her in her due position. And the Duke of Orkney, overhearing what they said, challenged to single combat anyone who so charged him; and the Lords consented thereunto; but the Duke of Orkney seemed cold in the business. The Queen sent for the Laird of Grange and told him that if the Lords would do as he had declared to her and give assurance for the Duke of Orkney, she would leave him and come to them, and the Lords, being advertised of this, assured her in their united names they would do as they had said.

The Duke of Orkney entreated the Queen not to put trust in the Lords, but finding he could not move her from her purpose he parted with the Queen, she having requested him to depart, and before parting he made known to her the design of her enemies; and the Queen advanced unto the Laird of Grange and rendered herself unto him, upon the conditions he had rehearsed to her in the names of the Lords.

That night the Queen was conveyed to Edinburgh, and during the journey the Lords separated all her servants from her, and she knew that she was now a prisoner. The Queen was taken to Edinburgh and lodged in the Provost's lodging, and as the Queen came through the town some of the common people cried out against Her Majesty at the windows. The Queen was shut in a chamber, and guards were posted on the stairs and at each door of the house, and some of the men-at-arms were without shame, and would not leave her chamber, so that the Queen lay all night long upon a bed without undressing.

And the Queen cried out to all who passed in the streets that she was their native Princess, and that she doubted not but all honest subjects would respect her.

The next morning the Queen showed herself at the window of the Provost's house; and she had rent her garments and her hair was wild about her face, so that many were moved to pity, save two soldiers, who advanced a banner whereupon the King was painted lying dead under a tree and the young Prince upon his knees, praying, "Judge and revenge my cause, O Lord." And at this sight the Queen screamed aloud and called upon the people either to slay her or to deliver her from the cruelty of the traitors who had deceived her, and by whom she was thus barbarously entreated.

And there were many who took pity upon her and spoke of unfurling the blue blanket.

And, as the Queen was looking out of the window, she saw Secretary Lethington pass, and she called him several times by his name and she wept, but the Secretary passed his way; whereupon the common people, angered at his behaviour, became riotous, and the guards removed the Queen from the window.

The bruit got abroad in the town of the Secretary's ingratitude, and for shame in the evening he came to visit the Queen. And the Queen asked him why she was being thus ill-treated, and what was in store for her. The Secretary said it was feared she would thwart the execution of justice demanded upon the death of the late King; and with fair words and promises he took leave of the Queen and went to confer with the Lords.

At nightfall the Earl of Morton came to the Queen with a message from the Council that the Queen was to be lodged at Holyrood Palace; but they designed to remove her further, and had waited until night, fearing the anger of the people. Thither was she led, betwixt the Earls of Atholl and Morton, on foot.

When she reached Holyrood Palace supper had been prepared, and the Queen's Ladies were with her.

When supper was scarce begun, the Earl of Morton bade the dishes to be removed from the table, and he told the Queen to be ready to mount on horseback incontinent. And the Queen asked the Earl of Morton whither they were going to remove her in such haste, and she asked that some of her Ladies and servants should go with her; but this request was denied her, and none save two *femmes de chambre* were allowed to accompany the Queen.

And the Queen was taken in haste to Lochleven, the house of the Earl of Moray's natural brother.

The Queen was taken in charge by Lord Lindsay and Lord Ruthven, the son of Lord Ruthven who led the insurgents on the night that Seigneur Riccio was killed. And the Queen was told by the way that her friends might gather forces for her rescue, and was advised to linger on the road, but there was always someone near who whipped her hackney to urge it on. And Lord Seton and others pursued the Queen with an armed body, but albeit the race was sharp, they did not overtake her; and the Queen was rowed in a boat to the Castle before her friends reached the water-side.

141

MARY LIVINGSTONE'S NARRATIVE

CHAPTER I

Soon after the death of King Henry VIII, the French Ambassador petitioned that the Queen of Scotland should be sent from the cloister of Inchmahome to France for the better safety of her person, since the times were troublous, whereunto the Council and Estates of Scotland assented. And in the month of August of the year 1548 the Queen, being six years old, embarked at Dumbarton in a royal French galley and sailed to Brittany; and with her were Lady Fleming, her Lady Governess, and her four child-ladies: Mary Beton, Mary Seton, Mary Fleming and Mary Livingstone. They landed on the twentieth day of the month of August in the year 1548, and were lodged in the Convent of St Dominic, and a *Te Deum* was sung at the Church of Notre Dame, whereat the Queen was present; and on the way back from Church, when the Queen had passed the gate of the town, the drawbridge, overloaded with horsemen, gave way and fell into the river, but without causing loss of life; and the Scottish nobles cried "Treason", but the Seigneur de Rohan, who was walking on foot by the side of the Queen's litter, cried: "Never was a Breton a traitor," and the Queen was undismayed. The Queen tarried there two days, whence she passed to the Palace of St Germain-en-Laye.

The Queen was well instructed in music, Greek, Latin, Italian, Spanish and French; she delighted in falconry and the chase; her uncle taught her to ride; and needlework and horsemanship came easily to her, as if they had been faery gifts. The Queen had been given, in lieu of Lady Fleming, Madame Parois for Lady Governess, who treated the Queen harshly, and what most displeased the Queen, Madame Parois would not permit her the credit of giving away a pin; and the Queen had to bear the shame of being thought niggardly; and this was a cause of exceeding bitterness to her, for she was over-generous and over-prodigal of her nature.

When the Queen was twelve years old she recited at the Feast of the New Year an oration in the Latin tongue before the King and the foreign Ambassadors, whereat the Court was in admiration. There were at the Court many poets and lettered men: M. du Bellay, M. de Ronsard, M. de Maison-Fleur and others, and the Queen loved to discourse with them of poetry, for she greatly delighted in the verse of poets.

The Court was guided at this time by Madame de Valentinois, the mistress of the King, and the Queen of France remained in the shadow, and the Queen of France from the first was hostile to the Queen of Scotland, albeit she spoke of her with admiration; but Madame de Valentinois was a true friend to the Queen: they were akin in beauty, in their love of fair things and in their native nobility; whereas the Queen of France knew that the Queen of Scotland was made of a finer substance than herself: and this filled her with envy.

The same year the Queen was entered into the estate which had been appointed for her, and was given a royal household; and two years later Madame Parois retired, at her own wish, after having caused the Queen much infelicity, which the Queen endured with patience. In her place Madame de Briante was appointed to be the Queen's Lady Governess; she had been a servitor of the Queen-Regent in Scotland, and, being wedded to Lord Seton, who died the year after the Queen arrived in France, was the mother of Mary Seton; and a year before she entered the Queen's household she married the Seigneur de Briante.

Madame de Briante was a wise woman, outspoken and fearless of speech, with a prompt wit and a swift discernment into the hearts of men and of women. She was a devout friend of the Queen, and maybe there was none who read the heart of the Queen so well as she.

When the Queen reached her sixteenth year the ceremony of handfasting took place in the month of April between her and the Dauphin, in the Great Hall of the Louvre; and the marriage articles were read and subscribed. The Queen was dressed in white, and it seemed as though she were clothed in light, so dazzling was she; but before this ceremony the King of France made the Queen sign an instrument by which she gifted him and his heirs with the succession of the realm of Scotland and her rights to the throne of England, should she die without surviving offspring, *"dans le cas qu'elle décédast sans hoirs procrés de son corps (que Dieu ne veuille!)"*, and the French King, by reason of his arrogant greed and clumsy craft, thus sowed the seeds of much trouble for the Queen.

The marriage between the Queen and the Dauphin was solemnized on the Sunday after the handfasting, at Paris in the Church of Notre Dame, and after the banquet and a ball in the Palace of the Archbishop, the Court passed in procession to the Palace by the Rue Saint Christophe, where, after supper, the tables were lifted and there was more dancing, and the Queen-Dauphiness trod a measure with Madame Elizabeth, the daughter of the King, while her train, which was six *toises* long, was borne by one of the noblemen through the maze of the dance.

In the month of November came the news of the death of Queen Mary of England, and the Queen of Scotland was the next in line of succession; the Princess Elizabeth, who succeeded to the Crown, having been declared illegitimate at the time of the divorce and execution of Anne Boleyn.

147

Nevertheless, the Princess Elizabeth was crowned Queen and declared to be legitimate by Parliament.

The King of France determined to challenge her claim; and at the justings which were held in the month of July at the Palace of the Tournelle, the King ordered the Queen of Scotland to quarter the arms of England and Scotland, and that the titles of King and Queen of Scotland and Ireland should be added to those of King and Queen of Scotland, which were borne by King Francis and Queen Mary. This act greatly wounded the pride of the Queen of England, although she herself was not willing to erase the arms of France from her shield.

For over a year the Queen-Dauphiness held a Court that was all enchantment. The hours were vocal, and the Court was haunted by fair women and gallant men, such as the King of Navarre and M. d'Anville.

Each of these was enamoured of the Queen-Dauphiness, and the Queen favoured M. d'Anville, who excelled all the other courtiers by his grace, his daring, his noble carriage and his joyous ways.

M. d'Anville loved the Queen unto frenzy; and she was more drawn to him than ever to any other before or since; but he married Mademoiselle de la Marck, because his father, the Connétable de Montmorency, so willed it, before the death of Henry II, King of France; and when this King was untimely and inopportunely slain at the justings, M. d'Anville sorely grieved, for the Queen would have married him had she been at liberty, and now this could be no longer be. The Queen-Dauphiness was now Queen of France; but this brought her small joy, and she fell into sadness and sickness; the realm was distracted with turmoil and strife, and the King was sickly. The crown and the business of ruling were too heavy a burden for one of his years and delicate frame, and he died at Orleans after he had reigned but a little over a year.

The Queen, now no longer Queen of France, retired little by little from the Court of France, not wishing it to appear, what was indeed true, that the cause of her retirement was the Queen-Mother's rigorous dealing and disdain for her.

In the first days of her mourning, when she kept to her dule-chamber at Orleans, she was clad in white robes, and a marvel to behold; and to one of her ladies, who said that it was sad to see the Queen in such doleful array, Madame de Briante answered, that the Queen knew it became her.

During her time of dule the Queen received a visit in secret from my Lord Darnley, the son of the Earl of Lennox, of the blood royal of England. My Lord Darnley was a tall and lusty young Prince, high of stature and straight; compared to the French nobles he seemed younger and fairer, and yet not ill-instructed. His carriage was seemly and his speech pleasing. He pleased the Queen, and she gave him gracious audience and a letter to his father and to his mother, thanking them for their condolence; and when he had departed the Queen told one of her Ladies that would she but wed that youth she should be Queen of England, but that never would she wed a man whom she must govern.

And Madame de Briante said that stranger things had happened; Her Grace might well marry one as young and as boneless. But to be Queen of England was a more difficult design to compass, for the Queen of England would suffer no rival so long as she lived.

But the Queen answered she might not live for ever.

And Madame de Briante said no more.

The French nobles who had come from Scotland resorted to the Queen and advised her to return to Scotland, rather than to endure the Queen-Mother's disdain, and be second person in France, where she had once been first; and they said she might well be first person in Scotland and in England.

They advised her to be familiar with my Lord James, Prior of St Andrews, her brother natural, and to use the Secretary

Lethington and the Laird of Grange, and to repose most upon those of the Reformed religion. The Prior of St Andrews came himself to France and entreated the Queen to return to her own, promising to serve her to the utmost of his power.

Lesley, afterward Bishop of Ross, came to her also from the Catholic nobles and promised if she would land at Aberdeen, where all were of her religion, he would meet her with twenty thousand men, and she should establish once more the old religion in the realm.

Other of her Scottish nobles paid their duty to the Queen while she was at Joinville with her grandmother, and among these was the Earl of Bothwell, who returned with her to Scotland.

The Earl of Bothwell was a claimant of high offices in Scotland; he was of the Reformed religion, but a devout servant of the Queen. There were many he failed to please, especially among the French nobles, but he would pass unnoticed by none; his countenance was well matched with his hazardous spirit, and albeit at times rough in carriage, and apt to be glorious, he had been well instructed in his youth, in France, and he was not without letters; and when he had the mind he pleased greatly; and his daring spirit pleased the Queen, nor did his rashness displease her. The Prince of Spain and the Earl of Arran were desirous to obtain the Queen in marriage, and the Queen, after visiting the Duke of Lorraine at Nancy, into which city she entered in high triumph, fell sick and passed to Joinville, and thence to Rheims, where she went into retreat in the convent of St Pierre with her aunt the Abbess Renée of Lorraine, and the bruit was abroad that she would never leave that seclusion; whereupon her uncles hastened to Rheims; but Madame de Briante thought otherwise, and said that the Queen was not born for the cloister, but for the Court and the battlefield.

As soon as the Queen was mended in health she passed to Paris, where she was honourably welcomed and entertained, with pleasures, pastimes and justings, and lodged in the Palace of the Louvre: the Queen-Mother, being now Queen-Regent, was now the first person at the Court, and the Queen yielded her precedence, as was befitting. The Queen now determined to return to Scotland, for since her uncles would not suffer her to remain in peace in the cloister, she had no mind to be second person in France: and M. d'Anville no longer haunted the Court. She bade farewell to Fontainebleau, where M. de Ronsard visited her and declared that she was yet fairer in her black robes of dule than she had been in her more sumptuous finery. "For," said he, "she knows how to wear veils more cunningly than other Princesses, and her black robes heighten her celestial pallor, which is that of a rose-leaf."

The Queen gave audience to the English ambassador, Sir Nicholas Throckmorton, and told him she was sending M. d'Oysell to the Queen of England to declare unto her good sister that she had determined to embark at Calais for Scotland, her realm, and that the King of France had lent her galleys, and she would ask for a passport to pass through England, and such favours as Princes use to do in such cases.

The Queen, while she was at Dampierre, received a letter from M. d'Oysell advertising her of the refusal of these favours, which he said the Queen of England had declared to him with wrathful expressions before the Spanish Ambassador and others of the Court; and the English Ambassador was on his way to declare his Mistress's pleasure unto her.

Those about the Queen entreated her to stay her voyage until the Queen of England should be better disposed towards her, saying that if she fell into the Queen of England's hands she would be in peril. But the thought of peril was ever as a spur to the Queen; moreover, neither now nor later would she believe that she could not win the Queen of England's goodwill in the end. She even welcomed the thought of being constrained to land in England. Thus the Queen, deaf to entreaty, passed to the Palace of St Germain, where she received Sir Nicholas

Throckmorton, who told her that his Mistress could not satisfy the Queen's desire nor grant her such other favours as she required. The reason being that the Queen had not ratified the Treaty of Edinburgh, which, if she was willing to do, the Queen of England would grant her the favours, and be glad to see her in the realm.

The Queen said she could not ratify a treaty without the advice of her own Council. And in the matter of quartering the arms of England, she declared that she had but obeyed her father-in-law, the King of France; moreover, since his death and the death of her husband, the King, she had neither borne the arms nor used the title of England: but the Queen's words were of no avail, and those about her once more entreated her to stay her voyage.

But the Queen would not heed them, and when a few days later the Ambassador took his leave of the Queen she said to him that if her preparations had not been so much advanced, peradventure the unkindness of the Queen of England might have stayed her voyage: but now she was determined to adventure the matter whatsoever might come of it.

"I trust," she said to the Ambassador, "the wind be so favourable that I shall not come upon the coast of England: and if I do, then the Queen will have me in her hands to do her will of me: and, if she be so hard-hearted as to desire my end, peradventure she may then make sacrifice of me – peradventure that casualty might be better for me than to die. In this matter God's will be fulfilled."

And, having received the Queen's embrace, the Ambassador took his leave.

The Queen departed from St Germain-en-Laye in the month of July, and with her went many nobles and Princes: her uncles and her aunt by marriage, and the bravest and the noblest gentlemen of France; among them the Earl of Bothwell and M. d'Anville, and with him was Châtelart, a Huguenot from the Dauphiné, and the great nephew of Bayart, who had been

M. d'Anville's confidant, and was even at this time, so Madame
de Briante, enamoured of the Queen himself, albeit he
concealed his passion, or rather masked it with the public odes
he made and the songs he sang to the Queen; for these were
thought to be but the usual forms of courtesy and homage from
a courtier and a ballad-monger to a Queen.

Châtelart was young and well-favoured: a friend of the
Reformed religion, albeit his master was a Catholic; but it is
doubtful whether his religion, if indeed he had any, were not
more Pagan than Christian, for he had been fed on the Latin
poets, and he often declared that the teaching of the Greeks
and the Romans was the true religion for a man, and that the
Christian Faith, whether that of the Catholics or the Reformers,
was meeter for women; and he would often say that after this
life he looked forward to a sleep without dream, and that any
word written in the Old Testament, or the New, he believed as
well a tale of Robin Hood. He was a skilful lutist, and M. de
Ronsard praised his verse, as much as one poet will praise
another, and an older a younger; and said he harboured high
hopes of him; but these hopes were not fated to be fulfilled.

During the voyage M. de Châtelart made the Queen many
sonnets, and when the fog thickened, as the galleys neared the
coast of Scotland, Châtelart said that they needed no beacon to
guide them over the dark waves when they had the starlike
eyes of this fair Queen, whose rays lit up land and sea and
brightened all they shone upon. But neither M. d'Anville nor
any of the courtiers marked aught of import in such profession,
save Madame de Briante alone, who said: "Châtelart is of those
who o'erleap all bounds and who fall into the precipice; for
there is in him no curb of reason nor religion to refrain his
unbridled desire and his insolent dreams." But the Queen was
so pensive with her sorrow at leaving France that she heeded
little else, and least of all Châtelart.

The Queen was now nineteen years old, and passing tall. She
was higher of stature than all the Ladies, and as high as a man,

and as her uncle; but her majesty and the grace of her motion caused all to forget her height.

Madame de Briante said that she was well aware of all her charms, and heightened them of a purpose. She seldom wore a mask, and even in processions she walked with face uncovered; and often she would eclipse the more glittering splendour of the other Princesses with an artful simplicity; her hands, her ankles and her small feet shod with rare science were peerless; her fingers long and frail: the delight and wonder of the poets; and all at Court imitated the changing shape and colour of her gloves. Her hair was fair, with a golden glinting in it, and cunningly busked. Here she had the aid of Mary Seton, who was, the Queen said, the first busker that was to be seen in any country. Her eyes were changing in colour; and under her long lashes, live with flame, they sometimes seemed hazel-colour and sometimes blue, but when lit up by anger they were like flashing swords, and when she smiled they were like stars.

M. de Ronsard said her smile was like the first blush of the dawn upon a rippling sea. And Châtelart said it was blinding, like a fair diamond. She wore pearls round her neck, and during her widowhood a veil with a stiff edging; and she carried in her velvet satchel a volume of Ronsard's poems, stamped with her arms, and mended by the poet himself, and a golden whistle. She had small need of a whistle to lure to her the hearts of men. Her voice was low and perfectly pitched, and its accents, when she was in a gentle or melancholy mood, were as ravishing as the tones of a well-played lute; and when she was in a choler they were rapid and sharp, and the words fell helter-skelter from her lips, like a cascade of golden moneys.

In playing on the lute she displayed the skill as well as the shapeliness of her matchless hands. She favoured rings, and had a number of them, well-chosen and wrought. Her delicate body was fashioned as it were of steel; she was impetuous and tireless, swift in the chase, and first in the gallop, and ready to ride all day and dance all night, and be fresh at the end as at the beginning of it. Those about her sometimes heard her say that she was sad, but never that she was weary. She was blent of subtle, rare and delicate elements, and there was about her a magical flame, a seductive fragrance that bound those about her with a spell: and in peril she was compact of ice and fire.

At every banquet and stately pastime she would devise some new fantasy of apparel with poetic invention, and while her fancy outsoared that of the poets, she embodied what they divined and surpassed their devising.

She wrote verse which the poets praised for its delicate lisping; but her words and her letters writ in prose were more eloquent, and showed more of her native fire, fervour and wit. Her spirit was great and troubled, and in her presence all felt a sweet or a sad confusion.

Her welcome in Scotland in the mists of Leith was rude; the Scottish nobles, the greater part of them being of the Reformed religion, came to meet her with suspicion, and with jealous glances for her foreign company: but she won them incontinent with her grace and her lovely ways, and many among them, and especially the young, were swept away by admiration: and Mr Knox, the preacher, marked sourly that those of the Reformed religion were not the slowest to welcome the Queen.

The Queen was quick to discern the men about her she must sue most carefully: chief among these was Lord James Stewart, her brother natural, who was bold in arms and crafty at Council; cautious, prudent and greedy, and a devout friend of the Reformers, in heart as well as in word.

There was the Earl of Morton, cunning, double-faced and callous, concealing a native savagery under a sanctimonious mask; Lord Ruthven, crafty and bold and used to Court withal; Lord Lindsay, ready to put Catholics to the sword, and the Earl of Huntly ready to do the same by those of the Reform. William Maitland, my Lord of Lethington, who seemed better fitted for the Courts of France and Italy, with his easy learning and his polished phrase: the Laird of the Grange, a man of war and a leader of men, famous throughout Europe; and Mr Knox, who kept aloof from the Court and kept his welcome for the pulpit, where he greeted the Queen with bitter and burning words.

There was banqueting in honour of the French nobles, and pageants and procession when the Queen entered the city at the palace of Holyrood House.

At the banquet given to bid farewell to the Queen's uncles in the month of October, there was a masque in which M. d'Anville took part. This masque was devised by Mr Buchanan, the famous poet; and in it Apollo and the twelve Muses marched before the throne, and told in verse in the Latin tongue how they had been driven by the war from their ancient haunts and had taken refuge in the lettered court of the Queen of Scotland. Each Muse as she passed spoke a compliment to the Queen; and the Tragic Muse bade the tragic cothurn be ever a stranger to the Queen. And it was at this masque that the Queen bade farewell to her uncles and to M. d'Anville, who returned with Châtelart to France, leaving behind them the younger of the Queen's uncles, M. d'Elbœuf, an ill-advised choice, as he was young and untutored.

After these pleasures and pastimes the Queen turned to serious affairs, and appointed her Ministers: these she chose from those of the Reformed religion, save the Earl of Huntly, whom she made her Chancellor: Lord James Stewart was her chief Minister, and Maitland of Lethington her Secretary of State.

The Queen was assiduous at the Council Chamber, but even there she had her table of sandalwood, and worked with the needles; but, busy at her needlework as she might be, her mind never wandered from the matter that was being deliberated.

CHAPTER II

When the Queen arrived in Scotland she was held in suspicion on account of her religion; and soon she perceived that her chiefest enemy would be Mr Knox, and she set about to disarm his enmity and to win his goodwill, for the Queen had claimed liberty of conscience for herself and her household before her advent; and even this was hardly granted, for the first time Mass was sung at Holyrood House there was broil and tumult, and oftentimes later.

The Queen clove to her own religion throughout her life; but in despite of what the Scottish nobles may have said, she was no fanatic, having seen the woes resulting from religious dissension and persecution in France, and this is proved by her deeds. It is true she would gladly have seen the old religion restored in Scotland, believing it to be the true religion, and she declared this to be her dream to the Pope; but she knew it to be a dream, and a dream it was, for she scarcely obtained freedom of worship for herself, and never for those of her subjects who were of her religion. Never once did she act against her subjects of the Reformed religion; never once did she encourage persecution; and she refused the aid and support of her Catholic nobles, who were powerful in the North, fearing they would be over-zealous, and knowing that those of the Reformed religion were for the time the stronger. It was but for herself and her household that she claimed the right to worship as she pleased, but she often petitioned and entreated that those subjects who were likewise of her Faith – and of these there were many – might enjoy the same freedom, but this was ever denied her, nor could she save them from imprisonment; for when Mr Knox and his followers spoke of liberty of conscience and freedom of worship, they meant the right to worship as they pleased, and the right to imprison and put to death Catholics for worshipping in their manner; for they regarded that manner and that Faith as being of the devil.

But the wisdom and temperate action of the Queen in this matter won her favour from neither side, for those of the Reformed religion said it was but deceit; while those of the older Faith in France and elsewhere accused her of being but half-hearted in her religion, because she shared not their fury and because she was wiser than they in these matters. The Queen-Mother spurred her to encourage the Catholic cause in Scotland, hoping that thereby she would meet disaster: for so little did the Queen-Mother care for the interests of those of her Faith outside her kingdom that she entreated the Queen of England, when it fitted with her policy, to imprison and to persecute her Catholic subjects: and of this Secretary Lethington was well aware.

Thus it was that the sweet reason of the Queen found but a deaf ear in Mr Knox; and when the Queen summoned him soon after her arrival and petitioned for his goodwill, he spoke to her of those of her Faith as the Hebrew Prophets spoke of idolaters and their abominations, and when the Queen said to him that she perceived from his words that her subjects must obey him and not her, and so must she be subject to them and not they to her, he said to her that God craved of Kings that they might be as fosters-fathers to His Kirk, and commanded Queens to be nurses to His people.

Whereupon the Queen said to him: "You are not the Kirk that I will nourish. I will defend the Kirk of Rome, for I think it is the true Kirk of God."

Whereupon Mr Knox said: "Your will, Madam, is no reason, neither doth your thought make that Roman harlot to be the true spouse of Jesus Christ."

And he began to expound to her a refutation of the Mass, but the Queen bade him depart from her; and he ceased not to preach against her in the pulpit.

Yet those about the Queen who could read her heart knew that therein was neither malice nor guile, but alone the desire to govern her realm peacefully and to live at peace with her subjects, nor could she understand such harshness nor such scorn.

The Queen sent Secretary Lethington to the Court of England and bade him renounce in her name all claim to the throne of England during her lifetime, but she petitioned to be regarded as the inheritrix of the English throne. Now Secretary Lethington had great credit at the English Court, and designed to beget a strict friendship between the two Queens, and at one time it appeared nothing was more desired by either of them than they might see each other by a meeting at a convenient place. This was the design of Secretary Lethington: and it was planned that the two Queens should meet at York, whereat the Queen greatly rejoiced; but Madame de Briante told her that it would never be, because the Queen of England envied the Queen and was jealous of her beauty, her youth and her accomplishment. And Madame de Briante spoke truly, for although the passport was signed and the horses made ready, the Queen of England at the end said she must stay the meeting until the following year, whereat the Queen grieved and even wept. Thus in lieu of passing to England the Queen visited the northern parts of her realm, and it was during this sojourn in the North that the Queen lost her most faithful and devout subjects: for the Lord James Stewart, who was now already

Earl of Mar, coveted the Earldom of Moray and the demesnes of the Earl of Huntly, and sowed suspicion into the mind of the Queen, so that she would not visit the Earl of Huntly, either at Huntly Castle or at Strathbogie Castle; and when the Queen came to Inverness, my Lord James, who now openly styled himself Earl of Moray, the Queen having given the Earldom in secret earlier in the year, took advantage of the folly of Captain Alexander Gordon, who, being Deputy Keeper of Inverness, would not surrender the fortress without the order of the Keeper, Lord Gordon; and Captain Gordon was hanged, and the Queen was angered with the Gordons, and rejoiced at their discomfiture, and when she was threatened with an ambush of a thousand men and all expected a battle, undismayed, she welcomed the peril and the adventure. But peril there was none, nor adventure, for there were no foes to encounter; and she passed to Aberdeen in safety, and there she was honourably received. The Earl of Huntly sent her the keys of his castles and a cannon that was in his possession, which the Queen had demanded, and he sent it saying that not only the cannon that was his, but his goods and even his body were at her disposal.

But the Queen was deaf to all protestations of loyalty from the Gordons, nor would she give audience to Lady Huntly, who came to offer the submission of her husband. And at last, led by an evil star, and in an evil hour, the Earl of Huntly took arms against the Queen and was defeated, and died incontinent after the battle, at Corrichie, and his sons were captured; and one of them was beheaded at Aberdeen before the Queen, which caused her great sorrow and much displeasure, for he was a gallant, noble man, the comeliest in Scotland, and it was said that he was enamoured of the Queen, and some said he had designed to carry her away.

In all this business the Queen greatly erred: for she had in Scotland no such loyal subjects, had they been treated with better understanding, and that this was not done was due to the greed and the craft of the Earl of Moray, who coveted their lands and who obtained them. And the doom of the Gordons was the first of the calamities that befell after the Queen came to Scotland, and this error led to others, and at the end to the downfall of the Queen herself.

Until the Earl of Huntly was defeated, and Sir John Gordon was beheaded, never had the Queen been so joyous and so free-minded; but, after that defeat and that beheading, her mind was clouded with questioning. For the Queen, albeit subtle in mind, and like a harp of many strings, able and apt to respond to every breeze and to sound unto any touch, was easily deceived, and she was slow at first to perceive the true nature of these Northern noblemen who were about her.

Because they were rough and daring, she thought they were single-minded: and she thought they were loyal subjects and devout friends because they paid her homage with their lips. She was accustomed to the men and the commerce of France and the French Court, and she was deceived by false semblances; for she knew not then that the Northerners were deceitful, nor suspected that they masked their thoughts and concealed ambitious designs.

The Queen paid heed to those who flattered her, and heeded little those who crossed her, nor for a long while did she discern the true nature of her brother natural, the Earl of Moray.

She knew him to be excellent in the field and at the Council Board, and a true servant of a strange Faith, but she marked not his ambition nor his covetousness, which he knew well how to dissemble.

And ever the Queen would think that the men who pleased her must needs please all others: and this brought her bane, for the Scottish noblemen disrelished the noblemen of France and all foreigners, and it was the foreigners who brought the Queen misfortune.

161

While the Court was at Montrose, a messenger came from France bearing a letter for the Queen from M. d'Anville; and the messenger was Châtelart, who was in M. d'Anville's service. Châtelart's name was now upon all lips in France, for he had become famous for his pretty swordsmanship and his courage at the Pré-aux-Clercs, as well as for his rhymes, and he brought the Queen a book of his rhymes, and the Queen gave him a sorrel gelding: but the purpose of his mission was to press the suit of his master; for M. d'Anville said he would put away his wife if the Queen would wed him: but the Queen was now distant from all such dreams.

Soon after his arrival the Queen and all the Court fell sick of a new disease, but this was but a passing ague, and the Queen held her feast upon her birthday, and there was dancing, and the Queen trod a measure with Châtelart. And the next day, after dinner, she was sitting in her chamber sewing with her Ladies at her little table of sandalwood, and Madame de Briante was reading from the Romance of Lancelot du Lac; and they lighted upon the tale of how Sir Tristram, having been sent by his Lord, King Mark, to woo Iseult of Ireland, became enamoured of her himself, which was a cause of woe to all; and Madame de Briante said to the Queen that she feared that Châtelart was in much the same case as Sir Tristram, and had forgot his master. And the Queen laughed, and said that albeit she was the object of Châtelart's rhymes and his homage, which were such as all French courtiers felt bound to pay to all women, and yet more to all Queens, Mary Beton (who was not present) was the object of his heart; and Madame de Briante shook her head and said:

"Men like Châtelart are not to be contented with the second best, and if Châtelart favours Mary Beton, it is because she has for him a borrowed glory."

And she advised the Queen to send Châtelart back to France; but the Queen said that Châtelart thought no more of her than he did of the Great Harry, and she would not be deprived of the sunshine she had those days, surrounded as she was by so many dour faces and so much gloom. He would be leaving in a month, and when he went, he would return no more.

But Madame de Briante said the sooner he left that place the better, for the man was sick for love, and hot-blooded and rash, and ready for all folly, nor could he be blamed, seeing that Her Grace had encouraged him and made much of him.

The Queen wept and entreated Madame de Briante not to blame her; for she had little occasion for mirth and pleasure; and she promised she would not encourage Châtelart, but keep him at a distance; and Madame de Briante, knowing that the Queen, for all her tears and gentleness, had a purpose as hard as polished diamond when she so willed, said: "Have your way, Madame, but I pray to God that you may not both of you live to rue the day that Châtelart came to this country."

The Queen continued to favour Châtelart, and she marked not that he was enamoured of her, or, if she marked it, she heeded it not; for she looked upon Châtelart as a servitor, and she believed him to be discreet.

Mr Knox preached a sermon against the dancing at the Palace, and prophesied that the wrath of God would strike the Court. The Queen summoned him to her bedchamber, where he rehearsed his words before the Lords and Ladies, and said he did not altogether damn dancing, if they did not dance like the Philistines for pleasure in the tribulation of God's people. If they did that they should receive the reward of dancers, which was to drink in Hell. For Mr Knox believed the Court had danced for joy at the sufferings of those of the Reformed religion in France.

And when he had departed, Madame de Briante said to the Queen: "That man is puffed up with conceit, and he believed no word of his harangue, which was addressed to the Lords: and what angers him is not Your Grace's dancing, which even his narrow creed forbids him to condemn, but that Your Grace, being a woman and but twenty years old, should speak to him of such subjects as an equal and worst him in argument, for he perceives that Your Grace has both heard and read; and he despises all womankind, but should Your Grace condescend to flatter him, he will be different, for vanity is his weakness."

Châtelart, under the pretence of pressing his master's suit, pleaded his own, and at last passion led him to a mad enterprise, and he was discovered under the Queen's bed with a sword and a dagger by the servitors.

The Queen was told of this the next day, when she forbade him evermore to appear in her presence: but Châtelart, instead of leaving Scotland, followed the Queen to Burntisland, and hid himself that night in the Queen's chamber, where he set upon the Queen with force and in such impudent sort that she cried out for help, and bade the Earl of Moray to stab him incontinent; but the Earl of Moray said he must be dealt with according to the laws.

Suit was made for his pardon, and the Queen was inclined thereto, but her Council dissuaded her, and it was whispered by Secretary Lethington that Châtelart had been sent by the enemies of the House of Guise to cast a slur upon the Queen's honour, so as to hinder her marriage with any foreign Prince: but the Queen, knowing well what M. d'Anville's purpose had been in sending him, and never suspecting Châtelart of double-facedness, paid no heed to this; nevertheless, she signed his death warrant, albeit she counselled one of the equerries to contrive his escape; but the gaoler could not be persuaded, and Châtelart was beheaded at St Andrews, refusing the aid of all spiritual ministers, and rehearsing rhymes of M. de Ronsard, and invoking the Queen as the fairest and most cruel of all Princesses. And the adventure of Châtelart and its tragic ending caused the tongues of slander to wag.

Those, and there were many, who misliked a foreign match for the Queen rejoiced exceedingly. For there were rumours in the air now that the Queen would wed the King of Sweden, and now another foreign Prince.

The same year, and about the same time, the Queen of England had been persuaded to summon a Parliment, and her Commons had petitioned her to marry; for she had the year before been grievously sick, and the Commons of England desired that the next heir might be known, if the Queen were to die without children to survive her. And they declared the foreign realms would set up a rival against herself, and they feared the danger to the Reformed religion, should that rival be a Catholic.

At the same time the Queen of Scotland had received a proposal of marriage from the Archduke Charles, and bade Secretary Lethington to advertise the Queen of England thereof. And when the Queen of England learnt thereof, she sent her Ambassador to Scotland and advised the Queen that she should wed one whom her subjects could approve, and who was likely to increase the friendship between the two Crowns; but when asked to say who that might be, he answered with ambiguous words; but at last he told the Earl of Moray that the man whom the Queen of England had chosen was my Lord Robert Dudley, the favourite of the Queen of England; and the Queen was amazed that, having refused so many foreign Princes, the Prince of Condé, the Duke of Ferrara, the Dukes of Anjou and Orleans and Nemours, she should be petitioned to marry my Lord Robert Dudley.

But it was now plain to all about the Queen that she had determined to marry; and on the Twelfth Night of that year the Queen told her Marys that she would release them of the vow they had taken, for they had vowed never to wed unless the Queen were the first to take a husband – for she was minded to wed herself.

On that Twelfth Night there was a great feast at Holyrood House, and the bean was hid in the cake, according to the French custom, and it fell to the lot of Mary Fleming, who was

acclaimed as Queen: and the Queen said that as she was Queen she should be Queen in deed and wear royal apparel, and she lent Mary Fleming her State robes of cloth of silver and her gems, with which she loaded her, and even the Great Harry, the diamond cross which had been given to the Queen by her father-in-law, King Henry. But Mary Beton was the fairer, with her hair the colour of wheat and her eyes as black as sloes, and no less fair was Mary Seton; and Mary Livingstone was present also.

Randolph, the English Ambassador, courted Mary Beton. Mr Buchanan wrote a verse in Latin in honour of the Queen of the Feast; and the Ladies wore their brightest apparel, all save the Queen, who wore but white and black, neither gold nor any jewel, save a ring hung round her neck; and Madame de Briante said she could have found no surer way to outshine the others, and outshine them she did.

At Shrovetide there was another feast at Holyrood House, when the four Maries served the Queen, apparelled all in black and white, and the last course was served by gentlemen apparelled likewise in black and white, who sang verses in the Italian tongue which had been rhymed by Seigneur David Riccio, sometime Secretary to the Marquis de Moretta.

CHAPTER III

Seigneur David Riccio, of the country of Piedmont, had come to Scotland in company with the Ambassador of Savoy not long after the Queen's advent. He had sung by chance in concert with the Queen's three valets at Mass in the Chapel of Holyrood, there being wanting a bass.

The Queen perceived that he was a good musician and was greatly pleased; and, when the Ambassador went from Scotland, he left Seigneur Riccio behind him in compliment to the Queen, who made him a Groom of the Chamber.

Albeit crooked in body, he was nimble in mind, and he pleased the Queen and many at Court with his drollery, for he could counterfeit the voice and gait of those around him, so that he could rant like Mr Knox, snuffle like my Lord Morton, blink like the Earl of Moray and scold like Madame de Briante. And when her French Secretary went from Scotland, which was towards the end of the year which saw the death of Châtelart and the assassination of the Queen's uncle, the Duc de Guise, the Queen made Seigneur David her Secretary in his stead: and from that moment he lost his discretion and began to make himself enemies; for he had a barbed tongue, and many of the noblemen misliked seeing him mock others of their kind and their kin, suspecting that what he did to these he would do presently to them, which was indeed the truth, for

Seigneur Riccio spared none. But he was a diligent, prompt and observant Secretary, and the Queen came to lean upon him more and more; and when the noblemen complained of his arrogance and familiarity, the Queen listened and said she would take order, but never did she.

In the matter of the Queen's marriage, which was now being debated in Scotland, in England and in France, Seigneur Riccio played no small part. The Queen had been asked in marriage by the Archduke Charles of Austria and by other foreign Princes, and the Queen of England, fearing a foreign match for the Queen, proposed to her my Lord Robert Dudley, her favourite, for a husband; and albeit the Queen declared her unwillingness to wed him, the English Ambassador continued to press the suit.

In the matter of these suits the Queen reasoned thus: she refused the foreign Princes because she knew they would be disagreeable to her subjects, and would have no means of enabling her to assert the rights of her succession to the throne of England. She could not risk offending her subjects for the sake, for example, of the Archduke Charles, who could not strengthen her authority over them, for she was herself without power or money, or even faithful counsel among them; and being, in a manner, estranged from them by having been brought up out of her own country, and by the difference in religion.

She therefore determined to wed in the realm, to which she was solicited both by Catholics and those of the Reformed religion, who plainly told her they would not permit her to do otherwise.

Lady Lennox had solicited her to accept her son, of the blood royal both of England and Scotland, and the nearest after herself in succession, of the Stuart name, and a name dear to the people of Scotland, which would be retained by the marriage, and of the same religion as the Queen: whereupon the Queen of England, being privy to the design, urged my Lord

Robert Dudley once more upon the Queen, and made him Earl of Leicester. But the Queen had no mind to marry him; moreover, she knew the Queen of England was not in earnest, for the Earl of Leicester had told her in secret, through Randolph, the Ambassador, that the purpose of the Queen of England was to abuse and retard her, and he showed her at the same time how she might induce the Queen of England, through fear, to give her consent by stirring up troubles in Ireland.

She had therefore sent Sir James Melville to London to see the Queen of England, and he, when back from England, had told the Queen to expect no plain dealing from the Queen of England, for there was in her nothing but dissimulation, emulation and fear; nor was she in earnest in offering her the Earl of Leicester. And yet she had feared at one time that he might find favour with the Queen, and she incontinent gave licence to my Lord Darnley to come to Scotland and gave him letters from herself.

Moreover, the Queen knew that the Earl of Moray sought to be made legitimate, and would have all the offices, strong places and the whole guidance of the realm in his hands, and hold her in his tutelage, and seek the authority of the Crown for the ruin of the Hamiltons, as he had once already sought and obtained it for the ruin of the Huntlys.

Reasoning thus, the Queen determined to take a husband and to choose him herself, namely, my Lord Darnley; and my Lord Darnley came to Scotland in secret, for the Earl of Moray, seeing the Queen was inclined to the marriage, made means in England for him to be countermanded by the Queen.

The Queen met Lord Darnley at Castle Wemyss in the year of God 1565, about the Saint Valentine, and my Lord Darnley found favour with her, and she charged M. de Castelnau, who was on a mission to her, to demand the consent of the King of France and the Queen-Mother. And, after tarrying but a few days at Castle Wemyss, the Queen came to Edinburgh, whither my Lord Darnley had come before her; and he dined with my Lord of Moray, where he danced a galliard with the Queen, and his behaviour was well liked and there was great praise of him.

In March of the same year Mary Livingstone was married to my Lord Sempill of Beltreis at the Shrovetide Feast, this being the first marriage among the Queen's Maries, and the Queen gave the bride her wedding apparel, besides other gifts, and furnished the bridal masque.

The Queen had now minded to marry; but my Lord Darnley, becoming impatient, proposed marriage to the Queen; which displeased her greatly, and she refused a ring which he then offered unto her, and she began to wonder whether her choice were wise, for my Lord Darnley was, without doubt, over-boyish and indiscreet, and Melville, whom she trusted, was averse to the match.

From France the bruit of this marriage brought to the Queen proposals from a number of Princes, and from the young King himself, and from his brother, the Duke of Anjou, for the French were afraid lest the two Kingdoms of Scotland and England should be united under one Crown. Nevertheless, besides those who opposed the match from policy, there were others who opposed it from regard for the Queen and her interests, as well as for their own, and among these was the Cardinal de Guise; and Madame de Briante, with whom the Queen talked of the matter, was yet more outspoken.

"Lord Darnley", she said, "has grace and comeliness, but no woman of spirit should make choice of such a man. He resembles a woman more than a man, beardless and lady-faced. He is rash and hot-headed, for he has no boldness; anger but no power. He is unstable, and will keep neither his counsel nor his head: and he will betray from weakness and not from malice. He is but at best a painted Prince, a reed to lean upon, and as easily guided as a weathervane, and as yielding as wax."

And when the Queen said she must needs wed for the sake of the Scottish Crown, Madame de Briante said it was for the sake of the Crown of England that Her Grace would be wedding, and she would do better to accept the throne of France.

It was at that time the Queen was being urged from France to wed the young King; but the Queen knew she could never be Queen of France so long as the Queen-Mother were alive, and she had no desire to be a puppet in her hands, and to go back to France now would afford her more pain than pleasure, yea, maybe pain too sharp to endure.

And Madame de Briante bade Her Grace beware, saying that if she should wed Lord Darnley, he would not prove strong enough to be a defence against the nobles of Scotland; and this marriage would fan the enmity of the Queen of England, nor ever permit her rancour to subside. The Queen answered nothing, but she thought, maybe, were she wed to Lord Darnley, she would be strong enough to defy the Queen of England.

And Madame de Briante held her peace, likewise fearing to seal the determination of the Queen.

While the Queen was still in two minds, my Lord Darnley came to fall in acquaintance with Seigneur Riccio, and he became his friend; and Seigneur Riccio would speak to the Queen in my Lord Darnley's favour, and try to convince her that no marriage was more to her interest than this, seeing it would render her title to the succession of the Crown of England unquestionable. For until she married, he said, she would have no peace from the Queen of England, and this match would make her secure enough against the Queen of England's machinations. And the Queen tried to persuade Madame de Briante that this was the truth; but Madame de Briante said that the Queen would never be freed of this English plotting; and this the Queen would not believe, for, being frank and outspoken herself, when she had declared to her cousin and royal sister that she wished her no ill-will, but was desirous only that the Queen of England should recognize her as the inheritrix to the throne of England, which she was in very truth, she could not but think the Queen of England would treat her with a like frankness and goodwill. But Madame de Briante said that the Queen of England was double-faced; and, moreover, she was one who lived ever in fear; she was jealous of the Queen's youth and beauty, and feared lest, if she acknowledged the Queen to be next in line to the throne of England, her subjects might chase her from the Kingdom, for she was not safely seated upon her throne. Nor did Madame de Briante think the Queen of England was so much opposed to the Queen's match with my Lord Darnley as she pretended. She had rather the Queen married my Lord Darnley, she said, than any foreign Prince; for the Queen of England, being sharp-witted, knew that from Lord Darnley she had little to fear: and M. de Castelnau was of the same mind.

But it was the advice of Seigneur Riccio that the Queen followed, and not that of those who were wiser than he: for now she trusted Seigneur Riccio alone among those about her, and as for Madame de Briante, she was used to being scolded by her from childhood upwards, and so she heeded not her displeasure.

So the Queen was married to my Lord Darnley, secretly at first, at Stirling Castle, and she sent to Antwerp for gold and silver cloth for the bridal robes which she would wear at the State wedding, after she should have put aside her robes of dule, which she had worn since the death of her husband, the King of France.

She sent Secretary Lethington to declare her determination to the Queen of England, saying she was acting in conformity with her directions in forgoing her foreign suitors and choosing an English consort; but the Queen of England manifested great displeasure, and albeit she had already heard the bruit of the Queen's marriage, and confined the Countess of Lennox to her apartment, but knew not whether to credit it or not, for the Secretary Lethington had not yet been advertised of it himself, she sent the Queen a fair diamond ring and begged her to be guided by her wishes.

The Earl of Moray was yet more displeased, but he told the Queen he would further the marriage, provided he might manage the matter in his own way, and thereby he designed to banish every Catholic from the Kingdom.

Before the marriage of the Queen the Earl of Bothwell had come out of England to Scotland without licence, and stayed on the Border, and the Earl of Moray petitioned to hold his law day with the Earl of Bothwell, and awaited him with five thousand horsemen; but the Earl of Bothwell remained away, sending a deputy and declaring his willingness to meet the charge, and the Queen ordered the Court to be broken up. In the month of May the Queen declared to her nobles at Stirling Castle that she had determined to marry my Lord Darnley; and the Queen of England's Ambassador, Randolph, came from England with Secretary Lethington, being desirous to interrupt the business in the Hall of Convention at Stirling.

The Queen gave him no audience until the business was at an end and the nobles had assented to her marriage; the message from the Queen of England being that the Queen had erred by unadvisedness, and that my Lord Darnley and his parents had failed in their duties to their sovereign by arrogantly enterprising so great a matter without first obtaining her leave. And the Ambassador advertised the Queen of England that the Queen was so far past in the matter as was irrevocable.

The Queen sent remonstrance to the Queen of England, that she had forgone foreign alliance, which if she abstained from, the Queen of England had told her she might take her choice of any person within the realms of England and Scotland; and she spoke of the sharp entreatment of my Lord Darnley's mother; whereat the Queen of England committed the Countess of Lennox to the Tower and summoned my Lord Darnley and his father to England under penalty of forfeiture and outlawry. And

173

the Queen made my Lord Darnley Earl of Ross and a Knight of the Thistle.

Until these events my Lord Darnley had been well spoken of by all; but now, secure in the Queen's love, for at this time she was still captivated by him, and being King of Scotland, he estranged all about him by his arrogance and his petulance: so that the Queen was abandoned by her counsellors, save Seigneur Riccio; and from this moment the nobles were resolved to rid the country of my Lord Darnley, and they planned to seize my Lord Darnley and his father to take them to Berwick, and deliver them to their Sovereign, who could inflict upon them the penalties of treason; and to shut up the Queen in the Castle of Lochleven: and this enterprise was hazarded when the Queen was proceeding from Perth to Callander House to attend the baptism of Lord Livingstone's son: but the Queen was advertised of the plot by a faithful subject, and she outwitted the rebels by her promptness. The Queen now pushed forward her marriage, which was solemnized in the Palace of Holyrood House, in the Queen's Chapel; and the Queen was married in the dule-robe of black, with a great mourning hood, which not until the Mass was over did she exchange for bridal robes, and even then she was hardly persuaded. And when the benediction was ended, and the priest said Amen, Seigneur David cried out:

"*Te Deum laudamus* – it is done and cannot now be undone."

My Lord Darnley was now Duke of Albany, and after the marriage he was proclaimed King of Scotland, but these honours did not satisfy him, and he desired the Crown Matrimonial, nor could he suffer that the Queen should pass before him; and soon after the marriage the Queen pardoned Lord Gordon, the son of the late Earl of Huntly, and the Earl of Bothwell. The Queen of England once more declared her displeasure at the marriage and summoned my Lord Darnley once more to England, nor would she recognize him as King of

Scotland; and she accused him of holding treasonable correspondence with her own subjects.

The nobles having failed in their design to take the Lord Darnley in the Queen's company now took them to the field, and the Queen pursued the rebels near Glasgow; and they entered Edinburgh, where they caused to strike their drum, but won small support; and the Queen pursued them, sparing not to ride twenty miles in a day, so that her Ladies, save only Mary Seton, were left behind her. The Queen entered Edinburgh and proclaimed the Earls of Moray, Argyll and others to be traitors, and gave audience to the Earl of Bothwell at Holyrood, and made him Lieutenant of the Border. The rebels were strengthened with three hundred English harquebusiers and vaunt of support by sea and land; and they assembled at Dumfries; and the Queen took the field against them, leaving her Ladies behind, all but Mary Seton; and she assembled at Biggar in Lanarkshire, with a muster of eighteen thousand men, and the rebel Lords fled across the Border, and the Queen entered Edinburgh.

CHAPTER IV

The change that was first manifest in my Lord Darnley after he became King grew now more marked. He estranged the noblemen of Scotland and of England, and thereupon he estranged the Queen: first of all with his wilfulness and afterwards with his neglect and his debauchery. He was a stranger to reason, and, like a child, what he desired he must have incontinent, howsoever harmful the instant fulfilment of that desire might be, even unto himself.

When the Earl of Bothwell was made Lieutenant of the Border by the Queen, the King claimed that his father should be made Lieutenant in his stead; a childish desire, for the Earl of Bothwell was a Captain; but the sharpest difference between the Queen and the King was the Crown Matrimonial, which the King and his father demanded in season and out; and the Queen was loth to grant this hastily to him, until she knew how well he was able to enjoy such a sovereignty; and as the time passed she was assured of his unworthiness therefor.

The King grew sullen, wilful and petulant, like a child that is crossed, and he brooded over his wrongs and nursed his ambition, his father fanning the flame of his discontent. And presently other and more crafty persons contributed to this business: George Douglas, named the Postulate, son natural to the Earl of Angus, who was father to the mother of my Lord

Darnley, the Lady Margaret Douglas, and the Earl of Morton, who was a man of craft, and Lord Ruthven, who pretended to the heritage of Angus.

After the feast of Christmas the King went to Peebles with his esquires, the brothers Standen, but came to Holyrood in the month of February, when the French Ambassador came to compliment him with the Order of St Michael. The French Ambassador had been urged in England to speak for the banished Lords (the Queen had stayed the Parliament which was to meet in February to punish them, until the month of March); but the Ambassador spoke against their recall. Now my Lord Morton and other of the Lords began to blame my Lord Darnley for the credit enjoyed by Seigneur Riccio, to which they said his favour had contributed. And this was true, but the King had now estranged Seigneur Riccio, as he had estranged all others, for he had begun to drink deeply of *aqua composita*, and pressed Seigneur Riccio to join him in his drinking bouts and other debaucheries, and Seigneur Riccio, being from the South, and no friend of fiery wine, would not join him. Then my Lord Morton and George Douglas began to whisper in his ear. The King was made Knight Companion of the Order of St Michael with much ceremony; and he put on a robe made of crimson satin guarded with black satin and black velvet, with gold aglets and a gold chain, and the French noblemen said that it became him well; yet he was ill at ease. Madame de Briante marked that his eyes were dull, and his hand of a tremble. And she said he was no longer the same Prince who had greeted M. de Castelnau but a few months before, and won his admiration, he saying then that it was not possible to see a more beautiful Prince.

And those about the Queen knew now that she repented her marriage, for she had lost the love of the King, and was no longer sure of his faith or even of his allegiance; and the enemies of the King and of the Queen plotted to foster the dissension between them.

After the ceremonies, the banquets and the masques, in honour of the Frenchmen, were ended, the Earl of Morton and George Douglas hatched their plotting and fanned the King's resentment against Seigneur Riccio. They whispered to him that he should force the Queen to resign the Government into his hands, and they promised to abet him, and they told him it was Seigneur Riccio who counselled the Queen to keep him without revenue, and that he would never obtain the Crown Matrimonial so long as Seigneur David were alive.

In the month of February the Queen and the King were entertained in a merchant's house in Edinburgh, and the King drank overmuch *aqua composita*, to which he had grown addicted; and the Queen pressed him to stay from drinking, and he heeded her not, but drank all the more and enticed the others of the company to drink with him; and the Queen whispered to him to come away, for the feasting oppressed her, and it was irksome, said she, for her present condition, she being far gone with child, and the King said out loud: "Never mind, if we lose this one, we will make another."

And one of the Lords present told him he did not speak like a Christian, and the Queen straightway wept and went from the house.

Soon after this the Earl of Bothwell was married to Lady Jane Gordon, and he would not be married in the Chapel Royal, albeit his bride was a Catholic, but in the Kirk of the Canongate; but the Queen gave the bridal dress, and there was much feasting; and these were the last feasts that were ever held by the Queen at Holyrood House.

Now the plotters hasted forward their enterprise. And the plot was made first of all against the Queen, and not against Seigneur Riccio, who was but a pawn in the game; for he was wooed by the King to be of the conspiracy, but he would hear nothing of it, and he warned the Queen that the King was plotting to seize the power from her hands. Bonds were drawn up which the King and his father signed, and a bond was signed by the Earl of Moray and the banished Lords for the slaughter of Seigneur David. And some of these bonds were secret and some public, and the Lords said they would procure for the King the Crown Matrimonial, and that in the event of the Queen's death he should be declared her successor; and in one of them the King declared, with the aid of certain of his nobility, he would seize and cut off some wicked and ungodly persons, especially an Italian, called David.

First of all they planned to slay Seigneur Riccio at Seton, and next while he should be playing tennis with the King; but one of the conspirators said Seigneur David must be slain in the presence of the Queen, and in her chamber, so that the people might believe that the King could do no otherwise than kill him for his honour's sake.

It was in the month of March, at the beginning of the great feast, on Saturday, the ninth of the month, about two hundred armed men entered into the King's chambers and told the King they were in readiness; and the King went into the Queen's closet, where she was at supper with the Countess of Argyll, and Seigneur Riccio was present among her other servitors. And Seigneur David wore a doublet of satin, a gown of black damask figured, and faced with fur, and a satin doublet and a russet-coloured velvet hose, and a fair diamond which the Earl of Moray had given him. And before supper they had music, singing in parts, Anthony Standen, the King's page, holding a torch before the music. And the Queen said to the King: "My Lord, have you supped? I believed you would have supped by now." And the King sat down in the empty chair beside the Queen and he embraced her.

Of a sudden Lord Ruthven came into the closet from the Queen's bedroom, in a nightgown of damask lined with fur, under which he wore mail, and a casque over his nightcap. And the Queen asked him who had brought him to this place in this hour, and who had given him licence to come there.

"It is yonder poltroon David who hath caused me to come, who deserved not such favours," said Lord Ruthven. And the Queen said: "What offence hath he done?"

And Lord Ruthven said to the Queen: "Ask of your husband, the King," and, turning to the King, he said to him: "Sir, take the Queen your wife and sovereign to you."

And the King stood amazed and spoke no word. Then the Queen rose upon her feet and commanded Lord Ruthven to leave her closet; and she stood before Seigneur David, he holding Her Majesty by the plaits of her gown, leaning back over the arch of the window, his dagger drawn. Meanwhile Arthur Erskine and the apothecary began to lay hands on Lord Ruthven, who pulled out his dagger and defended himself: and there was a clamour without from men who had forced their way into the presence chamber, and the Queen's servants fled.

And Lord Ruthven put up his dagger: and one of the armed men who had come into the closet had a small pistol in his hand: and the Queen said: "If he has done wrong, I will bring him before justice," and Seigneur David, still holding Her Majesty, said: "Madam, I am a dead man," and the man who had the pistol said: "This shall be your justice," and he took from his pocket a rope, and the King forced Her Majesty into her chair from behind, and held her, while the man who had the pistol pressed it towards her and against her, so that she felt the steel, and she said to him: "Fire if you respect not what I have within me." And the name of this man was Andrew Ker of Faudonside; and the board fell towards the wall, with the meat and candles thereon: and another man came into the closet and seized Seigneur David by the neck, and the Queen, albeit the King held her back, reached the door of the closet; and while Seigneur Riccio was in the doorway with the Queen and the King hard by, the King holding the Queen back, George Douglas took the dagger from the King's sheath and struck at Seigneur David over the Queen's shoulder, saying: "This is the King's blow," and the dagger stayed in his body; and they dragged Seigneur David from the closet into the bedchamber, leaving the Queen with the King. And in the bedchamber Seigneur Riccio clung to the Queen's bed, and Andrew Ker beat him on the arm with the butt of his pistol; and thereupon he clung to the chimney-piece, and they beat him upon his hands until he relinquished hold of it, and in the doorway of the bedchamber and the stair they slew Seigneur David, giving him fifty-six strokes with daggers and swords; and there being now no more need to hang him they dragged his body down the stairs.

And one of the equerries came into the closet, and the Queen asked whither they had taken Seigneur David, and at the same moment Lady Sempill, who was Mary Livingstone, came into the closet, and said she had seen the body of Seigneur David wounded to death and mangled, and that all had been done by the King's order.

And the Queen turned to the King and said to him:

"Ah, traitor! And son of a traitor! This is the reward which thou hast given to her who gave thee much; and these are thy thanks to me for having raised thee so high," and so speaking the Queen swooned incontinent. And the servitors of the Queen and her Ladies were banished from the Palace, nor were any of them suffered to wait upon her, save her servant, Margaret Cawood.

All night long the Queen's Ladies were kept from the Queen, and from the chamber below they could hear her footsteps.

And the Earl of Bothwell and others fought for a while to expel the King's party, but they were outnumbered, and they escaped by a window into the garden.

The King went up to her chamber by the secret stairway from his lobby, but he found the door locked, and he entreated the Queen to open it, but he was not permitted to enter. And he visited the Queen the next morning, and she besought him to let her Ladies come to her. And Lady Huntly, Lady Sempill and Mary Seton were allowed to go to her. And she asked first of all for the black box that held her foreign dispatches and her ciphers, which was in Seigneur David's room. And Lady Sempill bade her husband (John Lord Sempill) to search for this, which he did, and Lady Sempill brought it to the Queen: and the Queen wrote many dispatches to her ministers, to the Earl of Atholl, the Earl of Bothwell and others. And the Queen saw the King and spoke to him softly, and asked how she had deserved such ill-treatment of him, so that he repented him of his treachery and wept. And he revealed to the Queen the bond that had been made betwixt him and the Lords, and all that he knew of the plot; and the Queen devised a plan of escape, and, having been advised by Secretary Lethington thereunto, gave presence to the rebel Lords, all except unto Lord Ruthven, and promised them remission as soon as she should be released from captivity; and the King promising to keep the Queen that night in sure guard, the rebel Lords went from the Palace with their guards.

They went from the Palace deeming that the Queen was sick unto death; but she at the fourth hour after midnight left the Palace with the King through the office of the butlers and the cupbearers, all of whom were French, by a door which opened into the burial-ground, where Arthur Erskine, an esquire of the Queen's stable, awaited the Queen with five horses, one with a pillion; and the Queen mounted on a pillion behind Arthur Erskine, and crossed the cemetery, in which lay buried the body of Seigneur David, and almost over the grave itself: and the King was seized with fear, and began to moan, and the Queen, who knew not of the grave, asked what troubled him. And he said: "Madame, we have just passed by the grave of poor David. In him I have lost a faithful servant. I have been miserably cheated." And the Queen bade him be silent, lest he might be overheard.

After they were clear of the city, the King, taking fright at some guards, who were of the Queen's party, albeit he knew it not, galloped on and abandoned her in the open country, where she was overtaken by the Earls of Bothwell and Huntly. And they rode first to Seton House, where they were welcomed by Lord Seton; and with two hundred armed cavaliers they came to Dunbar at sunrise. And there, when the warder challenged them, and asked who they were, they made answer: "The King and the Queen." And the Queen entered the Castle and asked for a fire to be made to warm her, and for some fresh eggs, which she cooked herself; and being refreshed, she wrote incontinent to the King of France and her uncles, and the letter was sent from the port of Dunbar.

The next morning the Queen's Ladies were the first to discover that the Queen and King had fled, and the rumour was abroad that the Palace would be sacked; and Mary Fleming went to Secretary Lethington and told him of the Queen's flight, and asked him whether they were in peril, and he said there was no peril; and the news was spread through the city, and six days later the Queen came back to Edinburgh, where she was joyfully welcomed.

The Queen was now betwixt men who hated each other vehemently, and her task was to give quiet to the country. Was ever so great burden laid upon the shoulders of a defenceless woman? And the greatest obstacle of all was the King, who was hated of all men and trusted of none.

The rebel Lords hated him because he had betrayed them and because he had publicly lied in declaring his innocence, and had accused Secretary Lethington of complicity; those of the Queen's party hated him for his treason to the Queen; and the Queen knew that his treachery was bottomless.

The Queen set about to pardon; and first of all she pardoned the Earl of Moray, and thereafter the Earl of Argyll, Lord Boyd and the Earl of Lennox: the King would have had her pardon Lord Ruthven and George Douglas, the Postulate, but he durst not speak their names to her, and Lord Ruthven and Lord Morton fled to England, where Lord Ruthven died, repenting him of his sins, for during life he had practised the art of magic, and at his death he saw a concourse of angels; and some said these were the messengers of his pardon, but others that they were demons in false guise, anxious to delude him and to bear him to Hell.

Now that the time for her deliverance was at hand, the Queen passed to Edinburgh Castle, and she was anxious to prepare for childbed, and for the safety of her child; for she had been warned that the Lords designed to seize the child as soon as she should be delivered.

She knew there was dissension among all the Lords, and that were she to die these dissensions must widen: she knew that she could not entrust her child to the keeping of her husband, for, as Madame de Briante said, he was not to be entrusted to see a scullion cook an egg, nor not to cheat that scullion of the egg once it was cooked. So she determined to make peace as well as she was able between the Lords, and to bring them together, so that they might be atoned.

So peevish became the King at these pardons that he was minded to depart to Flanders. Well for him would it have been had he taken ship!

The Queen lodged the Earl of Moray in the Castle during her labour: and the Earl of Huntly and the Earl of Bothwell pressed to be lodged there as well, but the Queen would not suffer this, and they envied the favour the Queen showed to the Earl of Moray, and they took occasion to persuade the Queen to imprison him, saying that he and his dependants intended to bring in the banished Lords at the time of her child-bearing. And the Queen said this secret design showed but their own hatred.

The Queen made her will, of which three copies were made, one being sent to France, and she told her Ladies that none of them would be forgotten; that she had left her books, in the French, English and Italian tongues, to Mary Beton, for she was delighted in the verse of the poets: and to each of the Marys she had left a small diamond, beside other gifts, and to Lady Sempill a carcanet of coral.

On the nineteenth day of June, between ten and eleven of the clock in the morning, the Queen gave birth to a son, and the Prince came into the world with a large and thin caul that covered his face: and the artillery of the Castle was discharged, and the Lords went to St Giles's Church to thank God for having an heir to the kingdom.

Gentlemen were sent incontinent to the foreign Kings and Queens to ask them to be gossips at the christening. And some days after the childbirth, the Queen sent for Sir Anthony Standen, who was an English page in the service of the King, and whom she had knighted, for he had saved her when on the night of the murder of Seigneur David he had warded from her the pistol of Andrew Ker of Faudonside.

The infant Prince lay asleep with a cross of diamonds upon his breast, and upon this cross the Queen commanded the knight to lay his hand; she gave him herself the oath of fidelity to her only son with these words: "For that you saved his life." And saying this the Queen turned to the King and said: "What if Faudonside's pistol had shot? What should have become of him, and of me, or what estate would you have been in? God only knows, but we may suspect."

"Madam," said the King, "these things are all past."

"Then," said the Queen, "let them go."

During all the time the Queen was at the Castle, and during the time of her travail, the King led a disorderly life, and he went up and down alone, for none durst bear him company. And he resolved to go to France in secret and to live upon the dowry of the Queen, and the rumour of this design coming to the Queen, she spoke to the King of it with great frankness.

CHAPTER V

The Queen designed, both before and after the birth of the Prince, to quieten the country and to establish amity and unity betwixt her turbulent Lords (now that my Lord Morton had fled to England and my Lord of Lethington had retired to Atholl), the Earls of Atholl, Huntly and Bothwell, and the Earls of Moray and Argyll.

Maybe such a task was beyond the skill of a mortal Queen: but that alone by which she might have compassed the wise design was lacking, the support of a trustworthy husband.

The Queen, being a stranger to jealousy, could not mark nor understand jealousy in others. She believed that she had but to govern graciously: but Madame de Briante said truly that the Queen misread the minds of her Scottish nobles, nor did she fathom the hatred that was betwixt them: the Earl of Moray hated the King; the Earl of Moray suspected the Earl of Bothwell, and was himself hated of the Earl of Huntly, and the King hated all the allies of the Queen, and most of all the Earl of Moray.

Madame de Briante said that the King not seldom hit the mark he shot at in his guesses: but since his motives were ever unworthy or malicious, and his argument angry or foolish, nobody, and the Queen least of all, heeded him: for example, the Earl of Moray pressed the Queen to publish an Act of Grace

186

pardoning the banished Lords on account of the birth of the Prince, and the King in a choler said they were not to be trusted; that he distrusted the very shadow of the Earl of Moray. His words were prophetic, but they came from the mouth of an angry child, and the Queen knew that they were prompted by envy and malice, and heeded them not. Again, the Earl of Bothwell and the Earl of Huntly each of them pressed the King to bring about the utter downfall of the Earl of Moray and my Lord of Lethington, who was still unpardoned and dared not take the seas lest the Earl of Bothwell should intercept him; and, since they made the King the spokesman and the instrument of this design, it could not but fail. For the more the King pressed the Queen towards this end, the more the Queen, knowing the King's malice, came to lean upon the advice of her brother and give him the guidance of the realm.

It was necessity that pressed her, for the Earl of Moray commanded the allegiance of all those of the Reformed religion in the realm, and they the more powerful: nor could she forgo the wisdom of my Lord of Lethington.

All this the Queen knew well; nor could anyone gainsay her, or say that it was but wise: but Providence made of her very wisdom and prudence an instrument of her doom.

The Earl of Moray from the first designed that the banished Lords should be pardoned, and all at Court knew that once the Lords should be combined and the banished Lords restored to favour, the doom of the King would be sealed; for Lord Morton hated the King with a hatred greater than all the other Lords harboured against him, because the King had betrayed him.

Wherefore the King lived in fear, and more especially of the Earl of Moray, and he told the Queen that he would have him slain, and the Queen warned the Earl of Moray of the King's design; but she said he would never dare the deed; and for this warning the Queen received no particle of gratitude from her brother.

187

Peace there might have been, but for the King: and he was too foolish and too arrogant to permit the Queen to offer him amity: for humble himself he would not, and could not, nor ever confess that he had erred. And Madame de Briante said that if the Queen could but hate the King, all would be made easy: but, albeit she had plumbed the depths of his folly and scanned the heights of his arrogance, she was ever mindful that she had once loved him, and, whatsoever he did or said, the Queen, albeit she could not forget the ill he had done unto her, could not forget her love for him aforetime: nor did she ever until the end cease to regard him as a child that was in need of guidance and might one day grow to man's estate and reason.

Towards the end of the month of July the Queen, with the Earl and the Countess of Moray and her Ladies, and the members of her Privy Council, crossed the sea to Alloa, the house of the Earl of Mar.

But the King would not sail in the same vessel with the Earl of Moray, and journeyed by land. And the Queen and the King sat in Council at Alloa Castle, and there she gave audience to M. de Castelnau, the French Ambassador, who came from the French Court to bear a letter from the French King about the birth of the Prince.

The Earl of Moray pressed the Queen to pardon my Lord of Lethington, saying that he was her friend and innocent of the murder of Seigneur David: and the Queen gave my Lord of Lethington presence at Alloa Castle, and granted him remission for all offences: whereat the King was displeased. And this act of pardon caused strife between my Lord of Lethington and the Earl of Bothwell; for my Lord of Lethington, when under the ban of treason, had been stripped of the Abbey lands of Haddington, and these had been given to the Earl of Bothwell; and now the Earl of Moray said the lands should be restored to my Lord of Lethington, who was willing to consent to a division, but the Earl of Bothwell said that ere he parted with those lands he would part with his life, and the Earl of Moray declared that my Lord of Lethington should not be reft: and he warned the Earl of Bothwell that his life would not be safe if he held fast to those lands; and the Earl of Bothwell passed to Meggatland to prepare for the hunting of the stag by the King and Queen, where they had little pastime for want of deer, which had been slain by forest outlaws.

During this hunting the King and the Queen visited the house of the Laird of Traquair: and while they were at supper the King spoke of a stag hunt on the morrow, and the Queen, not wishing to gallop, whispered a suspicion into the King's ear regarding herself; and the King said what he had said to her before at the house of the merchant; and the Laird rebuked him, whereupon the King answered: "What! Ought we not to work a mare when she is with foal?"

But in despite of the King, my Lord of Lethington was made Secretary of State once more; and the greater part of the Council was filled with the friends of the Earl of Moray.

After these hunting excursions and visits, and one to Drummond Castle, the Queen passed to Stirling with the Prince until, in the month of September, at the request of her Council, she came to Edinburgh for the affairs of the Exchequer.

And now the King's behaviour began to be more strange than it had ever been heretofore.

The Queen was desirous that he should come to Edinburgh with her, but he liked to remain at Stirling, where his father came to visit him; and the Earl of Lennox wrote to the Queen saying the King had in view to retire out of the kingdom and across the sea, and for this purpose had a ship lying ready.

The same evening that this letter was brought to the Queen the King himself came to Edinburgh in haste and impatience, but, when he heard there were Lords present with the Queen, he would not enter the Palace: and the Queen went out to meet him and conducted him to his apartments, where they remained all the night. And he would not acknowledge to her that he had any cause of discontent.

And the next morning, hearing that the King was about to return to Stirling, the Lords of Council repaired to the Queen's chamber, where they spoke with the King, there being none other present, except M. du Croc, the French Ambassador; and the Lords asked the King in all humility whether he had formed a resolution to depart by sea, and upon what ground, and for what end.

If his resolution proceeded from discontent, they were earnest to know who or what had afforded an occasion for the same: and they professed themselves ready to do him all the justice he could demand. And the Queen entered the discourse and spoke affectionately to him, and made, according to M. du Croc, a beautiful speech.

M. du Croc entreated the King to unburden his mind of any troublesome stuff; but the King would not own that he had intended any voyage, or that the Queen had given him occasion of complaint; and as he took leave from the Lords of Council he said:

"Adieu, Madam, you shall not see my face for a long space."

To the Lords he said: "Gentlemen, adieu."

Although he acted as if he were still minded to go to France, the Lords said this was but a trick; and he sent advertisement from day to day that he still held to his resolution, and he kept a ship in readiness.

A few days later he sent for the French Ambassador to meet him between Glasgow and Stirling, and M. du Croc drew from him little by little the cause of his discontent, which he thought to be the reconciliation of the Lords with the Queen, and his fear lest at the baptism of the Prince the Queen of England would not make any account of him.

Thereupon the King wrote to the Queen, saying that he had two causes of complaint: firstly, that the Queen trusted him not with so much authority as she did at first; and, secondly, that no one attended him, and the nobles avoided his company. To these complaints the Queen made answer that he should blame himself and not her; for although he had been named as chief of the enterprise when Seigneur Riccio was murdered, she had never accused him but excused him; as for attendants, she had offered him her own; and as for the abandonment of him by the nobility, it was his own deportment that was the cause thereof; for, if he desired to gain their love, he must render himself amiable to them; and thus the King, not being able to compass his desire, which was thought to be the removal of Secretary Lethington, whom he alleged to have been guilty in the murder of Seigneur Riccio, took his leave, and although ever speaking of going, went no further than Glasgow.

M. du Croc said this discontent was caused by the favour shown to the Queen by the Lords, which he said wounded the King's pride; and Madame de Briante said that, although this were true, the King was in fear, seeing that his enemies were being one by one restored to power. For the Queen had brought about an agreement between the Earl of Bothwell and Secretary Lethington, by which the Earl of Bothwell ceded a portion of the Abbey lands.

Never, so said M. du Croc, had he seen Her Majesty so much beloved, esteemed and honoured, nor so great harmony amongst her subjects. And yet never until the present time was the Queen in so deep a dejection.

Madame de Briante said that the strange behaviour of the King was caused not only by pride and fear but also by the love he had for the Queen, which was mingled with hatred: so that Madame de Briante said she would not marvel if one day he were to slay her: and yet in her presence he was meek and full of entreaty, and yet a certain slyness never left his eyes.

In the month of October a Justice Ayre was opened at Jedburgh, and was carried on for six days, and two Privy Councils were held; and upon the eighth day the Queen rode to Hermitage Castle to visit the Earl of Bothwell, who had been wounded in an affray on the Border, so dangerously that it was thought he must die; and the Queen conversed with him some hours and signed many papers, and returned on the same day to Jedburgh; and the day after that journey the Queen was seized with a pain in the side. And soon the sickness seemed like to be mortal, and was attended with fits of swooning and fits of vomiting, and some feared poison. And on the third day the Queen recovered the use of speech, and prepared herself to die, and she summoned the nobles and exhorted them to unity and quietness, saying that by discord all good purposes were brought to nought, and she forgave her enemies and spake long of the Prince, her son; and she said farewell to the French Ambassador, and bade him petition the King of France and the Queen-Mother to pay her debts and reward her servants; and she asked that toleration in matters of religion be observed after her death, as it had been to the utmost of her power during her life; and she declared she had never persecuted one of her subjects on the score of religion, for she said it was a "a mickle prick to anyone to have the conscience pressed in such a matter"; as for herself, she would die in the Faith she had been nourished in, and repeated the Creed in Latin and in English.

On the evening of the ninth day of the Queen's sickness her limbs became contracted and her face distorted, and her body so cold that all, and especially her servants, thought she was dead; but her French physician bandaged and rubbed her knees, legs, arms and feet for three hours, until the Queen recovered again her sight and speech; and the fever abated.

The King, who had been at Glasgow hawking, did not come to Jedburgh until the tenth day; and he came nine days too late.

The Queen's health began to mend, and she went from Jedburgh to Kelso quickly, whence she paid a visit in state to the English border, accompanied by the Earl of Moray, the Earl of Bothwell, and eight hundred horse; and the Queen sending word to the Warden of Berwick, he marched out to meet her and conducted her to Halidon Hill, whence she could see the town of Berwick; and on Halidon Hill, where she was honoured

with shots of artillery from the fortress of Berwick, while she
was talking with Sir John Foster, the Warden, his horse bit the
Queen's horse, and kicked her thigh very ill; and the Warden
incontinent dismounted and knelt, craving the Queen's pardon;
and the Queen bade him to rise, and said she was not hurt; and
the English took leave of her with marks of homage, for at that
time all England reverenced her. But the Queen was compelled
to tarry two days at Castle Home, until she recovered again.

She wore that day upon Halidon Hill a little hat of black
taffety, embroidered all over with gold, with a black feather and
a gold bow.

Towards the end of the month of November the Queen had
returned to Craigmillar Castle, where she held a Court for the
Comte de Brienne, the French Ambassador Extraordinary, who
came to represent the French King as gossip at the christening
of the Prince.

At Craigmillar the Queen was at this season in great
dejection. She was still in the hands of the physicians, but those
around her thought that the principal part of her disease
consisted of a deep sorrow and grief, for she was often heard
to say: "I could wish to be dead"; and she told her Ladies, more
than once, that she grieved to have been so unfortunate as to
recover from her sickness.

The King visited the Queen at Craigmillar Castle, but he
stayed little more than a week, saying he would not be present
at the baptism of the Prince; and the King's deportment was
thought to be bad by all: and the Queen could not see a
nobleman speaking with the King but presently she suspected
some contrivance, for there was still a cunning look in his eyes.

It was whispered to the Queen that the King had written to
the Pope blaming the Queen for being lukewarm, and as not
managing the Catholic cause aright; and the Queen's sorrow
increased, and her health declined, so that some thought that,
like her father, she would die of grief. And all this was noted by
Secretary Lethington, who was at this time courting Mary

Fleming, and thus knew all that the Queen made manifest to her Ladies. The Secretary had been courting Mary Fleming for more than a year, ever since his wife had died: but at first Mary Fleming paid small heed to him, for she was loved of Sir Henry Sidney, who went from the country. The Secretary attended her day and night, and watched and wooed her, and all at Court thought this to be folly, for they were assured she would always love another better: but the Secretary persisted, and seemed to those at Court to show himself a fool or stark staring mad, until the courtship was broken by the murder of Seigneur Riccio and the disfavour of the Secretary. But as soon as he was restored to favour, in the month of September, the Secretary began his courtship anew, and with renewed fury, and his love prevailed. He was past his fortieth year, and Mary Fleming about four-and-twenty, and although less fair than Mary Beton, and smaller than Mary Seton and Lady Sempill, she was the brightest of the Queen's Maries, for her smile dazzled and her laughter was silvery; and the Queen of her Marys loved her the best.

Although Mary Seton was wiser, and Mary Beton more accomplished and lettered, the Secretary looked not at these; but when Mary Fleming laughed with him, or at him, and made merry, for she was fond of all kinds of jest, he was like a man bewitched.

It was arranged betwixt them now that the marriage should be solemnized at Twelfth Night.

And Mary Fleming told the Secretary that, unless a scheme be devised, the Queen would pine away, not for love but for the displeasure that the King was causing her. Thus it came about that the Secretary devised a scheme, and all knew that behind his eyes, which looked inwards but not outwards, and revealed nothing, there was plan and plot. And one morning, with the Earls of Huntly and Argyll and Bothwell, he repaired to the Queen's apartment, and they spoke with the Queen about the King's wicked folly, and pledged themselves to obtain a divorce on condition the Queen should restore their estates to the banished Lords: Morton, Lindsay and Ruthven. And the Queen said the divorce must be made lawfully, so that it should not prejudice her son: and the Earl of Bothwell said he himself had succeeded to his father's estates, although his father had been divorced from his mother. The Lords said the King, after the divorce, should remain in one part of the country and the Queen in another, or that he should withdraw to a foreign land; but the Queen said it were better for her to pass for a time into France. And the Secretary said: "Think you not that we of your nobility and Council shall find means that you be quit of the King without prejudice to your son? And although my Lord Moray be no less scrupulous for a Protestant than your Grace for a Papist, he will look through his fingers thereto, and will behold our doings."

The Queen answered him this: "I will that ye do nothing whereto any spot may be laid to my honour or conscience, and therefore, I pray you, rather let the matter be in the estate it is, abiding till God of His goodness put remedy thereto; that ye, believing to do me service, may turn to my hurt and displeasure."

When the Lords had left her, and she spoke of the matter to her Ladies, one of them said to another: "It is not only the King they purpose to withdraw to a foreign land – but I fear lest it be Her Grace as well, and to a land which is far, and whence none must return."

The King remained but a week at Craigmillar Castle, and he took his leave of a sudden, and went to Stirling, not to the Castle, but to the lodgings of Willie Bell in the High Street. And the Queen passed to the Palace of Holyrood House for her birthday on the 7th of December; and she was now four and twenty years old: and thence she passed to Stirling, taking the Prince, to be in readiness for the baptism.

CHAPTER VI

The Queen's health was not yet mended, nor was her spirit revived, and she continued sad and pensive. The Ambassadors from Savoy and England came to Stirling; the baptism was solemnized in the Queen's Chapel, according to the rite of Rome; neither the Earl of Bedford nor any of the Lords of the Reformed religion being willing to enter the Chapel, excepting the Countess of Argyll, who stood proxy for the Queen of England; and the Prince received the name of Charles James. The Earl of Atholl bore the baptismal taper of unsullied wax: the salt was carried by the Earl of Eglinton, and the chrism by Lord Sempill. The Prince was immersed in a silver font, which the Queen of England had sent to the Queen. After the baptism there was a banquet, and the meat was brought through the hall upon an engine marching, as it appeared alone, with musicians, clothed like maids, and singing and playing upon instruments; and there was banqueting, dancing and triumph daily, and masking and fireworks. And the Prince was given a title and belted Duke of Rothesay, he being now six months old, and the Queen invested him with mantle and coronet, and placed a gold ring upon his finger, and touched his heels with the spurs, and helped him to kneel upon her lap in show of homage, and bend his head to his sovereign. The King had given out he should depart before the baptism, but when the time came he stayed, keeping close within his apartment.

The Queen of England instructed the Earl of Bedford, her Ambassador, to advise the Queen to show the same demeanour towards the King as she had shown at her marriage, but she had demanded that the Queen should restore my Lords Morton, Lindsay and the rest to favour: and the Queen was pressed thereunto by all the Lords of Council, and by Sir James Melville, and she consented to give an amnesty to all, excepting to three who had threatened her life. The King in great choler thereat passed to Glasgow, where the smallpox was prevalent in the neighbourhood, and he fell sick of this disease.

Upon the Feast of Kings the marriage of my Lord of Lethington and Mary Fleming was solemnized. The Queen gave the banquet and the bridal robe, which was of cloth of gold; but there was no masking, and the Queen was too sick to be present at the feast: she had sent her physician to Glasgow to the King.

Rumours of plots were abroad, and it was said that the King was plotting against the Queen; but the plot was sifted and found to be baseless, and the Queen was once more reconciled with the King, and wrote him fair letters.

As soon as the banished Lords were pardoned, Sir James Melville told Madame de Briante that the Earl of Bothwell was packing a friendship with the Earl of Morton in secret, in order to strengthen his faction, and he said to her: "He is aiming at a mark of his own." She asked him not what mark; but that evening she talked for a long while with the Queen alone, and she came out weeping; and when Mary Livingstone went into the Queen's chamber to read to her, when she was in bed, the Queen said she would have no reading that night; and the Queen said to Mary Livingstone that Madame de Briante's scoldings were becoming ever sharper and more frequent.

And Madame de Briante, when Mary Livingstone spoke of the Queen, shook her head and remained silent.

The King wrote letters of repentance to the Queen, entreating her to come to him, with fair words, and sometimes with rhymes: but the Queen was kept back by sickness and by the advent of the Ambassador from the Duke of Savoy, and she held a Court therefor at Holyrood House; and there were some who advised her not to go to Glasgow, saying that the King's repentance and fair words were but the mask of further treachery; howbeit the Queen went midmost in the month of January; and bitter was the cold; and within a few miles of the city of Glasgow the Queen was met by Captain Thomas Crawford, who was in the service of the King's father, with excuses from the King for not coming to meet Her Majesty until he knew her mind further; for he feared he was in Her Majesty's displeasure, because of sharp words she had spoken to one of his servants in Stirling. Whereat said the Queen to Captain Crawford: "There is no receipt against fear. He would not be afraid unless he were culpable." And so, asking if he had no further commission, the Queen put an end to the performance, and rode on.

The Queen abode in the house of the Archbishop, and she told the King that preparation had been made for him to lodge at Craigmillar Castle, for he must not be with the Prince, lest he should give him the infection, and the Palace of Holyrood House would be too low and sunless, and Edinburgh Castle too high and bleak.

A few days later, being sufficiently mended in health to travel, the King went with the Queen to Callander and to Linlithgow, and thence to Edinburgh. The King had no will to lodge at Craigmillar Castle, and instead he went to the Provost's house near St Mary's Kirk of Field, where it was concluded he should stay until his cleansing time be fulfilled.

The choice of this lodging was made on the report of James Balfour, and was pressed by the Earl of Moray.

The King and the Queen were met on the road to the city by the Sheriff of the Lothians (the Earl of Bothwell), and they made entry into the city gloriously.

The Provost's house at St Mary's Kirk of Field had been made ready with ornament and furniture: a bed of violet-brown velvet, a passement of gold and silver with coverlid of blue taffety piqué; and furnished with roof head-piece and pandis, forty pieces of tapestry, large and small enough for the hall and the King's chamber and wardrobe; a dais of black velvet, and a double-seated chair of State, covered with yellow and red-rayed taffety. The King and the Queen were now reconciled, and the Queen would send for her musicians from Holyrood House to play in the gardens of the Convent hard by.

But there were some who said that this concord could not be enduring. Madame de Briante whispered to the Ladies that she feared for the Queen's life: for she said the King was ready to betray her once more, as he had already betrayed her, with a Judas kiss; and that the Lords would make use of him as they had used him already in the matter of Riccio's death, and then they would discard him when the business was finished; but this time he would not betray them, for his fear would be too great. She spoke of this to the Queen, who said she boded there was mischief afoot.

During these days the King would see no one, until his cleansing time should be accomplished; and he wore a piece of taffeta drawn over his face, and the windows of his chamber were not opened. The cleansing time, during which the King had gone into retreat, was to be ended on Shrove Sunday, and the Queen passed the night at the Kirk of Field on Friday night; and that night the King spoke to the Queen of plots against his life. The Queen questioned him, and he said that the Secretary Lethington was planning the ruin of one of them by the means of the other, and meant in the end to ruin the twain; to crown the Prince, and to commit the guidance of the realm to a regent: and the King promised to reveal yet more.

The Queen asked him whence such rumour came; and he answered slyly that he would tell her in good time: but she pressed him to answer her, and he kept silent: and she entreated him, and he whispered to her that he had been told of these plots by her brother natural, Lord Robert Stewart; and on Saturday morning, when the Earl of Moray and the Earl of Bothwell were present, the Queen sent for Lord Robert Stewart and commanded him to say what he knew; and Lord Robert said he knew nothing of any plot, nor had he spoken thereof to the King: and the King was wrathful, and there was discord between them; but the Earl of Moray appeased them.

On Sunday, the King's cleansing time being ended, he heard Mass; and the Earl of Moray took leave of the Queen to go to his Lady wife.

The King was to pass to Holyrood House on the morrow, and the Queen was to hold a Court for the Ambassador of Savoy to take his leave. On the morning of Sunday the Queen attended the marriage of Bastian Pazes, her servant, with Christily Hogg, and, at four of the clock a banquet, held by the Bishop of Argyll, and she was minded to pass the night at Kirk of Field: Bastian Pazes had petitioned her to be at his wedding masque and for the bedding of the bride. And the Queen had said to Bastian she would be there.

The Queen went from the banquet about seven of the clock, with the Earls of Argyll, Huntly and Cassilis, and with her gentlemen and her Ladies, and with them a muster of Gordons and Campbells and their servitors, and came to Kirk of Field. The Queen remained in the King's chamber while some of the noblemen played at dice, and presently the Earl of Bothwell joined them. The King was fond and merry, save when the Queen, talking of Shrovetide, said it was nigh upon a year since Seigneur David had been murdered; and as she said these words she looked at the King, whereat his brow darkened and he was amazed.

Between ten and eleven of the clock the Queen said: "It is late and I have failed to Bastian that this night of the marriage I promised him to be at the Masque, and to bed his bride," meaning she had tarried overlong; whereupon she rose and embraced the King, saying she would be with him anon, and she put a ring upon his finger, and, having called for the horses, she rode by torchlight to Holyrood with the nobles and all their train. And when the Queen reached the Palace she entered the room where the bridal was held, and after she had tarried there a little while, she passed to her chamber with the Earl of Bothwell and John Stuart of Traquair, the Captain of the Guard; and there they sat in talk until past midnight, when the Captain of the Guard came from the room, and, not many minutes later, the Earl of Bothwell came from the chamber; and thereupon he went to change his clothes, and he left the Palace.

The Queen said she would pass the night at Holyrood House, and she dismissed her Ladies.

About three or four of the clock in the morning there was a great noise like a volley of cannon, and the Earl of Bothwell came to Holyrood House with the Earls of Argyll, Huntly and their Ladies, and entered the presence of the Queen with tidings of disaster.

And the Queen commanded the Earl of Bothwell and the Captain of the Guard to hasten to Kirk of Field and bring her news of what had been done.

After daybreak the Earl of Bothwell came to the Palace and told the Queen that some powder which had been deposited in the King's lodging had taken fire and blown up the house and killed His Majesty and his gentlemen of the bedchamber, and that their bodies had been found at a distance from the ruins. The Queen kept to her bed, sorrowful and quiet, and Madame de Briante gave her breakfast about nine of the clock, when the Earl of Bothwell visited the Queen and spoke to her by her bedside.

Madame de Briante said to Lady Sempill that it was a lucky and a near chance that the Queen had not lodged that night in the King's chamber. The King's body was found, at a distance of about eighty paces from the house, clothed only in a shirt and a furred nightgown, in the orchard, and his clothes were unsinged; and it was thought that he, hearing the noise of men surrounding the house, had fled into the garden, where he was strangled with a cloth. The King had ordered his great horses to be in readiness at five of the clock, and it was thought that he was on his way to reach them. Madame de Briante disguised not from the other Ladies that the plot was designed against the Queen, and the King privy to it; that the Lords intended the ruin both of the Queen and the King: and that some knew a little and some all: and the King least of all; but although he knew not all, as was his wont, partly from fear and partly because of the dominion the Queen had over him, when they were face to face, he had blabbed incontinent somewhat of what he knew. Therefore the nobles had hasted forward the enterprise, and the Earl of Bothwell had saved the Queen, as he had saved her before, warning her not to sleep at Kirk of Field that night, and telling her that the King would be taken, and obtaining her warrant thereto. And Madame de Briante said he had done this, not from loyalty or devoutness alone, but because he aimed high, and thought to thwart the plots of the rest of the nobles; and she said the play was not ended, rather it had only begun; therefore the Queen was pensive and kept to her dule chamber. The gunpowder, which had blown the King's house, had been put in the cellars of the house adjoining that of the King, which was called the Prebendary's *salle*, but a small barrel in which powder had been placed was left of a purpose near the garden wall, so that some might be blamed: but all fell out differently from what had been planned. It was the Queen and the Earl of Bothwell against whom the barrel was brought as a witness of guilt; for later the Queen's enemies declared that the King's house had been destroyed by polks of gunpowder placed in the

Queen's room, but of powder there would not have been sufficient in such a barrel to produce so great a devastation; but as to the hidden machinery of the plot, and who was the deviser, and who were the instruments, save that all were guilty in one manner or another, the Queen and her Ladies knew not. But they knew there had been a plot against the Queen, and that there was likelihood that this plot was not ended.

The day after the death of the King, Margaret Cawood, the Queen's favourite maid of the chamber, was wedded to John Stuart, and the Queen furnished the bridal feast but attended it not, for she kept to her chamber until the King was buried, at the end of the week; and he was buried after the Palace gates had been closed, for fear of a riot, seeing he was to be buried according to the rites of Rome, and that there were rumours abroad; and there were present Sir John Bellenden, and John Stuart of Traquair, the Captain of the Queen's Guard.

The Queen up till now had been in her dule chamber, enjoying and using none other than candlelight, and her physicians pressed her to leave that kind of close life, which was doing her harm; so she passed to Seton, where it was bitter cold.

A few hours after the news of the King's murder was spread abroad, the Earl of Bothwell was suspected of having devised it, and placards were seen on the Tolbooth, naming both him and his accomplices. The Earl of Lennox importuning the Queen to prosecute the murderers, the Earl of Bothwell was summoned to trial; but he and the rest of the suspects were not put in ward, wherefor the Queen was blamed. The Queen regarded the Earl of Bothwell as her defender, and in him alone of the Lords she thought she could put her trust; and therefore Madame de Briante blamed her, and said she would rue it; but whether or no she should have been wiser at this time, and more discerning, she durst not have proceeded against the Earl of Bothwell, for now that the Earl of Moray was absent, the guidance of the realm was in the hands of the Earls of

Bothwell, Huntly, Argyll and the Secretary Lethington; and of these the Earl of Bothwell commanded the musketeers, as well as the ships.

In the month of April the Earl of Bothwell, in company with my Lord of Morton and Secretary Lethington, and a train of gentlemen mounted on horseback, and 6000 soldiers, went to be charged at the Tolbooth with murder and treason: there were neither witnesses not proofs, and the Earl of Bothwell was acquitted by twelve Peers, and afterwards declared by Parliament to be free from reproach, whereupon he published a cartel challenging to single combat any who should dispute his innocence.

A few days before the trial the Earl of Moray took his leave of the Queen, saying that he was in debt and wearied of public business, and the Queen entreated him to tarry in Scotland, and if he must go, to go neither to England nor to France, but to Flanders. The Earl of Moray went incontinent to Berwick, and thence first to the Court of England and then to the Court of France. Thus the Earl of Bothwell, after he was acquitted, ruled all.

The Queen's Ambassador in France was Seton, the Archbishop of Glasgow, and the day after the King's murder the Queen had a letter from him, in which he advertised her that the Spanish Ambassador had spoken and warned him that a formidable enterprise was in preparation against her: and now he wrote again, saying that the cost of putting himself and his servitors into dule habits had left him without a penny: and that the Spanish Ambassador, speaking of the warning he had sent before, had bidden him apprise Her Majesty that there was still some notable enterprise in hand against her, whereof she must beware in time. But more he had not been willing to say.

The Queen, although she feared the power of the Earl of Bothwell, feared not the man. Madame de Briante said that hitherto the Queen had, with good reason, feared no man; for ever Her Majesty had been the stronger, either because they had given her worship or because she had inspired them with awe: but the Earl of Bothwell, said Madame de Briante, would never give her worship, nor would she inspire him with any reverence: for he had the heart of a pirate and feared neither God nor Queen nor man; and what he desired, that would he obtain, by fair means or foul; albeit the consequence would be perilous unto himself: for he looked not far ahead, like the Secretary Lethington, but only towards that which lay near at hand, and what he needed now that must he have incontinent, and his present desires must be satisfied: and Madame de Briante said that he now gave the Queen such looks as made her fear for the future: and whether Madame de Briante spoke thereof to the Queen is not known: but the Queen was listless and doleful: for all thought with the Archbishop, who had written in his letter that unless the Queen should cast the foundement of her relief into the hand of God and in His mighty power, he feared this to be only the beginning and first act of the tragedy.

The Queen opened and dismissed Parliament, and passed to Seton, and the Earl of Bothwell convened the nobles to a supper at a tavern, where they signed a bond, wherein they pledged themselves to say that the Earl of Bothwell was innocent of the King's death, and to defend the Earl of Bothwell to the utmost, and to advance his marriage with the Queen.

As soon as this bond was signed, whereof the Queen was ignorant as yet, the Earl of Bothwell at Seton began to discover his intention to the Queen, and hinted at his suit, but the Queen answered not as he desired.

The day after the Queen went from Seton to Stirling Castle, and passed thence from Stirling to Linlithgow, and on the third day after she had left Seton, when she was within three-quarters of a mile from Edinburgh, she was encountered by the Earl of Bothwell, at the head of a great company, she having only twelve attendants. And the Earl of Bothwell took the

Queen's horse by the bridle, and she was taken to the Castle of Dunbar a captive, together with the Earl of Huntly and Secretary Lethington and Sir James Melville, and the rest were allowed to go free.

When the news came to Edinburgh that the Queen had been treasonably interrupted by the Earl of Bothwell, who had carried away with her her Lord Chancellor and her Secretary of State, there was fear and tumult in the city, and the common bell sounded, and citizens armed themselves with intent to rescue; but their purpose was prevented by the Provost; and the gates of the city were shut, and the Castle guns pointed; and the rumour was spread abroad that all had been done with the Queen's consent. The Queen's Ladies were at Holyrood House, and there was no Lady at Dunbar Castle, save the sister of the Earl of Bothwell. Madame de Briante bewailed the Queen's fate; and said she had brought disaster upon herself, for she had ever thought herself a match for any of her nobles, and feared none of them, and the Earl of Bothwell was to be feared. The Queen had not known the mark whereat he aimed, for he would use her as instrument for his ambition, which was to be King of Scotland, and cast her away as soon as this ambition should be fulfilled. The Queen was kept a week at Dunbar Castle, where the Earl of Bothwell made good his threat that he would marry the Queen, "who would or would not".

From Dunbar Castle the Queen was brought to Edinburgh Castle under a guard, and the Earl of Bothwell's men, when they entered the city, threw away their spears, fearing to be accused of treason thereafter, for having coerced the Queen: and the Queen turned her horse's head towards Holyrood House, but the Earl of Bothwell seized the bridle, and brought her to Edinburgh Castle, where the doors of her chamber were guarded, and none of her counsellors or her Ladies were allowed to go to her.

In despite of the remonstrances of many, and of the French Ambassador, and the denunciation of Mr Craig, the minister of the Reformed Church, and her own pleas for delay, the proceedings for the pretended divorce between himself and his wife were hasted forward by the Earl of Bothwell, and the marriage was solemnized in the Palace of Holyrood House, in the Great Hall. And a witch prophesied that the Queen should wed yet two husbands more, and live not a year more at the most, and die by the fiery death.

From the moment of the Queen's marriage the forebodings of Madame de Briante came true, and the Earl of Bothwell treated Her Majesty with disdain, and handled her with roughness; and she was without money, and was compelled to dismiss many of her servants, and send silver and gold to the mint to be melted; and she was sick in body, and fell often a-swooning, and mortally sick in spirit.

The Earl of Bothwell, who had now been made Duke of Orkney, became beastly and suspicious of the Queen, and suffered not a day to pass without causing her to shed abundance of salt tears.

The day after her marriage the Queen sent for M. du Croc, who had kept aloof from the marriage, although the Queen entreated him to be present: and M. du Croc was amazed at the change in her face, nor could he think she was that Queen who had once led the chase in the forest of Fontainebleau, and whom M. de Ronsard had sung; and he was amazed, too, at the strangeness between the Queen and her husband; and she said to him, if he saw her sorrowful it was because she could no more rejoice, not now nor evermore; for she desired death only. And, shut within her chamber with the Earl of Bothwell, she cried aloud for a knife, that she might kill herself.

The Duke of Orkney was now hated of all, and, knowing this, and that he could no longer trust those with whom he had plotted aforetimes, he desired to get the Prince, who was in the keeping of the Earl of Mar, into his possession, designing, if he captured the Prince, to be made Regent. And this design being known, the Earl of Morton and the Confederate Lords concluded at a secret meeting to crown the Prince and to pursue the Duke of Orkney for the King's murder; and the Queen, having made a proclamation for the men of the southern shires to convene at Melrose, and to proceed against the insurgents on the Border, they determined, with the aid of the Governor of the Castle, to seize the Duke of Orkney and the Queen at Holyrood House; but word of this was whispered to the Duke of Orkney, who fled in the night to the Castle of Borthwick, taking the Queen with him.

For a whole month long after her marriage the Queen was sick, and the citizens were displeased, because it was rumoured that the Queen was held in thrall: therefore the Duke of Orkney made the Queen ride abroad with him, and be present at pastimes, on the water at Leith, and at the mustering of troops; but the Queen, when she rode abroad, was ever guarded by harquebusiers, and few were allowed to draw near her person.

The Secretary Lethington was hated above all by the Duke of Orkney; nevertheless he had been, by Sir Robert Melville's persuasion, brought in again to Court, whence he had been absent long; and while he was at Dunbar, when the Queen was there in captivity, the Earl of Bothwell had thought to slay him in the Queen's chamber, but the Queen came betwixt, and said that if a hair of Lethington's head perished, she would cause Bothwell to forfeit lands, goods and life. And some weeks later the Secretary escaped to Atholl.

As soon as the Duke of Orkney went from the Castle the Queen sent a letter to the Governor of the Castle at Edinburgh, bidding him to hold it out for her, and she escaped from the Castle in man's attire; but, riding all night astray and in a circle, she was met by the Duke of Orkney, and he bore her with him to Dunbar, whence proclamation was made in the Queen's name, calling upon all loyal men to pass to the relief of the Queen: and it would have been better for her had she stayed at the Castle of Borthwick.

The Confederate Lords marched to Edinburgh and obtained the surrender of the Castle, and they took to the field, and met the troops of the Queen near Carberry, where there was parleying between the two factions; and the Confederate Lords offered the Queen allegiance if she would forsake the Duke of Orkney, for they said it was against him and not against her that they had taken up arms. The Queen said that she would embrace the overture if they would suffer the Duke of Orkney to pass unmolested from the field, and, the pledge being given, the Queen bade the Duke of Orkney adieu; and he left the field unpursued and passed to Dunbar, and the Queen rendered herself to the Laird of Grange, and to his honour. The Earl of Morton and the Lords received the Queen with reverence, but no sooner had they begun to march to Edinburgh than the Queen perceived she had exchanged one thraldom for another more close and more sharp. And the soldiers of the Lords cried incontinent: "Burn her, the murderer, burn the whore!" and used other reproachful words; and great was her anger.

A white banner with the picture of the dead King beneath a tree, and the young King kneeling and calling vengeance upon the murderers of his father, was held up by two soldiers between two pikes before her eyes: whereat she swooned and all but fell from her horse to the ground.

And, recovering from her swoon, the Queen's anger was great, and in lieu of conciliating the Lords she threatened Lord Lindsay of Byrnes, who had been her playfellow as a child, she would have him beheaded for his treachery; and on the road to Edinburgh she never spoke but to threaten to have the Lords all crucified and hanged, which angered them the more: and at ten of the clock in the evening she entered the city with the bloody ensign carried before her; the Earls of Morton and Atholl on each side of her; and she was wearied with fever and wrath, tear-stained and besmirched with dust; and the men and the women railed at her as she passed; and she was taken not to Holyrood House but to the Black Turnpike, the house of the Provost in the High Street.

Here she was reft of Mary Seton and Lady Sempill, and confined in a chamber that overlooked the street; nor was she allowed to change her garments; for the guards left not her chamber; and although she had eaten nothing throughout the day she ate nothing now for anger, weariness, and fear of poison.

Mary Seton and Lady Sempill were lodged in another chamber, but they were not suffered to enter the Queen's presence: and the guards railed at the Queen and said that she, being a murderess, would get her deserts: the fiery death; but when, in the morning of the next day, the Queen showed herself at the window, and cried to the people to help her, there were some who took pity upon her. And the Queen espied the Secretary Lethington walking in the street, and, opening the window, she called upon him by name and besought him for the love of God to come to her. The Secretary obeyed her entreaty; and he went to her in the course of the evening and spoke soft words. The Queen bade the Secretary explain the cause of the maltreatment she was enduring, and she told him what she had suffered from the hands of the guards, especially from Drumlanrig and Cessford, who had threatened her and addressed her unbecomingly; and she called to his mind how she had bestowed many favours upon him and how she had saved his life: all of which he admitted. And he begged the Queen to let matters tone down little by little, and he might yet do her some good service, and to give him permission to depart, and not to ask him to return to talk any more with her, for it would bring suspicion upon him, nor further her cause; for if his credit with the nobility be shaken, her life would be in peril: the nobles having many times proposed that she should be put away.

But very different was the account he gave of his audience with the Queen to the Lords, and at the Palace: to these he said the Queen would rejoin the Duke of Orkney as soon as she could, her only desire being that they two might be put into a ship alone to go whithersoever fortune might carry them, and that he had promised her that if she would abandon my Lord Bothwell she should have thankful obedience; but all knew well, the Queen being a prisoner, and the Earl of Bothwell a fugitive, such words and tales were vain.

In the evening the Earl of Morton came to the Queen with a message from the Council, and words of regret and penitence, and he promised to conduct her to her own Palace of Holyrood: and he persuaded her to speak from the window to her champions among those of low degree in the street, and to tell them she was under no constraint, and bid them disperse; but they dispersed not: neither those who pitied her, nor those who cried for her death.

The Queen was suffered to change her red petticoat and partlet for a nightgown of variable colours, and invited to partake of food, but she would not partake any food in this house.

She was taken on foot by the Earls of Morton and Atholl from the Black Turnpike to Holyrood House; and with her were Lady Sempill and Mary Seton, and some of the women of the Canongate reviled her, and there were others who pitied her; and this time the Queen no longer swooned nor wept, but bore her undauntedly, protesting her innocency, and crying out: "Good Christian people, either take my life or free me from the cruelty of the false traitors who have deceived you."

At Holyrood House she found her Ladies: Marie Courcelles, Madame de Briante, Jane Kennedy and Mademoiselle Rally and others, and supper was ready; and, after the roast was brought, the Earl of Morton told the Queen to prepare for her departure, and bade the esquire get ready the horses, and, withdrawing herself into her closet, the Queen bade Lady Sempill to send a sure messenger to the Captain of Edinburgh Castle, and to desire him to keep a good heart to her, and, wheresoever she might be carried or sent, not to render the Castle. The Queen asked that some of her Ladies and servitors might go with her, and these entreated to go; but the Lords would not permit them, save two *femmes de chambre*; nor was the Queen allowed to take other clothes with her.

Lord Lindsay and Lord Ruthven took her to Lochleven Castle, the house of the Earl of Moray's natural brother. And the Hamiltons and the Earl of Rothes collected forces for her rescue, and followed the Queen. She was advised of this by the way, and she lingered as much as she could, but the Lords perceived this, and whipped her horse.

And those who were in pursuit of the Queen arrived too late, and the Queen was rowed in a boat to the Castle.

MARY SETON'S NARRATIVE

CHAPTER I

When the Queen of Scotland went from her native country to France at the age of six, there went with her four chosen daughters of noblemen, each nearly of her own age, who were thereafter to be her Lady servitors, and each bearing the name of Mary. The first was Mary Beton, a niece of the Cardinal; the second, Mary Fleming, the daughter of Lord Fleming; the third, Mary Livingstone, whose father, Lord Livingstone, was one of the custodians of the Queen; and the fourth, Mary Seton, daughter of Lord Seton. Of these the most learned was Mary Beton, the fairest was Mary Livingstone, the most dexterous with her fingers, Mary Seton, and the most lively and most excellent, Mary Fleming; and the Queen loved Mary Fleming the best.

With the Queen went also her nurse, Janet Sinclair, and her Lady Governess, Lady Fleming.

The Queen was brought to the Convent of the Blessed Virgin at Saint Germain-en-Laye, where the Queen was so well-contented, and showed such relish of the Life Religious, that the King of France, fearing to lose her, and having other designs for the Queen, bade her pass to the apartments in the Palace. In the Palace the Queen was attended as before by her Lady Governess and the four Marys.

The Queen was well instructed and learned of the Latin and the Italian tongues: needlework came to her easily, but music she studied later: she sang sweetly and played passably on the virginals.

When the Queen was eight years old, her mother, the Queen-Dowager of Scotland, visited France and met her daughter at the city of Rouen, and she marvelled at the ripeness of her daughter, who enquired of her mother whether feuds continued to subsist in the noble families of Scotland, who among them were attached to the ancient faith, whether the English still harassed her native country; and whether the priests attended to their duties. She addressed a seemly compliment to the Scottish nobles who accompanied her mother, and spoke befittingly of the protection she had received from the King of France: all these things she had been instructed to say, but she surpassed the instruction.

The Queen and her mother passed from Rouen to Paris, where they were welcomed with carousal and triumph, and at Fontainebleau the Queen-Dowager bade adieu to the Queen, whom she was fated never to behold again upon earth.

The Queen studied with zeal and learnt easily and swiftly, and in her thirteenth year she recited at the Louvre before the King and the Queen an oration in the Latin tongue, wherein she defended the opinion contrary to that which was held by the vulgar, saying that it was seemly for women to be lettered, to practise the liberal arts, and to excel in them.

When the Queen had reached her sixteenth year the ceremony of handfasting with young Prince Francis, the Dauphin, was performed at the Louvre, with solemnity and banqueting.

Before the ceremony was performed the Queen was summoned by the King of France to write a testament in secret and to bequeath her birthright to the King of France, and to sign other articles, all of them favourable to the King of France, and to the country of France; and the Queen relished not the import of these deeds, and she divined the purpose of the French King and of those who were at the Court the more powerful: the House of Guise; and she feared, in despite of their persuasion, they were using her ill; but their persuasion, albeit fair, could not be gainsaid.

In her sixteenth year the Queen had attained to a marvellous ripeness: at the Court she was the highest, and she was made of unyielding stubborn substance, albeit her form and her limbs were delicate, and her skin white as alabaster, and her health variable, for she had frequent distempers and fits of sickness and swooning; ague, and later a pain in the side; and once before her marriage the smallpox, whereof she was cured by Fernel, the first physician to the King of France, who bathed her face with a water whereof he had the secret, and thus saved her beauty, which happy occasion was celebrated in Latin rhyme by Adrien Turnèbe. Strong she was at the core, and able to endure fatigue and hardship with the strength of a man; and throughout her life when she was sick she would be so that all about her deemed she could not live another moon, whereupon of a sudden she would put away her sickness and shine again out of the shadow as if she had been born anew: maybe, as some said, her tameless spirit triumphed ever over her delicate frame.

As she was in her sixteenth year, so she was throughout her life: single-minded and a stranger to fear; but rash at times in deed and imprudent in word; indifferent to ceremonious honour, but jealous of her estate royal; free in speech, pleasant and familiar, prompt to be avenged upon an enemy, and never forgetful of a friend, or unmindful of service rendered; a friend of courage in others, even in an enemy; and unable even in a friend to overlook or to palliate cowardice.

Impetuous she was, easily mollified, and sometimes easily persuaded; but once her purpose was determined, unyielding as a diamond: aflame for victory; and for victory's sake prepared to face pain and peril, and to hold health and other such things, yea, even life itself, cheap and vile.

Before the Queen married the Dauphin she would sometimes be prompted by her quick wit or by her choler, which was sudden and fleeting, to let fall a word which the envious would treasure and use as a weapon against her. Thus with the Queen-Mother she was careful and deferent; but once when she was rebuked by Madame Parois, who had become her Lady Governess in lieu of Lady Fleming, the Queen being desirous of giving away some clothing, and Madame Parois saying this was contrary to the Queen-Mother's wish, the Queen said that the Queen-Mother's ancestors having been merchants and Medes, she knew better how to hoard than how to give money away. And doubtless Madame Parois rehearsed these words to the Queen-Mother.

After the Queen's marriage with the Dauphin, which was solemnized six days after the handfasting, the Queen held her own Court; for a while the Queen tasted felicity, unvexed by the cares of State and protected from the contention of warring factions. She greatly delighted in the company of lettered men and of poets, especially in that of Monsieur de Ronsard and Monsieur de Maison Fleur; and lesser poets such as Monsieur Du Bellay and Châtelart; and already it was patent that her beauty would be a snare for men and cause of bane to herself: so that those who loved her were tempted to say her beauty was like a lodestar that attracted the hearts of men, but remained fixed, nor swerved from its orbit, and shone untroubled itself upon the shifting tide, as fair and as hard as a diamond. It is true that her heart was bright as a diamond, and hard in peril, conflict and disaster; but it is false to say that she was unmoved and unswayed by mortal passion. For, alas, the heart of the Queen when thus moved and wounded turned to those who were beyond her reach or unworthy of her love. Of such a kind is the mischief wrought by the darts of the blindfold gold.

Thus it was that when she was Queen-Dauphin she was loved by M. d'Anville, the son of the Connétable, a very comely and gallant nobleman, but who was wedded to another.

In the month of July following after her marriage, which was in the month of April, the King of France died of a wound at the justings, and the Queen was Queen of France and Scotland, and she hoped one day to be Queen of England.

But from time onward a shadow fell upon her life; the times were troubled: the King, her husband, was but sixteen years old: the guidance of the realm was in the hands of the Queen-Mother and the House of Guise, and the realm was distracted by religious quarrel, warring faction and civil strife: plot, counterplot and broil.

The young King had not been long upon the throne when the Queen of England sent her Ambassador, Sir Nicholas Throckmorton, to the Queen so that she might confirm the Treaty of Edinburgh, which had been agreed upon in the Castle of Cambray, to seal the peace between England and France, and by which the fortress of Aymouth in Scotland should be demolished and the French King and Queen quit their titles and arms of England and Ireland.

Sir Nicholas Throckmorton was given audience at Orleans, and pressed for the ratification of the treaty, whereat the Queen told him that her subjects in Scotland did their duty in nothing but what pleased them; therefore she would have them assemble by her authority and proceed in their doings after the Laws of the Realm, whereof they boasted but kept none of.

And the Queen having told him her mind was to return into her kingdom, he questioned her about the religions in her Kingdom and how she should deal with them: whereat she said the religion she professed she took to be the most acceptable to God, and neither knew or desired to know any other: that constancy became all people well, and none better than Princes. And who might credit her if she showed herself light in this case?

"I am none of those," said she, "who will change my religion every year; and, as I told you in the beginning, I mean to constrain none of my subjects, but would wish they were all as I am; and, I trust, they should have no support to constrain me."

Before these disputings were at an end the King of France died, from having taken cold at Mass. And with the death of the young King, the Queen, from being a Queen in name alone, became a Queen-Dowager. But albeit diminished in estate royal, she waxed in beauty's sovereignty. For when she retired into her dule chamber for forty days at Orleans, she wore a robe of white, and this became her better than her robes of State, yea, better even than the one she wore upon her wedding day, which was stamped with golden lilies and alive with jewels, like a robe of light; and the courtiers and the poets used to say that the whiteness of her face contended with the whiteness of her veil, and that the snows of her face prevailed, and that her spotless veil was discomfited. And the Queen was exceeding sorrowful, and her pallor was from that time permanent.

Maybe in the past there were fairer women than the Queen of Scotland, and maybe in the future there will be Queens that shall excel her; yet her beauty, whether or not it deserved praise or blame according to canon, or whether or no the poets and the gallants gave her more than her due, was of the kind that made men willing to endure exile, hardship and torment for her sake, and to face death gladly, whether they were old or young: and when she passed in procession or to Mass, or to the banquet, men murmured to see her, or shaded their eyes for the dazzle, and women were silent.

The Queen believed she would find no more felicity in France, for the Queen-Mother dealt rigorously with her, and she was removed partly by the Queen of France, and partly by other circumstance, from the sight and commerce of M. d'Anville; and at times she thought to retire to the Convent of

Saint Jacques at Rheims, where her aunt was abbess, and bid a lasting adieu to the world; for in those convent walls she had tasted of a freedom larger than that she had met with in the world hitherto, and immeasurable compared to what was in store for her. But she was dissuaded therefrom partly by the ambitious promptings of her uncles, and again by her own desires; for she being next in succession to the throne of England, that throne allured her, and she would often say that either she or a child of her own should some day sit upon the throne of England.

Nobles came from Scotland: her brother natural, the Prior of St Andrew's, and Lesley, who was thereafter Bishop of Ross, and the Earl of Bothwell; and they pressed her to come back to her native land: and while she was in her dule chamber at Orleans she received in secret the visit of my Lord Darnley, the son of the Earl of Lennox, who was the first Prince of the blood royal of England, a Stuart, and a cousin of the Queen; and it was patent that the Countess of Lennox, knowing that the hand of the Queen was already being sought after by many Princes in Europe, desired a match betwixt her, the Queen, and her son; and this the Queen perceived, and my Lord Darnley found favour with her, although she thought him over-boyish: but one of her Ladies, who had been her Lady Governess after Madame Parois – Madame de Briante, the mother of Mary Seton – said the Queen would one day wed my Lord Darnley, although she boded no good of the match: and although the Queen made merry at these prophecies, they did not displease her, and she looked pensively when they were said.

After the death of the young King, the Queen of England bade her Ambassador return, and sent yet another to congratulate with King Charles, the new King, and summoned the Queen of Scotland once more to confirm the Treaty of Edinburgh; but they could draw from the Queen no answer, save that she neither would nor could confirm the Treaty of Edinburgh without the Peers of Scotland.

The Queen, now having determined to retire into her Kingdom, sent to the Queen of England a Frenchman entreating her to give Her Highness leave to pass by sea into her kingdom: this the Queen of England utterly denied, saying the Queen had not ratified the Treaty of Edinburgh, which, if she should promise to do, she might freely pass either by land or sea. And Sir Nicholas Throckmorton spoke to the Queen of the great offence she had done to the Queen of England by usurping the name and arms of England at the marriage feasts of the King of France's daughter. And the Queen said to the Ambassador that her husband's father and her husband had commanded it: as soon as they were deceased she had quitted both arms and title; and she told the Ambassador that she was likewise a Queen, and grandchild to the sister of King Henry the Eighth, and had more right to carry these arms than others who had borne them, who were further off kin than she, meaning thereby the Marquis of Exeter and the Duchess of Suffolk.

When the English Ambassador pressed the Queen once more, she said to him that the articles of import of the treaty were already effected: the French garrisons were called back from Scotland, the fort of Aymouth was razed, and she had quit the arms: but the Queen of England was not contented; and the Queen determined to go to her kingdom, whether the Queen of England would or no: for the obstacles had but confirmed her determination.

The Queen sailed from Calais to Scotland, and with her went her uncles and M. d'Anville, and with him Châtelart, a gentleman from the Dauphiné, his servitor and confidant, a well-favoured and well-lettered gentleman, and a pretty swordsman.

English ships were sent to encounter the Queen's galleys, as some said to take her; for the Prior of St Andrews, the brother-natural of the Queen, when passing through England had counselled the Queen of England to do it for her own safety.

But the Queen, in despite of the English ships and the fog, returned with safety in to Scotland.

CHAPTER II

The Queen of Scotland entered into her kingdom ill-armed and ill-equipped for the warfare that awaited her. She came not as a meek dove to an eyrie of eagles, but rather as a royal eagle unto a haunt of vultures and other birds of prey, some of them noble, but all of them enemies; and among those that were the more formidable were they who seemed to be her friends. Chief among her enemies was Mr Knox; for whereas the others were busy with the schemes and plans which should gain them power and advancement, Mr Knox minded alone the things of the spirit and the business of another world.

Now the religion of the Queen in which she was nourished, and to which she held fast until the day of her death, was to him the abomination; nor was it that he blamed alone the instruments, the accidents and the crimes of those of the Queen's faith; but he blamed the Faith itself as being the cause of those faults, those frailties and those crimes, and of the sin original wherewith man is tainted.

Thus it was that it was in vain for the Queen to seek to be reconciled with him, or even to win the smallest share of his goodwill: for he was undeterred by the threats of men and impervious to the charms of beauty, and he swerved not from his purpose, which was to uproot Papistry and to abolish the Mass in Scotland.

For it was not the Papists alone that he wished away; but the Mass, which in his eyes was the cause why those Papists offended: the emblem of the harlot of Rome.

And the Queen came from France, she being the niece of uncles who were as militant and as full of hatred for a Faith not theirs as Mr Knox himself: and she came with the condition that, although she should change nothing in religion, she and her household should be allowed their own worship in her private chapel.

The Queen was acclaimed with joy, but the only light in the sky from the day of her arrival, and for two days later, came from the fires of joy at night.

On the Sunday after the Queen's arrival Mass was said in her chapel at Holyrood; and Lord James Stewart, the Queen's brother natural, kept the door, to prevent the Scots from entering, he said, but as well to prevent the priest from being murdered.

And, on the following Sunday, Mr Knox preached in St Giles' Church that one Mass was more fearful to him than if ten thousand armed enemies were landed in any port of the kingdom. The Queen was advised by her brother to give Mr Knox audience at Holyrood House, and she did it, in the presence of her brother and two of her Ladies.

And Mr Knox, who had reviled Queens, misliked being asked hard questions by the Queen, for he could not but mark that she was wise beyond her years, and he despised womankind. So no good came of the audience, for the Queen wept, and Mr Knox, having been led against his will to dispute, came away saying the Queen had a proud mind, a crafty wit and an indurate heart.

Two days later the Queen made entry into the city, and when she came forward to the throne of the burgh, where the butter is weighed, a boy of six years of age came through the portlet made of timber and delivered to the Queen the keys of the town, together with a Bible and a psalm-book and writings denouncing idolatry; and they had been about to represent a priest being burned at the altar at the Elevation, but the Earl of Huntly would have none of it.

The night following there was banqueting at Holyrood House; and on the following Sunday the Queen's chaplains would have sung a High Mass in the chapel, but the Earl of Argyll and Lord James so disturbed the quire that the priests and the clerks left their places with broken heads and bloody ears, which was a cause of merriment to the Scottish Lords.

The Queen was not slow to perceive troubles that might arise in a realm where so many various passions were dormant, and she set about to calm the spirit of the combatants as well as she could. She changed nothing in religion: she chose her Council from the Protestant Lords, all but the Earl of Huntly, and she made temperate laws and good ordinances.

She had brought from France many fair tapestries wherewith she adorned the Palace of Holyrood House; and a little sycamore tree, which she planted in the garden. In the month of October the French Lords took their leave, and before their departure the Queen held a banquet and a mask at Holyrood House; and there the Queen said adieu to M. d'Anville, who spoke of marriage to her, saying he would put away his wife; but the Queen told him to dismiss the thought, and that she had determined to be a Queen. She never saw him more, and he, albeit when his wife died he married another, and yet later another, never forgot, so it was said, the Queen; and once in one of the wars of religion in France, in the thick of a charge, he paused and bent him down, a target for the enemy, and thereby risking his life; for he had dropped a kerchief of Cyprus silk which had once touched the neck of the Queen of Scots.

The Queen comported herself with a wisdom far exceeding her age, and the Lords returned to Court, and the people wished her well, and she pleased all, save Mr Knox, who said that many were deceived in this *woman*.

And the Queen was wise and grave at the Council, and those nearest about her were the Lord James, her brother, and my Lord of Lethington, whom she presently sent as Ambassador to the Queen of England.

Lord James was of rude exterior and dealt bluntly with the Queen, wherefore she believed him to be honest, but he concealed both craft and greed and ambition. My Lord of Lethington was fine and delicate, subtle in mind and happy in speech and polished in manner, and the Queen liked his commerce more than that of any other Nobles, and in my Lord of Lethington she was to find her greatest friend and her greatest enemy.

Those about the Queen who were more elderly and who had a near knowledge of her nature and wit, said that she had done ill to come to Scotland, for that although she might rule over the hearts of men and win their love, even until death, and beyond, she might never conduct their affairs: for howsoever wise her intention, and howsoever true her aim, of herself she could accomplish nothing, and she leaned upon the strength and upon the advice of those about her, and not always of the wisest. Her own mind she was not slow to know, nor was it easy to bend her from her purpose; but in matters of government and all such as concerned the realm she listened to others, and she followed their bidding; and, had those nearest to her been loyal and open, all maybe might have been well, but either they were intent upon their own aims, or they set the interests of an alien sovereign before their own, consulting their own ambition and advantage.

But the Queen, albeit she was often since her advent into her kingdom mournful, and aware of the perils about her and the obstacles before her, was now as ever aflame for victory, and, being the lawful heritrix to the throne of England, desired greatly that she or a child of hers should possess that throne, and this desire was her doom.

Her brother natural, Lord James, was of the stronger quality; the Queen had privily exalted him to be Earl of Mar, and thereafter to be Earl of Moray; but the title was not yet complete, and the demesnes, although unawarded, were in the hands of the Earl of Huntly; and in order to obtain the demesnes of that earldom Lord James was instrumental in bringing about the ruin of the House of Gordon; the Gordons aiding thereunto by their folly, and, as some said, by their treachery; for the son of the Earl of Huntly, Sir John Gordon, was said to be enamoured of the Queen; but only as many of the young were thought to be enamoured of her, and as all the courtiers at the French Court had been thought to be enamoured of her, alone upon the evidence of a few sighs, a few piteous looks and unspoken words. The Earl of Moray, desirous of the demesnes, and bent on the Earl of the Huntly's ruin, perceived his opportunity, saying that the Earl had in his mind to capture the Queen for his son; and Providence favoured him, and decided against the Earl of Huntly, who in the end took arms against the Queen, with his servants and tenants, maybe from no desire to rebel, and with no treasonable motive save but to force his person into the Queen's presence, for she had been poisoned by the reports of her brother and of others, and she had never been willing to see him nor his wife, nor had she lent credence to his protestations of loyalty; and when she had come to the Castle of Inverness and had been refused admittance by the deputy, whose duty it was to give entry to none without the leave of Lord Gordon, the Castle was compelled to render and the Captain was hanged.

And after the Earl of Huntly and his men had been discomfited at Corrichie, and the Earl of Huntly had died incontinent after the battle, falling from horseback stark dead, Sir John Gordon was beheaded at Aberdeen.

And thus Lord James Stewart possessed the Earldom of Moray in very deed, and returned rich with the spoils of Strathbogie; and the Queen lost the second noble in the kingdom and the first of the Catholic Lords, and the sole support of what in the realm was Catholic.

The Queen had determined to favour those of the Reformed religion, and maybe her determination was wise, for they were the more plentiful and powerful in the realm; but the choice brought her neither felicity nor advantage; and thereby she lost, haply, the most devout if not the wisest of her subjects. Nor did she ever forget the execution of Sir John Gordon, which she was compelled to witness, whereat the executioner, shaken maybe by the comeliness of the sufferer, for he was the comeliest of the Scots, or the distress of the Queen, which was manifest, struck awry, so that the crowd murmured aloud.

And the Queen, who had started on that journey joyful, and had taken part in the roughness of the circumstance as merrily as a man in buckram, came back thoughtful, pensive and melancholy. Maybe she deemed she had erred, albeit my Lord of Lethington declared to the Queen that the guilt of the Earl of Huntly had been made manifest by certain papers and confessions; but the Queen said nothing thereof, neither at this time nor thereafter. The Queen was prompt to lean upon all around her, and she delighted especially in the commerce of foreigners. The Marquis de Moret had come from the Duke of Savoy as Ambassador, and he left behind him when he went from the realm his Secretary in compliment to the Queen, Seigneur de Riccio, from Piedmont, who had sung bass in the Queen's chapel.

The Queen made him a groom of the chamber; he was lively and quick witted, and he pleased the Queen by his drollery and swift apprehension, but the nobles, although he pleased them at first, grew to hate him later, for he despised them.

After the Queen had returned from the Highlands, where the ruin of the House of Gordon had been accomplished, she passed to Montrose, in the month of November, where Châtelart brought her a letter from M. d'Anville, wherein he pressed his suit once more, and said that he would put away his wife if the Queen would wed him; and instead of returning to France incontinent, he stayed all the winter, and was familiar in the Palace and admitted to the Queen's cabinet; and the Queen was pleased with his commerce, and he made her rhymes, whereunto she made answer in rhyme, and at the banquet they danced the *Purpose* together and made a matchless pair.

Several of the Court were displeased with his easy way, and Madame de Briante, who misliked him, said that he was *un gentil hutaudeau:* that the Queen would be unwise to put her trust in him, and that under the guise of pleading his master's suit he was pleading his own, with no good purpose. But the Queen heeded this not at all. And one night the Queen sat late in her chamber in conference with my Lord Moray and others of the Council, and those of her servitors who were in waiting in the Queen's chamber fell asleep, for it was past midnight; and Châtelart entered the chamber by stealth and hid him behind the bed, where he was discovered by the grooms of the chamber when they looked, as was their duty, behind the tapestry. The Queen was told thereof the next day, and ordered Châtelart from the kingdom; he made as if to go, and he went not, but followed the Queen to Burntisland and entered her chamber again when her Ladies were with her, Mary Seton and one other, Jacquellon, and he said that he had come to prove his innocence; and the Queen, in a greater choler, called upon the Earl of Moray to have him put in ward, saying that he deserved to die.

Châtelart was taken to St Andrew's and was examined; and my Lord of Lethington told the Queen that in his examination, which was rough, he had been suborned by the enemies of the House of Guise to cast a stain upon the Queen's honour, so that she might not marry a foreign Prince. And he was said to have spoken several names, and notably that of Madame de Curosot. The Queen was pressed to show mercy, but she did not pardon him, and his execution was hasted forward by the Council, and he was executed nine days later. He walked to the scaffold reading out of a book of Pagan poems, and he invoked the Queen as the fairest and most cruel of dames; and he died, said Madame de Briante, albeit bravely, like a player rather than like a knight.

But if it were true that a plot had been made to hinder foreign Princes from pressing their suit to the Queen, it was of no avail, for the Queen's hand was sought in marriage by the Archduke Charles and by Don Carlos, the Prince of Spain; and the Queen thought well of marrying with the heir to the Spanish throne, until it was whispered by the Spanish Ambassador to the Secretary Lethington that this Prince showed symptoms of derangement, and advised her to marry with the Archduke Charles: and this match was distasteful both to the Scots and to the Queen of England, and the Queen refused to have the Archduke. But already by this time she had determined to marry, for at feast upon the Twelfth Night, a year after the execution of Châtelart, the Queen said to one of her Marys that they would all be soon free to marry; for they had vowed not to marry unless the Queen led the way.

At the feast Mary Fleming was Queen of the Bean, and the Queen lent her State jewels and robe and crown; yet was Mary Livingstone the fairer, in her vaskenis of white satin pirnit with silver; and some said Mary Beton was the fairer that night, pensive as Eve, in a grey gown: but the Queen was the fairest of all, being unadorned.

The Queen was pressed on all sides, from all sides, to marry, and she was herself determined to choose a husband, but whenever a match seemed to be near there was remonstrance and distaste from those in England as well as Scotland.

The Queen of England was advertised of the suit of foreign Princes, for the Prince de Condé and the Duke of Ferrara pressed their suit, and the Dukes of Orleans and Nemours.

Madame de Briante said the Queen should wed the Duke of Ferrara, where she would find a Court that befittea her, and leave the barbarous country of Scotland to the birds and beasts for whom it was fit, and put away vain dreams of the English throne and of uniting the two kingdoms.

The Queen of England greatly misliked a foreign match for the Queen of Scots and summoned her to marry my Lord Robert Dudley, who was her own favourite; and soon the matter was debated.

But the Queen said it was beneath her dignity to marry a subject, nevertheless the Queen of England continued to press the suit; thereupon the Countess of Lennox asked the hand of the Queen for her son, my Lord Darnley.

The Queen of England, fearing a foreign match for the Queen of Scots, when advertised that the Queen of Scots made no account of my Lord Robert Dudley, summoned the Queen to give licence to the Earl of Lennox to go to Scotland. Now the Earl of Lennox had been banished out of his country for the space of thirty years. But as soon as the Queen of England learnt that the Countess of Lennox had solicited the hand of the Queen for her son, she summoned the Queen of Scots to take away her licence from the Earl of Lennox, and declared to the Queen that a marriage between her and my Lord Darnley was distasteful to all the English; and she advised the Queen to think of some other marriage, and commended unto her my Lord Robert Dudley once more, whom she exalted to the dignity of an Earl. She sent deputies to treat of this marriage at Berwick; and the English promised unto her amity and peace, and that she should succeed to the Crown of England if she married with the Earl of Leicester.

But the Scots said that it was beneath the Queen's dignity, who had been sued by an Emperor's son and by the King of France, to match with a new-made Earl and a subject of England.

It was doubted whether the Queen of England was in good earnest, and whether she did not propound this match to make it more excusable for herself to marry with Leicester.

While the Lords were treating of this marriage the Countess of Lennox obtained leave for her son to go into Scotland and to stay there three months: and some thought that the Queen of England gave this licence to my Lord Darnley because she feared the Queen of Scots had good liking to the Earl of Leicester, for he had written discreet letters to the Earl of Moray, which had pleased the Queen; and there were others, and among them the French Ambassador, who said the Queen of England might say what she would, but she, or rather Secretary Cecil, had chosen my Lord Darnley to be husband of the Queen of Scots; whether she feared more greatly the marriage of the Queen with a foreign Prince, or whether, knowing my Lord Darnley and the distaste many in Scotland would have for the match, she foresaw that troubles would spring out of this marriage.

Be that as it may, my Lord Darnley came to Edinburgh in the month of February in the great winter, and he was received by the Queen and bidden by her to abide at Wemyss Castle. My Lord Darnley was a comely youth of mild spirit and honest behaviour, and the Queen, who had already determined that no marriage would be more to her interest than this, seeing it would render her title to the succession of the Crown of England double sure, took well with him, as she had taken well with him when she saw him at Orleans. But she did not fall in love with him incontinent, and she perceived at the first that whereunto she was blind later on, for a time, that he was lacking in many qualities which are needful for the consort of a Queen, let alone for a King.

My Lord Darnley was well received at Edinburgh, and he heard Mr Knox preach, and danced a galliard with the Queen at the Earl of Moray's; and he was present at the marriage of Mary Livingstone with Lord Sempill of Beltreis, which was solemnized at the Shrovetide feast; and while the Queen kept the project of marriage with my Lord Darnley constant in her mind, the treaty for her marriage with my Lord Leicester was still debated, and there were many who urged the Queen to marry with my Lord Darnley, and others who entreated her not to do it.

My Lord Darnley jeopardized his fortune by proposing marriage to Her Majesty himself, and offering her a ring: and the Queen disrelished this greatly and refused the ring: for she said he should have known such behaviour was not honest, and it proved him to be indiscreet.

The Cardinal de Lorraine entreated the Queen not to wed with my Lord Darnley, and so did many others of those about the Queen; but Seigneur David Riccio, who had now become the Queen's Secretary in lieu of Raulet, for her foreign correspondence, and upon whom she leant willingly, pressed her to this match, telling her that thereby she would succeed to the throne of England, and maybe unite the two kingdoms; and he said that the Queen of England, or rather Secretary Cecil, was not minded that any of the marriages should take effect, but they wished to hold the Queen unmarried as long as they could. The Queen soon forgave my Lord Darnley his indiscretion, and she sought a dispensation from Rome for my Lord Darnley, he being near to her in blood; and she sent Secretary Lethington to the Queen of England to have her consent to marry with my Lord Darnley, and messengers to the Queen-Mother in France.

Before the dispensation came from Rome and before the messengers she had sent to France and England had returned, the Queen was married privily with my Lord Darnley in Seigneur Riccio's chamber at Stirling Castle.

This was maybe the second occasion in her life when the Queen gave proof of power; for albeit always courageous and full of fire, and able to endure, she had not the wise will of her mother, and she leant upon others, her favourites, whom she chose by chance. But when she married my Lord Darnley

she did so of her own will, and likewise when she would not
ratify the Treaty of Edinburgh; and the one act was wise, but
the other act pregnant with disaster.

CHAPTER III

The Queen of England, when she was advertised of rumours of this marriage, wrote to the Queen advising her to deliberate, and recommended Leicester again; and the Queen answered that the marriage was now past revoking, and that the Queen of England had no cause to be angry, since she had chosen an Englishman born of the royal blood of both kingdoms; and the Queen of England called back the Earl of Lennox and his son; but they excused themselves with letters and petitions. The Queen adorned my Lord Darnley with the dignity of Eques *Auratus*, and with the title of Earl of Ross, and not a month after the secret marriage she declared at the Parliament at Stirling that she would marry with her cousin, my Lord Darnley, whereunto she obtained the consent of the Peers: but the Earl of Moray, the Duke of Châtelherault and others murmured. And the Queen of England, knowing the waxen and unstable nature of Lord Darnley, and how the great ones of Scotland disdained the match, was inwardly content, albeit she made a show of choler and committed the Countess of Lennox to the Tower.

Hitherto, from the time of the secret marriage, the Queen had doted upon my Lord Darnley and done him great honour; but after the meeting of the Peers at Stirling the pride of my Lord Darnley waxed and became intolerable; and, not satisfied with the honours that he had received, he claimed to be made

Duke of Albany, to which honour the Queen was loth to exalt him until she had written to the Queen of England. But in despite of his arrogance, by which he estranged all those who were nearest to the Queen, and in despite of the petulant and choleric words that he spoke to the Queen himself, she continued to dote upon him. The Earl of Moray and the Secretary Lethington were away from the Court: the Secretary was busy courting Mary Fleming, and his work was done by Seigneur Riccio, who now worked all.

Although was there never a more diligent and observant Secretary, this was marvellous unwise of the Queen, seeing that Seigneur Riccio was hated and envied for his arrogance, and because, in the presence of the nobility, he would speak publicly to the Queen, saying that the Queen would not suffer him to carry himself otherwise.

My Lord Darnley grew ever more proud, disdainful and suspicious, and offended all who served the Queen; even her Ladies, who would tarry at home when my Lord Darnley rode abroad with Her Grace: for my Lord Darnley would treat them either with disdain or with over-great familiarity; and at one time he courted Mary Beton. And the Queen was in need of money, and sent to the principal merchants of Edinburgh; and she needed fifty thousand pounds Scotch, and asked them to become surety in ware for that sum, which they refused. And she was changed in face; for she knew that her brother and the Duke of Châtelherault and his friends were plotting mischief against her; and they designed to surprise the Queen, and to take my Lord Darnley to England and to put the Queen in ward until she should grant such conditions as they should demand for the Kirk and the realm.

But for the loyalty of a gentleman named Lindsay they would have captured the Queen when she was riding from Perth to Callander House, where she had promised to be gossip to the child of Lord Livingstone; but the Queen, being advertised of this plot, outwitted those who would be waiting for her in triple

MAURICE BARING

ambush, by setting forth earlier in the morning and by another
route; and peril, as ever, was to the Queen like medicine or the
salt air of the sea, and on this occasion, and during that
morning ride when she started on horseback at five of the
clock, she was like a drooping flower that has been refreshed
with rain and has come to life once more. She kirtled her skirts
and put on her blue Highland mantle, and her little grey hat
embroidered with gold and red silk, with a feather of red and
yellow, and as she galloped through the sleeping town of
Kinross and reached the banks of the Forth, men seemed
to spring out of the ground to welcome and defend her, and to
muster in her support and to acclaim her; and perhaps that was
the morning throughout all her life in which she tasted most
sharply the sweets of majesty, homage and worship; and the
ardour and the worship of her subjects were reflected in her
face and in her eyes, and she became once more and for a while
that Mary Stuart whom the poets loved to sing, and for whom
the brave and the young were glad to die. And she reached
Callander House full five hours before she was awaited, and
she was gossip to the infant son of the Lord Livingstone. And
hearing at Callander that the Lords, her enemies, were about to
bring their ensigns into the field, the Queen came to Edinburgh,
and she was still in high gladness and good health, for the wine
of danger was still in her veins and in her heart; and one
afternoon in a merry mood she walked up and down the town
with my Lord Darnley disguised until suppertime; and she was
recognized, for they were the tallest pair in the town, and no
disguise could conceal the Queen's stepping, for none trod the
ground as she. And this frolic caused men's tongues to chatter;
and Madame de Briante, who had entreated her with tears not
to go forth thus, said that little matters in a Queen's demeanour
were of import, for they are noted by the envious and the
malicious, and magnified and distorted; and what is an act of
frolic in a simple subject in a Queen becomes an offence. But
the Queen paid no heed, and her enemies wagged their heads

and their tongues. But never was the Queen so high-hearted as at this time. She summoned the Earl of Moray and his friends to come to her marriage; but they excused themselves and protested they would assemble to defend their lives and properties; and the Queen recalled into the realm the Earl of Bothwell, who had been outlawed since her advent into her kingdom.

The Queen exalted my Lord Darnley to the rank of Duke of Albany, and the trumpet sounded through the streets, and at Mercat Cross, setting forth the Queen's intent to solemnize the bond of marriage with Prince Henry, Duke of Albany: in respect of which marriage she declared him King during the time thereof.

But my Lord Darnley was not content with this honour, and demanded with passion the Crown Matrimonial, which the Queen would not yet grant him.

In the morning of the 29th of July, at half-past five of the clock, the Queen was led from her chamber between the Earls of Lennox and Atholl into the Chapel Royal of Holyrood House with her Ladies and the loyal among the nobility; and she was wedded by the Dean of Restalrig, according to the rite of Rome; but my Lord Darnley, after the marriage benediction had been given, would not stay for the Mass, but went out a-hawking; and the Queen came back to the Palace in her mourning gown, which she had worn, according to custom, until the ceremony should be ended. And in the Palace she laid it aside with a pretty reluctance; and every gentleman was allowed to take a pin; the Queen saying, with a smile, she had not been accustomed to be served by such noble servitors, nor to disrobe before so many; whereupon she retired and came back in festal apparel, and wearing a new robe which had lately come from Flanders, and was of crimson satin figured with silver and bordered with a silver fringe.

And there followed banquet, and largesse was thrown to the people; and the King in robes of State of rose-satin danced with the Queen after the banquet, and after supper there was more ceremony and dancing: but without the Palace there was tumult and broil, which lasted until the morrow, the people being angry at this Papist match and fearing for their religion. But the Queen summoned the burgesses into her presence and told them she could not abandon the Faith she had been brought up in, nor should her conscience be forced in such matters any more than theirs; and she entreated them, as they had full liberty for the exercise of their religion, to be content with that, and to allow her the same privilege; and the burgesses declared themselves content with her assurance, and the tumult was at an end.

At noon of the same day my Lord Darnley was proclaimed King in the presence of the Lords, but save his father alone not one of them said "Amen".

The King went in State to the High Church, where a throne had been made for him to listen to Mr Knox, who spake in his discourse of the wicked Princes who, for the sins of the people, were sent as tyrants and scourges to plague them, and of how God had sent this realm boys and women to govern them; and the King in a great choler walked down from the throne and went from the church, and, too wrathful to dine, went a-hawking for several hours.

The Rebel Lords now brought their ensigns into the field; and the drum was beaten through the streets to raise recruits for the Queen's army; and the Queen took the field and pursued the rebels and constrained them to fly into England before the English troops, which were promised them by the Queen of England, were arrived. And the Queen, braced as ever by the scent of danger and the call of adventure, in casque of steel and with pistols in her holsters, said to some of her nobles, who bade her to be mindful of her health and the bad weather, nor remain so many hours in the saddle: "I shall not rest from my toils till I have led you all to London." But to London she had no need to go; for the Rebel Lords were dispersed and fled without the firing of a volley.

The Earl of Bothwell was made Lord High Admiral and Warden of the Southern Marches; and the Queen of England, when the rebels had failed in their purpose, disowned and disdained them, and bade them, when they took refuge in England, go from her presence and repent them of their abominable treason.

The Earl of Moray, who had been proclaimed a rebel and who was cited to come before Parliament, in his defeat and humiliation asked pardon of the Queen, and sought to be reconciled with her, and sent Seigneur David a diamond ring; but the Queen was dissuaded from pardoning the Rebel Lords by the Cardinal de Lorraine; and the banished Lords, failing to win the Queen's pardon by soft means, designed to regain what they had forfeited without it. And the Earl of Moray wrote to my Lord Morton, a man of craft, that since the marriage was now accomplished, yet discord might be brought about between the Queen and the King; and soon occasion thereof presented itself. For soon after the marriage the King became suspicious and much addicted to drinking, which was harmful for him, seeing that his choler was already too quick to boil, and being malcontent because he had not the Crown Matrimonial, and because the Queen set her husband's name after her own in moneys and stamps. And they first designed to estrange the King from the Queen, and thereupon to estrange him from all the nobility and from the people. My Lord Morton sowed suspicions in the King's mind about Seigneur David, telling him that it was Seigneur David who dissuaded the Queen from granting him the Crown Matrimonial, but making no other calumniations, as the rebels thereafter declared; which they did, so that the King alone might be blamed for the conspiracy.

My Lord Morton dropped words of poison into the King's ear and pressed him to set the Crown upon his own head, saying that women were born to obey and men to command, and that the Queen had sworn at the altar to obey him; and the King listened easily to these promptings, for his mark was power and the Crown Matrimonial, without which he deemed he was but the shadow of a King. Thus he wrote to the banished Lords and promised to indemnify them from the Parliament; and George Douglas, the son natural of the Earl of Angus, was of the conspiracy; and Secretary Lethington, and others of the Queen's Council: but the Earls of Bothwell and Huntly and Atholl were untainted; and my Lords Lindsay and Ruthven were the leaders chosen for the execution of the plot.

On Saturday night, two days before the day upon which the Parliament were to assemble, the Queen, who was far gone with child, was at supper in her private cabinet adjoining her bedchamber; and there with her the Countess of Argyll, Arthur Erskine and the Lord Keith, the Master of the Household, her physician, and Seigneur David. And before supper they had been making music, Anthony Standen, the King's Cup-bearer, holding the torch, and Seigneur David was standing by a buffet-stool with the servitors, and eating somewhat sent to him from the table by the Queen, when the King entered through the arras by the winding stairway which led from his lobby to the Queen's bedchamber, at about seven of the clock; and he sat him down beside her in the double Chair of State, one seat whereof was empty.

And the Queen said unto him: "My Lord, wherefore have you supped earlier than your wont?"

And the King said he had supped early of a purpose, knowing that she was supping in her cabinet, and doubting but that she was sick; and he took the Queen's hand and he embraced her.

And incontinent my Lord Ruthven came through the arras boden over his nightgown, and with his sword naked drawn; whereat the Queen marvelled, for my Lord Ruthven was sick, and the bruit of the Court was that he was sick unto death. And the Queen said: "My Lord, I had designed to visit you in your chamber, being told you were sick, and now you come boden into our presence. What does this mean?"

And Lord Ruthven said to the Queen: "In very truth I have been sick, but now I am restored to health, and I have come in this fashion to render unto you service."

And the Queen, half-smiling and deeming that these words were born of his distemper, said: "And what service do you wish to render me at this hour?"

And he answered to her: "We have come for yon gallant," and he pointed to Seigneur David, "and we will no longer be governed by a servitor."

And the Queen said: "What hath he done?"

And Lord Ruthven said to her: "Ask the King, your husband." And the Queen said to the King: "What is this?"

And the King said: "I know nothing thereof."

And Lord Ruthven said to the King: "Sir, take the Queen your wife and sovereign to you." And the King stood all amazed and wist not what to do.

Then the Queen rose upon her feet and stood before Seigneur David, who held her by the aglets of her gown, and the Queen in choler bade Lord Ruthven leave the presence under pain of treason. But Lord Ruthven heeded her not; and Arthur Erskine and the Lord Keith, the Master of the Household, and the apothecary, began to lay hands on Lord Ruthven, who cried out: "Lay no hands on me," and drew his dagger, whereupon another came into the cabinet who carried a pistol; and the Queen said that if Seigneur David had committed any offence he should be brought to justice. And Seigneur David said: "Madame, I am a dead man."

And he with the pistol cried : "Here is the means of justice," and he drew a rope from his pocket. And Seigneur David clung to the gown of the Queen and called "*Justitia*".

243

Without there was a cry of men-at-arms shouting "A Douglas", and Lord Morton and others came up the great stairway through the presence chamber and the bedchamber into the cabinet, with torches, and the buffet-board fell to the ground with the meat thereon and the candles. And the Queen's servitors fled. And George Douglas, the Postulate, stabbed Seigneur David across the Queen's shoulder, so that the blood was spilled upon her gown; and the King dragged Seigneur David from the Queen, and the Queen would have defended him, but the King held her down in a chair from behind; and one of the assailants held a bended pistol to her, and she bade him fire if he respected not what she bore in her womb; and Patrick Bellenden, the brother of the Justice Clerk, offered to fix his poniard in the Queen's left side, which Anthony Standen turned aside and wrested the dagger from him. And another took Seigneur David by the neck and dragged him from the cabinet into the Queen's bedchamber, where he clung to the bedpost, and they beat him upon the arm with the butt of his pistol until he left hold; but again Seigneur David clung to the chimney-piece, which was further removed between the bed and the doorway, and they bended back his fingers until he screamed for pain, and dragged him to the far door of the outchamber; and George Douglas, who had been the first to strike him, laid hands upon the King's dagger and struck Seigneur David, and left the dagger in his side, saying: "This is the blow of the King."

The King dragged the Queen back into the cabinet; while in the far door of the bedchamber they gave Seigneur David fiftysix blows with daggers and swords, and they bound his feet together and dragged him back across the floor of the bedchamber, and threw his body down the winding stair into the King's lobby, and dragged it thence to the porter's lodge, where the porter, taking off the clothes from the body, said: "This hath been his destiny, for upon this chest was his first bed when he entered this place, and now here he lieth again, a very ingrate and misknowing knave."

The King was left alone with the Queen in the closet. And presently an equerry came to the cabinet, and the Queen asked what had befallen Seigneur David, and whether they had put him into ward, and where, and the equerry said: "Madam, there is no case to speak of David, for he is dead." And the Queen said: "May God have mercy upon his soul!"

Presently Lady Sempill came to the cabinet and said she had seen the body of the dead man, and that all had been done by the King's order; and the Queen turned to the King and said: "Ah, traitor, and son of a traitor!" And the Queen swooned incontinent.

Lady Sempill tended the Queen, who passed into her bedchamber followed by the King; and presently Lord Ruthven returned. And the Queen said to the King: "My Lord, why have you caused to do this wicked deed to me, considering I took you from low estate and exalted you?"

But the King was ashamed and said nothing, and my Lord Ruthven prompted him; and the Queen said to the King: "My Lord, all the offence that is done me you have the wite thereof, for the which I shall be your wife no longer."

Lord Ruthven sat him down upon a coffer and asked for a cup of wine, for he was sore felled with sickness. And the Queen said to him: "Is this your sickness, Lord Ruthven?" And Lord Ruthven answered: "God forbid your Majesty had such a sickness."

And Lord Ruthven chided the Queen with her proceedings and tyranny, saying it was not tolerable to the Lords, who had been abused by David Riccio, whom they had put to death, because he took counsel for the maintenance of the old religion, entertained amity with foreign Princes and nations and favoured the Earls of Huntly and Bothwell, who were traitors. And the Queen said if she and the commonwealth perished, she would leave the revenge of her cause to her friends, for she had the King of Spain and the Emperor for her friends, and the King of France, her good brother.

And Lord Ruthven said these Princes were over-great personages to meddle with so poor a man; and, if anything were done that night which Her Majesty misliked, she must blame the King; and the more angry she appeared the worse the world would judge her. And the Queen answered to him she trusted in God, who did behold this from the high heavens, and would avenge this vile contempt; and setting her two hands to her sides she said she hoped God would move that which was between her sides, meaning the child of whom she was big, to root him out, and his treasons, and all his treacherous posterity.

There was a knocking at the Queen's chamber door – Lord Gray declaring that the Earls of Huntly and Bothwell and others were fighting in the close against the Earl of Morton and his company.

The King would have gone down, but the Lord Ruthven stayed him, and he went down himself, leaving the King with the Queen: and presently Lord Ruthven came again into the Queen's chamber, having drunk wine with the Earls of Bothwell and Huntly, who had gone out of a low window and passed their ways. And the Provost of Edinburgh and a number of the men of the town in arms came with him in arms to the outer court of the Palace of Holyrood House, and demanded to see the Queen's presence and to speak with her and know her welfare; and the Queen was not permitted to give answer, but was threatened by the Lord Ruthven, who declared in her face the Lords would cut her into collops and cast her over the wall; and the King declared to them that he and the Queen were in good health, and bade them pass home. And the King declared to the Queen that he had sent for the banished Lords to return again; and the Queen asked the Lord Ruthven what kindness there was betwixt the Earl of Moray and him. "Remember you," said she, "what the Earl of Moray would have had me do unto you for giving me the ring?" For the Earl of Moray had told the Queen Lord Ruthven was a sorcerer and deserved the fiery death for his *maleficia*. And Lord Ruthven said it had no more virtue than another ring, and was but a little ring with a pointed diamond in it. "Remember you not," said the Queen, "that you said it had a virtue to keep me from poisoning?"

My Lord Ruthven, perceiving that the Queen was very sick, said to the King it was best to take leave of the Queen; so the King took his good-night. And all that night the Queen was detained in captivity, nor were her Ladies allowed access to her, and scarce any of her domestic servitors; and the King came to her chamber by the secret stair, but he was denied admittance. And on the following day the King was stricken with terror, because the Lords had told him he must follow their advice for his own safety as well as for theirs, for if he did otherwise they would take care of themselves, cost what it might. And they told him they planned to ward the Queen in the Castle of Stirling, where Lord Lindsay said she would have leisure to shoot with her bow in the garden, and for needlework; and to keep her there until she had approved their enterprises, and to give the King the Crown Matrimonial and the government of the realm, or else they were prepared to strike at the root and to put the Queen to death. The King visited the Queen. And the Queen greeted him kindly and spoke to him of his great fault, and of the great danger whereunto his aspiring mind was like to bring him; that he had nothing in Scotland but by her and under the shadow of her name; that the child she was about to bring forth might increase his power; and that if she were to die with her issue through these manifold outrages, let him not hope to escape the hands by whose persuasion he would bring about the death of his wife and his child; for the death of David Riccio would cry to God by his blood.

And the King was moved and affrighted by her speech, and with watery eyes he craved pardon of the Queen, and he discovered fully the whole conspiracy and revealed everything: what the Lords had agreed in their Council to do unto her, and likewise to the Lord Livingsone, the Lord Fleming and Sir James Balfour; and how they had designed to drown the Queen's Ladies of Honour.

And he told the Queen of the assistance of the Queen of England, and of the enemies of the House of Lorraine in France; and he told her he could no longer put trust in such cruel people, but attended no other thing than to accompany the Queen to her death, which was now agreed upon.

And the Queen said to him that in the last twenty-four hours he had done her such a wrong that not the memory of the past nor any hope he could give of the future could ever make her forget it.

And she feared he was driven to such repentance rather by necessity than by true affection; but since it was he who had drawn them to the marge of the precipice, he must now deliberate how they should escape.

And the King beseeched the Queen to devise some means of escape, and the Queen promised to do it, but he must bestir himself as well.

The Queen on the Sunday morning saw her brother natural, the Earl of Moray, and he declared he was ignorant and innocent of all the conspiracy; and the Earl of Moray shed tears and sued the Queen to pardon him and his complices from their first fault when they rebelled and fled to England; and he showed her the danger wherein she was if she did not appease those who had killed Seigneur David, which she could do by receiving them to mercy.

The Queen gave audience to the Earl of Morton and to Lord Ruthven in the outer chamber, for she would not admit Lord Ruthven into her presence; and she bade them to prepare their securities, which she promised she would subscribe when she was no more a prisoner.

The Queen, with the aid of Lady Huntly, received a letter
from the Earl of Huntly and from the Earl of Bothwell and
others who had escaped, telling her if she could escape they
would meet her with troops, and they bade her come in the
night upon chairs and ropes over the walls of the Palace. But
the Queen knew that the window was watched: she bade them
to meet her near Seton, and she devised another way of escape;
and, sending for the Laird of Traquair, she expounded to him
her plan, which was to escape through the burial-ground,
where Arthur Erskine should await her with a tall gelding and
a pillion. But first she must be rid of the presence of the guards.
These the Lords were loth to send away, and the Queen was
advised by Secretary Lethington to send for all the banished
Lords, and she did it; and the Queen spoke to the Lords and
told them that she owed justice to every one, nor could she
deny it to those who asked it in the name of the one who had
been murdered; whatever his rank may have been, he was her
servitor, and that honour should have protected him from
outrage, more especially in her own presence: therefore she
bade them not to hope for full pardon so speedily; yet, if they
should endeavour to blot out the past by service which they
now promised, she gave them her word she would try to forget
what they had done; but being a prisoner, all that she did now
was in no force or virtue; therefore she demanded to be set
free.

And she drank a cup of wine to the Lords as an earnest of
her goodwill.

And the Queen reminded them that from her youth she had
been blamed for being too easy in the matter of clemency; and
then, fearing lest she might say too much, she made as though
overtaken by the pains of childbirth, and summoned the
midwife; and the midwife and Arnault, the physician, both said
she was in danger of parting with her child, which they
believed, for the infant was near the birth. But the Queen,
in despite of her pains, had no fear thereof and rejoiced in

hoodwinking the Lords; and further debate on the matter was postponed until the next day.

And she bade the King to speak of the particulars of the pardon with the nobles and to obtain the removal of the guards; and at six of the clock the Lords gave to the King the articles for the security of the Lords to be subscribed by the King, which the King took in hands, as he desired the Lords to go from the Palace and to remove the guards, and to give to Her Majesty's servitors the keys of the Palace; and this the Lords were loth to do, saying they feared all was but deceit and that the Queen would fly with the King to the Castle of Edinburgh or to Dunbar, wherefrom bloodshed and mischief would ensue. But the King said he would warrant all and should guard her himself that night; whereunto the Lords consented; for they believed that in the extremity of her sickness the Queen would hardly live until the morrow.

At midnight that night the Queen rose from her bed and escaped from the Palace, as she had planned, by the gate into the churchyard, and mounted upon horseback behind Arthur Erskine, upon a pillion; and they reached first Seton and then Dunbar Castle, in company with the Earls of Huntly and Bothwell, the Lords Fleming, Seton, Livingstone and others.

CHAPTER IV

The Earls of Huntly, Atholl and Bothwell had gathered together some thousands, and the rebels fled; and the Queen came to Edinburgh and set about to appease the country and to reconcile the one faction with the other, which was like the mingling of fire and water. The Queen had proclaimed the King to be innocent of the murder of Seigneur Riccio, and this but inflamed the hearts of his fellow-conspirators, whom he had betrayed. My Lord Morton and my Lord Ruthven fled to England, and Secretary Lethington retired into Atholl. And the Queen subscribed remission for the Earl of Moray and some of his dependants; and this angered the King greatly; and he told the Queen that he had it in his heart to kill the Earl of Moray, whereat the Queen spoke sharply to him.

In the month of May Mary Beton was married with Alexander Ogilvy of Boyne, and the Queen and the King were at the marriage. In the month of June, the time of her reckoning being near, the Queen retired to Edinburgh Castle for her lying-in. The Earls of Moray and Argyll expelled the Earls of Huntly and Bothwell from the Castle; and they would allow none to sleep there but the King. The Earls of Huntly and Bothwell would have persuaded the Queen to imprison my Lord of Moray, alleging that he and his dependants designed to bring in the banished Lords at the time of her reckoning; but the Queen heeded them not, thinking this to be their malice. The Queen took to her chamber in June and made her will, and received the Sacraments, and on Tuesday, the nineteenth day of the month, the Queen gave birth to a son, with peril unto her life and unto his; and bonfires were lighted, and there was rejoicing.

The King, during this time, led a disorderly life, and threatened the Lords, and was offended with the Queen because she had asked the Queen of England to be gossip to the Prince; and his ill-humour waxed when in the month of August the Queen gave audience to my Lord of Lethington and was reconciled with him. And the Queen, after hunting the stag with the King in Meggatland, and after removing her son to Stirling, and leaving him under the care of the Earl of Mar, went in the month of September to Jedburgh to keep the laws days which are held there for the bringing of the Borders in order and to punish the robbers. The Earl of Bothwell, who had been sent there to pursue the robbers, had been wounded, and was grievously sick, and the Queen visited him with the Earl of Moray, in whose presence she conversed with the Earl of Bothwell, and returned the same day to Jedburgh. And on the day following she fell sick of an attack of the spleen: and the sickness increasing, she disposed herself as one at the point of death, and she called the nobles to her to receive her last commands, and exhorted them to unity and concord, forgiving those who had offended her, especially her own husband, King Henry, and the banished Lords; and she commended her son to the Lords and bade them keep the banished Lords from having access to him; and she spoke also with the French Ambassador, bidding him to recommend her to the Queen-Mother. She recommended her son to the Queen of England, his nearest kinswoman; and, having spoken her wishes, she recommended herself to God and prayed to Him for mercy, praying thus: "Grant me mercy, for I seek not long life in this world, but only that Thy Will may be fulfilled in me.

O my God, Thou hast appointed me above the people of this realm to rule and govern them; if therefore it be Thy pleasure that I remain with them in this mortal life, albeit that it be painful to my body, so that it please Thy divine goodness, I will give myself to Thy keeping. If Thy pleasure and purpose be to call me from hence to Thy mercy, with good will will I remit myself to Thy pleasure, as well deliberate to die as to live, and as the good King Ezekias, afflicted with sickness and other infirmities, turned him to Thy Divine will and pleasure, so do I the like."

But on the ninth day of the sickness, when all had given her over, Arnault, her physician, with skilful rubbing, brought the blood into her limbs, and fetched her back to life, and thereupon she began to mend.

And when later she returned to Edinburgh, and there vomited forth much corrupt blood, the cure of her body was complete. But albeit cured in body, the Queen was sick in mind, and often she would say to her Ladies that God had dealt sorely with her by calling her back to life: for she knew that, whether she looked to the right or to the left, she stood alone. She had drunk of the cup of treachery, as she thought, to the dregs, and yet that cup was not yet empty. She had measured the falsity of the King, and gauged his weakness and his folly; and yet there was a falsity more rank and a greater weakness, and a wilder folly awaiting her. And those whom she knew to be fittest to guide the realm could least be trusted, for either they were led by the lodestar of their own ambition, or they were guided by plans which would destroy her; and they would proceed upon their way without remorse. And she herself had within no fixed compass to enable her to steer her course and her kingdom, but she must ever lean upon others; and ever she must choose ill, for when she chose right for the realm she chose ill for herself; and when she chose right for herself she chose ill for the realm.

So had it been with my Lord Moray, who shot at the mark of the Crown. So had it been with Seigneur Riccio, who in public matters had been industrious and observant, and yet deadly to her, because he had incurred the hatred of the Lords; and so was it with her husband, the King, whom she had once doted upon, for there was no public act of his that brought not bane; and so was it with my Lord Bothwell, whom alone of the Lords she had come to trust in, for, no sooner trusted, he was inflamed by ambition, which was used by others more crafty than himself, and he brought about the Queen's doom and his own; and so, above all, was it with Secretary Lethington, whom the Queen knew to be the wisest of her counsellors; for he, albeit guided by wise designs, was overfull of policy, even unto treachery; there was no craft which was for him too subtle.

But now the chiefest evil was the King; for he had lost the trust of all; and while he lived there could be no peace among the other Lords. And the King, knowing this, went about as a man in dread, and spoke of going to Flanders or to France.

The Secretary Lethington, seeing there was no outgate, summoned the Queen to release the Earls of Morton and Lindsay and Lord Ruthven of their banishment, and he pressed the Queen to procure a divorce from the King. The Queen made answer that she would rather for a time return into France; not being willing that anything should be done to her son's prejudice or to her own dishonour. And the Secretary said that the Council would find the mean that Her Majesty should be quit of the King without prejudice to her son; but the Queen prohibited him to perform anything that might in the least blemish her honour or burthen her conscience. "Let things stand as they do," she said, "till God above vouchsafe some better remedy."

Thereupon there followed the baptism of the Prince, whereat the King would not be present, not being acknowledged to be King by the Queen of England; and a week after the baptism of the Prince, on the eve of Christmas, the

Queen released the Earl of Morton from banishment, and more than seventy others, excepting those who had offered her violence.

And on Twelfth Night the Secretary Lethington was wedded with Mary Fleming. And the King, greatly angered at the remissions that had been given to the banished Lords, and affrighted thereat, passed to Glasgow, where smallpox was prevalent, and fell sick of that malady. The Queen sent him her physician, and it was said by some who tended him that he had been poisoned. The King summoned the Queen to come to him; but she was sick, having fallen from her horse at Seton, but, after a space of time, she went to him.

When the sickness had run its course the Earl of Moray told the Queen it was needful for the King to be removed for the change of air, and he was to be lodged at Kirk of the Field without the town, being a pleasant place and in good air; but this was in despite of the wishes of the Queen, who would have had him lodged at Craigmillar Castle; he could not lodge at Holyrood House for fear of giving infection to the Prince. The Queen conducted him to Kirk of the Field and led him to the house of the Earl of Arran adjoining Kirk of Field; but the Earl of Moray bade her return and lead the King to the house of the Provost, which had been chosen by the King and had been made ready for him at the advice of Sir James Balfour, to whose brother the house belonged.

The King would receive no visit until the time of his baths should be accomplished, but he was visited often by the Queen, who slept some nights at Kirk of Field. The Queen had slept there on Friday night before Shrovetide, and upon the Wednesday night, and she had designed to sleep there again on Sunday night; and she had promised to her servitor, Bastian, to be present at the masque which was to be held at Holyrood House after his marriage with Christily Hogg.

And on Friday night, while the Queen was at Kirk of the Field, the King told her of a plot against her that had been devised by those who had slain Seigneur Riccio, for the King could conceal no secret, however perilous the revealing of that secret might be for himself; and when he was with the Queen he was like clay in the hands of a master potter.

The Queen asked him whence he knew of this plot; and the King said it was from Lord Robert Stuart he had heard of it. And the next morning, Saturday, the Queen sent for Lord Robert, who, in the presence of the Earl of Moray and the Earl of Bothwell, denied all; whereat the King was wrathful, and the Earl of Moray made concord betwixt them.

The Queen was now certified that there was treachery; but who the traitors were, and of the manner of the plot, she knew nothing; nor did she know how to trust the King's word, for he had betrayed her once with a Judas kiss; and she knew not whether the Lords were plotting against her life and using the King as an instrument, or whether the King was privy to all. But she showed no sign of fear, and spoke lovingly with the King and merrily with all.

Upon the same day the Earl of Moray took his leave of the Queen, saying that his wife was sick in childbed. And after he had taken leave of the Queen, the same evening as he was crossing the Ferry, he said to Lord Herries: "This night shall the King be cured of all maladies."

On Sunday morning the Queen attended the marriage of Bastian, her servitor, and later a banquet given in honour of M. de Morette; and attended by many of the nobility she went from the banquet at eight of the clock or thereabouts to Kirk of Field. And the Queen talked with the King familiarly in his chamber while the Nobles played at dice in the larger *salle*. And at about eleven of the clock the Queen took leave of the King, saying he should soon see her again, but whether she meant that night or on the morrow was not known. And she rode back to Holyrood House with the Lords and her Ladies, and with lighted torches; and the night was dark, and there was no moon.

When the Queen reached Holyrood House she tarried for a while in the room where the bridal was held, and then she passed to her rooms, and remained speaking with the Earl of Bothwell and John Stuart of Traquair, the Captain of the Guard; and her Ladies thought the Queen had designed to go back to Kirk of Field and to sleep there that night maybe; but she said nothing of her purpose until now, when she said she would sleep at Holyrood House, and she dismissed her Ladies.

The Earl of Bothwell changed his clothes and went from the Palace with his servants. About two hours after midnight the house wherein the King was lodged was blown into the air.

At break of day the Earls of Huntly and Bothwell came to the Queen and told her that the King's house had been burnt and destroyed, and himself found lying a little distance from the house under a tree; and there was not a hurt nor a mark upon all his body. And there were women who lived near the King's house at Kirk of Field who declared they had seen armed men around the house, and the King letting himself down from a window into the garden; but he had not proceeded far before he was surrounded by certain persons, who strangled him with the sleeves of his own shirt.

Early in the morning, after the death of the King, Robert Durie, an archer of the King's Guard, arrived at Holyrood House; he was sent from the Archbishop of Glasgow from France to advertise the Queen that some great conspiracy and enterprise was in preparation against her, whereof he had certain knowledge; but he spoke not of the names of the conspirators.

The day after the death of the King the Queen kept to her chamber at Holyrood House, and thence she passed to her dule chamber at Edinburgh Castle, where she tarried without light or air until the King was buried, five days later, in the Chapel of Holyrood, by the side of the late King, James V, the Queen's father. The physicians saying she was in need of freer air, she passed on the following day to the abode of Lord Seton,

257

accompanied by the Earls of Argyll, Huntly, and Bothwell and others, amounting to a hundred people.

The Earl of Bothwell was suspected to be guilty of the murder of the King, and some said plainly that it was he. Libels had been fixed in the market-place incontinent after the King's death, naming the Earl of Bothwell as the murderer; and the Earl of Lennox summoned the Queen to put the Earl of Bothwell into the hands of the justice, that he might be proceeded against by the order of law for the murder of the King, his son. And the Earl of Moray and his faction weaved their plot with craft, and they aimed at how to free the Earl of Bothwell. A session of Parliament was ordained, and the Earl of Lennox accused the Earl of Bothwell, who was commanded to appear before twenty days; and within that compass of time the Earl of Bothwell made his appearance, and, having my Lord Morton for his advocate, prevailed in the cause, and was sent away absolved by the sentence of all the Judges. Thus, although those who went upon the trial were of the Earl of Moray's faction, the Earl of Bothwell was absolved, not for any goodwill which they bore him, but to make the Queen to be suspected of the King's murder.

A few days before the trial the Earl of Moray told the Queen he must needs take a voyage into France, and he left his affairs to her protection.

And presently it was rumoured that the Queen would marry the Earl of Bothwell, who had six months before married the Earl of Huntly's sister, from whom he would obtain divorcement. Whereafter all good subjects were dismayed, but none durst speak in the contrary, save Madame de Briante, who had been the Queen's Lady Governess. She spoke to the Queen without fear, telling her of the reports that were going abroad of the Earl of Bothwell murdering the King, and how she was to marry him. And Madame de Briante said to the Queen that the Earl of Bothwell was a wicked man, full of vice and blinded with ambition, inconstant and easy to be persuaded; and she said that the nobles, the Earl of Moray and his dependants, had tickled the Earl of Bothwell's mind with fair promises and large designs by which he might satisfy his twain passions, which were ambition and his pleasures; but no sooner had he satisfied his pleasures by wedding the Queen, whereunto they had already led him half-way by persuading him to murder the King, than they would take care that he should not satisfy his greater ambition to be King of Scotland, but rid themselves of him incontinent. And the Queen made answer that the Earl of Bothwell had been all his lifetime a faithful servant of the Crown, a man valiant, and above all others for prowess; and that he had twice saved her life; firstly, when he had protected her after the murder of Seigneur Riccio; and, secondly, when he had saved her from the plot that had ended in the King's death.

Whatever the bruits might be, she knew from his dealings with her that he was the only one of the nobles whom she had never had cause to distrust, and the only one who had not yet sold her to the Queen of England.

As for marriage, the Earl of Bothwell had hinted of such a suit, but she had spoken to him frankly, telling him that not a second time would she marry with a subject, and he had taken her answer well.

Then Madame de Briante said to the Queen, the Earl of Bothwell might answer what pleased him, but she, an old woman, could read the desire and the intent which was writ in his looks for those who had eyes to see; and it boded ill for the Queen. And the Queen said there was not a subject of hers whom she feared; and Madame de Briante said the Earl of Bothwell had no reverence for Majesty when his passions were kindled; and that, bereft of Majesty, the Queen was a woman like any other. And the Queen in a choler bade her say no more.

And four days after the acquittal of the Earl of Bothwell the Queen rode to open her Parliament at the Tolbooth, and the Earl of Bothwell bore the sceptre; and upon the night the Parliament was closed, two days later, the Earl of Bothwell called divers of the nobility to a supper in the house of one Ainslie, where they subscribed and sealed a draft in writing declaring the Earl of Bothwell to be innocent of the King's murder, promising to take true and plain part with him to the maintenance of his quarrel, and pledging themselves to further and advance the marriage of the Earl of Bothwell with the Queen.

The Queen was counselled to go to the Castle of Stirling to visit the young Prince, and made the Earl of Bothwell acquainted at what time she should return; and when the Queen returned from Stirling, upon the Eve of St Mark, he lay in wait for her in ambush, being well accompanied; and the Queen, having but few persons with her, he encountered her at the village of Foulbriggs and led her to the Castle of Dunbar. And with her were Sir James Melville and Secretary Lethington, and the Earl of Huntly and Sir James Melville: the rest were permitted to go.

Captain Blackwater, one of his servitors, told Sir James Melville that what had been done was with the Queen's consent, and the Earl of Bothwell desired this to be bruited: but the Queen commanded some of the company to pass to Edinburgh and charge the town to be in armour for her rescue. And the men obeyed: and when they reached the town the citizens armed themselves; but the Provost caused the gates of the city to be shut, and the rumour was spread abroad that what had been done was with Her Highness' own consent, for that she was more familiar with the Earl of Bothwell than stood with her honour; and never a man in Scotland made any mean to procure her deliverance.

Albeit it was bruited abroad, as the Earl of Bothwell had willed, that all had been done with the Queen's counsel, and the news sent incontinent by the foreign spies to their Courts: yet the shame done by a subject to the Sovereign offended the whole realm; and the people judged that the Queen was detained without her liberty and against her will. And whether the Queen was not displeased to be carried away against her will, and still trusted in the Earl of Bothwell, or whether she already divined the truth, now it was too late, she knew not that he was already boasting that he would marry the Queen, who would or would not; yea whether she would herself or not.

CHAPTER V

The Queen was kept a prisoner at Dunbar Castle for a space of ten days or thereabouts, and she was without her ladies and without her servitors, and in the puissance of the Earl of Bothwell; and the Earl of Bothwell showed the Queen the handwrites of those who had signed the bond at Ainslie's tavern. And by persuasions and suit, but yet more by force, the Earl of Bothwell drove the Queen to end the work which he had begun; and seeing that the Nobles had yielded to his desire and that not a man had stirred to procure her deliverance, the Queen, revolve as she might many things in her mind, found no outgate but to make the best of it and to promise she would as soon as possible contract marriage with him: for she could not but marry with him after what had passed.

The Earl of Bothwell hasted forward the processing of divorce between himself and his Lady; and from Dunbar the Queen was carried by the Earl of Bothwell accompanied by armed men to Edinburgh Castle, and kept a prisoner there for six days, when she was taken to Holyrood House; and four days later she was wedded with the Earl of Bothwell, who had been exalted to be Duke of Orkney.

The Queen knew that the divorce was but a pretence, that she was a prisoner, and that the marriage caused everyone in Scotland and in other lands to surmise that she was guilty of the King's murder, and she desired nothing so much as death; and the Duke of Orkney, as soon as he was married with the Queen, treated her with disdain, so that sometimes she called for a knife to stab herself, and she was changed in face; and a whole month long there was not a day passed that she did not shed bitter tears.

The chief authors and counsellors of the marriage, the Lords who had signed the bond declaring that the Earl of Bothwell should marry the Queen, denounced the marriage incontinent, and the Queen, having summoned her lieges into Lidsdale, the malcontent Lords gathered an army upon the day before that appointed by the Queen, and would have surprised Her Majesty and the Duke of Orkney at Holyrood House, had not the Duke of Orkney received advertisement; whereupon the Duke of Orkney and the Queen removed to the Castle of Borthwick, the Queen taking with her a silver kettle for heating water, a cabinet and two thousand pins.

The Lords beset the Castle in arms, and the Queen and the Duke of Orkney escaped from thence to the Castle of Dunbar; and the Lords, entering the city of Edinburgh, published a protestation that they were forced to take weapons to deliver the Queen out of the thraldom of the Earl of Bothwell, the murderer of the King; and the Queen and the Duke of Orkney marched out of Dunbar and met the army of the Lords at Carberry Hill, not many miles from Edinburgh. And it was upon a Sunday, and in the month of June, and the sun was exceeding hot, and the Queen's troops were in want of water, but those of the Lords were well provided. The Queen's men were posted on Carberry Hill, where the Queen dismounted.

The Queen that day wore a red-and-yellow petticoat, a partlet with sleeves tied in points, and a black velvet hat and muffler, and she was mounted upon a grey charger; and Mary Seton, who was with her, was dressed likewise in red and yellow, but rode upon a small pony.

In the afternoon the French Ambassador, M. du Croc, passed from the rebels to parley with the Queen, and the soldiers, wearied from the great heat of the day, began to disperse in search of meat and drink. And the French Ambassador, receiving but haughty replies from the Lords, took his leave of the Queen and rode to Edinburgh.

The Queen on the hill sat upon a stone of granite in company with Mary Seton, and she awaited the advent and the aid of friends: the Earl of Huntly, Lord Fleming and the rest; and she looked ever westward in hope: but out of the west there came not one.

The Lords sent the Laird of Grange to ride about the hill with two hundred horsemen, and the Queen sent the Laird of Ormiston to the Laird of Grange to desire him to come and speak with her under surety: and the Laird of Grange came to the Queen, and while they were speaking the Duke of Orkney appointed a soldier to raise his harquebus and to shoot him, and the Queen gave a cry and said: "Shame me not with so foul a murder. I have promised him surety."

And the Laird of Grange said to the Queen: "All in this field, Madam, will love, honour and serve you, if you will put away the murderer of your husband." And the Duke of Orkney, having heard all or part of what the Laird of Grange had said, offered the combat to any who would maintain that he had murdered the King; and several of the Lords offered to fight with him in that quarrel: but the Queen said he should not fight with any of them. The Queen then sent again for the Laird of Grange, and told him that if the Lords would give assurance for the Duke of Orkney, she would leave him and come to them. And the Laird of Grange went to advertise the Lords thereof; whereupon the Duke of Orkney entreated the Queen to put not her trust in the Lords, for he knew their hearts to be full of treason, as she would find out to her cost; and he entreated the Queen either to let him fight and to abide by the decision, or else to retire with him to Dunbar; but the Queen would not be persuaded, and she bade him absent himself for a while until the issue of the Parliament should be known. The Duke of Orkney, finding he could not dissuade the Queen from her purpose, made known to her the design of her enemies; and showed her the handwrites of the noblemen: the Earl of Morton, Secretary Lethington, Sir James Balfour and others to the bond, agreed among themselves for the murder of the late King; and he gave this bond to the Queen and bade her take care of that paper.

Whereupon the Laird of Grange, having advertised the Lords of the Queen's word, rode up again and promised to the Queen in the names of the united Lords that they would do as they had said: and the Queen asked the Laird of Grange whether the Lords had given assurance for the Duke of Orkney, and the Laird said they had given him no authority to treat thereof, and he took the Duke of Orkney by the hand and advised him to save himself; and the Queen bade him retire to Dunbar, saying she would write to him or send him word what she would have him do.

The Laird of Grange saw the Queen part with the Duke of Orkney. She wept and she gave him her hand, and he turned his horse's head towards Dunbar. The Laird advertised the Lords thereof, and not a man went in pursuit of the Duke of Orkney; and they bade the Laird go up the hill again, and receive the Queen; and the Queen said to him: "Laird of Grange, I render myself to you upon the conditions you rehearsed unto me in the name of the Lords."

The Queen gave him her hand, which he kissed, and he led the Queen's horse down the hill unto the Lords. It was eight of the clock, and the sun was setting and the sky all glorious and gilded.

The Lords came forward to meet the Queen, and the Queen said to them: "My Lords, I come to you not that I fear for my life, nor yet doubting of victory, but because I abhor the shedding of Christian blood, especially of those that are my subjects. And therefore I yield to you, and will be ruled by your counsels, trusting you will respect me as your born Princess and Queen."

At first the Lords received her respectfully, but some of the men in buckram uttered reproachful words against her; whereupon the Laird of Grange and others struck them with their naked swords. And the Queen desired to send a message to the Duke of Hamilton; but this was denied her, and she perceived that she was a prisoner; and she asked whether this was indeed the truth; and the Lords made stern answer. And the Queen summoned the Lord Lindsay to her presence, and she bade him give her his hand, and he obeyed; and she in a great choler said to him: "By the hand which is now in yours, I'll have your head for this."

And now the men-at-arms no longer showed her any respect, but only reproach, crying out, "Burn the murderer, burn the whore!" This march lasted for two hours or more, the Queen riding between the Earls of Morton and Atholl; and her face was changed with dust and tears, and for faintness and grief she could scarce be holden upon horseback. Yet her sorrow did not overcome her anger, and she told the Lords she would have them hanged, yea crucified, and they durst not look at her. And before her the soldiers carried a bloody ensign of white taffety, standing between two spears, upon which was painted the King's picture as he was murdered, and in one of the corners the young Prince was drawn, newborn, crying to Heaven for vengeance against the murderers of his father. And this picture was prepared by Captain Andrew Lammie.

At eight of the clock the Queen entered the city, and she was lodged in the house of James Henderson of Fordell, being then the Provost's house, at the head of Peeble's Wynd, and called by the people the Black Turnpike. As the Queen entered the city the common people, who were gathered at the windows and on the stairs of the houses, railed against the Queen and uttered reproaches and despiteful language, which was a pity to hear, and the Queen was mightily overtaken with grief and anger; and she cried out to the people: "I am your born Princess and Queen. Let all honest subjects respect me as they ought to do and suffer me not to be abused."

Cessford and Drumlanrig the younger were set to guard the Queen, both of them cruel murderers, who ceased not to threaten her and to address her unbecomingly.

When they came to the house, she found the Lords there ready to sit at supper, and they asked her whether she would sup in their company, and the Queen said they had provided her with supper enough; and the Queen was locked up in a small upper chamber, which looked upon the street, and guards were posted upon the stairs and upon each door of the house; and some of the soldiers in their shamelessness would not leave her room, so that the Queen that night lay but an hour or two upon a bed without undressing.

The Queen was suffered to write two letters: one to the Laird of Grange and one to Secretary Lethington; and she asked to know the purpose of the Lords, and she offered to assist in the Parliament for the furtherance of justice; and she demanded to know wherefore she had been thus disrespectfully entreated, saying that where she was there she had neither bed nor furniture befitting her rank.

The Lords answered to her that, fearing she might do a mischief to herself, they had placed guards over her. And the next morning the bloody ensign was brought before her window once more, whereupon the Queen tore her dress from her person, and cried to the people in the street: "Good people, either satisfy your hatred and your cruelty by taking away my miserable life, or release me from the hands of such cruel tyrants." And the Queen espied the Secretary Lethington in the street, and she called out to him for the love of God to come to her; but the Secretary drew down his hat over his eyes and made as if he had heard nothing and seen nothing; whereat the people cried out at him and the guards removed the Queen from the window.

During all that day the Queen ate nothing but a piece of bread and drank but a little water; and her guards, Drumlanrig and Cessford, railed at her and spoke unbecomingly.

In the evening Secretary Lethington came to the Queen, and while she spoke to him he did not dare once to raise his eyes nor to look her in the face. The Queen asked him the cause of the ill-treatment she suffered, and what was yet to be, and she recalled to him all that she had done for him: how she had called him back from exile and supported him against the advice of the King and shielded him from his anger, and how she had saved his life when the Earl of Bothwell would have slain him. And he denied nothing. The Secretary said to the Queen that it was feared Her Majesty designed to thwart justice being done for the death of the late King: and that until proper investigation would be made, she must be held in ward: for the Council would never permit her to go back to the Earl of Bothwell, who, said he, deserved to be hanged, and against whom he spoke bitter words.

The Queen said to him: "You say the Duke of Orkney deserves to be hanged, but wherefore was he suffered to ride from Carberry Hill to Dunbar with not a man in pursuit?" For she divined that the Lords had privily admonished him speedily to withdraw himself for fear lest being taken he should reveal the whole complot: and that from his flight they might draw argument whereof to accuse the Queen for the murder of the King, and then seize on her person and entreat her ignominiously and with shame. And the Queen perceived the false pretexts the Lords were employing to carry out their evil designs upon her, by charging her with wishing to hinder justice being done for the murder they themselves planned and carried out, and she knew that there was nothing they feared so much as investigation. Wherefore the Queen told the Secretary she was ready to join with the Lords in the investigation of the murder. And as to the Earl of Bothwell, the Secretary knew better than she how the murder had been executed, he having been the adviser.

To the Secretary, who answered with slippery excuse, she spoke thus frankly: she told him she feared he and the Earl of Morton more than all hindered the enquiry into the murder, since it was they who had been guilty of planning it. The Earl of Bothwell had told her, as he bade her farewell, how he had acted by their persuasion and advice, and he had shown her the handwrites of the Lords to the bond. If she, the Queen, could be thus entreated because they suspected her of wishing to to thwart the punishment of the guilty, the Council could proceed with a greater certainty against himself and the Earl of Morton, who were the murderers in very deed. And the Queen told the Secretary that, if he would persist in this complot with the Lords, she would proclaim to the world what the Earl of Bothwell had told her of his doings.

The Secretary was greatly angered, and he said that if the Queen revealed what she knew she would drive him to even greater lengths than he had yet gone, in order to save his life, which, said he, "I hold dearer than all else in the world." This he rehearsed more than once.

For the present he must confer with the Lords, and the Queen must of her graciousness not summon him to her again; it did, he said, both herself and himself ill, for if his credit were shaken the Queen's life would be in jeopardy; for the Lords had often talked of putting her out of the way, and this he could prevent. So saying, the Secretary took his leave.

About nine of the clock in the evening the Earl of Morton came to the Queen and declared to her that Holyrood House had been chosen to be her place of abode, and thither she was bid to proceed. She was led on foot between the Earls of Atholl and Morton, with men-at-arms, while the women on the forestairs of the houses mocked her, and reviled her with ugly reproach. And the Queen was dressed in a very homely brown nightgown, and with her were Mary Seton and Mary, Lady Sempill. Thus they proceeded from the Black Turnpike to Holyrood House, while some cried: "Drown the witch, burn the whore, and let her suffer the fiery death," and showed her once more the bloody ensign; and others of the common people pitied her, and the Queen bemoaned her calamity and wept.

When the Queen reached Holyrood House supper had been prepared, and the Queen's Ladies were assembled to meet her; Madame de Briante, Marie Courcelles, Jane Kennedy, Mademoiselle Rallay, besides Lady Sempill and Mary Seton. Before supper was ended the Earl of Morton, who stood behind the Queen's chair, asked of an esquire of the stable whether the horses were ready, and bade the dishes to be removed and the Queen to make ready to mount: and the Queen asked whither they were to remove her in such haste, and the Earl of Morton spoke of a visit to the Prince, her son.

The Queen asked that some of her ladies and servitors should go with her, and they entreated that they might follow the Queen; but the entreaty was denied her and them, and none save two *femmes de chambre* went with the Queen, and there was much weeping and entreaty, but it was of no avail. Nor might the Queen take with her any clothes, save her nightdress, nor any linen.

It was ordered that the Queen should be transported to the fortalice of Lochleven, and Lord Ruthven and Lord Lindsay were to guard her; and of all the nobility none was more beastly. The Queen passed through Leith, which was full of soldiers; and the Queen was told by the way that the Hamiltons were riding to her rescue, and she lingered as much as she might; but the soldiers near her whipped her hackney, so that the rescuers overtook her not.

At the edge of the lake she was met by the Laird of Lochleven and his brothers, who conducted her to a small room upon the ground floor, with but the Laird's furniture; and the Queen's bed was not there.

CHAPTER VI

The day after the Queen was imprisoned in the fortalice of Lochleven the Lords took an inventory of the plate, jewels and other movables within the Palace of Holyrood House, and spared not to put hands on Her Majesty's cupboard, and melted the species and converted all into coin. And about the same time the Earl of Glencairn went into the Palace with his servants, and into the Queen's Chapel, and destroyed the altar, pulled down the pictures and tore into shreds chasuble, alb and stole, and altar frontals, some of which the Queen had worked with her own hands, and destroyed the illuminated missals.

And they took her wardrobe, from which she could not obtain one garment, nor even linen, until the return of the Earl of Moray, who bade his wife's tailor make the Queen a dress of violet cloth.

There were now but two *femmes de chambre* with the Queen: Marie Courcelles and Jane Kennedy; but presently her physician, Arnault, was suffered to go to her, and after him her Ladies, Mary Seton and others. Her guards within the Castle were the Lord Lindsay and the Lord Ruthven; the Laird of Lochleven and his mother, the Lady of Lochleven; the Lady Margaret Douglas, who aforetime, when Lady Margaret Erskine, was the mistress of King James V, and the mother of the Earl of Moray: and in the Castle were the Earl of Moray's half-brother, George Douglas, and an orphan (some said a son natural to Sir William Douglas, the eldest son of the Laird) named Willie Douglas, who was but sixteen years old, a page to the Laird; two children, a daughter and a niece of the Laird, as well as the Countess of Buchan, the betrothed wife of the Earl of Moray, whom he had forsaken for the daughter of the Earl Marischal; and he stripped her of her inheritance and confined her in this fortalice.

The Queen had not been long at Lochleven before she was visited by Sir Robert Melville, who came from England and delivered to the Queen a letter from the Queen of England to Sir Nicholas Throckmorton, wherein the Queen of England declared she had resolved to recover to the Queen her liberty, with the accord of her subjects; to procure a due punishment of the murder of her husband; and to have the royal Prince preserved from danger. But Sir Robert Melville was not permitted to talk with the Queen save in the presence of the Lords Lindsay and Ruthven and the Laird of Lochleven; and after eight days he came again and saw the Queen alone. Sir Robert Melville pressed the Queen to agree to a divorcement with the Earl of Bothwell, whereunto the Queen would in no wise consent: and he came yet a third time, bearing a letter from Sir Nicholas Throckmorton, summoning her to renounce the Earl of Bothwell and to divorce with him. But the Queen said she was likely to become by the Earl of Bothwell the mother of a child, whose honour would be stained by a divorcement, and sooner than cast a stain on her honour, and on that of her offspring, she would die.

But she told him she would not be loth for the Earl of Moray to be Regent, or to sanction a Council of the nobility, which should take the government from her hands.

The Queen sued to be moved to Stirling on account of her health, and so that she might see her son, saying that, if the Lords would not obey her as a Sovereign, they might yet call to mind that she was the mother of their Prince, and the daughter of the King of Scotland.

At Lochleven, those who guarded her, save Lord Lindsay, soon changed in their hearts from suspicion to worship. George Douglas was smitten with love for the Queen, but he kept silent; and Lord Ruthven threw himself at her feet at four of the clock in the morning, near her bed, and said he would set her free if she would love him. Whereat the Queen was wrathful, saying she was still his Sovereign and had given him no occasion for such infamous conduct, whereof she advertised the Lady of Lochleven; and the Lord Ruthven was sent from Lochleven for a while.

The Lords were now resolved to take advantage of what the Queen had said to Sir Robert Melville of her willingness to let her brother be Regent, and Lord Lindsay was sent with Sir Robert Melville, bearing with him, for her signature, three instruments to be signed by the Queen, containing her consent to have her son crowned and to relinquish the government of the realm, and to grant the Earl of Moray the regency during the minority of the Prince.

Before the Queen gave audience to the Lord Lindsay, Sir Robert Melville talked with her in private, and he entreated her to sign these documents, saying if she did not sign them her life would be in jeopardy, for her enemies would seek her life by every means, nor could her friends strike a blow for her until the Earl of Moray should return; nor need she be scrupulous to sign these instruments, for deeds extorted from her while in durance, and under the threat of death, were of no account. And the Earl of Atholl, in token of this advice, sent her a turquoise, which he had received from the Queen, and Secretary Lethington sent her a small golden egg, whereupon was pictured the fable of Aesop of the lion in a net gnawed by the mouse, and around it this device:

A chi basta l'animo, non mancano le forze.

273

And from the scabbard of his sword Sir Robert Melville took a letter from Sir Nicholas Throckmorton, telling the Queen that it was the Queen of England's advice that she should not provoke those who had her in their power by refusing this concession, and telling her that nothing she did in durance and under threat could be of any force hereafter when she was free; and he told the Queen that the Lords would bring her to public trial, and that they had handwrites of hers proving she had been privy to the murder of the King: but the Queen laughed him to scorn, saying that the only handwrites they knew were those that would prove their own guilt; nor would she promise aught, nor yield to his persuasion.

Thus upon the following afternoon, the twenty-fourth of July, the Lord Lindsay, in company with two notaries, came into the Queen's chamber; and the Queen was lying in bed, for she was sick, and the Lord Lindsay declared to her the mission wherewith he had been charged by the nobility: to summon her to sign away her Crown. And he bade her be pleased to read the instruments.

But the Queen, in despite of all she had heard from Sir Robert Melville, said nay, nor would she look at the instruments, nor listen to them.

When the Lord Lindsay perceived how the Queen was minded, he bade her rise from her bed, for he said he had charge to take her to another place, if need be; and several times she said nay, and several times the Lord Lindsay advised her to sign, saying that if she did not sign the instruments incontinent with her hand, he would sign them with her blood and seal them upon her heart, and throw her into the lake to feed fishes. Then, by threat and violence, bruising the Queen's arm with a gauntlet, he caused the instruments to be read by the two notaries, and the Queen to sign them, which she did: without reading the thing or heeding it as it was read, she signed the renunciation of the Crown.

And she protested that she signed the instruments against her own will and in opposition to her intent, and that the signature had been extorted by force and constraint. Therefore she would observe them no longer than she was in durance, and she called upon those who were present to bear witness thereunto.

Whereat the Lord Lindsay in anger said they would take care she should never have the power to revoke them.

The Queen was fearful after what the Lord Lindsay had said that the Lords were minded to remove her from Lochleven and to convey her to some unknown place; and she said she would rather be dragged by the hairs of her head than leave Lochleven of her own will.

And Sir Robert Melville, to whom the Queen spoke thus, told her that she would find no enemy in George Douglas, albeit Lord Ruthven had told her that of her enemies he was the bitterest; but this he did out of jealousy and because he divined that George Douglas loved the Queen in silence.

Soon after the Queen had signed these instruments the Prince was crowned at Stirling, and the oath was taken for him by the Earl of Morton and Lord Home; and upon that day the Laird of Lochleven bade the artillery of the house be discharged and bonfires to be lit; and he himself sang and danced in the garden. And when the Queen asked the cause of these rejoicings, the Laird entered her chamber and asked of her whether she would rejoice with them upon the coronation of her son, who was now King; and as for her, one might well say that "the Lord had put down the mighty from their seat". And the bystanders mocked the Queen, some in one fashion, some in another, taunting her and saying that she was reft of power and could no longer take vengeance upon them. Whereunto Her Majesty made answer that they had a King who would avenge her one day, and she prayed God that He would guard him and defend him against their wicked and damnable treasons; and she knew full well that if they had the means they would never suffer him to come to an age when he could show his displeasure thereunto.

And the Queen knelt down at the table and wept bitterly; and with her arms outstretched and uplifted she prayed to God thus: "O my God, Who seest the indignities that I suffer at the hands of those whom I have rewarded and exalted, seeing that I have always taken compassion upon the innocent and upon the afflicted, let it be Thy pleasure that before my death I may see my rebellious subjects brought to the same discomfiture, sorrow and desolation whereunto they have now brought me, and especially may it be Thy purpose before the year is ended that the Laird of Lochleven may be as sorrowful as I am now, and may he and his household be accursed."

And the Laird, hearing these words, was afraid, and he went from her chamber pensive.

When Lord Lindsay came back from Stirling to Lochleven the Queen was kept straitlier, and confined in a gloomy tower, and deprived of ink, paper and books, nor were her Ladies and attendants allowed to come to her; none save her two *femmes de chambre* and her physician. And the Queen fell sick, and Arnault, her physician, declared she had been poisoned: for she had violent pains in her body, which turned a deep yellow, and her heart beat weaker and slower day by day: but Arnault revived her with physic and with bleeding; and his skill, and the strength of her youth, for she was now but twenty-five, cast out the poison.

Presently news came that the Earl of Moray had come into Scotland from France; and he came with the Earls of Atholl, Morton and Lindsay to Lochleven. The Earl of Moray came riding upon one of the Queen's own hackneys, wherewith she was displeased and prayed it might break his neck.

The Earls came to Lochleven at supper-time, and they treated the Earl of Moray with honour, calling him "Grace", as if he were a King or a King's child; and the Earl of Moray entered instantly with Her Majesty in reproaches, and would not sup with her, nor would the give her the napkin, until the Queen said to him that aforetime he had not disdained to do it: and the Earl gave her such injurious language as was like to break her heart; and the injuries were such that they cut the thread of credit betwixt the Queen and him for ever.

· After supper the Earl of Moray walked in the garden with the Queen, asking first of the Lords leave for a private audience with the Queen, and saying to them, with a smile, that he would not betray them.

The Earl of Moray chided the Queen for her behaviour during his absence, which, even if she were innocent before God, was imprudent in the eyes of man. And he spoke of her marriage with the Earl of Bothwell, which he said was the cause wherefore people suspected her of being a consenting party to the murder of the King, saying it was not enough to avoid a fault, but the occasions of suspicion, for rumour was offtimes more potent than the truth.

The Queen said to him that she knew herself to be innocent in all that could be laid to her charge, and that she was ready to justify herself before her subjects, but was in no wise bound thereunto, seeing that she was their Queen; she feared neither the lying nor the slander of her enemies, for she knew that one day God, from whom she had concealed nothing, would make manifest her innocence and their false treasons. She had rather have spoken of her the evil which she had not done than have done evil which was never made manifest, for she had a greater regard for God than for man. Let him mind his duty towards God and unto his Queen, for not only was she his Queen, but she had been unto him more than a sister: now was the time for him to show his gratitude. Let him now repay to her somewhat of the debt which he owed.

The Earl of Moray asked advice of the Queen in the matter of the Regency, which he had been pressed to accept; but this, said he, he was loth to do, for, as she knew well, he shunned both greatness and ambition: yet the post must be filled; and maybe he, by filling it, might be of greater service to her. The Queen spoke to him frankly, and told him it became him neither for himself nor in regard to his duty towards herself, and she reminded him that her subjects had not been faithful to her whom they were bound to obey according to the laws of God and man, albeit she had neither oppressed nor wrung taxes from them; and if they were unfaithful to her lawful authority, they would not scruple to rebel against an authority that was unlawful; for he who keeps not faith where it is due will hardly keep it where it is not due: whereupon the Earl of Moray asked her who should be the fittest person to be Regent, naming her enemies one by one, the Queen not helping, in the hope she must at the end come to name him. And at last he was constrained to tell the Queen that he had already promised to accept the Regency and could not go against his promise.

On the day following, the Earl of Moray and the others took their leave, although the Queen entreated the Earl of Moray to remain with her for a day or two.

Before he left, the Earl of Moray caused the Laird of Lochleven and the Earl of Lindsay and Lord Ruthven to be summoned, and enjoined them to entreat the Queen with gentleness and allow her all the liberty that could be granted. And when the Earls of Morton and Atholl took their leave, the Queen said to them: "My Lords, you have experience of my severity, and of the end of it: I pray you also let me find that you have learned by me to make an end of yours, or at least that you can make it final."

Incontinent after his visits to the Queen, the Earl of Moray was made Regent of the kingdom and Sir Robert Melville visited the Queen, bearing her four ells of fine black silk; for the Queen was lacking in apparel and even in shoes: and she entreated him to send her a half-ell of incarnate satin and a half-ell of blue satin, some sewing gold and sewing silk: her doublets and skirts of satin, incarnate and black, and her skirt with the red doublet, and her maidens' clothes, for they were naked; and she asked him to send her some cambric and linen cloth, two pairs of sheets, some dry damask plums, a pair of shoes, and a dozen of raising needles and moulds.

Sir Robert Melville conveyed the memorial from the Queen to the keeper of her wardrobe, who delivered the three gowns into his hands and subscribed an acknowledgment. But the Earl of Moray came to Sir Robert Melville's house to see what clothes he had which were the Queen's, and among them was a knot of pearls, which he forbade Sir Robert to deliver; but a few days later they were entrusted to George Douglas to take to the Queen; but the three gowns were not sent to her until the following year, when she was at Bolton Castle, at the bidding of the Queen of England; but Sir Robert Melville sent her some Holland linen coverchiefs and handkerchiefs, and the gold and silver thread with raising needles and moulds, so that the Queen was enabled to work a tapestry.

In the Parliament, which met in the month of December, the Earl of Bothwell was forfaulted for treason and lese-majesty, and the herald, in obedience to the behest of Parliament, came in his barge to Lochleven and proclaimed the Earl of Bothwell, who had fled to the Orkneys and then put to sea, an outlaw for the high and horrible act of having devised the murder of King Henry and for having put violent hands upon the person of the Queen; for according to law, if a Peer of Parliament were put to the horns, the outlawry, together with the reasons thereof, must be proclaimed at any place where the Sovereign abided. The Queen, when she saw the herald and heard his fanfare, said she wondered the law were at pains to make sure of the sanction from an authority which they had done so much to make null.

During the winter-time the miseries of the Queen increased, but owing to the faithfulness of her servant, John Beton, without, and the services of George Douglas within, she sent messages to the world without, and received answers from friends, both those in Scotland and those in France. And the

Queen wrote to the Queen-Mother in France and entreated her to take pity on her, saying if she would send never so few troops, great numbers of her subjects would rise to join them: but they durst do nothing of themselves. And she declared unto her that the miseries she endured were more than she once believed it was in the power of human sufferance to sustain and live.

In the month of February the Queen fell sick...

[Here follows a page deleted in the MS.]

As soon as the Queen was recovered from her sickness she began to devise plans for escaping from the fortalice. The Lady of Lochleven, whose duty it was to watch the Queen, had at first entreated the Queen harshly, being ever mindful of the stain upon her own honour brought about by King James, the Queen's father, whom, the Lady of Lochleven would boast, she was the lawful wife to, albeit all knew this to be false. But the Queen conquered her enmity, so that even if she would not be party to a plan of escape, fearing ruin, she would be like to be pleased were it done in despite of her.

Moreover, she saw that her son, George Douglas, loved the Queen, and she dreamt of a royal match for him, for she loved him greatly.

George Douglas loved the Queen with a worship such as none had given her since M. d'Anville in France in the olden times, and he was resolved to live and to die for her: and the Queen looked upon him with favour, for he was comely and gallant.

When the Lords had shamefully entreated the Queen by forcing her to sign the instruments, he had wept tears, and he desired nothing so much as to see her set free: yet he had scruples about deceiving his brother; and at first it was devised to seize and man the great boat which belonged to the Laird, and with the help of those from without and those from within to assault the Castle and to carry off the Queen; but George Douglas spoke thereof to Will Drysdale, an officer in the fortalice, and he in his turn hinted thereof to the Laird, who laid up the great boat. Divers other plans were debated, and the Earl of Moray, hearing rumours thereof, came to Lochleven in pomp, and he spoke to the Queen discourteously and without shame; and when the Queen declared to him she should be discharged of the crimes whereof she was accused, and when she perceived his hateful obduracy that he was resolved to proceed as her mortal and sworn foe, she could no longer bear such monstrous ingratitude, and she bade him a lasting farewell, and said she would sooner live for ever in durance than that he should be the means of her freedom; and she hoped that God, the avenger of the oppressed, would deliver her to his lasting shame, discomfiture and ruin. Then, touching his hand, she protested in the presence of the Lords that one day he would repent, cost what it might, and so she left him. And before leaving the fortalice the Earl of Moray ordered George Douglas to leave Lochleven on pain of being hanged; and from that moment George Douglas threw aside all scruple and was determined to abet the escape of the Queen with all his might, nor to rest until she was delivered from durance.

When the Earl of Moray went from Lochleven, George Douglas followed him with a message regarding the Queen's business, and the Earl of Moray suffered him to carry an answer back, but sent a servant to Lochleven forbidding the Laird to receive his brother; but George Douglas discovered what the Earl of Moray had done, and forestalled his messenger and reached Lochleven and bade farewell to the Queen, advising her of the best means of escape, and telling her that through the man who had charge of boats upon the lake, she could learn what he and the other Lords of her side were doing upon her behalf; for Lord Seton and other Lords had sworn to forget their feuds and to serve the Queen. And George Douglas swore to her eternal fidelity, and carried a letter from her to Lord Seton, which she had written with the coal in her chimney, being reft of all ink. And as George Douglas was leaving he encountered his brother, the Laird, who forbade him ever again to enter the house or to come near it.

The Lady of Lochleven was much troubled, for she dearly loved her son George; but she dreaded ruin for the Laird, and thus she feigned sternness towards the Queen.

Divers plans of escape were devised, and some of them miscarried; but one of them came near to succeeding. The laundress was wont to come into the Queen early, and the Queen exchanged clothes with her, and, taking the laundress' fardel, she passed out with the muffler over her face and entered the boat to cross the lake; when they were midway in the lake one of the rowers said: "Let us see what manner of dame this is," and would have pulled down her muffler; and the Queen, to defend herself, put up her hands, which were very fair and white, whereupon the rowers became suspicious; and the Queen, undismayed, charged them, upon danger of their lives, to row to the shore; but they durst not, and they rowed her back to the fortalice, promising the Queen to keep the matter a secret, which they did. Albeit they said nothing, William Douglas came under suspicion, and the Laird drove him from the house for a while; and the Laird wrote to George Douglas, forbidding him to come near the Castle. Taking advantage of the expulsion of William Douglas, George came often to the village on the shore of the lake and debated with Willie Douglas about the means of escape; and George Douglas pretended that he was about to sail for France, and asked letters of the Queen, and the Laird and Lady of Lochleven were greatly troubled.

Towards the end of April, Willie Douglas, through the intercession of the Lady of Lochleven's daughter, was recalled into the house, and the plan of escape was devised, which was to come about of the second day of May. At first it was purposed that the Queen should leap from a wall in the garden, seven or eight feet high; but the Queen, who was fearful of adventuring herself without trial, two or three days beforehand pretended to be playing at follow-my-leader with two of her Ladies, and having reached a part of the garden where there was a wall equal in height to that she must needs leap in order to escape, one of the Ladies having leapt the wall, the Queen, who was on the top of the wall, to leap after Mary Seton, feared to injure herself; but, seeing she could not go back, she forced herself to leap, and, albeit she was caught in midfall by one of the gentlemen, she bruised one of her ankles, which were delicate: and fearing lest she should injure herself at the wall appointed for the escape, so that she would not be able to be moved, she warned those of her party who were to await her on the other side of the lake that, were she to be of a sudden injured, one of her ladies would make a sign to them from her chamber window, telling them to retire. And Willie Douglas, seeing that the Queen misliked this plan of leaping from the wall, since she feared to be kept back by injury, set himself to devise another way. On Sunday, the second of May, he called the household to a breakfast to be given in that part of the house furthest removed from the gate, and at the feast Willie Douglas dubbed himself the Abbot of Unreason, and bade the Queen promise to follow him wherever he went; thus the Queen and the Laird remained in this part of the house all day, and this furthered his scheme. In the afternoon the Queen retired to rest, and while lying upon her bed she heard a woman of the village tell the Lady of Lochleven that a great troop of men on horseback had passed through the village, Lord Seton being with them, on their way to a Law Day; and that George Douglas was in the village, having come to take leave of his mother before sailing for France. And the Lady of Lochleven went to visit her son, and persuaded him to return and to abide with the Earl of Moray; and, as George Douglas took leave of his mother, he sent to the Queen, by a maid of the household, Marie Courcelles, a pear-shaped pearl, which the Queen wore in her ear, saying it had been found by a boatman, who wished to sell it to him, and that he, having recognized it as his property, sent it to Her Majesty. This was the signal that all was ready.

An hour before supper-time the Queen retired to her room and put on a red kirtle belonging to Mary Seton, she being the highest of her Ladies, and over it she covered herself with one of her own mantles. Then, after walking in the garden with the Lady of Lochleven, whence she could see men passing on the further shore, the Queen ordered supper to be served; and when it was finished, the Laird, who was wont to wait upon Her Majesty at table, went to sup with the Lady of Lochleven in the great hall upon the ground floor. Drysdale, the officer who had chief charge of the establishment, and who guarded the Queen in her room, went out with the Laird and played with him at hand tennis.

In order to free herself from the daughter and niece of Lady Lochleven, the Queen retired to Arnault's room, which was above her chamber, to say a prayer. In this room she left her mantle and put on a hood, such as are worn by the country woman, and bade Jane Kennedy, who was to accompany her, dress herself in the same fashion. Mary Seton remained in the Queen's chamber, and the other *femme de chambre*, Marie Courcelles, stayed with the two young children to amuse them.

While the Laird was at supper Willie Douglas, as he was changing the Laird's plate, dropped his napkin over the keys, and wrapping them up in the cloth, took them away artfully; and as he came out of the door he gave the sign by whistling to Jane Kennedy, who was to accompany Her Majesty, and who was watching at the window. The Queen, hearing the sign, came down incontinent, and as she came to the foot of the stairs she saw several of the servitors of the household passing through the court, and she stood for a while near the door of the stairs; at last, in sight of them all, she crossed the court-yard, and, having gone out by the great gate, Willie Douglas locked it with the key, and the Queen and Jane Kennedy stood for a while against the wall, fearing they should be seen from the windows of the house; and at last they got into the skiff, where the Queen laid herself down under the rower's seat to escape notice or a cannon shot, should one be fired; and when they were midway between the island and the shore Willie Douglas threw the keys of the fortalice into the loch, and the Queen came from her hiding place and waved her veil, which was white with a red-and-gold border; and the watcher on the shore, one of George Douglas' servants, made sign to those in the village, the leader of whom was John Beton, and Her Majesty landed and was met and welcomed by George Douglas and by John Beton, who had broken into the Laird's stables and taken some of his swiftest horses.

The Queen left Jane Kennedy behind her, with directions to follow her incontinent, as soon as she could have an outfit. Two miles further on she met with Lord Seton and the Laird of Riccarton, and, accompanied by these she crossed the arm of the sea, about four miles from Lochleven, in an open fishing-boat, and landed above the town of South Queensferry, where she was met by Lord Claude Hamilton, son of the Duke of Châtelherault, first of the blood royal of Scotland, at the head of fifty armed cavaliers. And the Queen was conducted by Lord Seton to his Castle of Niddry, which was reached about midnight, and there she halted for the night. Here she rested but two hours; at dawn she was roused by the pipes and bugles of her subjects, and that day she was led by Lord Seton in royal fashion to Hamilton Castle, where she was welcomed by Archbishop Hamilton, and the nobility who were true in heart; among whom were the families of Livingstone, Fleming, Campbell, Bruce, Lord Herries, Lord Lochinvar and many others.

The Earl of Huntly and Lord Ogilvy were coming out of the north to the aid of the Queen; but they were a great way off, and the rivers were in flood, and they could not reach Her Majesty in time.

At Hamilton Castle she was Queen but for ten days, for on the eleventh day was fought a battle; and during those days the Lords, who were good in heart, entreated her royally and with great welcome and festal cheer, drinking to her health and to the prosperity of herself and of the realm, and swearing they would lay down their lives on her behalf.

One evening at the end of supper she brought the Nobles a dish which she said she had prepared with her own hands, and when she lifted the dish-cover on the dish there was a glittering pair of spurs, whereat the Lords burst into loud acclaim.

The Queen was advised to pass to Dumbarton Castle, and there await safe from her enemies until a better fortune; but the Regent, albeit he was first minded to fall back to Stirling, seeing that the Queen had mustered six thousand soldiers and he had but three thousand, changed his mind, being a crafty captain, as the Queen knew full well; and as the Queen had begun to retire to Dumbarton he encamped himself in a village called Langside, which the Queen needs must pass; and this the Regent was counselled to do by one of the Queen's party who had ever been a man with two faces: for the night before, having come to the Queen to betray the Earl of Moray, the next day, being privy to her plans, he deserted her; and the night before the battle this traitor, Lord Boyd, who, like Judas, followed to have the full bag, wrote to the Earl of Moray and declared to him that the Queen designed to retire to the Castle of Dumbarton till she had assembled all her forces.

The Regent incontinent sent the Laird of Grange with a footman to every horseman to ride to the head of Langside Hill; and the Laird set the footmen with their culverins at the head of a strait lane, where there were cottages and farmyards of advantage, to lie in ambush the way the Queen's soldiers must come, the Regent following with the main forces. The battle began with a skirmish between the harquebusiers; and the Queen's vanguard was led by the Hamiltons, divers of whose soldiers were killed by those of the Laird waiting in ambush;

and Lord Claude Hamilton showed courage and sustained the fight until the Laird of Grange, with fresh men, struck him in his flank and in his rear, and, seeing himself assailed by the whole force of his enemies, he was forced incontinent to give place and turn back; and the rest of the army was put to flight. And in the combat 57 gentlemen were slain, mostly of the name of Hamilton, and 27 prisoners were taken.

The Queen had halted, in company with her Ladies, upon a hill close at hand, and, perceiving the loss of the battle, she lost all hope and all courage, which she had never done before and which she never did thereafter; and she rode away from the field in company with Lord Herries, Lord Livingstone, George Douglas and Willie Douglas. She rode all night, and never drew bridle till she came to Sanquhar. She drew rein at Queenshill, at the head of the vale, where she drank from a burn, and she crossed the Dee at Tongland by the wooden bridge, which Lord Herries destroyed to delay her pursuers. The while he did this, the Queen drank a cup of sour milk in the house of a poor man. Thence Lord Herries took her to his house in Kirkgunzeon, and thence to Terregles, near Dumfries, where the Queen rested.

The Queen was twenty-four hours without food or drink, and endured famine, cold, heat and flight, not knowing whither, riding ninety-two miles across the country without stopping or alighting; she slept upon the ground, and ate oatmeal without bread, and was three nights like the owls, without a female to aid her.

After resting a day the Queen went thence to Dundrennan Abbey; but she slept not at the abbey, for the monks feared the vengeance of the Regent, but at Hazlefield; and at Dundrennan she held her last Council.

Some pressed her to remain in her present safety, or to seek a strong fortalice in the neighbourhood; and others pressed her to retire to France. But the Queen said she could not remain in safety in any part of her realm, not knowing whom to trust; nor would she go to France as a fugitive; but she said she would seek the protection of her good sister the Queen of England, to whom already, before the battle, she had sent one of her gentlemen servitors, carrying with him a diamond ring, in the shape of a rock, which the Queen of England had sent her aforetime in return for a diamond heart. And she recalled to the Queen of England the promise which her good sister had made to her when she sent the ring – that whensoever, howso-oft, the Queen should be in need of her sister's aid, she had but to send this ring as a token, and the Queen of England would come to the aid of her sister in person, or else send her assistance.

Thus, upon Sunday morning of the nineteenth day of May, the Queen embarked in a small fishing-boat in the bay of the Abbey Burnfoot, with twenty persons; whereupon, when she was already out to sea and in full sail for England, the Queen began to repent her, and said she was minded to sail for France; but, strive as the boatmen might, the wind and the tide willed otherwise, and the Queen was driven unwilling into a creek in Cumberland called Workington, where she disembarked before nightfall. And the Queen, as she passed from the boat, fell to the ground, which some said was a favourable omen; but others were of another mind.

REPORT SENT BY JANE KENNEDY TO MARY SETON

Fotheringay: February 8/19, 1587

...The Earl of Shrewsbury and the Earl of Kent, the High Sheriff of Northamptonshire and the Queen's other Commissioners, arrived at the Castle two or three hours before midday, and demanded audience in the afternoon. And the Queen, being indisposed, was preparing to go to bed; but they answering that it was a matter which would brook no delay, the Queen called for her mantle, and her Ladies made her ready, and she sat herself at the foot of her bed at her sandalwood sewing-table, with her Ladies and Bourgoigne in attendance. And when it was told to the Queen that Mr Beale was in the ante-room, she bade the Ladies open the chamber door, and the two Earls were introduced by Paulet and Drury, and, followed by Mr Beale, they entered and remained uncovered. Thereupon, in the presence of Paulet and Drury, Mr Beale, after first showing to the Queen a parchment, to which was appended the Great Seal of England in yellow wax, he began to read to the Queen the Commission, that the next day in the morning they would proceed to the execution, admonishing her to be ready between seven and eight of the clock. The Queen, hearing that with an unchanged countenance, made the sign of the Cross, and said: "I thank you for such welcome news. You will do me

289

a great good in withdrawing me from this world, out of which I am very glad to go, on account of the miseries I see in it, and of being myself in continual affliction. I am of no good and no use to anyone. I have looked to this, and have expected it day by day for eighteen years. I never thought that my sister, the Queen of England, would have consented to my death, seeing I am not a subject to your law; but since her pleasure is such, death to me shall be most welcome, and surely that soul were not worthy of the eternal joys of heaven, whose body cannot endure one stroke of a headsman." And, laying her hand upon an English New Testament which lay upon the table by her, she said most solemnly: "I have never either desired the death of the Queen or endeavoured to bring it about, or that of any other person."

The Earl of Kent objected that it was a Catholic Bible, the Papist version, and that therefore the oath was of no avail; whereat the Queen replied: "If I swear on the Book which I believe to be the true version, will not your Lordship believe my oath more than if I were to swear upon a translation in which I do not believe?" She entreated the Commissioners to grant her a little space and leisure that she might make her will and give order for her affairs, and the Earl of Shrewsbury answered her: "No, no, Madam, you must die. Make you ready between seven and eight of the clock in the morning. We will not prolong one minute for your pleasure." And to the Earl of Kent, who was desirous of giving her spirit constancy to affront this death, and who urged her to confess her faults and to embrace the true religion, she answered that she had no need of solace as coming from him, but she desired of him if he would minister comfort to her spirit to let her have conference with her almoner, so that she might receive the Sacrament of Confession, which would be a favour that would surpass any other; and as for her body, she did not believe them to be so inhuman to deny her the right of sepulture; and she asked to be allowed to see Melville, her steward, from whom she had been reft for two weeks. They denied her her Confessor, and offered her the Dean of Peterborough, one of the most learned in Europe, to comfort her, from whom she might learn regarding her salvation and the mysteries of the true religion. She had, they said, remained in that in which she had been instructed in her youth, for want of someone to show her the truth; and now that she had but a few hours to remain in this world she must think of her conscience and recognize the true religion, and not remain longer in these follies and abominations of Popery. And the Queen said: "I have not only heard or read the words of the most learned men of the Catholic religion, but also of the Protestant religion. I have spoken with them and heard them preach, but I have been unable to find anything in them which would turn me from my first belief. Having lived till now in a true Faith, this is not the time to change, but, on the contrary, it is the very moment when it is most needful that I should remain firm and constant, as I intend to do. Rather than be unfaithful to it, I would wish to lose ten thousand lives, if I had as many. For my consolation I beg you to let me see my own priest, so that he may help me to prepare the better for death. I wish for no other."

Whereupon the Earl of Kent said to her: "It is our duty to prevent such abominations, which offend God." And he pressed her to see the Dean.

And the Queen replied: "I will do no such thing. I have nothing to do with him, and I neither wish to see him nor to listen to him. It surprises me that at the end, when I have most need of my priest, they refuse him to me; I had asked to have him especially to assist me at my last end. The Queen of England had granted my request, and had allowed him to come to me; and since then they have taken him from me, and prevented him coming at the most necessary time."

Thereupon the Earl of Kent said to her: "Your life will be the death, and your death the life of our religion." And the Queen said: "I was far from thinking myself worthy of such a death, and I humbly receive it as a token. I must trust in the mercy of God to excuse the want of such rites as His Holy Church commandeth."

The Earls now rose to depart, and the Queen asked whether the Queen of England had sent any answer to her last letter; and the Earls said none. And she asked whether the Queen would allow her to dispose of such little means as they had left her for the discharging of her conscience towards her poor servants; and Sir Amyas Paulet said her furniture would be granted according to her disposition. And she enquired whether her son were well, and how he took her treatment; and, lastly, whether her Secretaries were alive or dead. And Drury said they were both of them alive, but that Nau was in close prison. And Bourgoigne pleaded with the Earls, if they were not touched with compassion for this noble Princess, to have at least pity on her faithful servants, who would be rendered destitute if the Queen were deprived of the means of providing for them, and for the sake of services he had rendered them and others of their family in time of sickness to grant a little respite. And the Queen said once more: "I have not yet made my will." And the Earl of Shrewsbury answered: "I have no power to prolong the time."

The Earls retired themselves from her presence, and the Queen's servants wept. And the Queen said to Jane Kennedy: "Up, Jane Kennedy. Leave weeping and be doing, for the time is short. Did I not tell you, my children, that it would come to this? Blessed be God that it has come, and fear and sorrow are at an end. Weep not, neither lament, for it will avail nothing, but rejoice rather that you see me so near the end of my long trouble and afflictions. Let each one be patient, and leave us here to pray to God."

The men retired themselves, and the Queen continued for some time in prayer with her Ladies.

Then she set herself to count her money, and, after dividing it into several parts in the little purses, put in each a slip of paper on which the name of each servant was written in her own hand. She then called in for supper, and supped very temperately; and as her servants, both men and women, continued to mourn, she comforted them and bade them to wipe their eyes, and rather to rejoice with her that she was now to depart from this gulf of miseries: and, turning to Bourgoigne, she said: "Have you not observed how powerful and great the truth is? For the common report is I am to die for conspiring the Queen of England's death; but the Earl of Kent told me notwithstanding even now that the fear they have of my religion is the cause of my death. Now this is no criminal act committed against the Queen of England, but the fear they had conceived of me which has brought about this slaughter upon me." And when supper was almost ended she drank to her servants, who in order, one by one upon their knees, took her pledge, mingling their tears with the wine, and craving pardon of her whereinsoever they had been negligent, and so did she likewise of them. After supper she sent for all her household, and, seated in her armchair, an inventory of her furniture and jewels in her hand, she examined the contents of her wardrobe and set down the name of such to whom she bequeathed anything, to everyone their share. And she distributed among her Ladies all that was left to her – rings, carcanets and ribbons, telling them that it was with sore regret that this was all wherewithal she had to recompense them. About nine of the clock she wrote to her almoner, praying him watch and pray this one night with her and for her, and asking his best advice what might be her best direction in her prayers this long night; and, after she had written her will, she finished a letter to the King of France, which she had begun on the previous day, all but the end and the subscription, telling him that she was to die on the morrow, and recommending her servants to his care. When she had finished, the night was already far spent. Her servants washed her feet, and she said she would take some rest; and she bade Jane Kennedy, her reader, read according to her custom from her Book of Hours about some saint who had been a great sinner. And when Jane Kennedy came to the penitent thief upon the Cross, the Queen bade her read of that example, saying: "In truth he was a great sinner, but not so great as I have been." And the Queen bade Jane Kennedy bring her a fair linen *Corpus Christi* cloth, which she needed for the morrow. Thereupon her eyes closed, yet her servants who sat round the bed for the last time thought that she slept not, albeit her eyes were closed, and her face was tranquil, and she seemed to be laughing with the angels. And from without came a noise of knocking and hammering, for they were making ready the scaffold.

When the night was spent and the day come, at six of the clock the Queen told her ladies she had but two hours to live, and bade them dress her as for a festival. And she put on her gown of black satin pointed, with the train and long sleeves, with its trimmings of acorn buttons of jet and pearl, and short sleeves of black satin cut out with a pair of sleeves of velvet; her kirtle of figured black satin, her petticoat upper body unlaced in the back of crimson satin, and her petticoat skirt of crimson velvet, her shoes of Spanish leather, the rough side outward; her green silk garters; her nether stockings of worsted-coloured watchet, clocked with silver, and a jersey hose. On her head she had a dressing of lawn; a pomander, chain and *Agnus Dei* about her neck, and a pair of beads at her girdle, with a golden cross at the end of them; and a great veil of white lawn fastened to her cowl, bowed out with wire and edged round about with bone lace, which hung from her head to her feet. As she was being dressed she said to her servants: "I had rather have left you this apparel than mine of yesterday, were it not that I must go to death more honourably. Here is a fair handkerchief which I have kept back also, and which shall be wherewith to veil my eyes when I come thither. And this I give to you," she said, speaking to Jane Kennedy, "for I would receive this last service from you." Whereupon she retired into

294

her private oratory, where she received from her own hands a Consecrated Host which the Pope had sent to her to use, should the necessity come about. And when she had ended her prayers, she finished her letter to the King of France. And, coming back into her bedchamber, she ordered her household to assemble. She seated herself by the fire, and Bourgoigne read her will aloud, after which she signed it and gave it to him to deliver to the Duke of Guise. Then, sending for the casket containing her money, she distributed the purses she had prepared on the evening before, and put aside seven hundred *écus* for the poor. When all was arranged, she spoke with her Ladies, and bade them farewell, consoling them and saying that the greatness of this world was as nothing, and that she should serve as an example thereof to all upon earth, from the mightiest unto the most humble; for, having been Queen of France and of Scotland, the one by birth and the other by marriage, after having been tossed about in honour and greatness, in triumph and vexation, now enjoying the one, now suffering the other, she was to be put into the hands of the headsman, albeit innocent; and this was nevertheless her solace, that the most capital charge against her was that she was to die for the Catholic religion, which she would never abandon until her latest breath, since she had been baptized in it. And she asked for naught else, not for any fame after her death, except that they should publish throughout France that she had remained constant until the end. And albeit she knew they would suffer heartbreak to see her upon the scaffold, she wished them to be witnesses of her death, knowing well she could have none more faithful to testify truly on what had come to pass.

And, going into her oratory, she remained there a long while at prayer, surrounded by her servants, who prayed and wept. And Bourgoigne, marking her paleness, and fearing for her strength, brought her a little wine and a piece of toasted bread, and besought her to partake thereof. And there were present

Jane Kennedy, Elizabeth Curle, Gillies Mowbray, Renée Rallay, Marie Paiges and Susan Korkady; and of the men Bourgoigne, Pierre Gourion, surgeon; Jacques Gervais, apothecary; Didier, butler; Hannibal Stouvart, *valet de chambre*; John Landor, the pantler; and Martin Huet, equerry of the kitchen. And, having said good-bye to her servants, she knelt down. They all knelt down and prayed with her for the last time. When the clock had struck eight there came a knocking at the door, and the High Sheriff struck against it with his wand. Being told that Her Majesty was at prayer, he went back and came again in a little while with the Earls. At the second knock the servitor who had charge of the door opened it, and the Sheriff entered, having his white staff in his hand, and said: "Behold, I am come"; and the Queen said to him: "Yes, let us go." And the Queen, Melville minding her thereof, took from the altar the ivory Crucifix and gave it to Hannibal Stouvart to carry before her ere she passed the threshold. And her servants, who now held her by the arms, were dismayed, and said to her they would serve her in all things, and even, if permitted, die with her, yet would they not convey her even to her death. And Sir Amyas Paulet lent two of his serving-men to lead her to the place of execution. For through long sicknesses and daily grievances she was brought so low that she was not able to go by herself. Then, supported by two of Paulet's soldiers, she passed to the door of the chamber, where her followers were stopped; and these entreated with tears that the Queen should not be reft of them, but in vain. And, taking the Crucifix from Hannibal, the Queen bade farewell to her servants, and they took leave of her with cries and lamentations, kissing her hands, some her feet, some her dress, while she, embracing them, was taken away alone. Then she descended the great staircase, where on the first landing the Earls awaited her; and at the foot of the staircase was Melville, who, when he saw the Queen, fell upon his knees, and uttered these words with tears: "Madam, it will be the sorrowfullest message that ever I carried when I shall report that my Queen and my dear Mistress is dead." And to him she said: "Weep not, for you shall shortly see Mary Stuart at the end of all her sorrows. You shall report that I died true and constant in my religion and firm in my love to Scotland and France. God forgive them who have thirsted after my blood as the hart doth for the water-brook. Recommend me to my dearest and most sweet son. Tell him for certainty I never did or attempted anything prejudicial to the kingdom of Scotland. Counsel him to entertain amity with the Queen of England, and be you his true and trusty servant." Whereat she made the sign of the Cross, as if to bless her son. The tears flowed from her eyes, and she repeated again and again: "Adieu, adieu, Melville!" who wept all the while no less lamentably. Then, turning towards the Earls, she entreated them that her servants might be gently used, and enjoy the things she had given them by her will, and might be permitted to be with her at her death. Whereat the Earl of Kent answered her: "That which you have desired cannot conveniently be granted, for it were to be feared lest some of them, with speeches and other behaviour, would be grievous to your Grace; also they would not stick to put some superstitious trumpery into practice, if it were but dipping their handkerchiefs in your Grace's blood." And the Queen said to him: "Fear you not, Sir. The poor wretches desire nothing but to take their last leave of me. I know Her Majesty hath not given you such strait commission but that you might grant me a far greater courtesy than this, even if I were a woman of far meaner calling. And I know my sister, the Queen of England, would not deny me in so small a request; for, for the honour of my sex, my servants should be in presence." And as the Queen uttered these words she wept the first tears since the reading, and to the Earls, whom she perceived to consent as for the men, but to be obdurate as for the women, the Queen said: "I am the nearest of her parentage and consanguinity, grandchild to Henry VII, Dowager of France, and anointed Queen of Scotland." Which, when she had said, and turned her about, it was granted to her to have two of her women and four of her menservants as she would nominate. Then she named Sir Andrew Melville, Bourgoigne, Gourion and Gervais; Jane Kennedy and Elizabeth Curle. And Melville carried up her train. Then, the two Earls and the Sheriff of the Shire going before, she passed out of the entry into the great parlour, in which was a great fire; and at the upper end whereof the scaffold was set up, twelve foot square and two foot high, spread over with black cotton, towards which she walked, with the like majesty and grace as if she were entering into the ballroom where aforetime she had been seen to advance in excellent wise; neither changed she her countenance then. The Sheriff of the Shire going before, she came to the scaffold, upon which was a chair, and a cushion, and the block, all covered with black. And the scaffold was surrounded on three sides by a rail, made low, and at the fourth side were two steps. Beside the block stood the two headsmen, both in long black velvet gowns with white aprons, and wearing black masks. And one headsman bore a large axe mounted with a short handle, like those with which they cut wood. And round the scaffold were a guard, men of Huntingdon, and in the parlour a crowd of onlookers. And when the Queen reached the threshold of the parlour and perceived the scaffold, she lifted the Crucifix which she carried high above her head, and advanced, in gesture, carriage and demeanour princely and majestic; unchanged and cheerful in countenance. And arrived at the scaffold, she mounted nimbly, Sir Amyas Paulet assisting, and, being come up, she seated herself and rested awhile; and, as soon as silence was commanded, Beale read the warrant, to which she listened attentively, as though it had been some other thing, and blessed herself when it was ended; whereat there was a shout of "God save the Queen!" and the Queen, looking at her Crucifix, was heard to say: *Judica me, Deus, et discerne causam meam.* "And the Earl of Shrewsbury, turning to her, said: "Madam, you hear what we are commanded to do." And the Queen said: "Do your duty." And she blessed herself once more, and looked at the assembly with a joyous countenance, her beauty more apparent than ever before, a bright colour in her face as aforetime in France. She entreated the Earls to have her almoner to come to her to comfort her in her God, which was refused. Then Doctor Fletcher, Dean of Peterborough, made a large discourse of her life past and present, and of the life to come. Twice she interrupted him, entreating him not to importune her, protesting that she was settled and resolved in the ancient Catholic religion, and ready to shed her blood for the same. Then the Lords, saying they would pray for her, she answered to them: "If ye will pray for me, my Lords, I will thank you; but to join prayer with you I will not: for to communicate in prayer with them which are of a different religion were a scandal and a great sin."

The Earls bade the Dean say on according to his pleasure, and the Queen, falling on her knees and holding the Crucifix betwixt her hands, prayed in Latin with her own people from the office of Our Blessed Lady. At the end of Mr Dean's prayer she prayed in English, for the afflicted Church, and for the Queen's Majesty, beseeching God to take His wrath from this land, and protesting, as she held up and kissed the Crucifix, that she hoped to be saved by and in the blood of Christ, at the foot of whose Cross she would shed her blood. Then the Earl of Kent interrupted her, saying: "Madam, settle Christ Jesus in your heart, and leave those trumperies." To whom she replied that it was to little purpose to carry such an object in her hand if the heart were not touched inwardly with remembrance of His bitter death and passion that died upon the Cross. "I think it," said she, "a thing most fitting for every true Christian to have it put them in remembrance of their redemption purchased by Christ, but especially they at that time when death threatens." And in the end of prayer she called upon the holy company of Saints in heaven to make intercession for her to Jesus Christ, and so kissed the Crucifix, and, crossing of herself, said these words: "Even as Thy arms, O Jesus, were spread here upon the Cross, so receive me into Thy arms of mercy and forgive me all my sins." Then the executioners, kneeling, desired her to forgive them her death, whom she forgave, saying: "I forgive you with all my heart, for now I hope you shall make an end of all my troubles."

And the headsman offered to unpin her; but she withdrew with a pretty reluctance, saying: "I have never had such grooms of the chamber to make me unready, nor put off my clothes before such a company."

She wore about her neck a gold pomander, chain and beads and *Agnus Dei*, which she would have given to Jane Kennedy; but the headsman took it and hid it in his shoe. And the Queen said to the headsman: "Let her have it; she will give you more than its value." And the headsman replied: "It is my perquisite."

Then, with her two women helping of her, she took away her coif and her ornaments, and they took off her upper garment, crying and lamenting aloud. And she, with joy rather than with sorrow, helped to make ready herself, and, being stripped of all apparel save her petticoat and kirtle, she stood up all incarnate. And her servitors beheld her with great lamentation, and cried, and crossed themselves, and wept. And she, turning to them, embraced them, saying: "*Ne criez pas, j'ay promis pour vous.*" Likewise she turned herself to Melville and to her other servants, who were piteously weeping, and she signed them with the sign of the Cross, and smilingly bade them all adieu. And Jane Kennedy took the fair linen cloth which the Queen had given her, and wrapped up the corner ways, and kissed it, and bound it fast to her head. Then the two women departed from the Queen, and she spoke aloud this psalm in Latin: "*In te domine confido, non confundar in eternum*". Then, groping for the block, she laid down her head, putting her chin on the block with both her hands, which the headsman espied and withdrew, which holding there still had been cut off. Then, lying upon the block mostly quietly, she stretched forth her arms and her body, many times ingeminating these words: "Lord, into thine hands I commend my spirit."

And the while one of the headsmen held her hands slightly, the other headsman struck awry, wounding her on the side of the skull, she making very small noise or none at all, and not stirring; and at the third blow the headsman cut off her head, and lifted up her head to the view of all, crying: "God save the Queen!" And Mr Dean said with a loud voice: "So perish all the Queen's enemies." And her dressing of lawn falling from her head, it appeared grey; and her lips stirred up and down for many minutes after her head was cut off.

The executioner placed the Queen's head upon a dish, and showed it from the window to the crowd in the courtyard; and this he did three times. And one of the headsmen, putting off her stockings, espied her little waiting dog, which had crept under her clothes, and could not be gotten forth but by force, but afterwards came and lay betwixt her head and her shoulders. And the dog, being imbrued with her blood, was carried away and washed. And the executioners departed with money for their fees, but without any one thing that belonged to the Queen, either of her apparel or any other thing that was hers; having been made to yield that which they had.

And every man was commanded out of the hall except the Sheriff and his men, who carried the Queen's body into a great chamber lying ready for the surgeons to embalm her. And her maids, through a little hole in the chamber wall, saw their Mistress' corpse covered with a cloth which had been torn from the billiard table.

August 5, 1587 – On Sunday the 30th July 1587 the Queen's body was borne in a chariot, covered with black velvet and set forth with the arms of Scotland, drawn by four horses, covered in the same manner, from Fotheringay Castle to the Cathedral Church of Peterborough, where, two hours after midnight, it was received by the Bishop of Peterborough in his episcopal robes at the entry of the church; who accompanied the body to a vault which had been prepared for it in the south aisle, opposite the tomb of Queen Catharine of Aragon. Upon the Tuesday following, being the first of August, in the morning about eight of the clock, the Queen's body was interred with princely funerals.

The interment was extremely magnificent.

The great halls of the Bishop's Palace were hanged with black cloth. And when all was prepared the procession followed the bier to the cathedral. And first went the Sheriff and then the Bailie of Peterborough; and after them two hundred poor women in white mourning, two and two; and then two Yeomen harbingers in cloaks; and after them the standard, carried by a knight; and after him forty gentlemen in mourning, and then the officers and servants of the Queen's household, her doctor and her almoner. These were followed by the Bishops of Peterborough and Lincoln in their surplices, and with their chaplains; and after them came the great banner, borne by Sir Andrew Nowell, followed by the Comptroller and Treasurer to the Queen of Scots, the Lord Chamberlain and the Lord Steward and others, with two Yeomen of the Guard in cloaks, with black staves in their hand. Then followed the Halm and Crest, the Targett, and the coat of arms borne by the Pourcyvants and the Heralds. Then followed the bier and the waxen image of the Queen, which was borne under a canopy by gentlemen and accompanied by other gentlemen and knights. Then followed the Garter King of Arms and the chief mourner, the Countess of Bedford, representing the Queen of England, and assisted by the Earls of Rutland and Lincoln, and twelve other Lady mourners, and other gentlewomen, both Scottish and English, and by the Yeomen of the Guard.

The procession entered the cathedral in this order, and in the centre of the choir was a catafalque, without tapers, and covered with black velvet, upon which were painted the arms of Scotland, the arms of France and of Lord Darnley. Under this catafalque upon the bier, covered with black velvet, was placed the waxen image of the Queen; and on a cushion of crimson velvet was the crown.

After the Bishop of Lincoln had preached a sermon, and the singing and the prayers were ended, the heralds broke their staves and threw them into the grave, and all departed after their degrees to the Bishop's Palace, where there was prepared a royal feast, and a dole was given to the poor. And the servants of the Queen, who had retired before the service, all except Melville and Barbara Mowbray, who were Protestants, were bidden by the heralds to come from the cloister, where they had remained, to the feast, and were prayed to eat well and to ask for anything they wished, such being the orders of their Mistress.

But the servants of the Queen remained in a separate chamber, and mingled many tears with their food and drink.

BIBLIOGRAPHY

Mémoires de Michel de Castelnau. 1731

De Vita & Rebus Gestis Mariae Scotorum Reginae. Samuel Jebb, 1725

Historical Memoirs of the Reign of Mary Queen of Scots. Lord Herries, Edinburgh, 1836

The Detection of Mary Queen of Scots. Buchanan, 1572

Les Affaires du Comte de Bothwell. 1568

Martyre de la Reine d'Ecosse. A Blackwood, Edinburgh, 1588

An Examination of the Letters Said to be Written by Mary Queen of Scots. Walter Goodall, Edinburgh, 1754

Memoirs of Sir James Melville. Edinburgh, 1735

History of the Affairs of Church and State in Scotland. The Right Reverend Robert Keith

Letters of Mary Stuart Queen of Scotland. Edited by Prince Labanoff, London, 1844, 1845

Œuvres. Brantôme

The History or Annals of Queen Elizabeth. Campden, 1625

Memoirs of Mary Queen of Scots. Miss Benger, 1823

The History of Mary Stuart. Claud Nau. Edited by the Reverend Joseph Stevenson, 1883

Mary Queen of Scots. David Hay Fleming

The Mystery of Mary Stuart. Andrew Lang

The Queens of Scotland. Agnes Strickland (Vols iii–vii)

The Tragedy of Fotheringay. Mrs Maxwell Scott

Mary Queen of Scots, Her Life and Reign. Robert S Rait

The Life of Mary Queen of Scots. George Chalmers

Mary Queen of Scots. Major-General Mahon

The Tragedy of Kirk o' Field. Major-General Mahon

Mary Stuart. Sir John Skelton

John Knox. E Muir

Queen Mary's Book. Edited by Mrs Stuart Mackenzie Arbuthnot

The Love Affairs of Mary Stuart. Major Martin Hume

History of the Reign of Queen Elizabeth. Froude

History of England. Lingard

Mary Stuart and Her Accusers. J Hosack

Histoire de Marie Stuart. Dargaud.

Histoire de Marie Stuart. Mignet

Histoire de Marie Stuart. J Gauthier.

"Mary Stuart", *Encyclopaedia Britannica.* Swinburne.

"History of Scotland", *Encyclopaedia Britannica.* Andrew Lang

Inventaires de la Reine d'Ecosse, 1556–1569. Published by the Bannatyne Club, Edinburgh, 1863

The Evidence of the Casket Letters. C Ainsworth Mitchell, 1927

MAURICE BARING

C

Baring's homage to a decadent and carefree Edwardian age depicts a society as yet untainted by the traumas and complexities of twentieth-century living. With wit and subtlety a happy picture is drawn of family life, house parties in the country and a leisured existence clouded only by the rumblings of the Boer War. Against this spectacle Caryl Bramsley (the *C* of the title) is presented – a young man of terrific promise but scant achievement, whose tragic-comic tale offsets the privileged milieu.

CAT'S CRADLE

This sophisticated and intricate novel, based on true events, takes place in the late nineteenth century and begins with Henry Clifford, a man of taste and worldly philosophy, whose simple determination to do as he likes and live as he wishes is threatened when his daughter falls in love with an unsuitable man. With subtle twists and turns in a fascinating portrait of society, Maurice Baring conveys the moral that love is too strong to be overcome by mere mortals.

MAURICE BARING

THE COAT WITHOUT SEAM

The story of a miraculous relic, believed to be a piece of the seamless coat won by a soldier on Mount Golgotha after Jesus of Nazareth's crucifixion, captivates young Christopher Trevenen after his sister dies tragically and motivates the very core of his existence from then on, culminating in a profound and tragic realization.

DAPHNE ADEANE

Barrister Basil Wake and his arresting wife Hyacinth lead a well-appointed existence in the social whirl of London's early 1900s. For eight years Hyacinth has conducted a most discreet affair with Parliamentarian Michael Choyce, who seems to fit into the Wakes' lives so conveniently. But an invitation to attend a Private View and a startling portrait of the mysterious and beautiful Daphne Adeane signifies a change in this comfortable set-up.

MAURICE BARING

THE PUPPET SHOW OF MEMORY

It was into the famous and powerful Baring family of merchant bankers that Maurice Baring was born in 1874, the seventh of eight children. A man of immense subtlety and style, Baring absorbed every drop of culture that his fortunate background showered upon him; in combination with his many natural talents and prolific writing this assured him a place in literary history.

In this classic autobiography, spanning a remarkable period of history, Maurice Baring shares the details of an inspirational childhood in nineteenth-century England and a varied adulthood all over the world, collecting new friends and remarkable experiences. It has been said that Baring's greatest talent was for discovering the best in people, that he had a genius for friendship, and in this superb book his erudition and perception are abundantly clear.

'A classic autobiography' *Dictionary of National Biography*

TINKER'S LEAVE

Reserved and unworldly, young Miles Consterdine and his epiphanic trip to Paris is Maurice Baring's first bead on this thread of a story based on impressions received by the author in Russia and Manchuria during wartime. From here Baring allows us to peek through windows opening onto tragic and comic episodes in the lives of noteworthy people in remarkable circumstances.

OTHER TITLES BY MAURICE BARING AVAILABLE DIRECT
FROM HOUSE OF STRATUS

Quantity		£	$(US)	$(CAN)	€
☐	C	8.99	16.50	24.95	16.50
☐	CAT'S CRADLE	8.99	16.50	24.95	16.50
☐	THE COAT WITHOUT SEAM	8.99	16.50	24.95	16.50
☐	DAPHNE ADEANE	8.99	16.50	24.95	16.50
☐	THE PUPPET SHOW OF MEMORY	8.99	16.50	24.95	16.50
☐	TINKER'S LEAVE	8.99	16.50	24.95	16.50

ALL HOUSE OF STRATUS BOOKS ARE AVAILABLE FROM GOOD BOOKSHOPS
OR DIRECT FROM THE PUBLISHER:

Internet: **www.houseofstratus.com** including author interviews, reviews, features.

Email: **sales@houseofstratus.com** please quote author, title, and credit card details.

Hotline: UK ONLY: **0800 169 1780**, please quote author, title and credit card details.
INTERNATIONAL: **+44 (0) 20 7494 6400**, please quote author, title and credit card details.

Send to: **House of Stratus Sales Department**
24c Old Burlington Street
London
W1X 1RL
UK

Please allow for postage costs charged per order plus an amount per book as set out in the tables below:

	£(Sterling)	$(US)	$(CAN)	€(Euros)
Cost per order				
UK	2.00	3.00	4.50	3.30
Europe	3.00	4.50	6.75	5.00
North America	3.00	4.50	6.75	5.00
Rest of World	3.00	4.50	6.75	5.00
Additional cost per book				
UK	0.50	0.75	1.15	0.85
Europe	1.00	1.50	2.30	1.70
North America	2.00	3.00	4.60	3.40
Rest of World	2.50	3.75	5.75	4.25

PLEASE SEND CHEQUE, POSTAL ORDER (STERLING ONLY), EUROCHEQUE, OR INTERNATIONAL MONEY ORDER (PLEASE CIRCLE METHOD OF PAYMENT YOU WISH TO USE)
MAKE PAYABLE TO: STRATUS HOLDINGS plc

Cost of book(s): —————————— Example: 3 x books at £6.99 each: £20.97
Cost of order: —————————— Example: £2.00 (Delivery to UK address)
Additional cost per book: —————————— Example: 3 x £0.50: £1.50
Order total including postage: —————————— Example: £24.47

Please tick currency you wish to use and add total amount of order:

☐ £ (Sterling)   ☐ $ (US)   ☐ $ (CAN)   ☐ € (EUROS)

VISA, MASTERCARD, SWITCH, AMEX, SOLO, JCB:

☐ ☐ ☐ ☐ ☐ ☐ ☐ ☐ ☐ ☐ ☐ ☐ ☐ ☐ ☐ ☐ ☐ ☐

Issue number (Switch only):
☐ ☐ ☐

Start Date: **Expiry Date:**
☐ ☐ / ☐ ☐   ☐ ☐ / ☐ ☐

Signature: ———————————

NAME: ——————————————————————

ADDRESS: ——————————————————————

——————————————————————

POSTCODE: ——————

Please allow 28 days for delivery.

Prices subject to change without notice.
Please tick box if you do not wish to receive any additional information. ☐

House of Stratus publishes many other titles in this genre; please check our website (**www.houseofstratus.com**) for more details.